I0691671

BEYOND TERRORISM:

SURVIVAL

Beyond Terrorism: Survival

THE NEXT ISIS PLOT

by

John Scherber

San Miguel Allende Books
San Miguel de Allende, Guanajuato, México

ACKNOWLEDGMENTS

Any book starts as an idea, and by its completion becomes a joint effort.

Thanks to my wife, Kristine Scherber, and to Lynda Schor, for editorial and critical help.

Cover Design by Lander Rodriguez

Web Page Design by Julio Mendez

Copyright 2014 by John Scherber. All rights reserved. No part of this publication may be reproduced or stored in an information and retrieval system without the prior written permission of the copyright holder. Reviewers may quote brief passages in a review.

This is a work of fiction. Any resemblance to actual persons, living or dead, is entirely coincidental.

ISBN 978-0-9906551-2-1

San Miguel Allende Books
San Miguel de Allende, GTO, México
www.sanmiguelallendebooks.com

Also by John Scherber

NONFICTION

San Miguel de Allende: A Place in the Heart
*A Writer's Notebook: Everything I Wish Someone
Had Told Me When I Was Starting Out*
*Into the Heart of Mexico: Expatriates Find Themselves off the Beaten
Path*
Living in San Miguel: The Heart of the Matter

FICTION

The Devil's Workshop
Eden Lost
The Amarna Heresy

(The Murder in Mexico mystery series)

Twenty Centavos
The Fifth Codex
Brushwork
Daddy's Girl
Strike Zone
Vanishing Act
Jack and Jill
Identity Crisis
The Theft of the Virgin
The Book Doctor

The ballot box is the fig leaf of unresponsive government.

-Derek Hamilton

I'm not sure if a man isn't wiser to do what he wants very much to do and let the consequences take care of themselves.

-W. Somerset Maugham

For Kristine

PRELUDE:
DARKNESS FALLS
June 25

Nate and Tiny, two kids already at loose ends in early summer, hovered at midblock with their hands in their pockets, leaning against the white stucco back wall of the town's only gas station, kicking at it with their heels. They were watching the meager midmorning traffic. The Marshy Flats grade school had been out just three weeks and they had already run out of things to do. Nate was eleven years old, and Tiny was ten months younger and one inch taller. They were best friends.

"I guess we could skip some rocks," Tiny said with a shrug, as if it didn't matter much. Of the two, he knew he was the better rock skipper; it was all in the wrist. To keep them outside getting some exercise, they were both barred from video games before dinner, and it looked like a long slow stretch until then.

Nate gave his blond head a single shake. Skipping rocks was a kid's game. He continued to stare down the street at the shore of the Gulf. With barely any wind and not much swell, the glassy water was perfect for skipping rocks. From up the street the whir and clatter of a garbage truck reached them.

Across the street and half a block down, a white van was parked behind Newton's Bait & Tackle. The back and sides were smooth, with no windows beyond the driver's. The passenger door had some writing on it, but it was too far away to make out. Nate thought he'd noticed this van before, making the rounds. A man came out of Newton's back door and set four small boxes down at the rear doors. He wore jeans and a blue work shirt. Looking comfortable, as if this was what he did all the time so he didn't have to think much about it, he didn't glance around before he opened the doors and stacked the boxes inside one at a time. He closed the doors again and went back inside Newton's without locking them.

"Look at that," said Nate with a smirk. "What do you think? How fast could that guy run if he saw us take one of those boxes?"

"You wouldn't dare." Tiny gave him a startled look that held a trace of awe.

"Just watch me then." Nate took off running flat out from the first step, even though his untied shoelaces were flying around his ankles. Tiny was at his heels. Both wearing shorts, their bare legs flashed in the sun. They only slowed to a walk three steps from the van. Tiny peered around the back toward Newton's door. Through the screen, no one was in view, although he could hear people talking inside. With a delicate touch Nate opened the back door of the van and lifted out one of the boxes. The four were all the same. He didn't bother to close the door as they ran away, turning up at the same corner they'd watched from, swinging around the gas station and sprinting three more blocks before they stopped, holding their sides and gasping for breath as they tried not to laugh.

Nate gave Tiny a wise look as he pulled out his pocketknife and sliced through the clear tape that sealed the top. "Let's see what we got here. I say it's money, all in paper too, a box full of twenties maybe."

Tiny looked around but saw no one coming.

Inside the box, cradled in a layer of bubble wrap, they discovered a yellow plastic fishnet float in the shape of a cylinder rounded on both ends. It was not much different from other floats they'd seen edging the nets on boats in that part of the Gulf. This float had a seam, however, running the long way around it. Because they'd never handled any of the battered floats that washed up around the tiny dredged-out harbor, this difference made no impression on them, nor did they realize that the weight of the float in their hands was too great to be of use in buoying up a net. Placed in water, this float would sink, because it had another purpose entirely.

"Crap," said Nate, disappointment wilting his features. It was too late to return to the van and run off with something else. The float could hardly be sold. It looked more like a toy, a candidate for kickball, one that would either spin like a rolling pin, or turn end over end. He and Tiny had a great time for twenty minutes or so knocking it about, but then the float ricocheted off a sharp fractured edge of the concrete curb and split open half an inch along the seam. When Tiny kicked it again squarely at the break, the two halves separated, revealing a plastic bag bulging with white powder. He picked it up and handed it to Nate, who opened his knife again. Hooking the point of the blade into it, he ripped open a cut three inches long. The powder erupted over the edges.

Nate was reminded of the white powder he'd sometimes seen in dozens of tiny plastic bags at his uncle's house. Of course, this one was much larger. Maybe his uncle would give them some money for it. He stuck a finger into it and touched it to his tongue, the way he'd seen his uncle do, but had never been allowed to do himself. He made a sour face at the bitter taste and spit it on the pavement.

"What is it?" asked Tiny. "I'm not going to taste it."

"It's garbage."

Tiny lifted the bag out of Nate's willing hand. The powder spilled out of the cut and over his fingers like flour. In front of the next building a pair of dirty tied-together high top sneakers hung from a telephone line, one above the other with the toes down. They appeared to be dancing through the air in slow motion. Tiny cupped the bag in his right hand and reared back as if throwing a runner out from center field. Streaming powder like a vapor trail, the bag flew in a powerful arc and sailed to the height of the sneakers, clipped the lower of the two and sent it spinning around the wire once more before it settled back again, still in second position. The bag plunged back to the street where it landed with the splat of a flyswatter hitting a table. A cloud of white powder the texture of smoke rose and dispersed in the air, lifting toward the smaller one spreading outward from the dangling shoes above.

"If you were trying to bring those shoes down, I would've gone for the higher one," Nate said, scrubbing his powdery palms on his shorts. "Next time *I'll* throw it. You'll see what I mean."

But the future held no next time for the two young friends. Five hours later Nate was dead after convulsively coughing up sprays of blood and mucus from his shredded lungs as he drowned in his own fluids. A reddish vapor hung in the air around him like an omen of the evil to come. Cradling him in their arms, it collected on the skin and clothing of his parents and grandmother as they wept. Tiny died in the same way half an hour later. Both of their families joined them in death later that evening.

While Nate and Tiny were the first ones to die in Marshy Flats, they were not the first casualties of the war.

PART ONE
EXODUS

1

A colorless haze hung over the Gulf of Mexico, visible mainly as a thickening of the air in the distance. Gulls traced loops against the flat windless sky, and on the simmering sand, shorebirds stalked about on stiff legs among the solitary tufts of beach grass. The single dock was empty of boats that morning, although three fishing rigs bobbed farther out in deeper water. It was no different than the way a lot of June days began in Marshy Flats, a day already pale and dense with the coming heat. Hurricane season was not far off, and some of the old timers there claim they can taste one coming in like a bitter coil at the back of their tongue.

On that morning a three-year-old white Chevrolet delivery van was parked at the small loading dock behind Newton's Bait & Tackle. The blacktop path coming up from the dock led past the entry door. The driver, a man in his later thirties, wearing jeans and a blue work shirt, had been in the habit of leaving the motor running if he was making only a single pickup inside, but he stopped that when he caught someone about to drive off in it one day. Even so, he still didn't always lock the doors. For three or four minutes inside the tackle shop, it didn't seem worth it—a thief would have to be walking down the shore at exactly the right moment, or following him, and Marshy Flats was not the kind of town for that.

The lettering on the door of the van read *Lightspeed*. Below it a bolt of lightning streaked across the white paint in electric blue, and under that came the man's name, Brett Wallace, and his cell phone number. On Tuesdays and Fridays, Wallace made a run up to the national parcel delivery service office in Bridger after gathering packages from all over that sleepy part of the Gulf coast the day before. Today was Monday, his collection day, June 25, and Newton's was his third stop of the morning. Newton handed him four identical boxes about ten by ten by fifteen inches. The same return address on all four typewritten labels said they hadn't come from his tackle business; they'd been dropped off for him to reship. In any week that was typical. Newton collected a buck apiece to store them on a corner table for Brett's arrival. He also supplied a manifest.

Brett Wallace of *Lightspeed*, one of whose core principles was to keep his life simple, didn't have an office and didn't want one—he relied on collection points like Newton's shop. He put the four packages in the back of the van and returned inside to collect three tackle shipments from Newton's own inventory; part of his business was online. Newton liked to chat a bit, especially when there was no one else in his shop, and Brett was inside for five or six minutes while they stood at the wooden counter. The weathered surface was scrubbed a salt gray color, part of an old hatch cover that had come ashore from a long-ago wreck one day after a storm. In the freshness of early morning, Newton often walked the beach before he opened. As always, they talked about fishing, the right gear, the wrong gear, the nuance of the ever-shifting weather, and although nothing marked that conversation as any different from a hundred others they'd had, that was how it all started that late June day in Marshy Flats.

When Brett returned to his van with the final boxes, one of the rear doors was standing open, and instead of Newton's four earlier packages, he found only three. The manifest revealed which one was missing. Scanning both directions, he saw no one on the street.

Feeling like an idiot, he locked the van and stomped back inside to explain to Newton that he'd already lost one of his packages. The fact that all four had the same typewritten Tampa return address had caught Brett's eye; he didn't see many typewriters anymore. Tampa isn't within six hundred miles of Marshy Flats—and the packages were each destined for a different city in the South. The missing one had been addressed to Little Rock. Newton explained that a fisherman his employee had never seen before had brought in the four boxes on the previous afternoon. Newton never worked Sundays himself. That's all he could say about their origin. He told Brett he'd notify the sender in Tampa and not to worry. This was something he liked about Newton—the man found little to worry about.

Yet Brett was still irritated as he drove off to his next stop. He had insurance for that kind of loss, but the declared value was only eighteen dollars. He decided he'd pay it himself rather than file a claim, since he didn't want the insurance company wondering how effective his security was. It wasn't like Marshy Flats was a tough town. Some kid with nothing else to do on a lazy Monday in June must have stolen the package.

The next morning Brett left his apartment for the drive up to Bridger on his usual Tuesday run. Carrying forty-six packages in the van, the black cargo net was stretched over them to keep them from shifting. This semi-weekly trip promised to be no different from any other, except for the missing box. A theft like that had happened only once before. He had no idea of the contents, but with such a low declared value, he wasn't worried. It was probably a sample of something.

As he left Marshy Flats, the traffic on Beach Avenue, the main north and south route, was oddly busy going out of town. Cars streamed in to join it from both directions where it crossed the coast road. Some days the traffic was worse than others, but Brett couldn't remember ever seeing it as busy as this, and June was not tourist season.

On his Bridger trip days, he never made any other runs. The distance is 155 miles, and he always had lunch at the same diner there after he dropped off the packages at the parcel service. This diner featured old chrome and Formica fixtures, and a not-so-young waitress with a quick wit and a pencil angled behind her ear in her hair net. The menu offered a succulent chicken fried steak and a cup of coffee they stood behind any time of day. When Brett finished lunch he never had anything more to do than take an easy slide down home through the heat of the afternoon. The simmering highway unrolled like a ribbon of soft tar beneath him as he played one of his Delta blues CDs. He was already thinking about which one it would be. Today, maybe the Mississippi Sheiks from the thirties. The CD he had was *Honey Babe, Let the Deal Go Down*.

Heading up to Bridger on that Tuesday morning, Brett didn't turn on the radio until he was already twenty miles above Marshy Flats, and only then because of all the traffic both behind and ahead of him. It was still flooding in from the countryside in both directions, because Marshy Flats isn't that big. No one at all was moving in the other direction, going south in the lane toward town. Driving for a living, he rarely got excited over minor delays, but this one looked like it could turn the day's program upside down. Like anyone in the delivery business, he worked hard to keep his schedule on track. All his customers knew *Lightspeed* was an exaggeration, but he still took it seriously.

One of the radio stations in Bridger focuses on Delta blues for an hour a day in the morning, but it always breaks in with current road and weather information if there's anything to report, especially in hurricane season. Brett switched it on. Even if nothing was happening, he was still in the mood for a little Lightnin' Hopkins or one of his friends with a twelve-string guitar. Highway 36 is a medium-use route that, although it has only two lanes, never travels at a crawl on a Tuesday morning, so Bridger was always the same distance away for Brett's run—two hours and fifty minutes. But when he switched it on, the station was playing something different that morning, a message that would change Marshy Flats forever.

"…now less than twenty-four hours since the first case was reported, and the toll has now reached sixty-four dead in and around the city of Marshy Flats. State health department spokesman James Esterbrook urged all residents to evacuate their homes and businesses immediately. The unidentified illness strikes any age group and is fatal within six hours. Avoid anyone you see coughing. If you have surgical masks available, wear them, but even if you don't, you must still leave the area without delay. Avoid contact with strangers. Wash your hands frequently. Safely dispose of any tissues used for nasal discharge. This is a public health emergency. Stay tuned to this station for further announcements."

Brett switched it off, his mouth open in shock at the idea of sixty-four dead in the small town where he'd passed his entire adult life after finishing college. He knew half the people by name. Wondering who had died, he covered his lips with one hand, and then jerked it away, asking himself what else he'd touched with it. He knew he hadn't been in direct contact with anyone that morning, but what might he have handled inadvertently that had been in someone else's hands first? He couldn't think of anything except the forty-six packages behind him. He pulled out his cell phone and checked, but he hadn't missed any calls. Brett lived alone and no one else had ridden in the van for several days. He'd picked up his last packages at 3:30 on Monday, but that was in Forrest Beach, eighteen miles to the west. He had left Marshy Flats three stops and an hour after he collected the seven packages from Newton's yesterday morning. He began to suspect that everyone else on the road was better informed than he was. Feeling that he didn't always need to be in touch, he often didn't carry his phone when he wasn't working.

The traffic on Highway 36 was laboring along in palpable frustration at less than thirty-five miles an hour, moving like a funeral procession with the vehicles nearly bumper to bumper. At that rate it would take Brett almost twice as long as usual to reach Bridger. His rearview mirror framed a solid line of cars and trucks as far back as he could see. He passed four bikers in fancy road gear on the shoulder, their knees pumping in the same rhythmic stroke. The terrain had been slowly rising for some time, and the highway was winding deep into the piney woods, which had begun to appear out of the flats about eight miles before.

Ahead the road drifted into a shallow curve, and about halfway through it a highway patrol car waited on the left lane shoulder with lights flashing. Two state cops wearing gloves and surgical masks gestured the northbound traffic into the empty oncoming lane with long sweeping motions, so that beyond, both lanes became one way going north toward Bridger. Brett stayed on the right side as the traffic speed briefly crept up to nearly fifty.

On the shoulder half a mile farther on, a station wagon was pulled off. To steady herself a woman braced her hip against the front fender as she doubled over and coughed violently. She grasped her chest with both fists knotted as if to keep it from cracking open. Her blood was sprayed over the gravelly soil at her feet, and over her shoes. Two young children gaped at her in panic from inside the car, screaming in silence, their palms and lips distorted against the glass.

This is what it looks like, Brett thought. It was an image he would never forget. For the first time he wondered if he was now a refugee himself. He began to lose the sense that he was at work, realizing that he was running too.

What would cause this? he asked himself. The radio had provided only a warning and an order to evacuate; it offered no explanation for what he had seen.

It must also be all around him, for surely if Brett had seen one, then there were more unseen victims in that woman's condition, behind the darkened glass of other cars, people who didn't know yet that they would die today on this highway, even if it might be only moments away. Six hours at the most, the health department spokesman had said, from exposure to death. Brett preferred not to think that woman's children would be next, but she was that far gone, and they'd been with her since they got out of bed. How could Bridger handle this migration of the doomed?

For the first time, he began to wonder if his normal mission to Bridger was still even possible. His customers knew he took their packages seriously, so how could he weigh the priorities in this situation? He flipped on the radio again. The death toll was now seventy-four. Ten more people had died in the past few minutes.

What was this plague? Brett understood that no one would know for a while. Lengthy lab tests couldn't be hastened because of need; they demanded their own pace, that of cultures maturing in Petrie dishes and the testing that followed. Once developed, a vaccine would be at least months away from injecting into real patients, and if it worked, then how much more time would pass before it could be manufactured in sufficient quantity? The American drug approval system was often an archaic crony process, and cued to favor old pharmaceutical houses, but even with their cozy connection to the FDA, clearances could still take months.

Yet, on this Neolithic timetable, in a hole-in-the-wall town like Marshy Flats, it was killing someone every minute. Why wouldn't the toll accelerate once it reached Bridger? As Brett drove north, the infected refugees from his town were distributing death further into the countryside. He was sure he didn't have it, but he knew that everyone else thought the same, and that was part of the problem. How strange to have it take root in the Flats, of all places. Was it the steamy climate, the swampy dunes, the brackish water? The mosquitoes that had propagated yellow fever and dengue in the past? Between the residues that flowed out of the Mississippi Delta, and the deep-water oilrigs, he had never trusted the day-to-day condition of the Gulf. The bugs never took a holiday, no matter what the season. Brett had read somewhere that an eighty-mile shroud of dead water spread out from the Mississippi Delta, not that far away. Statewide, life expectancy had fallen into the bottom ten percent of the national averages.

Humorous people, mostly older, liked to add that it was still damn good while it lasted. Like everyone else, Brett had always thought he'd beat the numbers. He worked at living a life with nothing to worry about, so it was obvious that he was a bad fit with this panicky crowd heading north. The sense of having made a wrong turn grew on him mile by mile.

Approaching the overpass at the Highway 51 interchange, streams of cars approached from east and west, compacting their lines on the cloverleaf onto northbound Highway 36 ahead. The southbound circles were empty. Traffic slowed to a crawl to absorb the flow. Now Brett could've kept pace on foot without breathing hard. Beyond the exit ramps waited a national chain gas station with a dozen or more pumps. There, what looked like 200 cars were massed on the shoulder waiting to refuel. Once finished, it was nearly impossible to leave because some cars had looped back from the highway and were trying to enter by the station's northbound exit. The off ramp was backed up to the edge of the blacktop with another queue of cars waiting on the shoulder. He realized that the gas supply could never last at this rate. He had filled his tank the afternoon before when he returned from Forrest Beach, and he always carried two five-gallon jerry cans full of gas strapped in behind his seat because he never knew when he'd get called out for some back country pick ups. Still, Brett was now filled with anxiety—the person who avoided worry as a lifestyle choice. The highway police were directing cars away from the station, not allowing any more to double up. He slowed to ask a question.

"Is the highway backed up like this all the way to Bridger?" he yelled across the passenger seat as he rolled down the window. Suddenly, it was vital to know.

The cop waved him on with a gloved hand, an impatient gesture. "Keep it moving, buddy, keep it moving, will ya?" he said through his anonymous antiseptic mask. Brett felt that his own naked face marked him as the enemy.

The air heated up by degrees, shimmering on the asphalt beneath his wheels. Brett rolled the window back up and bumped up the air conditioning two notches, wondering what effect the summer weather would have on this epidemic. He had come less than forty miles and now realized he didn't know what he was going to do next. Around him the other people were focused on evacuation, no one else was making a delivery. Never having made a decision to evacuate, he felt like he didn't belong there—Brett Wallace was still at work. He would've loaded a suitcase into the van if he'd had any idea he was fleeing Marshy Flats. As it was, he didn't even have a toothbrush. With both lanes only moving north, he could think of no clear way to go back home, and he didn't want to risk returning to Marshy Flats anyway.

On the opposite side of the road four people struggled to push a stalled car onto the shoulder. One was breathing hard, shaking his head, and his chest was heaving from the effort. Although he wasn't the oldest of the group, his face was flushed and contorted. At a glance Brett marked him as a dying man. He locked his gaze back on the road.

Most people Brett knew didn't always take the state government seriously. Corruption scandals and incompetence were often the rule. They reduced their expectations and accepted this kind of performance with resigned indulgence, an old tradition that was laughed at more often than condemned. Newspaper columnists joked about it in print almost every day. It was frequently a campaign issue that was never addressed after the election, no matter which side won. Yet the health and highway departments were responding early to this crisis, although Brett wondered whether it might have been better to quarantine Marshy Flats.

Even as he watched this, trying to digest it, Brett was growing increasingly twitchy at being locked into a grid of vehicles that could go no faster than a crawl. He couldn't imagine Bridger absorbing anything like this migration. The city counted a population of 70,000 people at most, and thousands now swarmed the highway both behind him and ahead. This exodus had to be drawing from a long stretch of the Gulf coastline, because Marshy Flats did not boast many more than eleven hundred souls. Given that all these people on the road were the advance guard of a new and virulent epidemic, he decided that if he were the mayor of Bridger, he would've summoned the National Guard and closed the highway.

Ahead, the traffic edged over the horizon and beyond.

Brett's impatience began to slowly unravel into near panic. He was accustomed to running his own business and his life, being proactive, solving problems as they appeared, and he needed to escape this useless gridlock. He had never in his life been a joiner, and he had started his own one-man van and shuttle service because he couldn't stand to take orders and didn't enjoy giving them. A free and independent lifestyle was his goal. Wherever the next exit went, he decided to be on it, and if he never saw Bridger again until this evacuation was over, so be it. He knew that a lot of businesses must have shut down already in Marshy Flats. Now *Lightspeed* delivery service was finished too. He hated that thought—for twelve years it had been his ticket to a carefree life.

By the time an exit to a small side road appeared after crawling three miles further, Brett's head was throbbing. At the turn, a hand-painted wooden sign promised unnamed delights at Blake's Nifty Store. With grim relief he swerved the van into the exit lane and then accelerated onto the side road.

Immediately a sense of solitude poured over him like a cool shower. Quietly among the thick stands of pine, he cruised on as if he'd returned to an untroubled world. His shoulders relaxed in stages and his neck rolled back against the headrest. Pent up air rushed out of his lungs. He felt like at the last minute he'd been taken down from the cross miraculously still breathing. He glanced into the rearview mirror to see who might have had the same instinct. Why was no one following? Why were people allowing themselves to be packed into a pipeline of no return and with no viable destination? A sign ahead read *Dundee 14*, a town he'd heard of but never visited, but he had a GPS and a stack of maps, some with strong detail. No matter how tiny Dundee might be, from the absence of traffic it looked like no one else was on the way there—it would be able to accommodate him, and it would be better than Bridger. Almost anything would at this point.

Brett realized he was streaking along at nearly seventy miles an hour down a road engineered for fifty-five. The sky was clear and blazing. It was freedom, and if it offered no predictable stopping point other than a tiny no-account town, at least it delivered a withdrawal from a dead end destination. His goal had shifted from accomplishment to escape.

Wondering about the current death toll in Marshy Flats, he switched on the radio again. The count hadn't been revised, but it still sounded like a war, one the state wasn't winning. Brett withdrew his foot from the gas and coasted back to a rational speed. No other cars were in sight. Oddly, after achieving his separation from the fleeing herd, he suddenly felt too much alone. The silence pressed in on him, now more like a vacuum than peace.

2

A short distance farther down the road, the same quiet reigned. A woman named Lee Carter sat waiting in her Volkswagen Beetle, parked in the weeds along the narrow shoulder next to the pines. She was waiting for another car to come by. None had in the twenty minutes she'd been stopped there, filing her nails in the steamy interior and glancing at her side mirror every minute or so. Her actions were mechanical and distracted. Had everyone been sucked into the unforgiving vortex of Highway 36? She considered walking toward Dundee, but she didn't want to abandon the car if there were any way to get it going again. That meant someone passing who would let her have enough gas to get to the next service station. She felt she was throwing herself on the mercy of the public, but no one was showing up to witness her gesture. Lee had no family in this part of the state. She had friends in Marshy Flats, but they must have all fled by now, just as she had. She hadn't tried to call anyone for help, knowing the traffic situation on highway 36.

Lee's thoughts were on the plague she'd left behind in town, wrestling with what could have brought on this epidemic. When she heard the evacuation order at nearly eleven o'clock the evening before, she'd called several friends. Only one hadn't already heard about it, and the others were all getting ready to leave. She suspected it was something invading the water supply, which sometimes tasted strange to her in the summer months.

Even after running out of gas, Lee knew she'd been right to join the exodus. She'd seen only one dead body, but it was someone she knew, and that was more than enough. She stepped out of the car and rested one foot on the bumper, tilting the brim of her hat against the sun. The road in both directions was no more than a sinuous ribbon to nowhere—she had never driven this stretch of blacktop before. Near the crest of the rise in the direction of Dundee a young deer scampered over the tarmac with legs flying, as if this were its first solo crossing. Lee was used to acting on her own, but she would've been more relaxed if she hadn't been facing a health disaster of unknown proportions. At least it was only local, and escape was still possible.

Lee pulled off her hat and fluffed her hair with her fingers. She examined her nails for the tenth time, hardly seeing them. The heat from the road shimmered up around her as she got back inside the car. She slapped a mosquito on her bare thigh, feeling her standards relaxing by degrees. At first she'd been certain that a woman would come by, and when no traffic at all developed, then someone of either gender would be OK. Now she was ready to accept anyone who wasn't a flat-out homicidal lunatic. Not that there was any way to tell in advance.

Five minutes later a flicker of movement in the side mirror caught her eye as a white van rose into view from a shallow curve, coming from the direction of Highway 36, just as she had. It was possibly a delivery vehicle, and that would likely mean a man driving. She put aside her feelings of vulnerability. Men were practical, most of them. She had no use for any that weren't, certainly now. After looking in the mirror and straightening the straps of her tank top and checking her eye makeup, Lee stepped out of the car, installed a smile on her face, and started waving. For a moment she detected no response, then the van slowed. She could see the driver's face through the windshield as he veered onto the shoulder and stopped. He was alone and he appeared skeptical, but not unfriendly, as he pulled up behind the Beetle. She walked over to his window with a more tentative smile. He looked like he was in his late thirties and he wore an expression that was serious, but still possibly accommodating. This guy could be the one to get me back on the road, she thought, trying to assume a positive attitude. Lee still had a long way to go and no gas to get her there. She hadn't been thinking clearly when she fled Marshy Flats without filling her tank; she had just seen something she would never forget.

3

Driving a cargo van whose only embellishment is a CD player, along nearly the same set of routes week after week, can be a mindless task, even when the driver possesses a polished taste for the local music and an active mind. Brett Wallace didn't care. In the solitude of driving he had nurtured his own mental life and he summoned it as needed. Often the music coming over the sound system seemed to be issuing from his own hands, on his own vintage Dobro guitar, which he now wished he'd brought along to pass the time as this all developed. He played now and then for his friends, although he didn't sing much in front of anyone else. In another life he would've been a great blues guitarist.

Music was not his only thwarted ambition. He had also once wanted to be a writer, but stumbled badly on two poorly conceived novels right after college, and had never found the nerve to try again. With a pair of painful failures back to back, it had seemed at the time too dangerous to risk a third. But Brett was practical and he had a knack for moving on when he had to.

Other than that, he was still open to new experiences, although few ever cropped up on these trips. Yet not far ahead on the right shoulder one was awaiting him in the form of a pale blue Volkswagen Beetle, blooming with rust on its fenders and roof from the salty, humid breath of the Gulf. It had an altogether dejected look. He wondered suddenly whether someone was about to stagger out and cough himself into eternity on the road. When he was still about 200 feet away and about to slow for a better look, the driver's door flew open and a young black woman jumped out waving with what he saw right away was desperation masked as welcome.

Even people of good will could now pass on the disease quickly without intending to; smiling like new neighbors, offering cheek-to-cheek kisses that rarely connected. Despite his anxiety, Brett thought it was more important, in this nightmare of indiscriminate threat, to simply be kind to another person as if they both were humans, the way it was done in the old days (meaning yesterday), when that idea still meant something.

He braked and glided onto the shoulder. Clearly it still meant something to this woman, because she continued to wave both hands until he rolled to a committed stop behind her car and cut his engine. He didn't get out.

"Hi, y'all," she said in a soft, candy-flavored voice, but with an uncertain smile. Brett rolled down the window and released a pale blue cube of conditioned air in her general direction. He wasn't used to getting even this much cheer from black women. She was still three steps away, and that was close enough. Her tentative smile began to grow in strength as if they'd known each other for a while, long enough to ask a favor with the hope of seeing it granted. Yet behind it, at the back of her eyes, he could see her uncertainty as well. Still, she was a pleasant surprise in an increasingly desperate world, and he thought that if she was that far off the road to Bridger, she was probably not infected, not that he could ever be certain. She might not have even come from Marshy Flats.

"I've got a really *big* problem," she finished.

This was a moment when, after what he'd unwillingly witnessed on the highway, *big* was a relative term. At least she wasn't coughing and she didn't sound hoarse.

"Let me guess," he said. "You've run out of gas."

"But I bet you've got a little in reserve, though, haven't you? You look like the kind of guy who has a better planning function than I have. But I *do* have this." Her hand came around from behind her back and she held up six feet of plastic tube to use as a siphon.

Brett's second thought was that she was working a little too hard to be his friend, but she might also be a refugee who had come through the same forty-five miles out of Marshy Flats that he had. She was wearing brief denim shorts with a burnt orange tank top. As she approached he noticed her strappy sandals. The woman looked about twenty-five until she got close enough to put her elbows on the sill and even as the shade of her straw hat darkened her face, he saw she was closer to thirty. She had short, layered hair with a touch of henna, and a medium complexion lit up by brown eyes that even in the shade still reflected a dancing luminosity. Her dimpled round face and soft lips reminded him that he hadn't spent much time with any women lately.

"I'll tell you what," Brett said. "I've got two full gas cans with me in the back, but I can't give you any until I know I can replace it. If I'm able to get more in Dundee, then I'll bring you back out here and we'll get you going, OK? I'm a little worried because it was impossible to get any more on the highway. I suppose you've had your radio on."

Her tentative smile fled. "I do know what's happening. I came up that way and they wouldn't let me stop to fill up. That's why I turned off here. My name's Lee Carter, by the way." She put out her hand boldly and shoved it through the open window. If Brett felt queasy about taking it, he didn't want to show it, and in truth, when he did, it had a warm, dry humanity that left him with no regrets. Still, she seemed almost too trusting in view of the slaughter behind them in Marshy Flats. He liked her look, but couldn't summon the same level of trust himself. He already felt the ground shifting uncomfortably beneath him.

"I'm Brett Wallace. Come on aboard and we'll check out Dundee." She returned to the front of her car and pulled out a suitcase.

"I'll take this along in case we don't come back this way," she said. "You never know now, do you?"

He found a place for it with the packages in back as she rolled up her car windows and locked the doors.

"Did you come up from Marshy Flats? You look familiar." She really didn't, but he wanted to be friendly.

She nodded. "I'm bound for Outpost."

"That's a long way up the road. You'll be out of harm's way up there, I imagine."

She nodded with a resigned smile. "That's the point, right now, for me. I'm trying to get as far away as I can. My brother lives up there with his family."

Outpost is a town in the northeastern corner of the state, small by most standards, but about ten times bigger than Marshy Flats. Nestled in the steep rocky hills the locals think of as mountains, it sits at the side of a 90-year-old dam and a small hydroelectric plant, with decent fishing in the lake behind and hunting in the woods above. The surrounding terrain is too stony and uneven in most places to support anything more than garden plots and rugged pasture. Brett had been there twice with his father when he was a kid. He still recalled the feeling of isolation, the sense of protecting walls around him on three sides. He hadn't visited again in twenty-five years.

Lee settled in with a grateful smile and they took off in silence.

After a while Brett made a gesture around the interior.

"Sorry it's not a little cleaner. I wasn't expecting company this morning, so I didn't dust."

Lee shrugged. "I'm glad you stopped. You're the first one that came by. I feel lucky." She gave him a sideways look as if to verify that.

The over-the-road bus only stops twice a week in Marshy Flats, so Brett took occasional passengers to Bridger or other destinations on his Tuesday and Friday runs, but he hadn't expected any today. The brown textured plastic of his dashboard was covered with a fine layer of gray road dust that collected more visibly in the ridges around the gauges. The world, at least his small corner of it, now felt hostile, and Brett could see that this woman felt it too. Without any gasoline, she was in a far worse spot than he was, so she'd have to deal with the dust. It would only be a detail now, like a pint of water in the bottom of the lifeboat, almost a relief to think about in the face of far larger threats.

Small homesteads nestled in the forest as they drove, seeking light within the thick interlocked texture of the pines. Most of them looked like retirement cabins, with no economic underpinning beyond a monthly pension check in the road-side mailbox. Sometimes as they passed, a bored and lonely dog rushed out to bark at the end of these lanes, with two front feet on the blacktop, as much in curiosity as in challenge. As always, Brett's eyes scanned the weedy fringes of the forest for signs of deer leaping up to skitter across the road into his path.

"When I turned off from 36 I was on my way up to make a delivery in Bridger, but now I don't think I can anymore."

"What'll you do?" She looked genuinely concerned. "I saw all those packages in the back."

"I don't know. We'll see how this plays out. It doesn't look like I'll be going back to Marshy Flats any time soon, either." He switched on the radio again but didn't get more than a garbled signal because they had entered a narrow, tree-clad valley.

"What do think really happened back there?" Lee

said. The way she dropped the tone of her voice suggested they were in this together. Brett wasn't sure.

"In the Flats?" He shook his head. "It must be a mutation of some bug we already had, that's about the only thing I can think of. It happens. Like it's only a gene or two off, but that's enough to leave us with no defenses against it. I don't know much about biology."

"Do you think it could be something in the city water? I never trust it this time of the year."

"I've been drinking it and I'm OK."

Lee shook her head. "I went to bottled water a month ago. I think this is going to rip through everybody who stays. Marshy Flats is going to be a ghost town. It's gotten down to leave it or die. Have you seen anybody die from it yet?"

This dropped Brett back a step. He gave her a startled look, but her face hadn't changed. It still didn't give much away. "No, but I saw a woman on the highway who looked like she was close, given what I heard about the desperate coughing at the end."

Lee remained silent for a while, rubbing the skin of her bare thighs with her palms. She kept looking down the highway.

"Are you too cold? I can turn this down."

"It's fine, I like it. I couldn't run mine while I was waiting." She shook her head and looked at him for a moment with an uneasy expression as if trying to make a decision. "My boyfriend died back there in the Flats. Well, he hadn't been my boyfriend for a while, but even so. I found his body this morning."

"I'm sorry. What happened?" He glanced at her briefly. The woman didn't seem to be on the verge of tears, although her hands were now locked together on her lap as if cradling her misery in a small package. She went back to looking out at the road without adding any more, as if she needed a moment to compose herself.

"When the message came out late last night to evacuate, I started packing up a few things and I called him. His name was Ted."

"I didn't have the radio or the TV on," Brett said. "That's how I missed it. I was reading through it all, if you can believe that. I left this morning thinking I was on my normal Tuesday trip to Bridger. No one called to tell me, and I don't have any family left. No one close, anyway."

She looked at him somberly. "I told Ted I'd come by this morning before I left to pick up a couple of boxes he was storing for me. My apartment's kind of small because I'm trying to save some money. I was going to bring them up to Outpost because it's cooler there at night and I thought I might need some heavier clothes. Ted and I used to live to-gether, but we never got married." She glanced at him briefly. "He was white."

They drove on in silence for a while. Brett didn't know what to make of her last comment.

"He hadn't decided yet whether to leave town or stay. He told me if everyone else left, or almost everyone, then it would be safe and the epidemic would be over. He said he'd given it some careful thought."

"That doesn't sound very practical." Thinking there would be many stories like this told and retold as people looked back on the Marshy Flats outbreak, looking back on the death of friends or family, Brett tried to give his voice a sympathetic note. It was a matter of what you were doing when you heard the news, like with 9/11, he thought.

"That's the way he was, though. He liked to wait and see what other people did before he made up his mind. He was a great follower. He thought of it as understanding crowd psychology, but to me, that was never his best feature." She didn't smile.

A white SUV sped by going the other way, the first vehicle they'd seen since Brett picked her up. Good luck, he thought. It'll put you right on Highway 36 going north to nowhere.

"When I stopped by this morning Ted didn't answer the doorbell, so I thought he might've changed his mind and already left. I felt that was smart."

"But you didn't go in, did you? I hope you didn't go in."

She shook her head. "I gave him back the keys when I moved out six months ago, but I still had his extra garage door control in the car, so I opened the overhead door. My boxes were stored out there." She again stared at the road ahead, neutral ground, with a firm set to her lips. "Ted was lying face down on the concrete on the side where I used to park, his arms stretched out ahead. He looked like he was trying to crawl to safety through his own blood. It was spread out in front of him in a fan shape."

"You didn't try to look at him any closer, though, I hope. I mean, you could see that much from standing outside the garage, right?" Brett looked at her carefully, trying to watch the road too; realizing he sounded like he was giving her a lot of advice when it was too late to be of any use. He imagined the fine spray of Ted's last convulsive moments misting the air in the garage, coating everything inside, a film collecting on the light bulb in the middle of the ceiling, and on the tracks the overhead door ran on, the inside face of the door itself, now over her head. Still, she didn't look sick.

Lee looked steadily out the windshield. "I could see both of my boxes but I didn't want them anymore. What if he'd coughed all over them? What if he was moving them closer to the front for me when he collapsed? I'm sure his hands had been all over them. He would've coughed into his hands at first. We all do that. I pressed the button to lower the door and tossed the opener inside as it closed. I heard the sound of the plastic sliding on concrete until it hit one of my boxes and stopped. I can get another sweater and a long nightgown in Outpost if I need them."

"I'm sorry you had to see that," Brett said.

"Then I drove away thinking scenes like that must be going on all over town. I wasn't even crying yet, but I was in shock. I heard on the radio as I drove out of town there were already forty people dead. Ted could've gotten it from someone last night in any casual contact, someone who looked as healthy as he did. Health was a big deal for him. He was a vegetarian, although he would eat fish and eggs now and then. A lot of good it did him. He was only thirty-one. I know he must've already had it when I talked to him, he just didn't know it himself yet." She paused and looked at her hands as if she almost didn't recognize them. "He was younger than you, sorry. That kind of thinking isn't going to save anyone now. I'm really scared, and I don't scare easily. They'll never be able to handle all the dead from this."

Trying to digest what she'd been through, Brett couldn't add anything.

"I don't think the ambulance would come anymore if you called," she continued, "and they'd be traveling from Forrest Beach anyway. What could the crew do, except put themselves in danger? That was probably the first service that stopped responding." She folded her arms tightly over her chest. "I didn't start crying about Ted until I ran out of gas. That just really did it for me; brought it all to a sharp point, and that was the first time I felt like I was next. I always rely on myself, but this is going to be worse than we think. You're all right aren't you...Brett? You're not coughing even a little? You don't have a sore throat or anything?" She looked at him narrowly, leaning away instead of closer.

He shook his head. "I'm OK. I haven't seen a soul since yesterday afternoon, until you. I'm really sorry. I hope you weren't that close to Ted anymore."

"Not at all. It was really over, but I still don't want him dead. You seem healthy, though. You look OK. You really do." She turned away. "What do I know?" she said in a softer tone.

"Don't ask to look at my tongue. What time this morning was it when you saw him?"

"A little before nine o'clock. Almost three hours ago. I think I'm all right. I feel good, anyway." She stuck out her hands and wiggled her fingers as if that was where it started, under her nails and in her smaller joints.

35

"I'm not a doctor."

"But you've got an opinion. You can see what you're lookin' at."

"I'm guessing that enough time has passed for both of us to be in the clear. We would've shown some symptoms by now if either of us had it." Brett wasn't sure this was true in her case, but he wanted to say something upbeat.

"That's good, Brett. Then we'll make it through this day alive. But we'll still have tomorrow to think about, like everybody else around here will. How far does this thing travel out of the Flats? We mainly need some distance here. I guess we're getting it now."

She gave him a pale smile. Her presence beside him reminded him of how isolated he'd been feeling since he left the highway. He liked her wide mouth and even teeth, and her dimples, although he couldn't decide whether she was only putting on a brave front, or if she was really fairly strong and resilient in a crisis. She was watching the road again, her arms folded. Her fingers dug into her shoulders as if massaging a band of knotted muscles after a scuffle.

"How tough are you?" he asked.

"Same question I've been asking myself." She didn't look at him.

"Do you know?"

"Not yet, but I know I'm damn well going to find out, and so are you."

Brett left Lee with her own thoughts as they approached Dundee. She seemed to be handling it, given what she'd walked into with Ted only a few hours earlier. He also knew that much more difficult times were coming if the disease were to spread beyond Marshy Flats, and it would be better to reserve some resources for the bigger bumps down the road. He was thinking about Bridger and all the people heading north.

Back on Highway 36, he'd pictured himself taking this side road alone no matter where it went, the way he did everything else, even though this crisis was more extreme than anything he'd ever experienced. He'd never been driven out of his home before. How bizarre it was that his no-account little town on the Gulf was the one to be targeted with this disaster when nowhere else was, although he still didn't believe it was from the water. It was more like bad luck.

Lee still looked healthy but other than that, he didn't know what to make of her. Probably they'd find some gas in Dundee and he'd take her back to her car. That was the best solution. He could see them parting company as she headed north, and he genuinely wished her well. Brett suddenly wondered how much of their current small connection was only that they both appeared to be healthy and had been thrown together in the evacuation. He shook his head; that might be the standard going forward in this part of the state. She was watching him now, but he didn't volunteer anything. He didn't want to get too close to her if she would soon be moving on.

Brett and Lee descended gradually from the wooded hills as if they were reluctant to take the next step, and then more steeply as the valley settlement called Dundee came into view. Blake's Nifty Store awaited them at the edge of town. Fifty feet beyond, a WPA bridge dating from the 1930s crossed a narrow stream, the concrete guard rails weathered and cracked, exposing in places their rusted steel ribs, but still holding up well enough for the state to keep it in use, since the roadbed looked well maintained. Only fourteen miles from Highway 36, Brett hoped they'd entered a land of practical people, isolated and not minding it, inclined to take care of themselves rather than depending upon others to bail them out. Quite possibly, this was a skill that was about to come into its own.

"Let's find some gas," Brett said. While that was what she needed to be able to go her own way, which wasn't his, he couldn't have said anymore what his was. She was the one with a plan; he was the refugee, unexpectedly running. He could see better now from her example that he needed to form a plan for himself, as if survival was a business that could be managed, but nothing came to mind. Hopefully, once he was farther away from Marshy Flats, the problem would fix itself through sheer distance.

The road over the river bridge dwindled into the somnolent main street of Dundee, which meandered in a slow curve parallel to the streambed about a block in from its course. The town went on for three blocks, after making an unpromising start at the Blue Bayou Inn, which was topped with a blue plastic-tiled mansard roof like every fast food road stop and gas station had to have in the seventies. Several warped shingles had fallen from its rusted framework onto the drive below. It created the effect of random missing teeth, more skull than grin.

Halfway through Dundee, a gas station appeared as an abandoned relic of itself. The sign above the weathered canopy called it *Red's*, with two pumps under the rusty corrugated metal. From the absence of glass in the windows, it must have been closed for several years. At the street, a taller sign read, "2.79 Reg Help Wanted Week nds. Go Saints¡" The weary exclamation point said it all.

As they continued under the drooping trees, Brett was searching for a place to stop and wait out the exodus north from the coast, nothing more. Dundee didn't look like much of a refuge. When the three blocks ended, he saw little beyond except the same empty highway as it drifted back up into the wooded hills on the way to nowhere.

"You know, that Beetle wasn't a bad little car," Lee sighed. Her voice was a whisper of resignation as they turned slowly back into town past the small white clapboard houses. The three or four that were more upscale boasted a veneer of thin red brick on their lower façades. She stared back at the gas station when they passed as if the sign had her fate written on it. "I had it for six years. It isn't worth much anymore, so maybe it'll still be there when I get back. Of course, if you keep them up, those cars go on forever." She paused with a crooked grin. "Where are you off to now, Brett? I'll go along with you for a while if you can stand my company, although I suspect you're kind of a loner." Her face held a frankness that was neither desperate nor coy. She slipped off her sandals as if that settled things. Lee appeared to have the ability to smoothly adjust to changing circumstances when they weren't going her way.

Brett had already made a choice. "I'm thinking about settling in right here for a while, hoping the highway will clear. I noticed that Blue Bayou Motel on the way in. I haven't seen another one, and I don't know how Dundee could support two of them. Maybe by tomorrow morning the highway traffic will be sorted out and things might make more sense. If we can find some gas on 36 tomorrow, I'll help you get back on the road again. Then maybe I can at least drop my packages off in Bridger. That's what we all want, right? Just a little bit of normal?" It struck him that he didn't know what to do next if that worked.

Lee nodded without comment, lifting her bare feet up on the front edge of her seat and wrapping her arms around her knees.

They returned through Dundee in the direction of the bridge and pulled into the crumbling blacktop driveway of the Blue Bayou Inn. No bayou exists within fifty miles of this town, and they're usually more muddy than blue, but sometimes a business needs a hook with a local flavor. Brett had once seen a restaurant out that way, but still on Highway 36, named *True Grits*. Coming originally from Kansas City, he knew he had to put up with things like that, and although many old traditions survived, not everyone down that way was a good ol' boy, or wanted to be.

Walking up to the office door, anyone could have guessed how it would feel inside from the streaming film on the interior side of the windows. It wept cloudy tears down to a paint-blistered sill spread with sun-bleached hunting magazines. He could barely make out the antlers. Inside on the sound system, Reba McEntire cycled through her collected hits, currently wrapping up *Only You*. A woman in scarlet hair and a blue sleeveless blouse that clung to her body like a second skin stood behind the counter waiting for them.

To Brett she resembled a snake coiled at the back of a cave, although an oscillating fan at the end of the counter lifted one side of her hair every eight seconds.

"Ah know, Ah know," she waved. Defeat kept her hands fluttering in the space before her eyes. "The AC is down and Ah cannot get ahold of the repair guy because of all this disease business. Y'all heard about it, I guess?"

"Just some things on the radio." The sweat ran down Brett's forehead into both eye sockets.

"Where y'all from?" The woman's gaze traveled neutrally from Brett to Lee and back as if she didn't notice any special difference between them.

"Bridger." He didn't look at Lee as he said this. "We were on the way down to Forrest Beach, but the state patrol reversed the direction of the southbound lane on 36. We thought we'd sit it out here till morning and see if the traffic clears. Maybe we can get down there yet tomorrow."

Shaking her head, she gave them the smile of an insider. "Well, Ah wouldn't be goin' on down to Forrest Beach right now if Ah was you, just sayin.' Y'all said you already heard about Marshy Flats?"

"Terrible. But Forrest Beach is eighteen miles west from there. I'm sure it's different."

She waved this thought away like a moth going for her hair. "Not different enough to make it safe. This thing'll be over there next, the way it's goin' around. It's up to 173 dead now. Ah don't know if you heard that. Marshy Flats is never goin' to recover from this, if you ask me. What's the population there? Don't suppose y'all would know, neither, not bein' from there." Leaning on her elbows, she stared over the counter into Brett's eyes as if she suspected he really was a lifetime resident of Marshy Flats, but wouldn't own up to it in a tight spot.

Brett knew the answer to her question about population, but he settled for a shrug. About 1100 people had lived in Marshy Flats before the epidemic. It now would be more like 900 on a good day, of which none were expected going forward. By morning it would be down twenty percent from that, the way it was ripping through. Lee was blowing upward with her cheeks puffed out and her ample pinkish lower lip extended, trying to lift the hair off her forehead without scraping it away with her fingers.

In profile she had a slightly upturned nose. Brett looked at her, appreciating her unpretentious humanity, suspecting that humanity of any kind would soon be in short supply in the Flats.

"Do you have a room?" he asked. "The sign on the road said you've got a vacancy."

"Only one, but Ah guess that'll be enough. It's got two beds, though. Air's not working over there, neither."

"I'm not surprised. We'll take a long dip in the pool, then, once we're settled in. That'll help some on a day like this." The vacancy sign had advertised a pool in both French and English. Brett lacked a bathing suit, but his boxers were dark blue and he thought they'd pass if he didn't dive much. Anyway, how deep could the pool be? He saw them both paddling around in four feet of chilly water with a cool drink waiting on the edge. He wouldn't object if Lee also had only her underwear to swim in. These were tough times and you had to make allowances.

"There's no water in it, though, sorry." With her eyebrows lifting, the woman shrugged with a resigned smile and a casual wave of her hand. "Damn thing has a crack acrost one corner of the bottom wide as your arm and about eight feet long. Ah'm sure you'll be fine, though. That'll be twenty-eight dollars. Cash or Visa? It's thirty-one fifty-eight with the tax. Check out time is at ten-thirty, but Ah hope you'll stay on some. Why not settle in for a spell? We're awfully hospitable around here, even when things are goin' all to hell around us." She managed a hoarse laugh.

"Is there a café in Dundee?" Lee asked.

"No, but old man Blake next door over to the Nifty has got some sandwiches that his wife makes up and some deli meats you can buy separate."

"She didn't even ask if we were married," Lee said as they walked back down the strip of four rooms. None of them looked occupied.

"I would've told her we've been married for a dozen years and still lovin' it." He laughed at the thought.

"You're bad. I was only sixteen then, going on seventeen."

The climate in their room was as oppressive as in the office, although not as moist. The first thing Brett did was slide the two windows open a foot to get some air moving. It was no cooler outside; he was only looking for circulation. Thin plywood paneling, stained the color of weak coffee, faced all four walls. Every few inches it was scored to suggest planks. To Brett's touch, the cloudy finish felt dull and sticky, as if it had been dissolving for years under the attack of the humidity. The yellow window curtains featured tiny red diamonds every four inches in a diagonal pattern. Beige vinyl tile squares covered the floor. Many were puckered on the edges.

Lee switched on the television to see whether the local disaster was getting any coverage in the wider world. Marshy Flats was a backwater that had been nearly leveled by hurricanes twice in the last forty years with no special media mention. The Blue Bayou had satellite service, so the reception would be better than the van radio had been in the valley. The set was twenty years old, as deep as it was wide. The screen slowly came on to display a map of the United States from the Centers for Disease Control and Prevention. The legend at the bottom announced that one orange dot represented 10,000 deaths.

At the same instant Lee and Brett both slumped down in shock on the edge of the bed, mouths open, staring at a scale of disaster they'd never imagined. Lee clutched his left arm with both hands; her nails bit into his skin. The map was shot-gunned with angry orange dots from coast to coast, where the concentrations were particularly dense. The New York, Boston, and Philadelphia axis was a blaze of orange that throbbed with only a few gaps down through Florida.

To the west, the Seattle-Portland area pulsed an angry orange, and after an interruption as it moved southward, it bloomed crescent-shaped again in the Bay Area, and from there, almost continuously down the coast into Los Angeles and San Diego. In the interior, the effect was more scattered, with Chicago, St. Louis, Denver and other big cities all hit hard. Large dark voids appeared between. Sioux Falls, South Dakota registered a single orange hit. Lee and Brett struggled to understand what they were seeing.

"My God, Brett! Is this the end of the world? I thought it was only Marshy Flats?"

Brett was in shock. He could see his entire life unraveling, and Lee's too. "To me, this looks like a terrorist attack spread across the country. You could never get such a pervasive outbreak like this otherwise. It wasn't about Marshy Flats after all, although it felt like it when we left."

He scanned their small section of the Gulf Coast, but of course, Marshy Flats didn't possess the population to merit its own orange dot. Even a thousand deaths would have nearly wiped it out, yet not registered at all on the screen. In the space where it would've appeared, nothing now interrupted the darkness. "Why did we think the Flats was at the center of this disaster, when it wasn't even a sideshow?" As they watched in shocked silence for a while, paralyzed, a new orange dot appeared every half minute or so.

"As terrible as this is, do you know what's odd?" Lee said, jumping up with a frown and mopping her face with a tissue from the pocket of her shorts. Brett wasn't sure whether she was clearing away tears or perspiration. Her voice had turned oddly calm, as if she possessed an analytic function that was now recording the event from a less personal distance. She pointed at a series of locations on the screen.

"Look at Atlanta here, then the Alabama Gulf coast, then go up to Memphis, and on the other side, Phoenix, Austin, Houston, Tulsa and Oklahoma City. They're all burning with orange dots, ruined." Her voice dropped a note. "But in other places you can see several sections of the South that have no problem at all, at least not on a scale big enough to register an orange dot on this map. Nothing is happening in Dallas and Fort Worth, and it's all clear in New Orleans, Corpus Christi, and Little Rock. No other major population centers in the U. S. have escaped this. If this is a terrorist attack, which it certainly looks like to me, too, then somebody has failed badly on his delivery system in our part of the country. Don't you think that's the only thing this can mean?" She stood with her index finger bent on Little Rock, smudging the screen, waiting for his response.

Blinking rapidly, Brett suddenly felt like he had slipped under water, and he couldn't find his voice for a moment. Confusion flooded his brain. His mouth hung open while he tried to process what he was seeing, his mind suddenly overloaded, his thinking blurred.

"Little Rock?" he finally said in a hoarse whisper. His voice ended in what was nearly a squeak as the crushing realization came into sharp focus. He saw what she was talking about, but it told him a different story entirely.

Lee was waiting for his answer. "Brett? Are you all right? You're not going to cough now, are you? Please don't cough!" She moved toward him but didn't touch him.

He slowly shook his head. His voice was low and clear. "No, I'm not all right, but I'm not sick either. It looks that way because Little Rock never got its package." He could hardly articulate the final word. "That was the box that was stolen from my van in Marshy Flats yesterday morning, and then it must have been opened there by the thief, probably only a short time later. It had to be." As if it was still in his hand, he could see on his clipboard the manifest he'd gotten from Newton as they stood at the hatch cover counter in his tackle shop. "That Little Rock package is what's now killing Marshy Flats, Lee. The other three matching packages were destined for Corpus Christi, New Orleans, and Dallas. They were part of my cargo heading up to Bridger this morning."

Lee stood by the side of the television set; her arms limp at her sides, her eyes huge as she watched him struggle.

"You can't be serious!"

"*I* was their delivery system, Lee, don't you get it?" As he yelled, she stared at him as if she didn't understand a word he was saying, as if she were paralyzed. "The attack on those cities failed because I never delivered those boxes up to Bridger to be reshipped at the parcel office. I'm sure of it, because although the Little Rock box was stolen, the other three are still outside in my van at this moment. If I had left yesterday, which they probably thought I would, I could've gotten all the way to Bridger, and they would have been delivered to those cities by now. The orange network we're looking at would be complete, except for Little Rock, because it was the contents of that box that destroyed Marshy Flats." He pointed at the screen as if it offered proof of this.

Until that moment Brett and Lee hadn't really looked at each other, aside from a few casual glances in the van, at least not with the kind of real depth that they did then.

"You're not kidding, are you," she said. "Those three boxes are *really* still in your van? Outside this room, right now? And we were driving up here with them?" She pointed a rigid finger at the filmy bay window.

"Yes. I'm not kidding, but here's something we can do about this ourselves. We can influence the way this goes. Come on." Brett seized her unresisting moist hand and pulled her out the door.

4

An instant later the *Lightspeed* van swung out of the driveway ahead of a spatter of gravel and sped down the main street back through Dundee. Lee looked over the seat into the rear, where, secured with forty-three other boxes by a black mesh cargo net, rested the death warrant for ten million unsuspecting Southerners. At sixty miles an hour, they flashed past the abandoned gas station, past rows of silent, white-painted and brick houses. No one stood on the street to watch them leave.

Back on the highway beyond the far edge of town, Brett slowed, searching for country lanes with mailboxes at the roadside. Each time they saw one he came to a stop, and both of them peered in through the gap in the trees, searching for activity. It didn't surprise him that this redefining moment of his life was happening on the road. That was where most of his life happened when he didn't have a guitar in his hands.

Cars were parked near the first two houses. The third had none, so they turned in at the drive. They had come only three quarters of a mile from the Blue Bayou Inn.

"There's no garage and you couldn't live out here without a car," said Lee. "This could be what we want."

The house where they pulled up looked more like a cabin. At most it might have held a closet-like second bedroom if the other rooms were also small. The construction suggested it had been built a hundred years before, the exterior later veneered with faded asbestos siding that had been banned for decades. The window shades were all lowered, and the gray cedar shingle roof sprouted patches of moss and darker areas of rot. Around the far side, across the weedy cleared lot, a stained square of concrete supported a rusty steel drum perforated with one-inch holes all around near the bottom. It was well away from any trees and brush. Country areas like this had no garbage service, and like most, the owners were people who burned their trash, or had when they still lived there.

Lee climbed the three steps to the door and knocked, standing on her toes to look through a small square window near the top. Brett came up behind her and pointed out the closed padlock on the jamb that reinforced the deadbolt. "Right," she said, and walked out to inspect the trash drum. Brett backed up the van and parked it closer, but still a safe distance away.

From the edge of the pine forest thirty yards off they picked up seven or eight brittle branches with reddish brown needles and stuffed them into the bottom of the drum. Shoving them in scraped the sides and chipped off half-dollar-sized flakes of rust, as if over time rain and fire had the same effect in eroding the metal. From the back of the van Brett pulled out the three fatal boxes and slashed the clear tape on the top of each one with his ignition key. His fingers felt the float shapes inside the bubble wrap. He already had the destinations and the sender's return address from Newton's manifest, not that he believed any sender lived at that address in Tampa. If any of those boxes went astray, no one would want them back. The recipient at the destination address would be waiting in vain for his lethal package. Would he be planning to drop it into the street from the observation deck of a Dallas skyscraper? Again Brett wondered for a moment whether Newton or any of his other friends in Marshy Flats had survived. He was in no hurry to start going down *that* list.

"What does that look like?" Lee asked, approaching warily, but with a militant expression. "How does the potential murder of millions of people present itself? I want to see it. This is the new hoard of storm troopers, the new concentration camps, the new Siberia, the new atom bomb. This is extermination for our century, and if it works here, then it will anywhere. We're just the biggest target." She pointed a rigid finger at the boxes, as if she would later tell her children and grandchildren about this moment. As if she would survive.

"If we live to tell anyone about seeing it," Brett said. He peeled back the bubble wrap in the Corpus Christi box to expose a yellow foam plastic cylinder that resembled a fishnet float. From others he'd seen at the tiny boat landing next to Newton's, he knew they weren't usually seamed like this one. Having a seam was only an invitation to leak and fill with water. It looked like it had been constructed, or at least altered, to be a container. The weight of the package reinforced that.

"Obviously, I'm not going to open it any further," he said. He set it with the others atop the dead branches in the barrel and wiped his hands on his jeans, wondering if he'd already touched it more than he should.

Pulling out one of the jerry cans of gasoline, Brett poured some over the dry pine boughs in the bottom third of the drum and lined up the boxes on top, leaving a small space between each of them. Immediately he started gasping from the fumes. His vision was clouded as, through the open box lids, he poured enough gas into each one to fill it, and then liberally splashed more around the drum's interior. The fuel immediately began to soak through the boxes onto the branches below. He worked as if this was a task he understood, one he'd been prepared for, one anyone might have to do. Moving back from the drum, he poured a little more gas on a pinecone at the end of a long branch and lit it. Staying as far back as he could, with Lee behind him holding onto the back of his belt as if she would anchor him when he was blown away, he pitched the flaming end of the branch into the drum on the first try.

The instantaneous rushing noise stunned both of them, as if all the air had been instantly sucked out of the yard in a roar and concentrated at the ignition point of the gasoline. It looked like an inverted rocket launch targeted at the center of the earth, with a trailing pillar of fire piercing the air more than twenty feet high. As if they'd unleashed a battalion from hell, the atmosphere seemed crowded with angry, hissing demons. Scores of birds leaped from the surrounding branches, squawking in panic from the treetops. Lee and Brett staggered back farther and watched, shading their eyes. Flames shot out of the holes in the base. After a while, the drum began to glow red-hot as if it were alive. Above it the air danced and quivered like a boiling, transparent fluid. Over ten minutes, the pillar of flame gradually retreated inside.

"I can't imagine that any living thing could survive that," he said.

"You're a hero. There aren't many around anymore." Lee's voice expressed astonishment more than admiration, as if she still didn't believe what she'd gotten into, or that she was standing there with him at that moment, as a person who had simply run out of gas.

"Maybe we're survivors too. I'm more like an ineffective deliveryman turned Boy Scout. We've caused no explosion, and no material has been blown clear. I'm sure they wouldn't have done it this way at the Centers for Disease Control, but what the hell, we're improvising, right? Anyway, they must be awfully busy in Atlanta at the moment."

"I think they're mainly trying to survive themselves," Lee said. "You saw how it looked on the map. Atlanta had a huge cluster of yellow-orange dots, like they'd gotten two fish-net floats."

Brett had noticed this too, as if the CDC had taken an overdose of the organism. That might well be the measure of epidemics in the future. Would it be a single float disaster, or two? He put the jerry can back in the van, strapped it down, and secured the cargo net. From what he'd poured, he estimated he'd used about a gallon of gas, maybe a little less. After a few more minutes elapsed he approached close enough to lean over and look inside the drum, keeping his hands well clear of it, clasped behind his back. Only a fine white ash remained. The slab and the metal were still radiating waves of heat, and sweat broke out on his face and dripped into the drum, vaporizing before it landed. From the surface of the concrete heat seeped through the soles of his shoes. By the time they drove away ten minutes later, when any danger of forest fire had passed, the scene looked exactly like it had less than half an hour earlier. It felt like an oddly historic moment, mainly because of what hadn't happened with the three deadly canisters. Little Rock and the other spared cities would now have some chance to protect themselves. With this opportunity, a national recovery might coalesce around them. It would all depend on the federal government's ability to take advantage of their spared condition and use them as a base for its response.

"This is horrible," she said as they climbed back into the van. "I didn't want to be a player in this, I was just trying to get up to Outpost. I was trying to get *away* from it."

"Looks like the choice is between player and victim.

Did you ever feel like you were chosen for something?"

"No. I don't believe in fate. I make my own choices. It's a luxury my people didn't always have. Very often they still don't."

Brett looked at her for a moment before starting the engine. This was a question he'd thought over a number of times in his adult life, but he'd never found a better answer than hers. Driving back to the steamy room at the Blue Bayou, he felt like they'd been through the first real moment of this crisis—real for them, because the huge numbers of dead behind them on the road and throughout the country were almost abstract. It was a self-centered thought, but striking a blow at something so monstrous and huge, rather than only running from it as everyone else had been doing, hadn't seemed possible until he tossed the flaming pinecone on the end of a branch into the waiting drum.

"Who are you, Brett?" Her voice was suddenly lighter. "I'm starting to suspect that your delivery business is only a smokescreen." She regarded him with new interest as they flew down the road back toward Dundee. "I think you're CIA, just a guess. It's a damn good cover, anyway."

He shook his head. "Now I'm just a vagabond foot soldier, and I think we're going to need a few more things for the road." Brett was not someone who ever needed to triumph over anything more than traffic, and the feeling the burning drum left him with was different from any other in his life. He wanted to talk to Lee about it, but that would have to wait until they knew each other better.

They passed the motel and crossed the old concrete bridge, where they pulled into the graveled parking strip in front of Blake's. No other cars were there. The building was deeper than it appeared from the road and resembled a twenty-first century version of a general store.

Brett watched Lee walk in ahead of him, feeling more connected to her after the fire. She had great legs and a graceful walk. They'd been partners in something important, for half an hour, anyway.

Inside, snacks and overheated coffee were available near the entry, and a cooler along one side offered milk, soft drinks, beer and wine, cold cuts and packaged cheese. The manager had chilled both the red and the white wine. A rack at the cash register held cellophane sacks of salted peanuts and cashews. A locked glass-front case behind the cash counter offered a dozen pistols and a variety of ammunition. The wall next to it displayed dozens of liquor bottles, all of a size to fit in a back pocket. Most of the essential consumer needs were covered, since this was Dundee's principal emporium.

Toward the back, beyond an assortment of screws and nails boxed by the dozen, hardware cloth and window screen by the roll, stacks of folded jeans and shirts lined the wall. Brett found a couple sets of boxer shorts, socks, and tee shirts in his size, and closer to the front, some toiletries. He hadn't brought a toothbrush, knowing he'd be on the way back home directly after lunch, so he assembled a kit of necessities. He didn't like any of the shirts on offer. This made him wonder how choosy he could afford to be, but he knew he wouldn't look good in plaid with mother of pearl buttons and big pocket flaps that dipped to a point in the middle.

Lee met him at the front carrying a basket holding a package of sliced turkey breast and a half-pound brick of cheddar. She also had a bag of tortilla chips and a tub of jalapeño cheese dip. Brett went back and pulled a bottle of white wine from the cooler. He hadn't thought about dinner until that moment. The future didn't invite consideration—it was entirely crowded out by the present.

5

"In the morning we'll be able to see better how this is going, won't we?" Lee asked as Brett unlocked their motel room door.

Reality had replaced heroism. Brett understood the required response and gave it, privately thinking it would be quite a while before things improved, if ever, but she wasn't asking for good news, only his perspective.

"Are you a realist, Lee?" he added, looking deeply into her eyes. Burning the three cylinders had created the start of a mutual exploration of some kind between them. They were antiterrorists, but what else wasn't clear. Maybe nothing.

She gave him a firm nod. "I try to be. I'm a single woman, so realism is the only thing that works for me. Fantasy is more for couples, where you've got someone else to depend on and you don't have to be objective and factual all the time. Of course, then you're going to be disappointed a lot. Since I left Ted I've gotten used to doing everything myself again. I don't mind." Her expression didn't support this statement.

That left Brett wondering whether Ted had always filled the Volkswagen's gas tank for her. He dragged his smoky shirtsleeve across his face.

The bathroom at the Blue Bayou Inn was furnished with a large square fiberglass tub that might have been featured in its advertising forty years ago when the motel first opened. The shower was darkly separate behind a vinyl curtain clouded with soap film. Twenty minutes after their arrival the tub was filled with cool water. Lee and Brett were stretched out inside facing each other head to foot with their bodies parallel. She had put on a turquoise two-piece swimsuit from her suitcase and he was in his navy blue boxers. Only her head and shoulders protruded from the water. She had fixed a leopard skin print band around her hair. More than anything they needed to relax and get some perspective. Lee seemed willing to connect a little more, but Brett found he still couldn't read her. An individual could save the lives of millions of people and then return to a cheap, steamy motel room with a woman he hadn't known two hours before in order to sit in the tub with her and soak the heat away. This was the new reality, or maybe it was only that something, at some level, needed to work since everything else had collapsed, or was about to.

"You didn't answer my question out there, Brett. Who *are* you? At this point, I think I need to know, since we're sitting in the same bathtub. It's not like this is singles night in Vegas, and with this epidemic, it's surely no Internet dating service hookup."

Not usually shy, Brett found he was reluctant to characterize himself. "What do you see?"

"A guy pushing forty, still in decent shape, maybe because his job is physical. The hint of a dimple in his chin gives some punch to his smile. Not that I've seen it much today. And why would I?" Here she paused for a gentle grin. "I sense a mental life that I'm only glimpsing the edges of. Maybe with a little more trust I'll get further inside, right? I think you've got opinions and insights about things."

"You're pretty much on track. Like you say, I'm a delivery guy, but I'm a big reader. That's how I missed getting any news of this."

When he didn't offer any more, she said, "And do you furnish deliverance?"

"If it comes to that; *Lightspeed* is a full service company. You're right, I've never been married but I'm not gay, I'm thirty-eight years old, I rent an apartment, and I don't own a vehicle other than my van. I play a little blues guitar and I lead a simple life by choice. I've got a few bucks tucked away that I inherited from my parents. It's a decent cushion but it's not a ton, and I don't have any debt. I pay off my credit card balance every month. If I have a bad week in my business, it doesn't matter. A better one will be waiting down the road and it'll all smooth out. Mainly, I don't worry about anything. That's how I choose to live. I always feel like I'm in control of my own life, although I guess that's become kind of a joke now and going down from there." He wondered how that sounded to her. It carried an element of independence that he liked, but it came up short on the achievement end.

Lee's eyes probed his face for a moment, the tip of her tongue visible between her lips. She began to shake her head slowly.

"Now I wonder if a worry-free life will ever be possible again. You must have had a *whole* lot to worry about at one time. Most people aren't that scared of being worried. They get used to it. I know I have, even though I still worry a lot."

"I could never get used to it." She had unerringly hit a sore spot. "It wasn't that I ever had a lot to worry about myself, but I saw the effect of worrying about money all the time. Oddly," he paused here, not sure he wanted to start down this road, "one thing I learned was that you worry about it the same whether you have any or not. Most people think that's not the case. Once I got free of it I decided not to travel that route myself."

He wondered how Lee had picked up on this. Maybe he wasn't that hard to decipher, and no one had tried to read him closely for a while. Lee looked at him, waiting as if she thought he might say more, but he didn't. Perhaps he might when he'd gotten to know her better, if he ever had a chance to. They might both easily be dead in the morning. What if the clerk at Blake's had been infected? Brett thought about the change in his pocket. When he got back to his jeans he could just pour it out on the floor without touching it again.

"How's that worry-free position going to hold up with all this?" Her look was curious but not unsympathetic, and the greenish light from the two florescent tubes edging the medicine cabinet mirror gave her face an alien look.

"It's already over, I'm afraid. When I saw that CDC map, I knew this epidemic was far beyond what anyone could ever control, even if they'd had some warning. I think it's going to run its course because no one will know how to stop it." He wondered if she was waiting for him to say more, something vaguely personal, but even though they were sharing the same bathtub, just as they'd shared the bonfire, he didn't feel he knew her well enough, and there were more obvious barriers as well. Wasn't it just the need to have something feel normal, anything? He couldn't trust that either now.

One of Lee's knees surfaced above the water line and

without thinking Brett capped it with his hand. She didn't flinch. It had a solid feel, one he didn't mind at that moment. The appeal of being a loner was rapidly receding in light of what was happening across the country. At his touch her face changed in a subtle way, as if they'd encountered a fork in the road, one they both knew was coming but hadn't expected quite yet.

"I'm not going to sleep with you, Brett," she said after a moment, her face neutral and her look steady. "So let's just step over that little hurdle, that speed bump in the road we're on. You're too old for me, for one thing—nearly ten years— and anyway I don't know if I want to hook up with another white guy again. On top of being a woman, it only gives me one more way to come in second all the time. But mainly, there's too much at stake here to be fooling around when we need to be payin' attention. You know that too."

Brett wasn't put off. His gesture had been spontaneous and had surprised him as much as it did Lee. "That's right. I was just thinking of contact, what it means with this situation. I wasn't making a move on you."

"Don't worry about it. In my job I've got guys coming on to me all the time. I'm used to it, but I'm not going to be anybody's party. It doesn't flatter me when they ask, but I'm not offended, either. It's only a part of the terrain, like predators and prey."

He frowned. "I really wasn't thinking of myself as a pred…"

"Here, give me your hand again." Her face softened.

Brett hesitated as he stuck out the same one he'd placed on her knee. She took it and put it back, just as it had been a moment before.

"There." Her voice softened. "I don't mind being connected to you, but now we've set the terms, so we can go on from here."

"OK. Who are *you*?" he said, just as eager to move on.

Lee's face took on a slightly tentative look. As if to frame her answer, she glanced away at the wall tiled with pink plastic squares, where segments of the grout had fallen away in dots and dashes like Morse code. It didn't adhere well to plastic over time, and the densely humid atmosphere worked like a solvent. She looked like she was afraid her answer would disappoint him. Not that his answer had been impressive, and the passage between had been awkward.

"Right now I'm a waitress and a part time student. I'm working on my master's degree in psychology at one of those online universities."

"You're ambitious."

She shrugged. "I thought so until this happened. Now maybe I'm just derailed. Anyway, that's what I meant when I said men were coming on to me all the time. After three drinks they're all irresistible, even if I'm not after six hours of waiting tables with my hair plastered to my sweaty forehead."

"OK, I'm impressed. Any family in Marshy Flats?"

"No. My parents have both been gone a while, and I have a brother who lives up in Outpost with his wife and daughter. I think I mentioned him. That's where I'm going now because he said I could use their house while he's in Corpus Christi. His wife's family lives there."

"In *Corpus Christi?*" The name had an unexpected, almost chilling, aura to it.

Nodding slowly, she gave him an ironic smile. "That's right. I didn't say anything before, but we burned their package a little while ago. You probably saved my sister-in-law's family. I owe you a big one."

Brett shook his head to deflect her sense of obligation. "Don't worry about it. Let's save ourselves next. That's going to be tougher because we're right in the middle of it."

"We need a plan," she said.

He thought for a moment. "After what we saw on TV, I think we should go back to Highway 36 tomorrow morning and see how it looks. If it's moving well, we can decide then whether to take it up toward Bridger or do something else. What do you think?" The forty-three packages remained in his mind, as if he were still working, although that didn't make much sense given the present state of the country. No one would now care as much as he did about that pile of boxes in the back of his van.

Lee sank further into the water and her knee disappeared like a tiny island at high tide. Brett's hand floated on nothing. Submerged up to her shoulders, she gave him a skeptical look. "I'm wondering what Bridger will be like by then. Even if the highway traffic is moving again, the city itself will probably be a bottleneck. All those refugees will be getting processed, whatever that means under these conditions."

"You think we'll be interned if we go that way." It wasn't a question; Brett could see it happening. What if the highway patrol sealed all the exits from both northbound lanes and channeled everyone into Bridger? No one could escape like they had earlier.

"How else can they handle that many people? They'll need to cobble together some kind of camp, and we'd all have to be confined there so we don't wander through the city and spread the disease. Wouldn't they need to take those precautions? Obviously, they can't tell who's infected and who isn't, just by looking at people driving in." She shook her head slowly. "It doesn't sound inviting to me. How about a glass of that wine while we're still free and alive? We've still got some choices, Brett, even though I feel like a lot of things are coming to an end now, more than we can anticipate."

Brett had set the bottle and two plastic glasses next to a corkscrew on the top of the toilet tank before they climbed into the tub. Leaning forward to retrieve them he noticed a subtle mark on the base of Lee's neck, a linear scar with a hint of darker color beneath the surface, just at the beginning of her right shoulder. He felt a sudden chill move over his skin: Lee was a *chippie*. He would never have dreamed she'd be one of those who had voluntarily gone in and had a microchip ID implanted in her body. It reminded him of the conformist nineteen-fifties. Resistance to doing that had spiked quickly after the revelation of domestic spying by the NSA. A difference in kind had instantly grown up between those who already had the chip, the *chippies*, a term coined by the news media, and those who hadn't and never would. As distrust of the government ratcheted up geometrically, the latter soon became known as the NC, the *nonchippies*. Brett knew that the percentage of chippies among African Americans was far lower than whites. Why had Lee done it? Now he was far from being able to ask her. Be careful, he said to himself. Although his jaw was tight, Brett said nothing as he uncorked the bottle and poured two glasses. His movements were suddenly slower and more thoughtful. He found himself searching for something harmless to say. With the varnished dark oak lid down, the toilet made a convenient side table and he set the bottle on it.

"I've always liked oval furniture," he said, as if taking a survey, "even the more informal kind. Anyway, I think you're right. Back in Bridger we'd be lumped in with everybody else. I would hate that. I can't do crowds, especially when they're so infected you can't risk coming close to them. Even before this, I was never a joiner." He watched her reaction to this. She was no longer quite the same person he had entered the tub with.

Without noticing his withdrawal, her eyebrows went up. "Crowds in tents with nothing to do but gripe as they slap mosquitoes, and always at the mercy of field toilets and rationed showers."

"They'll be standing in line for both of them, but the toilet paper is already gone when they get there. Babies screaming in tandem with the dogs yapping in the night."

"Think of the constant coughing with the stink of disinfectant hanging in the air all the time," she said. "And then we'll all die anyway because no one knows how to stop this thing." Wrinkling her nose, she lifted her glass with a laugh and touched it to his. "I know I shouldn't laugh, but sometimes I feel like I'm about to freak out from this. Sorry, but you're funny. Here's to micro-cooperation. Two at a time works best for me, I mean it." Her frank gaze held his for a while but sagged as the pause lengthened. "Brett, I'm flat out scared to death."

Brett took a sip of a wine that was only average. "I am too, because they still won't be able to stop the disease from entering Bridger, unless they quarantine people en masse before they let them into the camp. Then it'll rip through everyone standing around waiting for admission. It'll only take one who's got it, and you know that dozens or hundreds must have it. They'll be walking into a group cell on death row."

"The CDC must already have a game plan in place for this kind of disaster," she said with an ironic frown. "Wouldn't they have a planning function? I think prevention is even part of their name now."

"I'm sure they do. It is part of their name." Even as he said this Brett realized how many organizational names said the opposite of what they did, like the *United* Nations, or the *Republic* of Cuba. "But that's only PR and big budgets. With a little thought, anyone in that business could've seen this coming. The logistical problems for terrorists in bringing a one-ton nuclear device into Manhattan are too formidable; even though I'm sure that would be their dream project. But the stuff we burned this afternoon could be carried in an envelope."

"Or in a fishing net float. I think that was brilliant. Why would you look at it twice anywhere here on the Gulf? This comes from some sophisticated people."

"You wouldn't ever look at it." Brett wished for some music to set the mood. Delta blues offered plenty of depressing tunes. Many of them were about survival, in their own way. "But here's the choice for us." Brett leaned closer to her face. "We're either inside their plan, like at the camp we're imagining in Bridger, or we're outside of it, making our own way. How strong can you and I be, the two of us? You said you liked the number *two*. Do you really think survival can work on such a small scale?"

Her face took on a grave look. "We won't know until we see what we're up against. Who do you trust, Brett? That's what it comes down to. You don't know me well enough to trust me. Maybe I'm only after your van because it's got some gas left in the tank and mine was gone. Maybe your main attraction for me is your fossil fuel, those jerry cans. You'll wake up in the morning and find me and your keys gone forever."

Their eyes locked together again. "Maybe, although I haven't heard that one before. I think you know what I'm going to say."

"You trust yourself. So do I." As she sat up the cool water streamed off her shoulders, glistening on her cinnamon skin. "Let's take a chance and do this together anyway. I can be a gambler. God knows I've done it before."

"Are you sure? Because I can drop you back on Highway 36 in the morning and the cops will see that you get a ride into Bridger. With the shortage of gas, other people will be traveling on foot; you wouldn't have to be alone. Maybe we're wrong about internment and quarantine, although I can't imagine what else they could do now."

She pulled back slightly. "And can anybody vouch for the people in the car they put me in?"

"Of course not, but that's true of everybody now."

"So is that what you want me to do, after what I said? Think before you answer. You don't owe me anything, and I'm not offering you anything but collaboration, so say what you really want. That's where this has to begin." She gave him a level gaze as if she were expecting to read between the lines of what he was about to say. Her look suggested a history of having little trust for commitments made and sealed.

Looking back at her, Brett couldn't speak for a moment. All he could think of was that they were two people thrown together by chance. "No. I want you with me, but you might be safer in a crowd because the larger number of people will attract whatever aid is available. If it's only the two of us, no one is going to bail us out in a rough spot. But if you went another way, I'd only worry about you, and you know how I hate worrying."

A ghost of a smile crossed her face. "Then I'm OK with the two of us going on our own. We could stay on the side roads and try to make it up to Outpost. That's the only other option I can see." Her voice took on a conspiratorial note. "It's so far out of the way no one would ever find it if they didn't know where it was. It's a town on a dead end road bounded by water on one side and mountains on the other. My brother left for Corpus Christi this morning. I realize Outpost was my destination all along, but you were going nowhere."

A devilish grin came over Brett's face. "Lee, how long have we known each other?" He was more relaxed than at any moment since he picked her up on the highway.

"A few hours. Not nearly long enough." Water splashed up between them as she came closer and wrapped her arms around him. He hugged her tightly, feeling her face on his neck, surprised at how much it meant to be close to this woman he hadn't met even six hours before. It was no venue for romance, and she had made her views clear, but it was still a startling connection that could never have happened in normal times. He couldn't remember when he'd had an ally in a crisis before. Not looking at her neck again, he rose to his knees and poured them another glass of wine, even though it was too soon to toast the future.

Or even to imagine one.

6

"…and with the national death toll now standing at 1.4 million, it's the kind of challenge that brings out the best in all right-thinking Americans."

Later that day the President of the United States paused for a moment with his index finger in the air, staring gravely back at the camera. That must have been where the teleprompter was, because his eyes didn't look quite focused, although this didn't undermine the sincerity of his expression. Brett and Lee were sitting on the edge of the worn sofa at the Blue Bayou Inn. "I'll repeat that word—*right-thinking*

Americans, and there is a difference. Therefore it is with great frustration that I have to inform you that the Republican leadership in the House of Representatives has blocked emergency funding for the CDC's effort at controlling this catastrophic outbreak. This leaves the average working American with no protection whatever from this disease. It's a level of exposure that I find totally unacceptable."

He paused to let this sink in. The viewers in the Blue Bayou certainly had no immediate response.

"While it is true that the necessary funds would require another extension of the national debt ceiling, this is most definitely not the time to resume the same contentious debate over cutting government expenditures. In fact, my administration will refuse to consider any further cuts at all, for anything, in light of the current emergency. Leadership demands that we draw the line somewhere. Our national survival requires immediate and unrelenting action, not politics as usual. I ask that every one of you watching this broadcast call or email their congressman and urge priority action on the solution to this crisis. Thank you."

With a firm set to his jaw that bordered on a scowl, the President stalked off the podium without permitting any questions. He might have been alone in the room, aside from the media crew. The commentator came on to introduce the response from the Republican Speaker of the House. The motel room's remote control was missing, so Brett got up and switched the television set off. It wasn't because he was a Democrat—he had long been disillusioned with both parties for their legacy of perpetual gridlock, and he didn't want to listen to another pointless debate while the members of Congress acted from the highest of principles to prevent each other from doing anything at all for the people who had elected them.

"Sorry," he said, turning around. "That was only my reflex. I can switch it on again if you want to listen to some more. I can't stomach it. Since when is doing nothing in our best interest?"

Lee shook her head. "I believe I've heard it all before, although I didn't think they'd do this again, particularly now, I really didn't. Why does every problem have to be used as a political football? Don't bother to answer that, because no one can." She handed him the final slice of turkey from Blake's. She had rolled it up like a cigar. The cheese was already gone. The last of the wine was in their glasses, and their wet clothes hung over the shower curtain bar in the bathroom. There was no likelihood whatever they'd be dry by morning.

"I'm sure it's the same on every channel," he said.

"It's the same in every crisis. I'm glad we decided to do this alone, because we're not going to get any real help, are we? I can't believe this! Can't you trust anyone? I didn't vote for him, you know." She looked at him from under long lashes, as if waiting for him to challenge this.

"What?" Brett was stunned.

"I didn't vote at all, OK? I thought he was a strange choice for the nomination, and I couldn't stand any of the others."

"Because he was…" Brett couldn't finish the sentence.

"Because he's of African descent, but he isn't descended from slaves, and he grew up in a white household. He just didn't have the same experience. I don't know; it's complicated. You probably wouldn't understand."

She was right. "What would have worked better for you?"

"If his family had been slaves four or five generations back it would've come full circle, that's all." She made a vague helpless gesture.

"So you're looking for some kind of expiation in this? It's only politics." He didn't want to say it, but he thought of American party politics as an amusement for the light-minded.

Her eyebrows went up. "Call it that if you want. I don't need to call it anything. I do know that if it ever works itself out I'll recognize it. We're not there yet, and this guy doesn't do it for me, OK? I feel like, well, he's not his own man somehow. In order to get this far, someone has bought him and probably more than once. Think of where he came from—the same political machine that offered his Senate seat for sale when the chair was still warm."

Brett shook his head, knowing he'd be going over this conversation later in his mind. "I'm not disappointed or surprised by the inaction in Washington, but I've been on my own since I left home at seventeen and I'm used to having no one come to my aid. If he works for people other than me, I'm not surprised. No one has ever worked for me but me." They talked for a while longer, but they were both exhausted, more from stress than activity. They had done nothing more than take a short drive, do a little shopping, build a fire, and watch some TV. It was too steamy to go outside and walk through town, which they might have done in more normal times.

Lee came out of the bathroom wearing a pale green tee shirt that came to mid thigh and Brett had on his new underwear from Blake's Nifty. In place of a Gideon's Bible, which he was not looking for, he discovered a copy of *Gone with the Wind* in the nightstand. Lee had brought a book of her own, Truman Capote's *In Cold Blood*.

"Do you really like that book?" he asked. "You must have started it before this happened." What kind of cold blood, he was thinking, did it take to kill millions of people you didn't know?

"His style is powerful. It's gritty."

"No doubt, but it's awfully graphic, too."

"I'm already past that part with the shotgun. Anyway, what we're headed into is going to be even more graphic. I'm thinking of Ted on his garage floor now. We'll see a lot more of that, I suspect."

They read for a while in silence. Brett flipped through the thick volume trying to discover how Scarlett O'Hara had responded to a series of devastating threats. Usually it was with a tantrum, but she always got through in the end. Finally, with a brief, awkward hug that spoke of the need for new connections more than anything else, they retired to their separate beds. There they occasionally glanced at each other in silence across the five feet that separated their faces in the partially darkened room as they slowly fell asleep.

On Wednesday, after struggling with a breakfast of stale sweet rolls and watery coffee improvised from Blake's, they checked out of the Blue Bayou Inn without regret. Brett handed the manager forty dollars in cash to store the rest of the packages from the van, promising he'd be back through Dundee within four days. He didn't believe that himself, and he could see that she didn't either. Looking at the two twenties before she slid them into her jeans pocket, she didn't question it as he piled the remaining forty-three boxes into her back office. Brett was thinking that if he didn't reappear to reclaim them, the growing chaos would provide a ready excuse. The money he gave her would be incentive to hang onto them for a while longer. Whether she herself would survive was yet another contingency, one of too many to deal with. For her as well, life was speculative, but forty bucks in her pocket was a sure thing.

The Blue Bayou had served its purpose because they now had a plan they talked through again as they ate breakfast. Even without knowing the specifics of what they might be, they were still sure they didn't want to depend on the federal government's efforts to save them. And how long could anyone wait? The administration's delay in launching any effort at all spoke volumes. Even before this the people in the government had seemed so far removed from what was happening outside Washington that they didn't grasp what anyone else needed. How could they rise to this when their main experience in public service was repaying the favor to those corporate interests that paid for their election campaigns?

Still, Brett and Lee had the beginnings of a relationship of trust, nothing more, and one that would inevitably be subjected to some heavy testing down the road. A quick scan of the television news that morning revealed the only change was that the number of orange dots had grown. Hawaii was not yet on the map, and the political rhetoric had gotten even more shrill. As a firm matter of principle, neither side would move as they both beat the drum about how critical it was to respond without delay. Were they each seeing some campaign value down the road in being able to blame the other side for this failure? The November elections were a little more than four months off. Brett couldn't imagine any other reason to make this the proper time to set their positions in the concrete of principle. He took all of this to mean that whatever provision was being made in Bridger to accommodate refugees was being handled by the state health authorities on their own, not the CDC, which itself might still be under siege in Atlanta. No one had mentioned the name of FEMA, the Federal Emergency Management Agency, or made reference to their rumored sinister detention camps. Who would be put in them, and if this wasn't an emergency they should be dealing with, what was? It felt like business as usual as the government sailed on without response, aloof and self-absorbed. Ship of fools, Brett thought. If they had thought to bring any lifeboats, they were keeping them for themselves.

Once Lee and Brett got back on the road, they found the Bridger radio station was sputtering like a near-drowning victim, which meant, at least, that it was still broadcasting even if a coherent signal was beyond its capability. Once they got out of that valley they might be able to listen to it again.

Brett's map revealed a sparse network of small roads that could lead them up to Outpost without crossing more than one major highway. As always, his instinct was to avoid crowds. The trickiest intersection would be at Highway 84, which approached Bridger from the east. If it was clotted with traffic it might be tough to cross, depending on the type of interchange it had. The route they were on wouldn't be the quickest, and would definitely require more gas at some point. His hope was that in this snaky maze of little-used back roads a gas station might still be operating with pre-disaster innocence. Did such a thing still exist? It would have to be a throwback to the conditions of forty-eight hours before. Brett's dream was to buy another jerry can, or as many as he could, and fill them, as well as top off his tank.

"I've got my laptop with me," Lee said. "If the radio and TV stations go down, we might still be able to pick up the Internet from Outpost. I'm glad we bought all that water at Blake's." They also had sandwiches for lunch and snacks for the afternoon.

"You don't really think the media could go down?"

"Like my daddy always told me when I was little, and he'd be repeating it now if he were still around, 'Look at the trend line, chile'. It ain't nothin' but down, and it'll have to hit bottom and bounce off 'fore it comes up again.' Ask me that again after we see the bottom."

Brett turned away. "I don't want to think what the bottom of this might look like." Part of the bottom would include what he or anyone was capable of.

Because they'd come so far off track, they were still about 125 miles south of Bridger, and much farther north they would be passing it about 45 miles to the east. Several links on that route were identified on the map not as paved, but as "improved." To Brett, who had spent most of his working life driving, this meant a dirt road with the tree stumps cleared, and a layer of gravel spread and rolled out over the graded soil. Their current condition would be subject to whatever maintenance these routes had received since the map was printed. Fortunately little rain had fallen in the past month. All the towns on their route were tiny solid black circles on the map; this meant none were larger than what Marshy Flats had been last week, when it was still alive and healthy. As they pushed on, the air's initial freshness was fading under a developing blanket of the day's approaching heat.

"I wish we had sleeping bags," Brett said. "In an emergency we could pull into the woods and stay out of sight, sleeping in the locked van."

"Given what you said about the Little Rock package,

I wonder if it wouldn't have made more sense to quarantine Marshy Flats and keep people from leaving," Lee said. She had kicked off her sandals again and put her bare feet up on the dashboard. Her toenails were lime green, which worked well with her skin tones.

Brett had already considered this. "The death toll would be higher, I suppose," he said, "among the townspeople we know, but even so they could've contained the outbreak instead of spreading it north by driving people up to Bridger. This way they'll be mixing a contaminated population into a healthy one."

"I can see that, although they're probably thinking they can isolate the refugees more easily up there since Marshy Flats doesn't have anywhere to put them. Bridger would have more facilities and resources."

"Do you suppose they felt isolating the Flats would've looked heartless, as if they had written us off? You're the psychologist."

She shook her head. "It wouldn't surprise me. You can have a department of the state government called public health, but it doesn't mean their policy decisions are all made for public health reasons. Everybody in government is sensitive to public relations. Anyway, I'm not in clinical psychology; my area is testing. I'm looking to get into human resources in Bridger, or, better, maybe New Orleans in some big company, once I finish. I lived there when I was in school." After a moment of silence, she added, "*If* I finish. I never thought before that anything could derail me."

Brett was silent, thinking that human resources were getting scarcer by the moment. The country would soon be full of job openings where businesses hadn't collapsed completely. It might turn into a jobseeker's market and many companies would need someone like Lee, with her screening credentials.

"You might be a hot item once this is over." She looked at him as if uncertain what he meant. "This is going to be a crucible for both of us. What skills would you test for today that would help us survive?"

"Good judgment," she said without a pause. "Attention to detail combined with the ability to take the broader view—that's a rare combination. Then would come intelligence, intuitiveness and creativity. Organization, since the ability to prioritize tasks would be critical."

"A sense of humor?"

"Absolutely, but finding that might be a stretch under these conditions."

"Some men in the trenches acquire it in wartime. It's a great help to be able to laugh in the face of death."

"Ha-ha," she said without smiling. "Maybe that skill only comes on recollection, once the war is over."

"You're a survivor. I think I already knew that."

"That's my plan. It doesn't hurt that we're two people focused on exactly the same goal. You don't always find that in business. Plus, what we want is uncomplicated. Keeping our objectives simple is going to count for more now."

"Sure," he said. "Give me all your food, for example."

They drove on for a while without speculating further about their chances. The sky developed a hazy cast ahead and to the west, promising some relief from the heat. Half a mile further the road began to rise slightly. The pine forest still flanked the route on both sides, randomly interrupted by small meadows that, from the vegetation, suggested they sheltered a marshy layer. From an old full-size Ford sedan parked on the shoulder ahead where the rise began, a young woman stepped out of the driver's door, waving with no special urgency. Mentally, Brett noted how different her manner was from Lee's on the road where he picked her up. The sun was behind the van, and the woman held up her other hand to shield her eyes to get a clearer look as they approached. She wore jeans and a nondescript tee shirt whose printed message was too washed out to read.

"You're not going to fall for that old trick again, are you?" Lee said with a grin.

"Not this time." Without looking at her, Brett's eyes had narrowed. Even as he was slowing, shadows were sitting

JOHN SCHERBER

upright in his mind, locking in on the situation. He'd also
glimpsed movement inside the car. The short hairs on his neck
began to rise. Suddenly he knew this tableau was not about a
woman alone and in trouble on the road. He was still going
forty miles an hour, but it felt to him like everything around
them was happening in slow motion, even as the situation accelerated into crisis. The woman still waved in rhythm to some
need within herself, but her eyes did not seek his face as Lee's
had on the road to Dundee. This woman seemed oddly distracted, as if waiting for something else, knowing more than
he did what was about to happen.

The van reached the bottom of the dip and climbed
toward the car. The door on the Ford's passenger side opened
as if on cue. Brett felt the tension knot the muscles in his hands
as he gripped the wheel too hard.

"Lee, get down on the floor, fast!" His tone was hushed
but emphatic. Without delay or comment, she uncoupled her
seatbelt and slid off her seat. Her bare legs squeaked against
the leather. From the angle of their approach, the glint of
sunlight from a glassy or metallic material scattered over the
blacktop flashed into view next to the Ford. It could have been
broken bottle glass or nails. From the passenger side, a man in
a baseball cap emerged. He turned toward the approaching
van as he stood upright, both his hands down and out of sight.
To keep them in doubt, Brett held a steady course at the same
speed until they were about fifty feet away. Then he stomped
hard on the gas pedal. They jerked forward and lurched onto
the unpaved shoulder of the oncoming lane, mowing through
the weeds, slapping them down. As the man turned to face
them, his hands rose and rested on the roof of the Ford.
Together they gripped a gun. Brett held his focus on the road
as a shot hit the van. A muted squeal came from Lee as she
rolled further under the dashboard. The rear of the van fish-
tailed as Brett pressed the gas pedal to the floor. Gravel arced
into the air behind. The bullet didn't lodge inside either of
them.

Another shot sounded from the rear but didn't hit the

70

van; short-barreled pistols don't have much effective range.

As they accelerated up the hill, Lee exhaled as if she hadn't thought to do that for a while. "You're not so bad," she said. She climbed back into her seat and dusted off her knees and elbows.

"At least he didn't have the sense to shoot at the tires. Aside from hitting me in the head, that was his main chance."

"Maybe they wanted the van with the tires intact. They'd leave us at the side of the road."

"Still standing?"

"I doubt it. Who travels with a pistol?"

"I wish we did." This came out in a long sigh. "We're going to need one. Blake's Nifty had a dozen of them."

Lee glanced into the side-view mirror. "I don't like them. So, what was *their* problem anyway, other than a bad hair day in her case?"

"Same as yours was, I think. They must be out of gas, but they're not as polite about it as you were." Brett still gripped the wheel hard to not reveal the sudden tremor in his hands.

She relaxed back into her seat, rubbing on her legs. The stiff weave of the floor mat had imprinted diamond grid patterns on her knees and elbows.

Brett was impressed that Lee could smile so soon after being shot at. Behind them, far enough back to be harmless, the woman who had waved and the three men now standing beside her were still looking after them. Her limp arms hung at her sides. Maybe when the next vehicle came they'd get it right. Driving up the road, Brett wondered for the first time in his life how far he was prepared to go, and suddenly realized there would absolutely come a point when he had to answer that question with no chance for reflection.

"That's how it's going to be now," he said quietly.

When they reached the crest of the rise and started down, the failed ambush disappeared behind the hilltop, and in the dip ahead, the haze thickened with a suggestion of impending rain. But studying the sky for a while, he decided the layer didn't look like rainclouds. It was uniform in a way that suggested environment more than weather.

"You're going to find this interesting," Lee said, as she brightened with increasing relief. "I've decided that you're a lot like my dad," as if she'd arrived at a judgment that had been in doubt. This was a competition Brett hadn't realized he'd signed up for. Perhaps any woman you were spending time with entered you into it without your knowledge.

"He played the guitar?"

"Harmonica. Anyway, you can improvise at the drop of a hat, and you're dependable in ways that Ted never was. After a while with him, I realized how important that is in a man. I wasn't sure I'd find it in anyone else. Maybe I had stopped looking."

Her voice trailed off as she said this. Lee gave Brett a covert look that he pretended not to see, but he felt it on the side of his head, and it made him think that by following his instincts, he'd unknowingly done the right thing. This hadn't always worked in the past. Maybe he was better in crisis than in daily routine.

"So I'm dependable," he repeated in a flat tone. It was one of his core values, but it didn't sound very exotic coming from her.

She gave him a look of surprising serenity, given that they'd just survived an ambush, and shook her head. "Maybe you're aiming at being something else, I don't know, but I think basic things are going to matter more now in these conditions. You should take it as a compliment. We're going to see more gunfire like that down the road, aren't we?" she added, sounding like she was trying to keep the anxiety out of her voice.

"I'm sure you're right. I should have gotten the armored version of this van, but who knew?"

"But we already have some things they can't take from us, though, don't you think?"

"If we're moving fast enough. Everything else is up for grabs now."

7

Three miles farther on, the radio sputtered back to life on higher ground as it captured a signal from the Bridger station.

"...and from the section of the city above Seventeenth Street and east of Sampson. To evacuate by this route, proceed along Twentieth. All other routes must remain clear to give fire and rescue vehicles free access. The National Guard has announced they will shoot looters on sight. A tent city is being erected on open ground south of the Tyler Johnson Implement Company, two miles east of the city limits. There, food and water will be available, sanitary facilities, and an emergency medical station. However, and take special note of this, if you show any symptoms of the current epidemic, including severe coughing, rapid heartbeat, or fever, proceed directly and without delay to..."

The broadcast abruptly went silent. Brett filled in the last three unvoiced words. "...the nearest cemetery." The gray layer now covered the sky like a high and level shroud. "This must be smoke from Bridger. They're evacuating whole sections of it."

"It's a city made of wood," Lee said. "That's always been a risk."

Brett suddenly wondered if they were already burning the dead, but he didn't bring it up.

Like so much of this part of the state, most of the small-scale commercial and home construction in Bridger had long been driven by easy access to the surrounding pine forests, whose pitchy wood products were never suitable for furniture or interior trim, yet worked well as cheap and abundant framing lumber. Protected from termites and moisture, it would last for many decades. Bridger's inner-city neighborhoods were densely built with Victorian homes of the mid and late nineteenth century. Set on narrow lots, they had originally provided housing for a growing middle class of whites. Now many of these old-fashioned houses were divided and run down, the gingerbread millwork rotten or missing, front porches boxed in for an extra bedroom, and the environment mixed and restless. In the current month of dry weather they made for perfect tinderbox conditions.

"We were so smart not to go to Bridger," Brett said. "Imagine the city flooding with refugees even as it burns."

"But maybe that's why it's burning. That influx of potentially diseased people might have been the spark that touched off a situation already poised to explode."

"Maybe, but I go up there twice a week and I've never noticed much tension."

She faced him directly. "Brett, you don't live in Bridger, and you probably go to the same handful of places every time you're there, am I right? I think the racial situation is usually in balance around here, even with some of the usual issues, but if you upset that equilibrium, like by this evacuation of that whole strip of coast, you tip things too far one way or another. Tempers flare. Passions erupt. Worst of all, bad memories return."

"You mean like if the state health department decided to locate the quarantined refugees next to a poor black neighborhood. How that would be perceived."

"Something like that. You know how things are, or maybe you don't—race is often no more than an uneasy truce."

He looked at her face without discovering much nuance.

"I thought civil rights had made a lot of progress in the last few decades." Brett wondered where this was going. He was no fan of politics, and race was a sore point often and easily abused. Politicians on both sides who campaigned on healing such divisive issues later picked it like a scab for their own uses.

"Yes, but it can still be a raw spot, and I know that well. I don't think there has been a single day in my life after the age of two when I wasn't reminded in some way that I was black. Sometimes I feel like I don't belong here. I don't always know where I do belong."

Brett wondered about the microchip again. Had it been a way of belonging when she signed up for it? Had he been too quick to judge her for that?

"Tell me if I'm wrong, but I always thought that the race issue was an effect mainly felt in large numbers. There was slavery, then emancipation, the Jim Crow laws and then segregation in the schools. It was all about labeling large numbers of people in groups. That's how we disrespect each other most easily, with labels. But as individuals, like you and me, traveling together to escape the latest plague, it goes away, doesn't it?"

Lee shook her head slowly, pursing her lips. "That's where the rubber meets the road, Jack, like they say in Detroit City. It's one on one that's the worst. That's where you stick it in my face."

This took Brett by surprise and silenced him for a moment. He looked at her as if checking her color, a blank expression in his eyes. What else was Lee but another person? To him, this was a call so subtle that it could hardly matter in this kind of situation, yet it was still a current issue to her. Her tone of voice said it always would be. His idea had long been that people were individuals before they were members of any race or nation or religion. He didn't articulate this because she seemed to have worked it out in her own way, based on her own experience, something everyone had to do. He felt Lee must have some mixed race background. Her skin tones were medium. For himself, Brett didn't feel that having one parent who'd been a Methodist of Scottish background, and another who was a nonbeliever, defined him as a half-Methodist, a half-creed. Even so, he knew this analogy wasn't the same as what Lee was talking about since he had never suffered any discrimination for it.

"I hadn't thought about it that way, Lee. I guess it's easier for me to not think about it than it is for you. Is this going to be an issue between us?"

"Not if you don't want it to be. Maybe this mess will let us reinvent ourselves. Who do you wanna be?"

"I'll be a fugitive from injustice. Neither of us belongs here. We're only movin' on. Actually, when you came up to the van yesterday and said 'Y'all' in that sweet potato voice you can do so well, I thought you were a true Southern belle."

"That accent is something I can turn on and off. After a couple glasses of wine I do French and Vietnamese too, on demand. With a little work, my hair could be Irish. Nothing else is, but I'm OK with who I am. If you are too…"

For a few miles they didn't speak. It seemed to Bret that merely traveling with her had opened the door to some issues he hadn't anticipated.

"What's that fire going to do to the flood of refugees coming into Bridger from the east?" she asked, after a while. "I'm thinking of that crossing at Highway 84 that you mentioned might be difficult."

"We won't know till we see it. That's our mantra now about everything."

Brett switched on the radio again but it pulled in no more than deadly silence from the Bridger station. This was their only local source of information. He tried a few more distant stations and picked up nothing else. Cruising the dial at the high end brought up a couple of broadcasts with national news. The nationwide death toll was now nearly two and a half million, greater than the entire population of some small states.

"I can't listen to any more of that," she said, switching it off. "The epidemic keeps on spreading and we can only run. Do you have a siphon?"

"No. That would be handy now, wouldn't it?"

"I left mine in the car. We need a better planning function. I don't know what I was thinking. I packed my suitcase yesterday morning and the night before, mostly some clothes and toiletries. I thought everything else I'd need would be in place at my brother's house, even though they'd already left for Corpus Christi. Coming into Outpost, I'd pick up a pound of coffee, some sliced turkey breast and a loaf of bread. A quart of milk for cereal, a stick of butter, a couple of tomatoes and a grapefruit, and that would be it. Maybe a half pound of bacon and some lettuce, but I wasn't ready for the end of civilization as we know it."

As they drove farther north, the smoke layer thickened. It grew darker and more ominous, although the smell was still too high to reach them. That far above Marshy Flats the prevailing winds traveled from the west and slightly north, rather than swirling up from the Gulf. They would have to be considerably above the latitude of Bridger before a clear sky appeared again. The country of tall, scabby pines, straight and densely packed, stretched in a solid fabric all around, where the only functioning branches were near the top, closest to the light. If anyone wanted to harvest telephone poles commercially, this would be the place. Privately, Brett wondered how long any phones would still be operating as the casualties piled up. Who would show up for work only to risk death by exposure to his neighbor's coughing?

"What's next for our route?" he asked. The gas needle was inching down toward the halfway mark. This meant it was really closer to three eighths. That gauge was always the most optimistic part of any vehicle. On the other hand, when it read empty, enough gas usually remained to go another twenty miles.

Lee lifted the map out of the glove compartment and unfolded it. Brett had earlier marked their devious course with a red felt tip pen like the cut line for a surgeon in an exploratory operation, scrubbed in with scalpel in hand. "I see a crossroads a few miles up, it might be three or four? I can't tell exactly. Then we turn right toward a town called Kirby, like the vacuum." She turned to look at him. "Are you nervous? I am." Her eyes were more expressive than he remembered. Her tentative grin asked for his support.

"About being in a town again? It's probably a nowhere place like Dundee. I'd be happy to see another gas station. It could happen, since we're a long way now from Highway 36. Maybe it's untouched by the epidemic out here. We've crossed over into the recent past. This road might be a time machine. The farther you go, the deeper into the past you are. Does that sound too hopeful?"

"No, because that's my dream," Lee said softly. "The farther away we travel from Bridger and Highway 36, the more normal things become. You're right. Somewhere out there it's 1990. Just ahead on this road we're on, people are still laughing and shaking hands with each other. They're hugging and touching each other's faces with their fingertips, and not holding back in fear. In large areas further on everything is totally unchanged, and we're leaving behind us a throbbing rotten spot named Bridger." She was sitting quite still, with her hands folded in her lap, a childlike expression on her face. It was as if she were alone in her tiny schoolgirl's bedroom and staring out an open casement window at a rainbow. Brett imagined that this was how she had looked as a solemn child, feeling the weight of responsibility early.

"Dreamer," he said, knowing that too much responsibility could make a dreamer out of anyone, and to no good effect in a crisis, "but I hope you're right."

"And here's our turnoff."

Their route ended in a tee at another paved road. A convenient sign ventilated by three bullet wounds read *Kirby 4*. One of the puckered holes dotted the i perfectly. Brett swung around the corner and paused. No other traffic moved in either direction.

"Have you ever been married, Brett? Just asking," Lee asked softly, as if shifting gears.

"Ah," he couldn't help grinning as they pulled onto the new road, "now the lady questions are coming. I can tell you that I came close twice, once in college, and once again right after I turned thirty."

"So I guess you're still a virgin. What happened?"

"I feel like it some days. I bailed out of the first one just in time. It wasn't that I got cold feet, but one day I looked at my fiancée in a way I never had before. I won't reenact the detail, but it was an odd situation that came up with no warning, and the way she reacted surprised me. Shocked me, really. Thinking about it made me wonder what else I hadn't noticed about her, so I suggested we postpone the wedding while I sorted things out for a few months. I truly just wanted to think without that date approaching, but she was offended and broke it off right there. It was like we'd already printed the invitations in her mind. Looking at it now, I can't blame her. She felt insulted by my sudden indecision."

"I think she was hiding something from you and she was afraid you'd found her out."

"Maybe. I shouldn't have been surprised that she acted that way, although I was at the time. Eight years later, when I was ever so much more mature," here Brett smiled almost involuntarily, "my second fiancée cancelled the next wedding, which took me totally by surprise. I felt my role was reversed. Looking back now, I think each of us was right on both counts. I liked both of those women a lot, and I still do, because I run into them now and then in Marshy Flats, like in the Gulf Shore Market, although now I don't think I was ever really in love with either of them. They both married other men, but I thought I still could've gone down life's road with either of them for a while. But at the first serious fork, I'm not sure any of us would've taken the same direction. I can see that better now, but I didn't at the time of the second one. I was flat-out blindsided when she left me."

"You must've been hurting badly at the time."

"When I think about it I can still mainly feel the shock, and now I realize I had shocked my first fiancée in the same way. Anyway, I don't dwell on it."

"You don't show it."

"No, I like my life pretty well most of the time." Except, he thought, that he didn't trust his judgment quite as much after going through that failure twice. He believed he still wanted to end up with someone he loved, but also wondered if that would ever happen now, since the current dilemma skewed the odds even further. How could you objectively connect with a woman when everyone was growing more desperate every day? Would you find yourself in a relationship or a rescue?

"But isn't it difficult to be alone all the time? I lived with Ted for two years, and it's been hard to get used to being by myself again, although it never made me want to get back with him. Still, I feel like I'm missing some things by being alone."

"I know what you mean. I always felt I enjoyed my solitude. But in the last few years I've often wished I had someone important in my life. I've had a few relationships, but nothing that ever seemed permanent. You know how it is in a small town. You've already met almost everybody and it's hard to get excited about someone you've known since kindergarten. Maybe if this hadn't happened, I might have seen you on the street tomorrow and we would've walked right past each other without a glance. We probably have already, more than once. How was it that you and Ted never got married? Don't tell me if you don't want to."

And Lee did not answer immediately, apparently walking through it in her mind, and not for the first time. "I really think we both knew early on that it wasn't going to work long term, but at the same time it wasn't bad enough to end it. It was that same small town thing. Who would you rather be with? It was comfortable, and I couldn't answer that. I had never wanted to date anyone I met at the restaurant. They were only surfing for the evening's entertainment. Anyway, people don't always get married now like they used to. Ted and I had a lot of good times, but after a while, neither of us ever mentioned marriage anymore. I think I gave up. Naturally, I wondered if he had backed off because of the race thing. Maybe at first it was even kind of cool for him to have a black girlfriend, not that he'd ever marry her."

"And was it cool to be one?"

Her small shrug answered this. "Sometimes it was, OK? There was a little bit of power there, like I could go either way if I wanted. It was up to me for once." Her tone was calm and fluid, but her face was turned to the side window and he couldn't see her expression. "But when I moved out I felt tired more than anything else, and I told him I'd met someone else, although that wasn't true. Ted never asked me who it was, and I don't think he believed it. Things between us weren't ever terrible, but they weren't great either, and I couldn't figure out any other way to explain leaving. It seemed so complicated, and all the reasons I thought of to tell him why we were breaking up weren't exactly the real ones. I didn't want to lie, but when I wasn't able to tell him the real reasons, that somehow confirmed it was time for me to leave. I don't know. I think I didn't want to settle for that little, for whatever it was, which I couldn't have said if someone asked me. You know what? OK, I'll say it. I was better than that, and I always have been. It's still complicated. His dying certainly didn't settle anything. Imagine how full of loose ends and unspoken feelings this country will be when this is over. If it ever is."

"Still, for reasons other than that," Brett said, "I think it's a simpler game now for both of us. It's called survival. Ted's gone. You no longer have anything to explain to him or anyone except yourself, and I've got no one with me. We're homeless, more or less, so we also divest ourselves of our psychological baggage as well as we can. We pool our resources, which includes our brainpower. We're not lovers, but we can give each other some emotional support. The more complicated things fall away. The simple things will become harder, like finding gasoline, and eventually, I suspect, food. Have you thought about where all this might be going?"

"Yes," she said, "and it doesn't look attractive to me."

"I know. But you didn't give me the impression you were looking for anything more than survival in Outpost."

"What's wrong with that? Even without complicating it by anything else, that seems like a tall order."

Brett turned to study her face, and failing to find more

than determination, looked back at the road.

She regarded him with raised eyebrows, seeming about to rephrase something she'd said earlier. "I felt vulnerable in the bathtub, before, OK? Now I feel like I was rude. Maybe it was only because I didn't want to give you the wrong idea. I'm sure you've got other things on your mind than going to bed with me. Everybody at my job thinks I'm available, so I didn't want to seem desperate, because I'm not. I never have been. But this is a different kind of reality—each hour we're together is like a day. Maybe now we're all desperate for different reasons. But still, don't read it wrong. I'm looking to survive just like you are. When this is over maybe I'll date you, OK, if you want to? Call me then. I'll give you my number. If you're lucky it'll still be working, if anything is, which I doubt." Lee turned and her face softened as she watched his reaction to this. After a moment they both laughed softly. Lee touched his hand on the wheel for a second, and then her statement and the moment were both gone.

As they approached Kirby the scenery didn't change. The hills rolled on in shallow waves as if a once flat and wider landscape had been compressed in an ancient cataclysm between two unyielding walls, restructuring the terrain into the character of a reluctant washboard.

"This is going to be one of those forks in the road again, isn't it?" Lee said, her face suddenly more serious.

Brett wasn't sure which one she meant—he could see six or seven such tipping points in his past, so he took a chance. "Yes it is, but you and I have made our choice. It looks to me like it's the biggest fork of all, and not only for us. We can joke about it a little, when we have to, as we try to stay sane, but the choice we made is either going to kill us or save us. At least by avoiding Bridger we made one, and win or lose, we've got only ourselves to blame for the outcome."

"And is it easier to make that choice when neither of us really knows the person we're with that well?"

He didn't see much future for them after the epidemic passed, if it did, but he found he didn't mind this discussion;

it was better than thinking all the time about their next meal or who would be shooting at them around the next curve, or about gasoline, the essential medium of flight.

"It felt like it was easier to make that choice this morning. I'd have to say yes. It doesn't scare me, anyway, because I think that together we add up to more than two. How about you?"

"You don't scare me at all," Lee said, her chin tilted upward. "You never did."

"I haven't tried yet. Is that your answer?"

"It is right now. Ask me again later."

"Then let's take Kirby by storm."

As promising as this sentiment was, however, two miles farther down the road Kirby looked as if it had already been taken by storm by someone else. Parts of its leading edge resembled a tornado of violence.

As they approached the edge of town, what they saw first was a normal white-painted house. In the local style, the roof extended over the lawn in deep overhangs. The door of the screened porch stood open, as did the overhead garage door. The space inside was empty of vehicles. As they slowly drove closer, the jamb at the porch door displayed needles of splintered bare wood at the lock edge. Even more than that, the two dead bodies beyond a low hedge in the front yard set the tone as they came into view. Brett's stomach tightened while he slowed the van to take a closer look. They were lying face down, but no sprays of bloody mucous stained the soil around them. The small flows of blood that darkened the soil were not near their heads. Their skewed positions suggested they were already dead when they fell. Unless they were lying on their guns, they hadn't been armed when they died. Several triumphant grackles stalked about hopefully, heads acutely cocked, surveying the scene with one eye here, one eye there. They had won this round and were now working out the division of the spoils. Lee was breathing heavily through her open mouth, both her hands over her ears as if the guns were still blazing.

JOHN SCHERBER

Seeing this, Brett's first thought was that they needed a gun now more than ever, and although he didn't want to say this to her, if he had seen one at this scene, free of bloody mucous, he would've jumped out and picked it up. It was sad to be reduced to stealing from corpses, but it was becoming a scavenger's world, one that would increasingly belong to predators that were flexible in their prey. The most skillful, determined and unscrupulous among them would survive. The others would have their belongings picked over, and ultimately, their corpses. It wasn't the best and smartest that would survive, it was those who could maintain a grin and stop at nothing.

"We're looking at an execution." Awe edged Lee's voice. It was indignant, but still calm, although her face was contorted in a grimace. "That's what this has come to now. Can you believe that? I mean, so soon? I thought it would take longer for everything to break down. It hasn't even been forty-eight hours."

"People can see what's coming," he said. No one else was in view on the street. Brett began to understand the prism of the racist experience through which Lee viewed things. He felt he had somehow been part of the other side of that equation, but without ever feeling it or knowing it. How ironic that it took something like this for him to break out of that bubble. No one had responded to these killings. No yellow crime scene tape stretched from the hedge to the trees. That fact was almost as alarming as seeing the bodies themselves. No one was in charge in Kirby; no one was present to object or even to throw a sheet over the remains. There was no law here, and no order.

"Do you want me to stop?" he said, inching along.

"What? No! No!! Do you? Why on earth would you? Christ!" She looked at Brett like he had lost his mind. Instead, he felt his thinking was growing cooler and more focused. By asking he had only taken the pulse of her reaction.

Picking up speed, he drove on for half a block, feeling like they were being attacked by another disease: the phobia of getting involved in hopeless situations, the fear of being the next victim in a world crowded with victims. Or maybe that was only another name for prudence

"Here's a grocery store," she said, pointing to the right. "We could use a few things."

Brett opened his mouth to laugh, but held it back in time to turn. "So now we're going shopping. Let's pick up a TV Guide and some Skittles." He knew there was some bitterness in his tone, but he couldn't help it.

Lee gave him an impatient look. "Being sarcastic about it won't help us survive this, Brett," she said, shutting him down as they pulled up in front of the store entry and got out. "Practical is what's going to make it through. We need to eat." He felt like he should take his hand off her knee again, not that it had ever been there since their cooling bath.

"You're practical," he said to her back.

They walked up to the door and she faced him for a moment and pulled herself up to as close as she could come to his height.

"You're damn right, I am. Try being black without being practical some time. I know a lot of folks who do it that way, but believe me, it never works. You can't depend on anyone. I didn't put it on my list of survival skills before, but I can see now that I should've. I couldn't see then what was coming as well as I do now. This is going to take more than I thought, so yes, let's do some shopping here. Forget about what we saw back there. We're probably going to have more to forget about than we can imagine, and being able to change gears quickly is going to help. This is a stick-shift situation, OK? Maybe you're too used to running on automatic."

They stared at each other stiffly for a moment before she walked into the store. He watched the way she moved past him. Nothing was going to get in her way.

The grocery resembled many old-fashioned mom and pop businesses that have mostly been forced off the street by larger chain stores. The absence of any nearby town sizable enough to support a supermarket may have helped this one last beyond its normal life expectancy. Coming in, they found three aisles running from front to back with coolers and freezers sharing one long wall. The inventory held a lot of variety without much depth. The checkout counter was on their left. Although the ceiling lights were switched on, no one else was in the store. It was so quiet they could make out the subtle hum of one of the florescent ceiling fixtures. Lee picked up a basket near the door and started down the first aisle as if this were somehow normal. Brett waited for her near the entrance, shifting his weight from one foot to the other, as if it were a trap and someone was about to jump out with a chainsaw or a shotgun. His eyes flickered warily over the aisles while she collected groceries. He visualized himself as the single sentinel goose in the flock with his head erect while all the others fed on the grass at their feet.

Five minutes later they were still alone with the makings of dinner and several other meals. At the counter she set the basket down while Brett leaned over and studied the floor behind, expecting a body protruding feet first from beneath the shelves, but he didn't find one. The drawer of the cash register hung open and empty of anything but a few pennies. Was the owner lying behind the store in a pool of his own blood? They looked at each other and shrugged. It wasn't indifference, only the inability to judge what they were looking at.

Stepping behind the counter, Brett found a stack of handle bags and packed the groceries. It felt more normal than anything he'd done in some time. One bag was enough for everything. Peeling off a piece of paper from the printout reel, he used it to lift the cash tray without touching it. Placing a twenty and a five under it, he pushed the drawer shut, listened to it click, and they walked out of the store.

"I wish they were all that easy, even though I'm not sure what was happening there," he said, shutting the back door of the van. "Next we'll find a gas station if our luck holds." He didn't believe it would.

"What's going on with this place? I've seen the way

you're taking it all in," she said as they pulled out into the street. No other cars were in sight.

"Here's what I think, after what we've seen. What if the breakdown in public health is only the leading edge of the axe, and it's followed immediately by the collapse of civility and law enforcement?"

"I'm used to that."

"This isn't the same."

"Why not? Maybe it's less discriminating this time. Maybe everybody's a minority now."

For Brett, this didn't compute. "To me, it feels like all restraint is gone, so we have to adjust our expectations, that's all." They sped off down the street.

"Now I'm worried about Outpost," she said, then raised both hands. "I know, it's no time to worry, and life goes where it's going no matter what we do."

"Not bad," he said. "You're sounding like me."

Yet, like an apparition from a more intact past, two blocks away they saw a gas station from a major chain. It possessed only three pumps, but the lights were lit inside the convenience store. They seemed to beckon, as anything that still functioned would. Brett pulled up to a pump as if it was something he often did, and walked inside, assuming the manner of the road weary. This was natural enough, given the way things were going. He might have just driven non-stop from Biloxi, or from Tampa with another load of deadly fishing floats. A tall, sunburned man at the counter, his face framed by long white sideburns and a handlebar moustache, looked at him carefully and greeted him with a curt nod without speaking. His western-style hat was tan and fairly clean except where sweat had darkened the felt around the inner edge of the brim. On the counter a sawed-off shotgun rested within easy reach of his right hand. To save time, it was pointed toward the customer facing him. His palm rested flat next to the trigger guard, and his fingers were extended and subtly crawling in place as if a low-level current was flickering uncontrollably through their nerve endings. Brett recognized that facing this man was like a quick-draw of the mind, where any miscalculation could be fatal, and no more than one could occur.

"Where is everybody?"

"They've gone lookin' for easier times, I guess."

"Do you have any gas left for sale?" Brett said carefully, enunciating like he was attempting to speak an unfamiliar language for the first time. Under normal conditions, this would have been the question of an idiot, but the world was new and all bets were off.

"Only till it's gone. Then I'm gone too." His eyes rested on Brett's hands.

"Do you have a lot left?" He took a moment to banish the glee from his voice.

"More than I need for myself. Take however much you want. I haven't jacked up the price none, either. I want to sell it all to whoever wants it. Unlike some others in this town, I still believe in this country. It's the folks who're still holdin' their heads up and acting like they're human through all this that make it great. That's the way it's always been, too."

Brett nodded slowly, not wanting to make any quick movements. Like a lot of other things, too much affirmation could get you blown away in a situation like this. "And do you also have any jerry cans for sale?" He articulated each word as if it might have explosive tendencies.

"I think I might still have one. It's a five-gallon. Look over there by the restroom doors." He canted his head in that direction. While his hands didn't move at all from their position, they were ready to, and one of them didn't have far to travel.

Brett found the jerry can and brought it back to the counter. "I'm going to take this can and fill it outside, with gas," pointing through the window as if to show he knew where that was. "Then I'm going to fill my tank and top off another jerry can I've got in the van. OK?"

"You got it, buddy. Pay me for this jerry can here, and then use your card outside at the pump. Then we'll all be square."

"What will you do when the gas is gone?" Brett removed some bills from his wallet. Maybe he'd want to come back at some point, since this visit was going so well.

"I'm going to take all my money in a big bag and head for Canada. I hear they're still sane up there, some of them, anyway."

"Of course they are, and they're known for their sanity, so good luck with that." After their experience on the road, to Brett this sounded like the man was planning to drive across hell in a snowmobile, but he realized that not everyone comes up with the same solution to a new and unique set of problems.

"Same to you, buddy." The man pushed the change across the counter with his left hand. Brett scooped it up and walked outside with the empty jerry can. Lee was leaning against the van with her arms folded, watching the street, where nothing was moving. The tension in her bearing suggested she might be ready to break into a run. Clearly she didn't know what to expect, but when she saw the jerry can her face lit up and she took three steps toward him.

"You are a minor genius," she said.

"Minor?" He slid his credit card into the slot and started the pump.

"I suspect some tougher tests are still to come, but the first round clearly goes to you."

Later, as they pulled away from the pumps, he paused on the apron and looked into her face, trying to read it. "We're at another crossroads here, Lee. We can now go back and get your Volkswagen, or not. This question is only about getting your car back, OK? I still think we should do the rest of it together."

Although that would've been a long drive through territory that would likely be even more uncertain now than earlier, Brett didn't go into any more detail, like whether they would still go to Outpost if she retrieved the Beetle, driving separately, or split up, or any of the other options. This was a tipping point he hadn't thought of earlier. It didn't take Lee long to decide. She put her hand on his arm.

"I can't go back that way after that ambush and what we just saw. How many more bodies would be lying on the ground by the time we picked up my car, put some gas in it, and came up this way again? If it's even still there, how many more roadblocks would there be coming back here now? Who else would be dead in this town? And would this gas station still be open to refill our tanks? I still feel like we have to go on together, don't you? I think if the question is about one car or two, I vote one, if only because we would need that much less gas."

"That works for me, too." They stared at each other for a moment in silence, each seeing something meaningful in the other's eyes. Neither of them could've defined what it was. A moment later they were cruising up the highway again, heading north with a full tank of gas and fifteen gallons reserve in the jerry cans.

"I wonder how much longer we'll be able to use a credit card given the way things are deteriorating." Brett wished now that he had five of them like many other people did, in case they didn't all shut down at the same time. He had always limited himself to one and settled out the bill at the end of every month. He had called it prudence, but that now looked like a strategy for a more stable world that was gone forever. People who had run up huge debts would now do well, since few creditors would survive to collect them.

8

Next, dirt was visible beneath their wheels, real dirt, with its flighty offspring, dust. After all those miles of blacktop, the paved road came to an end, but at least Kirby was a mixed memory fifty uneventful miles back. No corpses had since appeared, no fires, and little traffic. The tone of the sky lightened and their mood rose with it. They had gasoline and food, and they were alive. They'd been through two small towns after Kirby that were apparently intact, although few people were in view. One had another working gas station. Brett topped off the tank without incident. The owner didn't have a jerry can for sale, and they got back on the road immediately without starting a conversation, happy to hope that an increasing distance from Bridger and Highway 36 might mean increasing normality. They hit the Highway 84 intersection that went into Bridger and breezed under it with no distress. The traffic overhead moved freely, but heavily, in both directions, neither of which was theirs. Brett began to have visions of Outpost as a final destination. It needed to be too far away to matter to the vandals and murderers, yet big enough to have working communications. Maybe by tomorrow or next week no place would be that far away, but for now it looked like their best bet. This was a crisis best managed by inches.

"And you know some people in that town, other than your brother and his family." He didn't have to say where he meant.

"Of course." The dismissive wave of her hand suggested how much like a second home it was. "I've been to Outpost lots of times. I always spend my vacations and holidays up there; it's where I go when I'm ready to freak out, like I was when Ted and I split up. Doug and Holly live next door, they're good neighbors, and Clayton and DeShawn are right across the street."

"I wouldn't mind having lunch or dinner with you when we settle in, if you're ready to get off the road for a while. I know I am," he said, in a neutral tone. "I think we need to celebrate survival, just as friends and allies. Did you bring along anything great for going out to dinner?" He suddenly realized how much he needed something like this.

"Maybe you, if you behave. I wouldn't mind getting out of the van for a while myself."

This sounded like she was inching toward him a bit

more. As they started around a curve he glanced at the rear-view mirror. Their own dust cloud fanned out in billows behind, but after a nearly clear interval behind them, Brett made out another cloud, fronted by a black and white car moving much faster than they were. Feeling like he had let them both down in his distraction, he sped up in response.

"Let's look for a quick exit," he said, "any small lane will do. This might be something we don't want to deal with." They were bouncing over the ruts. It was another panicky mile before they found a place to turn off. Lee was ready as he whiplashed for a hundred feet along a gravel-topped private lane before regaining control. With the aerodynamics of a shoebox, the van was not the proper vehicle for this kind of maneuver. As the lane widened and curved, Brett slipped behind some pines and shut down the engine with a gasp. Behind them a new concrete slab and several piles of building materials awaited carpenters and masons.

"You're panting," she said. "Good job."

"That was hard work." He waited a couple of minutes for the car to follow them in, then got out when it didn't appear. They peered through the trees down the lane and saw nothing but hanging dust. After a while they drove back out to the road. Far down on the right an ocher dust cloud was ripping along at a clip far too fast for the condition of the surface. The cop was on his way to address a serious problem, and they had no choice but to follow. Brett drove slowly to allow the dust to settle ahead of them.

"I wonder if I'm getting paranoid now."

"It'll probably be another shooting," Lee said, folding her arms. "I'm bracing myself for it."

"Resources will be getting more scarce now, I imagine. People are thinking they can get through today or tomorrow, but next week will be a different issue."

Lee turned in her seat to face him. "Do you really think we can survive this? Tell me the truth."

"I don't know. As it stands, we're too exposed. In the end we're going to need a community that's been able to resist the chaos we've seen and is willing to take us in. Does that describe the Outpost you know? I haven't been there in twenty-five years."

"It could be, but we won't know until we see how it's responding. If isolation is helpful, then it's got that. Not a lot of people are going to end up there by accident, and no one will be passing through because the highway ends right above the dam by the water treatment plant."

Another mile ahead, the road dust had mostly settled. They saw a police car on the shoulder, canted off at an angle as if it had slid to an unexpected stop. Brett couldn't tell whether it was the one he had seen. As they approached, a brown pickup with a battered box came into view turned on its side in the ditch beyond. No one was nearby, although the acrid scent of violence still hung in the air. Maybe it was in Brett's mind more than in his nose. He hadn't opened the van windows.

"I'm going to stop," he said. "A lot of these police cruisers carry a shotgun clipped to the dash and we need a weapon now. One of these times we're going to have to defend ourselves." He was recalling the sawed-off shotgun in the gas station. The owner had been ready for anything. He and Lee were only ready for flight.

"Brett, don't! Please don't get into this. Will having a gun really help us?"

"Sorry." He could hear how dismissive his tone was.

He had already pulled off without looking at her, not ready to argue at that moment. He jumped out of the van and ran over to the passenger side of the car. No one was inside, and no shotgun hung on the dash, but on the ground next to the car a sheriff's department officer was lying on his back. A clean round bullet hole perforated his forehead about half an inch above his left eyebrow. His lips remained parted as if from a final exclamation of surprise, and his eyes were half open and vacant. His pistol, a revolver, was still in its holster, although the flap was unsnapped as though he'd been reaching for it when he was shot. Brett pulled it out, and on the man's belt, among a half dozen other small packs of equipment and supplies, he also located the nearly square leather pouch he was looking for. Inside was a clip of ten cartridges. In a heartbeat he was back in the van. It was only as he drove off that he began to feel queasy at what he'd seen. His hands were a little unsteady on the steering wheel.

"Tomb robber," Lee said in a tone between outrage and admiration, staring at the revolver now tucked into his belt. Her look was grim. "You must have found a dead cop. He wouldn't have walked away from his gun. Are you sure he was dead?"

Brett nodded without speaking, remembering again the pistols and ammunition for sale at Blake's Nifty Store at normal prices. What babies they were then, he thought, only yesterday. They'd innocently bought wine and cheese and sliced turkey as if going on a picnic, but this was no picnic. A hundred fifty feet further on, four county sheriff's cars were scattered around an unpaved church parking lot. Six deputies huddled in their shadow. The church was an old-fashioned white clapboard affair with a bell tower and cheap amber and red tinted glass windows in diamond panes, two of which had been shot out. No one was firing at that moment, and only one of the cops glanced back at the van as they went by.

Two and a half hours later, after encountering no more problems, and seeing almost no one else on the highway as they drove farther and farther from civilization, they passed through a tiny town called Davis Junction. It appeared to be calm and undisturbed, so normal it was almost shocking. Five miles later they arrived on the edge of Outpost as dusk approached. Brett didn't remember a thing about coming into it years earlier. Lee grabbed his arm.

"We're here! We made it! Brett, do you realize that? I feel like we're safe now, after all that! Don't you?"

But they weren't home yet. Two Outpost squad cars were parked nose-to-nose blocking the road ahead before the buildings began. As they pulled up, a black officer with a flat-brimmed trooper's hat and rigid creases in his olive shirt sauntered up to their window as if he had nothing much on his mind.

"What is your destination today, sir?" he asked politely through his germproof surgical mask, as if there could be any doubt. Yet Brett had the sense that the next question would not be so polite if his response was wrong in any way.

"We're here in Outpost to find…"

"Hey, Leon! It's Lee. What's happenin', babe?" Bracing one hand on Brett's thigh, she leaned across his lap with an arresting display of cleavage and reached for the cop's gloved hand, which quickly met hers. A nice level of caution in an epidemic, Brett thought. Her accent was again closer to the Southern belle candy voice she'd used the first time he saw her on the road outside of Dundee. He wondered again whether he might be too trusting of her, the way she could turn it on and off.

Leon broke into a broad smile, only evident from the way his ears moved beyond the mask. "Your brother already left yesterday morning, darlin'."

"I know. He called me. But he also said we could come up and use the house until this damn thing blows over. Did he tell you that too?"

"No, but you can go right on through, Lee. Who is this with you? We have to ask everybody." He pulled a notebook from his shirt pocket.

"This is my friend Brett."

"Last name?"

"Wallace." Lee had never asked him. He realized he didn't remember hers. Survivors were all on a first name basis.

Leon turned back to Lee. "Have you known Mr. Wallace more than six and a half hours? I have to ask that too, sorry. We can't have people bringing in hitchhikers." He followed this with what might have been an apologetic smile under his mask.

"I believe I have, but it seemed like a hell of a lot

longer today. We went past some trouble south of here."

Leon took this to be a bitter joke and waved them through, peering at a pickup pulling up behind them.

"You're connected already," Brett said to Lee, pulling away through the gap left when at a signal from Leon, one of the squad cars backed up and made room for them to pass. "That's another survival skill we didn't think of."

The highway became the commercial strip, with a gas station and attached auto repair garage, then a supermarket and a fire station farther down. Homes mingled with commercial properties. The street curved away from the lake toward steep stony hills dotted with scrappy stands of pine. On the right, a fork led down toward the dam and a boulevard that hugged the rampart above the water. It felt calm and normal, as if they'd come home.

"This is going to be a lot easier now, Brett," she said, putting her hand on his shoulder. "More than you know. This ol' town is my home away from home. You'll see what I mean once we get settled in. God, I'm so glad to be here; I feel like we've escaped. Doesn't it look great?"

PART TWO
SANCTUARY

1

Call it holing up, or call it coming to earth. Brett called it living another day. With her history in this place of refuge, he couldn't be sure what Lee called it. It was already obvious that going forward the future would be quantified in smaller bites, whether Outpost was home or not.

"I'm calling it simple survival," Lee said. Her hands danced in the air as if she were conducting her own emotional life while she directed the way to her brother's house seven blocks beyond the checkpoint. After they pulled into the driveway she found the key under a clay pot of rosemary at the corner of the concrete entry platform. With a flourish, she swung the front door open like a realtor and held out her arm in a sweeping gesture. "Notice how different this private home is from a cargo van. Although it's not mobile, here we have actual rooms: a bathroom and a half, a kitchen, a master bedroom, a second bedroom, a laundry, a living room, and a patio in back with a barbecue and a picnic table under an umbrella. A garage with concealment for a vehicle that's been shot at recently."

Brett looked from room to room, already thinking about settling in one place. It made him feel vulnerable, as if depending on other people was a strategy that had become too risky. Certainly it was unfamiliar.

"What I like is that it's a familiar place, and I have

some history here. It's not being on the road where you don't know what's coming at you from around every corner. Thank you for getting us here. I mean it." She seemed to think he needed some encouragement, so she pulled him closer and briefly put her arms around his neck. "I'm feeling *so* much better." He noticed an emotional flutter in her voice.

Brett pulled her suitcase in and closed the door, setting his plastic bag of clothes and the bag of food left from the abandoned grocery store next to it. Lee was already moving through the other rooms. He stood motionless for a moment, his feet suddenly heavy, remembering the vacations he'd taken as a kid with his parents, their arrival at a rental cabin on a tree-lined lake somewhere in the north, Minnesota or Wisconsin. The fishing rods and a landing net would be leaning in a corner by the door next to his father's tackle box. He'd always felt a moment of disappointment coming in, as if to say, So, this is it? This is all it is after waiting a year? It never smelled like home, although his parents didn't stint on these summer places; they had more than enough money. These cabins simply weren't familiar, and neither was this place. He realized that nothing else would be going forward, either. Still, he didn't miss Marshy Flats.

The house was a single story faced with wine-red masonry, long, thin bricks like the Romans used, with white painted trim. The façade framed a sealed picture window, but it was flanked by two screened casements that opened on cranks. The shallow pitch of the roofline allowed for deep overhangs supported by inexpensive wrought iron uprights anchored in concrete rounds in the grass. With grapes and vine leaves in stamped metal rusting along the edges, every outside corner had one. The deep lawn sloped gradually down to the front sidewalk. Other than a box hedge along the front wall, the house lacked any other attempt at landscaping. The shade from a few trees would have been welcome. It was an entry-level lower middle class house from the early 1970s, with no special distinction other than its current value as a refuge.

The living room furniture could have come from a

store that used the word *barn* as part of its name. The sofa and two easy chairs were upholstered in a nubby blue and ochre print. The master bedroom was large enough to have two dressers, and faced the front yard next to the living room. The kitchen, smaller bedroom, dining room and the half bathroom all looked out on the back yard, which resembled the front in its plainness, except that it had a six-foot-high weathered plank fence at the back and sides, and a corrugated metal storage building in the rear left corner. It looked like a cheap cartoon version of a miniature barn. Brett felt at once relieved and disappointed.

A moment after Lee disappeared the air conditioning began to hum. An instant later she returned, but soon vanished again with her cell phone at her ear. Brett went out to the back yard and sat at a picnic table at one end of a concrete slab. At the other end a hammock hung from two steel uprights. At the far corner was a kettle barbecue. Dusk was collecting in the neighbor's trees, which provided the only shade. It began to thicken around the house and crept along the lower edge of the back fence. Brett was curious about the condition of the rest of the country, but he didn't want to look at the television, reluctant to dispel the illusion that he was back in the America of three days before—a different place and time entirely. It was reassuring that aside from the gatekeepers as they came in, nothing else seemed unusual once they were inside Outpost.

After a few minutes Lee came out and set two glasses and an open bottle of wine on the table. "I told my brother we'd arrived and everything looks fine. They made it into Corpus Christi and his in-laws are great, although they're worried about me. Once they got away from the influence of Bridger, they had no problems on the road. I couldn't find any white wine, so it's going to have to be red tonight."

"That's OK. Thanks for this."

She wrinkled her nose and moved a step closer. "I don't feel like going out, do you? I want to stop running now. We've still got those things from the self-service grocery, and I found some ground coffee in the fridge for tomorrow morning. I want to settle in here and pretend we don't live on this earth anymore. Does that sound good to you? I feel bad that you had to drive all day."

"Sure. I'm a little beat too. It's not the driving itself, it's driving under those conditions. Seeing three dead bodies and getting shot at wears you down."

"I'm just relieved to be here." Lee gave him a cool look, as the throbbing of insects grew louder in the grass.

To Brett, they didn't sound like a familiar variety. The dune-like terrain of Marshy Flats doesn't encourage lawns, and the insects, although plentiful, are less vocal, as if they need to work harder to make a living in the thinner vegetation. He wondered how many people had died there now, how many he knew, and who would be left to bury the dead. Lee was quiet, looking up into the slopes.

Brett sipped his Chilean red wine and tried to find some higher purpose in this disaster. He was no believer in fate, nor did he think everything happened for some higher purpose, or that events always worked out for the best. Doubtless the people who had launched this epidemic had done so from the loftiest of principles. Brett was a practical man with a strong set of functional ethics, but abstract principle had never filled his gas tank and he rarely thought much about it. He had seen it too often used to flog other people.

"Can you see a future out there for anyone?" Lee's voice cut across his thoughts as she sat down. This reminded him of something she'd said before.

"Only for determined survivors. The idealists will soon kill all the rest."

When the mosquitoes began to drift in, they retreated inside.

"TV?" he said. "There's probably only one show on tonight, and it's not *Happy Days*."

Lee put on a cheery voice. "Is it *Survivor*? I think I'd like to see that. Maybe we can pick up some practical tips."

"I have mixed feelings about looking in on this, but we

do have to know what's happening." He switched it on. Lee's brother had a decent Sony flat screen with a remote. They sat next to each other on the sofa as the station came up. On the bottom left side of the screen was a running tally, as with election results, but no one was winning this one. The death toll was now over 4.7 million and constantly changing. The national grid of orange lights came up, and New Orleans, Corpus Christi, Dallas, and Little Rock were all still dark.

A moment later a commentator in a white coat was explaining that the organism causing the epidemic appeared to be a variant of the tubercle bacillus, which existed in many variations. Because of the rapid onset, and what he called its *fulminant* course, he thought it probable that this strain had been genetically engineered. He went on to explain that the word *fulminant* meant severe and rapid. It was spreading so fast that no response could be developed to slow it down.

Even a government that was both nimble and effective, Brett thought, would be stretched to its limits, and that was not the caliber of leadership Washington had displayed within anyone's recent memory.

They managed to watch for another five minutes. No mention followed of any actions by the federal government or the Centers for Disease Control, but they may not have stayed with the station long enough, and it might still have come up after a while. However, the phrase *local authorities* was used several times. The focus then turned to fires raging out of control in several cities, the result of riots and looting. Prominent was St. Louis. Brett recalled the pillar of flame from the drum in the forest lot yesterday. Lee gently took the control from his limp hand and switched the television off. Her body slumped against his. He realized she was silently sobbing, and he put his arm around her waist.

"Lee, you're not alone here. You've got me, and you've got this town behind you, with whatever it can bring to the struggle. It's not a big city, but I haven't seen any bodies here. Nothing is burning, and people aren't coughing their lungs out. As a team, we weren't too bad on the road today. At least we're armed and dangerous now. More than anything else, I think we have to straighten up and face what's coming."

He thought he sounded upbeat and optimistic, but she turned and buried her wet face in his neck. "I don't want to die, Brett."

By ten o'clock that night the ongoing chaos in the country had drained their energy. Maybe it was only the absence of any good news, because they hadn't watched much television. Brett came out of the bathroom to find Lee pulling apart the two single beds that had been joined when they arrived, remaking them both with fresh single linens and three feet between them.

"I would rather have you in here with me, if that's OK. I'd just feel safer. If you have to know, I'm too damn scared to be alone, even here. If something changes suddenly I want you nearby."

"And what's the scariest part?" He already knew what scared him.

"The unknown. That's simple enough. Who's going to be able to fix this? When I think about Washington, nobody powerful comes to mind. They make speeches but they can't act." She stood up and put her arms around his neck and they said goodnight.

As Brett edged toward sleep he recalled her statement that she didn't like to depend on anyone. That, he thought, would serve her well as this went forward. But how well would it serve him?

2

They awakened to a bright and promising day. Brett stood up and pulled on his shirt. Looking into her face as it opened to him and to the morning, it took him a moment to remember the condition of the country. When he did, the light took on a harder edge and the shadows grew more sinister. Pulling her long tee shirt further down on her legs as she sat up, Lee went into the bathroom. Because everything had been so intense, both of them found they needed some time alone—no surprise after so many hours together without intermission. It was hard for Brett to think about their new collaboration in her presence, and he felt like stepping back to do that. There was nothing wrong in their connection, but he missed his old solitude and he needed to examine the condition of Outpost in more detail. He thought she must need a little time to herself too. They hadn't left each other's company in nearly forty-eight hours. It made for a long first encounter. It was almost surprising that they weren't screaming at each other after what they'd been through. Brett gave her a light hug and left for a walk through Outpost to get a feeling of how it had changed after twenty-five years. This was his habit, he said, and Lee didn't ask to go with him.

Their house was on Fourth Street, and at the intersection, Brett looked down a gentle slope toward the artificial lake behind the dam. It appeared to be a little more than a quarter mile wide at that point. The dam had been built at a much narrower part of the valley not far to the south. Few people were on the street as he walked down toward the embankment. It felt good to walk after all the driving the day before.

For two blocks the neighborhood still resembled the small rambler-style development of Fourth Street. The area nearest the lake had older construction in the designs of the twenties and thirties. The boulevard at the water line was named Shoreline and was edged by an embankment of rustic dressed stone that rose to about fifteen feet above the water. A block closer in, a vista point had been built out with parking for half a dozen cars. Across the lake, where nothing had ever been constructed, the forested slopes, scarred by stony ravines, climbed another 500 feet, as they did on this side to the west beyond the town.

Not many cars roamed the streets, but this was the dam end of Outpost. Ahead appeared a promontory that held the commercial district, and behind it a small marina provided launching and rental for boats. Nearby had once stood a restaurant with good water views. On Brett's last visit it had specialized in fish, mainly from the Gulf. When he was thirteen, his father had taken him there for lunch.

Brett had reached the vista, where no cars were parked to take in the view. He was stepping off the curb when an Outpost police cruiser turned in and cut across his path as it stopped. Brett paused and waited. The cop who climbed out was not Leon of the evening before, although he wore the same kind of surgical mask. He was a younger white kid, tall and lanky, with reflective sunglasses and more attitude than the job called for on a fine Thursday morning with no threat in view. He gripped a clipboard in his left hand.

"You got some ID with you, sir?" His tone suggested he had somewhere else to go, and Brett was slowing him down.

Brett was immediately irritated by his attitude, although he realized rules were being bent everywhere because of the emergency. He was also a guest in this town, but he still didn't like being called *sir* by people who meant no respect by it. It was only a label.

"I thought only blacks got carded just for walking down the street," he said, looking into the blank aggressive glare of the officer's bronze sunglasses.

"Very funny. Maybe back in your day. We even got 'em on the force now. What's your name, please?" Brett wasn't certain, but he could detect no sign of a grin behind the blue facemask.

"Brett Wallace. I'm staying at 217 Fourth Street." He reached into his back pocket and pulled out his wallet. When he offered the cop his driver's license, the man took a step backward in alarm. Brett suddenly felt he'd been identified as unclean.

"Hold it up so I can read it, please. Turn it a little

more into the light. Thank you."

The cop leaned forward and squinted at it. Saying please and thank you didn't make him polite. After a moment he scanned the list of names on his clipboard, made a check-mark bear the bottom when he found Brett's, and drove away to more important matters without further comment.

With both hands clenched in his pockets, Brett remained in the street for a moment before he decided to give the cop credit for doing his job. He had already realized that anyone in authority was going to have a much tougher time of it going forward. He kicked some gravel into the drainage grill nearby. Being stopped by the police is never much fun, but in these times what this officer was doing, despite the authoritarian way he did it, might help protect them all by keeping the town safe from casual invasion by infected refugees. He and Lee only wanted to live, as did everyone else, of course, and they knew they weren't infected. Don't kill the messenger, Brett said to himself, just because the message is unwelcome, or delivered in an offensive tone. He ended up thinking this encounter was barely OK, but oddly, it made him long for Lee's company, where her acceptance was at least warm and unambiguous, if nothing more.

Brett looked at his watch; he'd been gone less than half an hour. Reality was now unstable, its half-life too brief before it broke down and separated into components too new to be familiar. The commercial district could wait. He turned and walked back down Shoreline toward the dam. He felt foolish for running back so soon, but he was in no mood to deny his needs, which had taken on a more basic character since Tuesday morning, when making a delivery had last topped his list of priorities.

As he approached the house, he slowed when he noticed a tall black man standing on his own front lawn watching him from across the street. He was leaning on the upright handle of a rake, with one hand cupped over the other. No pile of leaves or dead grass was accumulated near him. Brett felt the need to explain his presence in Outpost, since the man was a neighbor, and no one would want a stranger living across the street in times like this. He walked as far as the edge of the man's lawn and held out his hand from the neutral pavement.

"My name is Brett. I'm here with Lee, staying in her brother's house." He didn't add anything about coming from Marshy Flats. It would be like saying they were visiting from hell, looking to take a break for a while from the unseasonably warm weather there.

"Clayton," the man said, in a musical mahogany voice. "Welcome to the neighborhood."

He looked to be about sixty years old, with short white kinky hair and a highly lived-in face. His skin was the color of ginger with a dash of darker freckles over his nose and cheek-bones. A look of ironic serenity framed his eyes.

"I guess you plan to be with us for a while, then," he added.

"I've been in worse places lately."

"Ain't that the truth? Did you and Lee come up from Marshy Flats? I heard from her brother she was still livin' down there."

"I was hoping you didn't know that."

Clayton waved this off with a smile. "Do I look worried? If you'd brought anything lethal out with you, you wouldn't have made it up this far. It's more than a six-hour drive. I still shook your hand, didn't I, and you better believe I plan to survive this."

"I'm happy to be here. What's Outpost like now? I haven't been up this way in more than twenty years." Brett felt his attitude loosening.

Clayton looked down Fourth Street toward City Hall as if that's where the answer lay. "It's been holdin' pretty well up till now. We haven't had any cases here yet. The town's got a mayor still in his first year, name of Emmett. He's a vigorous guy, a businessman coming up on forty. He says he's got a handle on this." An ironic grin formed on Clayton's lips. "Course, that's what we all need to hear. For starters, the city government isn't going to let anyone into this town they don't approve of."

"We saw that coming in last night, but can they do that legally?"

"They're going to try, legal or not. Who's going to take them to task for it? Not the folks who live here, sho'ly, and the state government has got way too many other things on its plate right now. At least for the moment, I think Emmett can do whatever he wants. There are times you're going to feel reassured by a firm hand, even when it's in the act of pushin' people's civil rights aside. That's been done before, and I 'spect it'll be done a time or two again before this is over. If it ever is."

Brett tried to keep the surprise from his face, but he was getting a far better perspective from Clayton than he expected. "Lee and I drove through a few places south of here that could've used a firmer hand. The way we came up we saw more people dead from gunshot wounds than from the epidemic. It seemed like no one in law enforcement was home."

"I'm sure you did. We'll see more of that, too, now. It's all breakin' down. The main task is going to be to keep this thing out of Outpost. Not only the disease, but also the social breakdown. At least Mayor Emmett knows that. We all thinkin' locally now."

In the silence that followed they studied each other for a moment. "What do you do here, Clayton?"

"I'm a mechanic in the city garage, helpin' to keep their fleet running. I'm on vacation this month because I'm set to retire in the fall and I'm using it up first. Started this morning. That was no coincidence."

"Wouldn't they give you your vacation pay at the end if you hadn't used it all?"

"Yes, they surely would, and they did offer me that, but I want to make certain they're still here to do it, so I'm takin' it now. Who knows what we'll have in September? I've done right by them for thirty years, and now they can do right by me for thirty days."

Brett thought about this for a moment, thinking Clayton was pretty calm for a realist in these times.

"How big is Outpost now?"

"Right around 10,000. It hasn't grown much the last few years. Housing is still cheap. That place you're in now across the street wouldn't quite fetch six figures in a normal market, not that we've recovered yet, nor ever will, by the way it looks. My place might go for $75,000 in good times. Of course, if the population should drop sharply, a lot more places will be available."

"You have a family here?"

"My son DeShawn is livin' with me at this time. I taught him what he knows about cars, and he works for the city too. When his mother died of cancer two years ago, DeShawn moved back home to keep me company. He's not married yet."

Brett considered this for a while, studying the man, noting how much he sounded like sanity after what he'd seen on the road. "After the chaos we went through on the way up here I think we have to stick together now, more than before. I've got a gun with me, Clayton, a police .38. If you need any help as this develops, you let me know, OK? These are strange times."

Clayton offered no more than a firm nod as they shook hands on that, and Brett went back into the house. His offer was as much for Lee and himself as it was for Clayton and his son. Brett felt they'd seen too much lawlessness on the way up to Outpost—now they needed a support group. Fear and need were rapidly dissolving the social glue that held humans together. Brett could easily anticipate that starvation would be the next cause in line, and from there it would get worse.

The smell of fresh coffee lifted his spirits on the way into the house. How many more times would those small moments of normalcy happen? Normalcy was part of the receding past. The screen door flew shut behind him with the irritating smack of aluminum on aluminum. The sight of Lee in the kitchen wearing a floral print apron almost broke him up. Somehow he wasn't ready for it. She paused with one hip and one shoulder thrust out.

"You're too normal for words this morning," he said. "I don't know where you find it. I couldn't." He approached her carefully and put his arms around her shoulders. His first instinct had been to grab her in delight, but he held himself back.

"Maybe that's my way of dealing, OK? We've got toast and coffee, no butter, but we do have jam, and we brought cheese and sliced salami, so we can fake breakfast." She pointed here and there. "You just take a seat now and I'll pretend I'm at work again. Let me find a pencil to put behind my ear."

"And I won't have to pretend you're about the most welcome sight I have ever set eyes on." This was no stretch. Brett sat down as instructed and she poured him a cup of coffee with a broad smile. She had found no less solace in normalcy than he did. He thought he saw a subtly seductive look in her eye.

"You've been over talking to Clayton. I saw you two out the window. He's my sweetheart."

"I'm not surprised. He's a good guy, I think, but something is different about him. I don't know exactly what. Maybe if I talked to him some more. I'm sure I will."

She set down the coffee pot. "I *know* you will. I can tell you what the difference is. Clayton is a true observer, and that's about three levels up from only being nosey. He likes to understand the context of things. Do you think he was out raking this morning before breakfast? No way. He wanted to know who you are and why you're here. I'm sure he saw you leave. The rake was only so he'd appear polite about asking. Part of it was that he's looking after me. He wants to know whether I'm with someone who'll treat me right while my family's gone."

"And are you?"

She shrugged. "So far, and counting. He didn't like Ted."

"Well, I told him why I was here. I also offered to help them out if they had a problem. They might do the same for us, you never know. If things collapse above us, we have nowhere to go but this community."

"That man would help. I feel better this morning. I think we're going to make it."

"Why? Only because it's morning?"

"Partly that. It does look different in daylight. I had a chance to think while you were gone."

"So did I." He wasn't sure where she was going.

She leaned back against the sink counter with her hands on her apron. "I'm going to trust you, Brett. I'll say that again, even if I can't say why, but I'm good at improvisation. I have a gut feeling that if we make it at all, it'll be because we're together. And that's not sentimentality. I'm not a sentimental person."

He was about to suggest she should be more cautious about him, but he kept silent.

But that was all; that was as far as she went. Later, while Lee was in the shower, Brett turned on the television. He wasn't trying to shield her from anything by waiting until she left, but he knew it would be easier to remain calm if she didn't know all the detail of what was happening. The story running at that moment concerned the evacuation of the civilian population of Washington, DC. The government had gotten out first—that much was expected, to brace up confidence that it was still functioning, the spokesman announced, but the reporter did not reveal where it had gone. Like so many other things, that information was classified.

The scene showed that the broad thoroughfares, always ready for a parade, were free of nonmilitary traffic, with Army checkpoints at intersections, tanks grouped in ranks at key buildings, jeeps everywhere. The inbound bridges and roads were all sealed. Every visible person was masked, and the city was locked down. The announcer said that house-by-house searches were turning up bodies in the tens of thousands. Disposal crews in grotesque protective gear were loading the dead onto military transport. No attempt was made to screen the gruesome sights from the camera's eye. They resembled scenes from World War II of troops liberating the Nazi death camps, except that the clips were shown in color and the dead were mostly still dressed. In their disheveled piles, they clearly weren't being taken to the nearest mortuary for embalming and makeup. Coffins were out of the question. Somewhere outside of Washington, the Army had set up an industrial crematorium. The announced intention was to use a specially trained crew separate from the regular troops to disinfect the city and make it a safe zone from which "to rebuild American democracy for a stronger future." While this made sense in some ways, it also had the ring of a public relations handout. Was the epidemic being spun into a cleansing process, a reaffirmation of traditional values? Still, for the first time it bore the appearance of competence. Something, at least, was in *motion*.

As he watched this, an unanswered question came into Brett's mind: why not choose one of the four large survivor cities in the South and start again there with a new national capital? Judging from the continued absence of any orange dots on the CDC map, all of those four were still disease free.

Dallas and Fort Worth certainly offered the banking, transportation, ranching, and manufacturing resources to be the logical candidate. Texas was usually scrapping for a fight like the one the country now found itself in. San Antonio, Austin, and Houston had been badly hit, but other than that, a large part of the state remained substantially intact, both in terms of population and infrastructure, which were still formidable. And as they had often declared, they didn't care to be messed with. This was the ultimate mess, and they had to be watching the paralysis in Washington with chagrin, and probably outrage, which Texans were rarely subtle about expressing. Furthermore, they'd started out as their own nation in the mid 1830s with no problem other than the Alamo. Recently, some had even talked of returning to that status.

Watching this, Brett thought he knew why those survivor cities had been passed over: all four lacked the *symbols* of power. Real economic clout and near normal function weren't enough. To be the seat of national government required the lofty domed Capitol, the revered White House, the U.S. Treasury, the Washington and Lincoln Memorials. These were buildings that had all appeared on the reverse side of paper money for generations. Those icons couldn't be abandoned to the fate of St. Louis, Berkeley, Trenton, or Chicago, now severely damaged by the flames of civil unrest. To lose the Capitol and the White House would be to virtually lose the country, psychologically, anyway. Al Qaeda had understood this well during the 9/11 attacks. The fourth hijacked plane, the one that crashed in a field in Pennsylvania, had been headed either for the Capitol or the White House, both iconic targets.

Brett changed the channel. For once they had a choice of programming. Here was the disease grid again, and the death toll was now 11.9 million. An authoritative voice in the background was explaining the reasons behind the occupation of Washington by the U.S. Army. The first item on the list was to secure the safety of the First Family, members of Congress, and the Supreme Court. The anonymous speaker repeatedly stressed the word *continuity*. A banner running along the bottom of the screen identified him as General Edwin A. Parker III, but his image was not shown. He was only the spokesman in a crisis, probably a medical person, Brett thought. An inset in the upper right corner displayed an anchoring image of the White House with the Stars and Stripes still proudly flying in the background. It could have been a film clip from Flag Day in the 1950s. It had a consciously old-fashioned feel, and Brett couldn't quite think why they were using it, since the ongoing disaster was distinctly twenty-first century in character.

It was now Thursday morning, seventy-two hours since Brett had picked up the four fateful boxes at Newton's Bait & Tackle, and forty-eight hours since he'd picked up

Lee on the road to Dundee. As he switched off the television screen she walked into the living room wearing a light cotton robe.

"Is it any better now? Out there, I mean."

"No. The military has taken over the city of Washington to save it, and they're starting to clean it up. That's something, I guess, but that's all. Nothing from the CDC yet."

"How many...?"

"Eleven point nine million."

"Jesus! Why the military? Doesn't that scare you?"

"Yes, so add it to that list. It must be because they have the budget in place already. They're not deadlocked about anything. The Army has the forces on the ground, and we're paying them to sit around anyway. No debt-ceiling increase is needed to put them to work. We're already feeding them and tucking them in at night. Of course, they're not going to cure the epidemic, but at least no one can argue about having them do something useful in response when no one else is."

"And I guess they won't be spending anything on ammunition or missiles."

Thinking about drones, Brett wasn't as sure about this. "Not unless they have to use some of what they've got for riot control."

"Right, because how could that happen? I'm sure everyone at the highest levels of government has got a firm handle on this. That's what they're trained for, isn't it? The National Security Council will be all over this."

Brett didn't feel like mentioning the riots in St. Louis and other cities. Was she being ironic? They hadn't heard anything from the National Security Council, yet wasn't this an obvious act of war? It suddenly occurred to Brett that the Justice Department would probably want to try the perpetrators in criminal court. He and Lee could be charged with destroying evidence. Fortunately, there had been no witnesses to what he had regarded as a patriotic act.

They looked at each other in silence. There were times when he felt like they'd been together for months and knew each other so well that neither could stumble. At other times they seemed like strangers sharing the seats of a shuttle van on the road to a place they'd never heard of. Putting his hands on her shoulders, he wondered to what degree he was deceiving himself. He could almost feel the softness of her skin through the thin cotton. What else was real now, other than one person to another? He suddenly recalled the chip implanted in her neck. Sometimes he almost didn't care anymore.

"Just hold onto me," she said softly. "Nothing else matters."

"I've got you, Lee. I won't let go. Together we can do this." He pulled her against his chest, suddenly recalling the lyrics to an old Lead Belly tune he had played many times; *Black girl, black girl, don't lie to me, Where did you stay last night? In the pines, in the pines, where the sun never shines…*

What baggage we all carry as we approach each other, he thought. What use was any of it now?

3

Brett stood there wondering how this was going to work going forward. Certainly because they were a man and a woman together in a life-threatening crisis, there was an emotional component. That made sense. Yet, while he appreciated what he regarded as her frankness, he wasn't sure how well she knew herself in a crisis situation. He had to fight the approaching life-or-death battle at her side, and while he welcomed her style and her spirit, her timing and consistency were still unproven, at least to him. In combat everything was about trust, as it had to be, and trust was now about the fact that they had only known each other forty-eight hours. And he had never forgotten that she was a *chippie*. That was something they still had to work out. He was still surprised at how strongly he'd reacted, but at the time, the *chippie* controversy had defined a real and surprising gulf among people. It had established an unanticipated line in the sand.

This was now connected to the fundamental problem of any war, as every combat grunt either learns first hand or ignores at the cost of his life. His existence depends on people he doesn't know well enough to trust, and on how they will act in situations full of stress and panic on a level they've never experienced before. Although the next crisis could be coming at them at any time, Brett had to admit he didn't know himself what he might do in a panic situation. As they already had, they both could talk about trust and how much they wanted and needed it, but in a pinch it was mainly going to be the quality of their improvisation under heavy pressure that mattered.

In an odd mockery of ordinary reality, they spent the morning shopping for groceries and clothes. Brett felt like this was merely a lull in the battle; they had fallen through the cracks of the chaos in the towns around them. Stoddard's Supermarket was crowded. Signs at the checkout station announced a limit of $100 per person, and no more than six of anything packaged individually. This was surely the hand of the mayor, Emmett. No fresh fruits or vegetables remained in the produce department, and no one in a white work apron was present to say whether or when more were expected. That was answer enough.

Lee didn't need anything to wear, since the cooler weather wardrobe she'd abandoned at Ted's was unnecessary, but at a store in a tiny neighboring strip mall, Brett bought two pairs of jeans, three shirts, and more underwear and socks. He had no idea when they'd see Marshy Flats again. What would it be like if they did? Aside from a large and visible police presence for such a small town, Outpost had an eerie feeling of near-normalcy, one that couldn't last. Soon all these products would have to be resupplied, and only the four major urban complexes that were untouched had any extras now. How would those cities make their choices, when restocking presented the same problems every other place had? They would obviously prioritize their own needs first. Or would the federal government, which had its own unannounced priorities, commandeer their small surplus resources? It could quickly become a wartime economy, because war it was.

Although they'd been able to resupply their pantry for the near term, they drove out of the parking lot with a feeling of systems failing around them.

"Maybe we should be walking to the store in the future," Brett said, thinking of gasoline, even though Stoddard's was less than a mile away.

Still, the federal government's example of inaction was not universal. Some people at the city level were taking action. Brett and Lee arrived home to find a sheaf of papers slid under the front door.

"It's a questionnaire from the city," Lee said, scanning the first page as Brett put away the groceries.

"About what?" As a measure of the future, the refrigerator still looked sparse and tentative.

"For starters, they want a list of current adult residents, with their ages, highest year of education, skills and work experience. Everyone over sixteen."

"I see what they're doing. Outpost is going to try to become self-sufficient. I like it."

"'Do you have a well? Did you serve in the military? If so, what was your highest rank?' I'm on the third page now. 'Do you own firearms? Please list them below, together with ammunition on hand. Are you able to volunteer for a local militia? Describe your primary vehicle. What other vehicles do you own? Do you have a supply of gasoline?'"

"Wait! That's way too thorough for me. I don't think we should admit to having a gun. That's my first instinct. It belonged to a dead cop, and what if they can trace it? What if they want to take it away from us? We should also hide the gas cans."

An awkward silence followed. Lee's lips were pressed together. "So right away we're turning into hoarders? I guess that's the normal instinct, but aren't we better than that?"

With a frown, she lowered the papers onto the counter and looked up as if this were a test question.

"You can call it that, I suppose, if you want, but once it leaves our hands, we can't control who gets any of that stuff, Lee. If they know what we have, some city bureaucrat will decide where it *really* belongs. And what would happen if the state government comes into Outpost and collects all these survey papers from the city? Then they'll decide that the people of Bridger need our stuff more than we do, because they're desperate and they probably really do. They have tens of thousands of homeless, many of them about to die, while we're out here behind the house drinking wine by the barbecue as if nothing has happened. You're over in the shady hammock with your shoes off, painting your toes while I refill your glass. Their first question will be why the hell do we think that's fair when the country is hurting so much? How can we rationalize that kind of behavior in this situation? They're going to say we're both Republicans and members of the one percent."

Lee turned and looked at him with both her hands on her hips, one of them still grasping the forms, which were crumpling under the unconscious contraction of her grip. She had never before been called a Republican, yet at this point it suggested a level of entitlement she didn't object to.

"I do like that backyard image, but this is how things start to break down, isn't it? What's happened to our sense of community? Was that the first casualty of the epidemic? You said you told Clayton we'd help them if it came to that. Were you just blowing smoke?"

"Yes I did say that, and I meant it, but how much community did you ever have outside of your family? What I always hear from you is about your separateness. You take the outsider's view on everything; you're the classic shutout. What if the city decides to make the next food handout cut on the basis of color as this goes on? Would that be a *surprise* in this part of the world, and where would that leave *you*? Yes, please step forward Mr. Wallace, but who is that with you again?

Hmm, let me check my list."

Lee looked at him more than coolly. "Maybe that's why I want to nail it down so much now. Maybe for once in my life I'd like to feel some domestic support, and that question did not appear on this form. It might've also read, Do you have a real partner at home? But I didn't see that one on these pages, either."

Brett let out a long slow sigh. Some parts of this he was not able to answer. "I think we're losing our way here. My question is whether we can trust the government to have that sense of public good too. I'd share our stuff with Clayton and our other neighbors long before I'd give it to City Hall." He was pacing back and forth between the refrigerator and the dishwasher.

"You just want to keep some control over it. I've seen that before."

"Yes! Yes, I do! What's wrong with that?"

"It's that you don't think anyone could be wiser than you about how it's used, isn't that it? Isn't this a little too much like *Father Knows Best?*"

Taking a step back, he considered this for a moment. Her statement had an undeniable element of truth. "I'm sure that some would be wiser than I am, but others would be corrupt, selfish, and mistaken in their judgments. Worse yet, others would simply be political, and they would redistribute our stuff to get votes or popularity to stay in office, and that would bug me more than anything else. The trouble is that I wouldn't be able to tell them apart in advance when they rang the doorbell with their hand out, as I'm giving up all of our stuff, including the wine and the nail polish."

"And the gasoline out in that shitty tin barn out there," she said, her voice ratcheting upward.

They were both silent for a moment. Lee looked like she was working up a further response, but Brett wasn't finished. Suddenly he could see the *chippie* side of her coming out in this crisis. She'd probably always be siding with the authorities.

"I'm not paranoid, Lee, I'm only an observer. Maybe I'm a bit like Clayton. I've watched what happens at all the levels of government for years. Here's the bottom line—it's been decades since any of them could handle a big challenge, other than collecting taxes and invading Asian and Middle Eastern countries."

Lee stared at him but said nothing for a while as she went back and scanned the rest of the document, five pages in all, as if there had been no interruption. "Listen to this! At the bottom of the last page, it says, 'Eligibility to receive distributions of food, water and other supplies, including electricity, will be limited to those who have completed and returned this form.' We only have twenty-four hours to turn it in. They're providing two drop boxes at City Hall."

"Some are already becoming more equal than others," he said, "and this is the first cut. With the city owning the hydro plant, they can make good on the electricity threat easily enough. We'll have no laundry, and no freezer or refrigerator, so our need for food will become even more complicated and immediate. We'll only be able to handle what we can eat right away, or dry things we can store. We'll have no TV for information, whatever that's worth, and no air conditioning. We'll end up in the bathtub again."

Lee set the pages on the kitchen counter and for a moment placed both hands palm downward next to them. Then she turned and showed him the face of a moderator. "Let's think calmly for a minute. Maybe this is the way it has to be now. How else can the city get everyone pulling in the same direction? Even though your first instinct about not going into Bridger worked out fine, I don't think this is the right time for rugged individualism anymore. Outpost is going to survive based on what we can put together as a collective effort. Doesn't that make sense? Think of the broader view now. It's not only about us."

Brett shrugged. "I genuinely don't know. What happened to that idea of two?"

"You're the one who said we needed a support group.

This is it, and it's easily the best thing we've seen."

"That sounds logical, but it still makes me queasy. I can see what might come next—under the city's right of eminent domain and the current emergency, they'll abolish private property within the urban boundary lines. They could put us out of this house because someone needs it more than we do, and who defines that need? What if Emmett's niece has always admired it? She walks past it every day on the way to her cushy City Hall job, and she can't wait to move in and put a couple of flowerboxes full of petunias under the front windows to spiff it up a little. Maybe a pale, putty green trim color might work better than white against the dark red brick, or it needs a backyard pool. Besides, it's three blocks closer to work than where she lives now."

"It would never come to that, Brett. Now you sound like you're starting to flip out." She stepped away from the counter with her arms folded. "You don't *know* this town like I do. These people you're talking about in the city government are our friends and neighbors. You haven't lived with them like I have. Clayton and his son both work there. Doug next store is one of their accountants. That's who the city government really is, people like them—*people like us*. They welcomed us in, so try to think of them as individuals rather than some monolithic bureaucracy. Outpost is too small and too personal to ever be that."

Brett took two steps closer. "A reassuring thought. It's only that I don't see what would put a limit on this process once it begins, and it's already started, because it can all be justified by the circumstances. Tyrannies are often launched with an emergency decree, in a *genuine* crisis like this one or 9/11, trying to address people's real needs for security. Then the decree remains in effect for years or decades. People get used to it, and month-by-month the grip is always tightening. They're already spying on everybody. They're looking at our emails and our Facebook posts. They're recording our phone calls. Once they have that power they never give it back. Where does it go after that?"

Lee shook her head. "But I want to *survive* this, Brett! Maybe that's what it's going to take. Maybe we all have to give a little, including *you*."

"I want to survive this too." His voice was exactly as quiet as hers had been shrill. She was still talking like a *chippie* and she didn't realize it.

"But what if this is the only way to do it? You saw what it was like on the road coming up here yesterday. It was the Wild West all over again, but you can't find the sheriff anywhere now. We have to furnish our own sheriff in Outpost."

"And you're saying that the man wearing the star and carrying the six shooter is named Emmett."

"Yes I *am!*" Her voice again climbed a notch in pitch and volume. "His name is Emmett, and the only guy who gets to be the sheriff is the one who's *able* to do it. Screw the law and the city charter, because I don't care anymore. That was all made for normal times. We've only got one chance for all of us here. If we don't get it right the first time, we might as well be sitting in our tent now back in Bridger wondering how long it's going to take the fire to reach us, or will we cough ourselves to death first? At least Emmett's program is *preventive*." Her thumb and index finger came together at the tips as if they were down to the short hairs of this issue.

Brett took a sudden step toward her and they locked themselves together like two pieces of a jigsaw puzzle that didn't quite fit. Still, they touched at key points. "I'll do whatever it takes to save us," he whispered into her cheek, but thinking that wasn't the same as doing whatever the government wanted. Any plan of City Hall would be aimed at saving the largest number, after the office holders saved themselves. Brett understood that he and Lee were only two grains of sand at the edge of the pile. He released her reluctantly with a sudden sense of how important she had become to him.

After a moment they went into the living room and parked in front of the television. That's what the crisis had done for them. They'd become news junkies, reacting to events and numbers more than acting on their own, and watching as someone else who had never met them or tried to understand them except as a statistic, decided what would happen in their lives.

The national channel they'd been watching earlier had gone off the air, which Brett thought odd, but he couldn't guess what might be happening as the signal ricocheted back and forth through the failing infrastructure between New York and Los Angeles and Outpost. This town was strictly the end of the line, and how many relay stations and satellite links were required to keep that signal from drooping from exhaustion as it crisscrossed the nation? Switching to the only other network, they caught what must have been a tape loop cycling over and over through some announcements by the same General Edwin A. Parker III, the spokesman they'd heard from earlier. As before, the general's face was not shown, only a series of disastrous images of urban panic and chaos. Maybe he's shy, Brett thought, or in this crisis, he'd been running for his desk as he knotted his tie, and he hadn't had the opportunity to shave that morning.

"...times like this that test the very fiber of our souls. Our faith in God is as critical, of course, as ever, but that too can only take us so far. Our survival will ultimately depend upon what we do for ourselves. This moment demands greatness and sacrifice from all Americans more than any event in our past ever has. Knowing history as I do, I am sure that we are up to it!"

It was a like a voiceover at the end of the world. Bret could see it as an announcement that echoed endlessly from loudspeakers mounted on thirty-foot poles even when all potential listeners were dead in piles around them. The final patriotic victim would've dragged himself onto the nearest mound with his last breath before he expired. The general paused as if for applause, but none was heard. From the images, the soundtrack would have yielded nothing more than groans and coughing in the background.

Brett heard the words accurately, but what he was seeing was the dead bodies on the road coming up to Outpost.

That was the real character of the public response. No one had been praying. Preying, perhaps.

"Fortunately for all of us, the days of partisan deadlock in Washington have now passed. Even as we speak, the President is meeting in an undisclosed location with a joint session of Congress to formulate a series of measures that will halt the course of this epidemic once and for all. Budget obstacles that formerly looked insurmountable have been cleared by acclamation. The first of these decisions has already been implemented with the evacuation and restoration of Washington. Our capital city is once again the symbol of all our hopes. The American flag, the emblem of our highest aspirations, as it has always been in the history of this republic, is still flying above the dome of the Capitol.

"In my role as Commanding Officer, I will keep the public informed of all significant developing events as we return this country to its rightful status as the most powerful nation on earth—the only remaining superpower. On all sides, I have heard speculation about what evil and cowardly enemy lurks behind this bio-terror plot. Let me assure you that this question will be foremost in all of our minds, right after the complete recovery from this attack, which is our main priority. We have a short list of possible culprits, but until we are certain, I shall have nothing more to say on that score, lest we commit an injustice of the same kind that was visited upon us. God forbid we act in any way unjust. Yet, once in motion, our vengeance will be swift and certain."

Here the Commanding Officer coughed softly, as if briefly overcome by emotion. It did not sound in any way like the coughing they'd seen and heard on the road to Outpost.

"One final word before I finish. I well know the suffering that has been visited upon our people, and I am not alone in this respect. Like the shepherd of a large and diverse flock that he is, the President has asked me to convey a personal message directly to you, even as he works undistracted day and night in the background. His tie was gone and his sleeves were rolled up when I spoke with him briefly earlier today.

'Ed,' he said to me, 'I want you to tell this to the folks at home: the days of quibbling and uncertainty are over. I mean that. Even as we bury our dead and mourn their passing, a powerful new day is rising in the East. You have only to raise your eyes from the ruins around you to see it. A new era blossoms throughout the land. The righteous shall surely triumph, and the evil be cast down to perdition. Amen.'"

Here the Commanding Officer paused for effect.

"I'll leave you now with that glowing testimonial of faith in our future. It was so in our President's personal style to share that with me, because he has always been a man of great faith and compassion."

The doomsday numbers reappeared at the bottom of the screen, spinning like a roulette wheel. The lives of more than fourteen million people had now been lost. Brett muted the sound.

"But does the army really have a rank called the *Commanding Officer*?" Lee asked with a wrinkle in her brow a moment after the announcement ended. She pushed out her lips, touching her index finger to the center of the lower one.

"I think it would be a job title more than an actual rank. Maybe it's like Surgeon General of the United States. You could have that position without being either a surgeon or a general."

"OK, but that still doesn't tell me who this Parker guy is. Do you know?"

Before Brett could answer, not that he understood it himself, a commentator came on as the disaster photos faded to black. They saw a familiar face from PBS, although this wasn't her network. Perhaps the surviving network personnel resources had been pooled. With the incessant bias on both sides, it had always sounded like chaos before the epidemic. To get a truer view, the viewer had to boil off the rancor and simmer it into a calmer paste of averages.

"As I said earlier," the commentator began, "we will at regular intervals again be airing this message from the Commanding Officer, General Edwin A. Parker III, or the CO, as he likes to be called less formally."

Two other talking heads came on. The first one spoke with an insider's smile. "Bill, I do have to say that I liked the CO's folksy style today, didn't you? As serious as the message is, his informality somehow makes him more accessible, more human, almost like a father figure."

"Absolutely. He almost reminded me of Franklin Roosevelt today. He has that same kind of ironic chuckle."

"I know, and he's not there to put anyone off. I feel like I could almost play golf with him, at the right club, of course. It's reassuring to feel he's with us in the trenches moment by moment, although we don't know exactly where he is now, do we?"

He shook his head with an admiring grin, as if to say, those people sure have gotten it together on such short notice. The other head wore a more sober look. "No, we don't, Chet, and our efforts to discover the present location of the government have been blocked. I almost think that's proper in times like this, although, as a reporter, it certainly can be frustrating." Here the glare from his teeth as he smiled distracted Brett from the impact of these insights. "Yet, it's not like he could ever have a press conference under such wartime conditions. Of course, everything is about security now, isn't it, and rightly so? If those bastards attacked the whole country in such a general way, what would they do if they had access to the leaders who are holding it all together in such difficult circumstances? No one would be safe. Of course, I'm perfectly happy to take the risk myself, here, right in the newsroom as we're doing our jobs."

"Well, I guess *where* our government people respond from is not nearly as important as *what* their response is, right, Chet?"

Chet tapped the eraser end of his pencil on the glass desktop for emphasis. "I think that the CO made an interesting point earlier when he said that the survival of those four major cities in the South, free as they are now from any trace of the epidemic, is a clear testimonial to their religious faith, more than any other reason you could imagine. Surely, their hygiene is no better than ours is right here in New York City. After all, it's the South, isn't it?"

"You think they were literally saved by divine intervention, is that what you're telling us?"

Chet responded with a noise between a chuckle and a snort. "Well, you notice that neither Los Angeles nor San Francisco was spared in the least, and certainly not Las Vegas. While I've never been much of a believer myself, in this context I do have to wonder whether some greater power isn't involv…"

Thinking that the crisis had encouraged a level of reverent informality he hadn't seen in the media before, a subtle twitch in Brett's fingers decapitated Chet's thought. The screen dissolved to black and he set the remote aside, squaring it with the corner of the cabinet.

"So that's how those four cities were all spared," he said with a slow nod. "That's good to know." It made bizarre sense that he was merely the unwitting agent of a higher power, as was the thief who had taken the Little Rock package from his van and probably died for his trouble only a few hours after he opened it. He waited for Lee to respond, wondering whether their principal remaining channel was now going to be used strictly for sanctimonious spin, but she said nothing. He could tell from the feel of her ribs under his hand that her body had grown more rigid than it was when they started watching.

She sometimes voiced doubt that the two of them were powerful enough to survive on their own without help, and he wasn't sure himself, although he trusted that idea of outside help less than she did. He still preferred that the help come from nearby, like down at City Hall, rather than a thousand miles away by decree. But even then, as the statement at the end of the mayor's questionnaire suggested, it was still likely to be conditional on loyalty and compliance.

"That Parker guy is a little strange, don't you think? I'd like to see his face as he says these things."

"Situations like this will bring out the worst in any-one," she said, standing up to face him. Was she referring to the position he'd taken on the city questionnaire? She had a way of throwing her chest and one hip out at the same time that made him fear she'd lose her balance. "He might be fine out on the golf course or at the dinner table when he lets his hair down. Maybe he listens to the Grateful Dead or Jay-Z in his chauffer driven jeep. But who else is doing anything? That's the real issue."

"He says the President and Congress are on it."

"But we don't see anything yet, do we? It's not like they have a lot of time to fool around with this."

"Now *you're* getting radical. I think we should check out the CO on the Internet." He said this in a neutral way, mainly to encourage her.

"You'd like to know who General Parker really is, too."

"More than that, I'd like to know who he's become in the last few days, since Monday, to be precise."

They stared at each other in silence for a moment, but neither of them got up to boot the laptop. They'd had enough government announcements, so instead they went to lunch, leaving the CO's background for the afternoon. Suddenly it had become too much to engage, and they agreed it would be easier to look at it again on a full stomach. Brett had already noticed that their ability to grapple with their situation came and went in waves, and at times it was easy to feel power-less. For now, research could wait. He was possessed by curios-ity about what the town was like under these conditions, not having seen it in detail in a long time. If survival was possible, it would happen there in Outpost.

4

They walked down Fourth Street to the commercial area. Eating someone else's food ration seemed like a great idea. Restaurants could hardly stay open much longer. On the way, the neighborhood looked nearly the same as theirs—well kept, lower middle class houses from the fifties and sixties. A few boasted a naked flagpole in the front yard, but lacked any fancy embellishments or serious landscaping. Not many people were about. Looking up onto the slope on their side of the lake, Brett realized that the town had been built on a nearly level platform that could have been the result of quarrying stone for the dam's parapets and the lake's surroundings. That would explain why it was so flat, although it had a gradual slope that provided drainage into the artificial lake. The dam itself would have been made from poured concrete with steel reinforcements.

"Your brother's house doesn't have a cellar, does it?" He was thinking about being on a stone platform with topsoil graded over it.

"No. It's on a slab built right over the rock. He has to water the lawn a lot because the soil's not very deep."

"What does he do? You never said."

"He's a teacher. They both are."

"Then they were on summer vacation when this began."

"Right. They were already planning to go to Corpus. Oddly, this didn't change anything for them other than move up their departure by a single day."

Downtown Outpost occupied three irregular blocks built out onto a bulge at the lakeshore. The small shady square next to the courthouse held a wrought-iron bandstand with an Art-deco feeling, and in one corner, a squat ten-foot granite obelisk on a four-foot high base. Approaching, Brett assumed it was dedicated to men from Outpost who had died in World War I. When they stood before it, he saw that the men, nine of them, had died instead in two accidents while constructing the dam in 1921.

At both front and rear courthouse entrances stood the drop boxes awaiting their questionnaire.

They crossed between two commercial blocks lined with two-story buildings dating from the thirties on the way to

Dante's, the fish restaurant by the water. It hadn't been called that when Brett ate there years ago with his father, but it was the same yellow glazed brick building, unaltered but for the neon sign and the tinted windows on the eastern front. They settled at a table outside with a view over the boat landing, the only one on the lake. With a scalloped edge fringed in white, a maroon canvas awning shaded that side of the restaurant. Brett felt more at peace than he had in three days.

"Thanks for bringing me here. If Outpost isn't what we need to survive, we can still catch our breath."
She shrugged as if the last part were irrelevant. "I feel like that too. I'm trying to have no long term expectations."

He looked ar her. "Do you ever think about life?"

"Whether it's sustainable on earth?"

"No, your own life. Where it's been, where it's going."
She looked at the tablecloth for a moment. "That's usually an old man's question, but I'm no different. I've been think-ing more about death lately. I'm wondering if you're the last person I'll ever see."

With a wry smile he took her hand for a moment.

A waiter slid two menus across the table as if this were no different from any other day in his boring life. "Anything to drink for starters?" He looked at their intertwined hands and brightened. "Special occasion? An anniversary?"

They both started to laugh helplessly. Coping is strange, Brett thought, when he recovered. "Yes! We woke up alive this morning," Brett said. The waiter's smile sagged into a straight line. They each ordered a glass of chardonnay. After he left Brett leaned closer to her.

"I can't imagine why I didn't meet you in the Flats earlier. I can't think of any place I don't go to now and then. What restaurant do you work at?"

She gave him an engaging smile. "It's not in Marshy Flats. I work at Paul's Place in Forrest Beach."

"The blues bar."

"Right."

Brett had long ago stopped going to Paul's Place

because he wasn't fond of the musicians who played there regularly, but he didn't say that. He thought of them as belters, purveyors of rasping voices and whiny tones. To him, vocals with a blues guitar required more finesse.

Three boats moved slowly around the lake, trolling because the bottom was too deep to take the bite of an anchor.

"Remember how I said I wanted to live my life without worrying?" he said. "I think I'm still going to try that in spite of this. Maybe we'll make it, and maybe we won't, but whatever time is left to us will not be improved by worrying."

"Good luck," she said softly.

The lunch was good if not amazing, but Brett could tell from the texture that the fish had been frozen. He never saw this in Marshy Flats. The thought passed through his mind that this might be their last restaurant meal.

Afterward they walked the embankment from one end to the other. Pausing to turn at the north edge of town they suddenly noticed a column of dark smoke rising above the distant end of the service road. No buildings other than the water plant had been built out that far. Lee said the road existed mainly to give access for maintenance of the embankment, and to service the plant. The air over the water was calm, and the people around them looked relaxed and unthreatened as well.

"I'm not as uncomfortable having the Army in charge in this epidemic as I was with the federal government," he said. "It's because the Army is not paralyzed; it has a clear chain of command, and because of that, it can agree on its mission. You do what you're told or you end up in the stockade without argument or negotiation, no tradeoffs. Best of all, no debate or gridlock."

"So you admire authority? And don't remind me of what I said about the sheriff."

"No, not for its own sake, but I appreciate the ability to act when it's required. General Parker can tell us how the President and Congress have resolved their issues and are now acting together behind the scenes, but we haven't seen any outcome from it. We have seen the military occupying the streets of Washington. We have seen a cleanup begin. Removal of the dead is underway. The city's being reclaimed. If it can happen there, it can happen in other cities as well. That's a start. It's now Thursday afternoon, and this began Monday morning in many places. Action is way overdue."

"The terrorists planned this to start on Monday, didn't they?" Lee asked. "It's the first day of the work week, everybody has gotten on the subway, the trains and buses, commuting to the office. The disease spreads wildly through the crowds as people bump up against each other. It's too early for them to suspect anything is wrong. As it takes hold, they start to cough in each other's faces. Even breathing does it. It's sick. Where do you think all those people from Washington are now, the people who lived there?"

"That's a great question. I suppose some large percentage of them must be dead by now. Fifteen percent? Twenty? Did the authorities find some other places like Bridger and disperse the rest into camps? I don't know."

"No one says anything about that."

Back at home Brett switched on the television to find that the death toll had accelerated and broken sixteen million. He shut it off again. Lee went to bring out her laptop to research the CO, but at that moment, the doorbell rang. Brett opened the door to Clayton.

"I hope I'm not interrupting anything?"

In one hand he raised a bottle of Haitian rum whose label Brett knew, Barbancourt, but he'd last seen it available in Bridger in better times. The selections in the food market in Marshy Flats had been limited to a few bland white rums.

"You are interrupting the demise of civilization as we know it," Brett said. "I'd say that's a welcome break. I'm curious to see what'll still be standing at the end, and who. Come on in. Is your son here? Bring him over, too."

Lee ran up and hugged Clayton. "Thank God for a few sane people," she said.

"DeShawn is working this afternoon, like he worked

this morning, and will be working this evening until God knows how late. Emmett is hauling out from storage some older vehicles he thinks we're going to need in this crisis, and he's getting them altered and tuned up. The city is calling up the police reserve. DeShawn is piling up some serious over-time pay, although it's not clear what he'll be able to buy with it once he gets it."

"How many reserves can they have?" Lee asked.

"Eight men and two women, all retired, and with their uniforms, if they can still squeeze into them. The main thing is that they all still have their own guns and ammunition."

"What's the issue?" Brett said. "Civil unrest? Fishing without a license?"

"Well, you can laugh, but according to DeShawn, Emmett thinks that perimeter control is going to be the main problem now. We have to keep the riffraff at bay. That's not only the infected, but also other people fleeing to a place where the resources are more intact than where they came from. He thinks we can be easily overwhelmed if we're not ready. I don't know if you heard, but we had our first case today."

"What!" Lee leaped up, her arms gripping her shoulders. "I thought we were safe here."

"It was a fifty-one year old woman from Bridger. They got her information from her license plate number. She pulled over and died late this morning about a quarter mile before the checkpoint. DeShawn helped tow her car away, without touching it, of course. He said the driver's window and the windshield were sprayed with blood on the inside."

"But the police would never have let her in," said Lee.

"No, because they didn't know her and no one could've vouched for her, even if she wasn't showing the symptoms yet. They towed away her car with her body in it and burned it north of town. They broke in the back window and doused it with gasoline inside. DeShawn said that's the only way to be sure. They never even touched the doors."

From personal experience, Brett also thought this was the only option. "We walked the embankment downtown today and we saw the smoke. I'm glad we didn't go up that way any further. It looks like you could easily get ashore almost anywhere along the watery edge of the city, but there's no other boat launch on the lake. No road on the other side, and here you'd have to come in through Outpost to get to the landing."

"That's why we've got a reasonable chance to do this," Clayton said.

Brett led them into the back yard. "And that's also why we're celebrating?"

"We are treading water, and that's not half bad right now. I'm not sure what a celebration would look like at this point, but I do know that one bottle of rum wouldn't do it justice."

They adjourned to the concrete patio slab. Brett opened the sun umbrella, although the neighbor's trees now shaded most of the table. Lee brought out a covered ice bucket and three glasses, and Clayton poured a round.

"I don't know if you ever knew this, Lee, but I've been a ham radio buff for a long time. It was always my hobby since I was a teenager. Part of it was living up here in such a remote place and trying to stay connected beyond what was on television. Later, my wife thought it was silly, like an over-age Boy Scout thing, but I didn't mind her thinkin' that. Now it might be important as a way of getting information that doesn't come from an official source."

Brett and Lee looked at each other.

"You're starting to sound like me," Brett said.

"Is that important, though, the unofficial part?" Lee asked.

"Oh, more than ever, now," Clayton said. "The way I feel, I want to understand how to interpret what I'm hearing, and the best way to do that is to also know where it's coming from. Isn't the source always part of the news?" He raised his glass. "Health and long life in difficult times."

"We've been listening to that new Commanding Officer, General Parker," Brett said after he set his glass down.

"As have we all because you cannot avoid him. That's a case in point about sources. And who, by the way, was the previous CO? I can't recall his name at the moment, can you?" He snapped his fingers twice as if trying to call it up without success.

They both gave Clayton a blank look, not sure whether he was being ironic. "We were going to look him up on the Internet."

"Not a bad idea. That'll tell you who he was a year ago or five, and who his family is. He can't change that. As for who he is now…?"

"So, these changes are too recent," Brett said.

"That's right, but I've already been talking on the radio about him with some people in Dallas. The CO's grandfather was a man of the same name, but without the numeral at the end, General Edwin A. Parker. I didn't remember him, either. In 1963 he was a retired senior army officer in the habit of going on the road and speaking in favor of the John Birch Society—a far right organization that ruffled the feathers of a lot of liberals in its day. In April of that year, Lee Harvey Oswald tried to kill General Parker with a Mannlicher Carcano rifle that he'd bought by mail order at a quite reasonable cost. Although the bullet missed General Parker's head by inches, it was a rehearsal for something more important to come later that year. Or at least a good pretext for charging Oswald with another crime, one far more successful."

"And you're suggesting that this current general, the grandson, was somehow damaged as a younger man by this experience?" asked Lee. "Or what is it?"

"Who can say that for certain? Maybe, being a small child then, he doesn't even remember it. But if the CO, as he prefers to be called, has a taste for order now that extends somewhat beyond that of most other people, we could easily understand why, right, given his family history? After all, where are we seeing him? Not that we are actually shown his face. It's not on the golf course. He's not out sailin' off

Hyannis Port. Yet, the President must be calling him Ed for good reason. Parker has found his way into the inner circle. If we should all decide to look for salvation, and why wouldn't we, we will apparently find it from the new CO, and not the President, whose ways are now even more mysterious than when he was still visible. He is a man now speaking all his lines from offstage."

Brett was starting to appreciate Clayton for his insights, but he could've come up with a more comfortable neighbor, perhaps one not as willing to so bluntly state his views. Not that comfort was going to save anybody. Comfort now mainly meant dying quickly in bed without much coughing.

"How much do you trust Emmett?" Brett asked. "Because I'm starting to think the local leadership is going to have more effect on us than Washington can ever muster, CO or not. The feds are getting farther away every day. This epidemic has badly distorted the map, and the distances that separate us are no longer measured in miles, and growing daily."

Clayton pursed his lips and made a vague gesture. "I believe that Emmett will do what he says, insofar as he can, but I also believe he'll do things he hasn't said he was going to do, things he doesn't want to share with us in advance. That might be where the problems develop."

"Things he should be asking for our input on?" said Lee.

"That wouldn't surprise me." Clayton looked up into the neighboring trees. Brett wished for a few in the yard where they sat. "They must've dug a little deeper into the rock on that lot next door," Clayton said. "You need more top soil for big trees here."

"That lot does stand four or five feet higher as it moves away from ours," Lee said. "And today Emmett burned that woman's body and her car on his own authority."

"Realistically, I would've done exactly the same thing," Brett said. "It's a public health emergency that overwhelms most other concerns, especially things that are no more than normal procedures, like trying to notify the next of kin under these conditions."

"DeShawn told me they're already talking about setting up a reinforced checkpoint a hundred yards farther out from town, something you couldn't rush or force your way through without a tank. They'd use those concrete highway dividers—they weigh over twelve hundred pounds apiece. That came out of Emmett's visit to the scene while they were towing the victim's car away today. They're also going to patrol the waterline. Someone has donated an old Chris-Craft to the police."

"How could anybody get a boat into the water without coming through town to begin with?"

"I know, but it's the vulnerable side nonetheless. I suppose they could come over the ridge here too, but that's a rugged climb, especially if you're short of breath from some developing health issues."

"Where is this all going to go, Clayton?" Lee tilted another dash of rum into his glass. She preferred the bottom line to a lot of discussion.

"It would take a much wiser man than I am to answer that. It's all a matter of layers. At the top, with the federal government, it's tough to read. I think the President and the Congress have collapsed already. Their only agreement was that they're both doin' nothing. Nobody is sayin' that yet in Washington, at least not for public consumption, but you have to ask why the spokesman is always in a military uniform now. You don't see anybody else from the government, like Congressmen from either side of the aisle, or even the President's press secretary. Where's he been during all this? Is he on vacation in Bermuda? Isn't it his job to give out news from the White House and to reassure us by answering questions? Maybe he was cut down by the epidemic on the first day. It's only the CO that's keeping us briefed on what the military is up to. Not that his version is complete by any means."

"You think that's alarming?" asked Lee. "Maybe the uniforms can be mainly a way of expressing authority, of giving us the sense that someone solid is in charge. A uniform also suggests we're at war. It has instant credibility, giving us all the impulse to stand up and salute."

"Maybe uniforms make us all content to do the same thing," Brett said. "That's how they're supposed to affect the people who wear them. Nobody stands out except by their medals and campaign ribbons."

"And they reduce the obvious differences among us, which, I believe, is what's happening out here as well."

"I think it's reassuring, which it's meant to be," Lee added, "although it's scary at the same time because of all the things we're not being told."

Clayton took a long, slow sip of his rum and stared off into the tops of the neighboring trees as he smiled. That was where the heat lived and bred fiercely on long Southern afternoons. If his eyes were watery, it wasn't from sentiment.

"To me it shakes out this way," he said slowly. "Power is much like youth—it is a fugitive condition. If you have power, you need to exercise it regularly, or it flies away unnoticed. The first time someone else exercises it for you, even just by usin' your name, it has left your hands and passed to those of that other person."

Here Clayton grinned like one who has not been taken in despite many people's best efforts. His right hand reached out as if to pinpoint a fallacy, to underline it. "This notion of the President and the Congress getting together behind the scenes is no more than insulting nonsense to grownups like us. These people we're listening to now view us all with contempt. We're supposed to believe they're doing it that way so they can make an agreement without losing face, I guess, but I'd like to know where they really are. As the CO is showing us, this is the time to exhibit both the appearance and the reality of power simultaneously. Just ask yourself who's been doin' that best lately. So you're right, Lee, it is about expressing authority. You are lookin' at the real thing now, and for the first time in quite a spell. I'm talking about decades. These last few presidents have all been figureheads fronting for big money."

"But the CO never shows himself," she said. "Why

does that make any sense? How does that make him different from the civilian government in this situation? Aren't they both equally invisible now?"

"I think the CO hasn't shown himself yet because he doesn't need to. He's still covering his real role under the veil of the President's authority. Instead, what he's showing you now are the ruins piling up in every direction, the rioting cities burning to the ground. In St. Louis only the blackened arch and a few gutted skyscrapers are still standing downtown. Soon the smoking pyres of the dead will appear forty feet high. All those orange lights on the map are little panic buttons that cause a corresponding flutter in your brain. How close were they getting to you in the last report? They might be down the road only a block or two now. Marshy Flats doesn't have its own orange blip, and you've said how bad it is there. The effect is to make you desperate for salvation. The CO is referring to God in every other sentence. That shows the man is well connected, he's got the right friends in the highest places. He knows his way around at a time when no one else can predict what will be goin' down in the next hour."

A squabble among several grackles erupted in the trees, causing Clayton to pause for a moment as if heckled from the stands for these uncomfortable views.

"By the time we *do* finally see his face," he continued, "I'm sure we're gonna want to weep because the CO looks so normal, so strong, so competent—why, the man isn't scary at all! It would be like the return of the ghost of JFK at the moment when we need him most. We are suddenly certain that we would have voted for the CO in a heartbeat, had he been on the ballot—*not that he ever was or needed to be.* I'll bet he's even good lookin', and his smile will be what it has to be in these times—reassurin' beyond all belief. The women will take to him first and then persuade their men."

Clayton flashed them a blazing smile of his own. Brett could have rolled a quarter on edge through the gap between his upper front teeth, and the effect would've remained undiminished.

Lee had caught the thread, and was nodding through-out this. "And then he will tell us next," she said, "every good thing we were hoping to hear. I already have my own list. Brett knows some of it." She tossed him a nod over her shoulder. "The CO is like the good-looking guy with wavy hair slither-ing up on the bar stool next to the lonely chick late in the evening at Paul's Place. It's only an hour from closing time and last call is sooner than that. The band has got one, maybe two more tunes on their playlist before they pack it up. No one has hit on her yet and she's getting a *leettle* bit desperate. The shape of her nose is kind of fleshy, and her hair needs some attention, but she's got big boobs and she has chosen a top that shows them off well. Even turning down some loser would make her feel a whole lot better. He could buy her maybe one drink, and that's it. She wouldn't even have to take him home to get most of the uplifting effect of shutting him down."

Hearing this, Brett glanced at Lee's glass, not that he saw any close parallel to the CO. It was empty, so he added a couple more ice cubes and refilled it to the midpoint.

"We all need to feel good some of the time," he said, "like that girl, even if we don't have much reason to. I know I do."

"So you tend a little bar over to Paul's Place, do you?" Clayton said, studying the slopes again.

"No, but I'm down at the end of it picking up drink orders a lot. I see how it goes every night, and there's not much variation in the program. Even when we've got the blues out front, it's like a dance without music, and the choreography is well known by all the dancers."

A few moments passed as each of them processed this image.

"So you're suggesting that we've already had a coup in Washington, an overthrow of the government," Brett said quietly, making a moist row of fingertip marks like little round footsteps on the table, quietly leaving a trail from the scene of the crime. They started to dry up in sequence, like ten little Indians being knocked off one by one.

Clayton nodded slowly. "That is what I am suggesting, and if it's true, that would be the first coup since late in 1963 by my count, but I'd give it a few more days to be sure. This is late on Thursday afternoon. I'd say if we have not *physically* seen the President of the United States by this time on Sunday, lookin' like himself and talkin' about what's actually happening on *that* particular day, then we have a new military government in power. Long live the generals. Welcome to Argentina, *amigos.*" He lifted the depleted remains of his drink as the index finger of his left hand tapped the tabletop for emphasis.

"Wow!" Lee whispered, as if her eyes were taking in a vision she never thought to see in her lifetime.

"Of course, the present administration will not have changed at all on the face of it," Brett said.

"Exactly. It'll be the same President and the same Congress. The same diligent Supreme Court will rubberstamp everything that's bein' done on its behalf and in its name by the CO. None of us will have any reason to feel threatened, other than by the epidemic. And whose fault is that? We're all on the same side, right? We all *patriots* now. It will mainly be a call to hang together against a cowardly enemy with a strange and foreign religion supported by no scruples or morality whatever. When they kill us it will be because God ordered them to do so. They'll put it up on YouTube and laugh. Nothing new there, I guess. It's like Christianity was 800 years ago, but with better weapons and publicity. You don't need to burn people at the stake anymore when you have surface to air missiles, suicide bombers, and bioterror. To me this has all the mark of ISIS, or the IS as they're calling it. And if that's the case, it's especially outrageous, because Washington has watched it growing and developing for two or three years now and done nothing at all about it."

Silence fell for a moment or two. Brett was thinking about how insecure the southern border had been lately.

"But then what happens in the fall?" said Lee with a frown. "This is an election year. We're going to have an accounting at some point, and it's only four months away. People in office will need to get out and campaign. They'll have to come out of their sanitary shells and be visible again. How can they fake that?"

For a moment Clayton didn't respond, looking off into the sharply climbing hills, where the thickening shadows could have concealed a battalion of nimble terrorists, or even desperate neighbors foraging for food. "Don't quote me on this part, OK? My guess is that the November election will not be cancelled, because that would be unconstitutional, right? It will only be 'postponed' for a short time at first, and later, indefinitely. That's unconstitutional too, only it doesn't sound so bad, in the way that *maybe* sounds better than *no* when you're taking your date home at the end of the evening."

As he said this, Clayton's weathered face bore the same benign and reassuring look he must have expected to see from the CO once the man finally appeared before the camera.

"The most elaborate respect will then be paid to our Constitution, far more than in the past. In fact, a new series of postage stamps will probably be issued in its honor, possibly ten issues featuring the Bill of Rights one by one, assuming enough of the postal service has survived and can return to work. If you think about it, the Constitution is approaching 230 years old fairly soon—a good time for a celebration. But it will be announced that the crisis requires an interim government comprised of the same people who were previously elected. Isn't that the very next thing to legitimate democracy? They will reoccupy the same chairs that would be still almost warm from their own backsides, had they shown up to do anything. I 'spect that several references will be made to Franklin Roosevelt being elected to a fourth term during World War II, principally to carry us to a victory that was almost within our grasp. *Stay the course* will be the slogan of the day. Besides, don't large numbers of people traveling to their polling place constitute a major health risk? All those dangerous grubby hands yankin' on the same set of levers one after another? Lordy! You cannot allow that kind of health risk!"

"Never change horses," said Brett.

"Exactly. Continuity in government will be the watchword of the day as if that was the same as continuity in our lives, something we're all missing right now. It will be a convincing argument, so who could object to that?"

"Clayton, I feel like you've been reading their play-book," Lee poured a little more rum into each of their glasses. Looking at her closely, Brett sensed her unwinding further.

Clayton chuckled without humor or bitterness. "As some of you know, when you're black, you don't have to read it because you already lived it—you *are* the other side. Growin' up without power, I learned to study it by watching it move away from me, 'cause that was the way it flowed. With money as its bedfellow, it always aggregates toward a center, and the military is already the greatest aggregation of power we have remaining, perhaps the only one. Think of it as a magnet on a table full of rusty nails that now have nowhere else to go. You'll find they can even travel uphill, using the proper laws of attraction."

"A phrase we've all heard before." Brett studied Clayton's hands. His knuckles were scarred from their close relationship with engine steel and wrenches, the dark burn of dirty oil. Like his mind, his skin was clean but well worn, and marked by decades of experience.

They all looked at each other for a while, sharing a dangerous secret, one that had come upon them unasked and unwelcome, but nonetheless could neither be ignored nor denied. Brett wondered what was happening at the state and local levels, and how it would be affected by this theory, if it were true. The federal government had long exercised so much input with the state governments, both in regulation and from funding grants over the years, that it seemed likely that the states could only change course and go on their own if the feds broke down completely. Was that release of control now happening?

"As much as I'd like to, I don't think I can contradict anything you've suggested," Brett said. "Do you see a parallel with what you describe in Washington with what we're now getting in the Outpost city government? Call it the local layer. Lee and I had some discussions about that when the questionnaire came around. I'm sure you saw it too."

Clayton raised his glass with a knowing smile. "You are both a scholar and a dangerous man," he said. "Not a rare combination historically, but I would certainly watch my back at this point if I were you. Our man in City Hall has a great deal on his mind right now, and he is not likely to welcome even a hint of dissent or opposition on the home front. He would feel that asking questions is no more than a distraction during a nightmare like this, and therefore a risk to the local community. Watch how disloyalty becomes the unforgivable sin as this goes on, worse even than the epidemic itself."

"And as we've been saying," Lee said, "this is the community that now supports us. It's the only safety net we've got."

5

In the midst of this, the bright blond head of a young woman popped up at the top of the unpainted plank fence on the north side of the property. A hand already waving shot up beside it. She was standing in the lot with real trees, those that were now shading the patio as they absorbed the withering sunlight on their opposite face. "You're back, Lee! Hi, Clayton. Are y'all bein' so world-weary again? Do cut me some slack now, OK? Because I believe I have acquired the most compelling need for a drink."

"Only as called for, Holly," Clayton said. "You cut us some too and then we can all be loose enough to talk."

"Well, I'll go first because I've got one *bummer* of an announcement. Doug was laid off today by the City of Outpost! Can y'all believe that? Right in the middle of this crisis business, too."

"Why?" Lee said, jumping up.

"Well, I guess they don't need a second accountant anymore because of the epidemic. More security is a higher priority. Tough budget choices for the good of Outpost, they called it. Do you believe that? He was only there half time anyway. I'm going down to see Emmett tomorrow morning and pound on his desktop. I'll make his damn coffee jump right over the side of his cup. Maybe I can get some results. He's always had a thing for me. I'll just lean over his desk."

"Then make sure you'll wear that same outfit," Clayton said drily, shaking the ice noisily in his glass as if it needed to be cushioned by more liquid to keep from shattering.

"What outfit?" Brett said, perhaps prematurely. He'd only seen Holly's head. The others appeared to know already.

"You'll see when she comes around the fence," Lee said in a grave undertone. "She really only has one, with several variations—too short and shorter. It's all about the heat, you know."

Holly started to step down from whatever had provided her height, but stopped as if she'd thought of something else she should do.

"Did Emmett tell you outright he had a thing for you?" Lee asked.

"No, but I always know when men do. Don't you? It's in their eyes. But I think I may have been rude. Who's your friend?"

Lee introduced Brett to Holly after she tiptoed through the gate at the end of the fence near where it disappeared between the houses. Her espadrilles lifted her on five-inch wedges. Brett could see why Emmett, or any man, might have a thing for her. Cascades of wavy blond hair framed a sensuously mischievous face whose detail he hadn't been able to make out at the top of the fence because the light was at her back. Her scooped white cotton top traveled with a tiny vertical stripe in the fabric weave that in the angled light was stretched like a contour map over a compelling landscape. Her shorts set a new standard in brevity. Holly still seemed ready to party in spite of Doug's bad news. Brett glanced at

Lee as he took this in and found her watching him narrowly. The only woman he'd ever encountered before when he was with Lee was the proprietor of the Blue Bayou Inn. Maybe he was already on a short leash without realizing it. It made him wonder what their relationship really was. Most of the time he would've called it fellow travelers over rough terrain with a common destination, one they couldn't always define.

Holly turned down some dark rum on the rocks and accepted instead a Diet Dr Pepper on ice mixed with a jigger of vodka to bump it up.

"Where's Doug now? How did he take it?" asked Lee.

"He's at home brooding like a goddamn five-year-old who dropped his ice cream cone upside down on an August sidewalk. He doesn't know what he's going to do. It's not like he could leave Outpost now and find a job in a neighboring town. At least we're only renting, so we don't have a mortgage. The landlord lives in Bridger, so good luck even collecting it with no more mail deliveries. The way it's going now, if Doug leaves town, he's not likely to even get back in anymore. For myself, I prefer to stay in. As y'all know, I'm very well connected here." Holly tossed her hair back as she said this. No one felt like contradicting her.

Her shoulders rose in a refined shrug as her eyes locked onto Brett's. Even from across the table he couldn't fail to notice how long her lashes were. He also felt that Holly's arrival was somehow affecting his relationship with Lee, moment by moment, in ways he couldn't easily read, but would probably be called upon to sort out later.

"It's *terra incognita* out there," said Clayton.

"Right." Holly shrugged again as if she didn't know what that meant, and then looked back Brett's way with an elfin smile. "And what do you do, Mr. Brett, when you're not running from the plague?"

"I used to run a delivery business, but that's finished until this is over. I'm going to hang out here for now and see what develops."

He rejected a first impulse to say he was both CEO

and chairman of the board of a transport fleet whose reach extended from Dallas to New Orleans, and from Little Rock to Corpus Christi. A firm whose roots were regional, yet whose impact was national, whose goals were not only success in business, but also to extend and enhance the quality of life for its customers and their neighbors. Some had even speculated in the media that his mission was divinely inspired.

That would have been a spin, but not a total lie. He could also have said he'd saved the lives of millions of people within the past few days, far more than anyone in the government or the CDC had. Even the Army and the CO. Yet he modestly reigned himself in. Holly's presence was stimulating, and to have her questions focused on him nearly made Brett stutter. Because it was difficult not to look at her, he decided a better choice was to look mostly at Lee. He wasn't sure she was fooled, although she may have appreciated the effort this refocus required.

"And do you think you're going to be safe in this town, Mr. Brett?" Holly asked, in a voice that caressed his ears like honey. "Is that why you came to us? Is our little Outpost a secure refuge for y'all now?"

Although her voice had become soft and fuzzy, she also sounded like she was calling his bluff, a tone he recognized. As for safety in Outpost, Brett would've guessed that no male was safe next door to her, or within a hundred yards downwind, but that wasn't something he could say in this company. He noticed Clayton was watching him with amusement, as if the entertainment value of this encounter was worth the price of the rum, and he had a front-row ticket.

"We saw some places coming up, and not too far from here, that are much more dangerous," Brett said carefully, not believing it for a moment, even where they'd driven past bodies spread-eagled on the ground. "Anyway, this was Lee's choice and I don't mind backing her up." Holly returned a long, cool gaze through lowered lashes, as if she were accustomed to sipping life through a straw, every subtle nuance of it rolling over her pink tongue, like a character from a Truman

Capote novel. Lee and Clayton both appeared to have taken premium seats on the sidelines to watch this joust between two armored and helmeted opponents.

"A noble thought, I'm sure," Holly said slowly, "but can y'all still define danger? If you ask me, you look like you might still nourish a certain veiled taste for risk yourself, one that might only emerge in a crisis such as this. Sho', you look all cool and composed drivin' in your truck, but don't you often find there are times when you surprise yourself just a bit? I know I do, and way too often for my own comfort. You never know what I'll come out with, and neither do I. Just askin', OK?"

Her lips and chin thrust forward saying this, and her look invited him to challenge this statement, or even to imagine it in detail. Even throwing down this lace gauntlet, Holly continued to skim the thoughts from the surface of his mind, like foam from a simmering and turbulent soup. What was she referring to at this moment? Three rums did not help Brett to respond. He felt that someone should have warned him. Billed as a place of safety, Outpost clearly was not without its homegrown species of risk. Probably nowhere was safe anymore. That was the new normal.

Later, when the guests had gone and they'd washed the glasses during a ponderous silence, Brett and Lee stood in the kitchen filling out the rest of the Outpost questionnaire with the kind of dense focus that helped them ignore the more obvious issues that hung in the air around them. They'd gotten through the education section with no problem and were working on sketching in their employment history. That part was going quickly too. Being self-employed, Brett couldn't offer much to slow it down. Certainly he had no references other than satisfied customers. Since he'd left home at seventeen he'd never had a boss, which was part of his strategy in leaving. After avoiding supervision in all of his working life, he sensed he had run into it now, and without meaning to.

"You find bad girls kind of attractive, don't you?" Lee

said in an offhand way, seeming to study the small print even as she puzzled over the question about what last year's property taxes had been.

This did not surprise Brett. "So that's on the form, too? I haven't gotten that far. Is the question you're reading about having the bad girl right next store and coming over the wall, or only in the city at large?"

And was the question a test of courage or moral fiber? Was it designed to establish what their connection was turning into, as if anything could? Avoiding his first response, which was that the lure of bad girls had powered much of world history, and that, after all, was their intent and their glory, he replied, quite innocently, but with a smug sense that he'd dodged a bullet, "And is Holly a bad girl?"

Lee looked up at him serenely, but with an underlying layer of tension in the set to her jaw. "Well, you didn't have to ask who I was talking about, now did you?" Had she been crushing grapes between the firm set of her lips, the seeds would've ricocheted off his forehead.

Brett paused a moment to clear his mind, which was still barely possible. Living alone hadn't required him to be this nimble with some of these issues, and the stress they had suddenly found themselves under was like nothing either of them had ever experienced. "Let's say that I think Holly knows who she is."

Surely this was neutral enough, if a little lame. It even had a supportive twinge of feminism to it, and it encouraged him to extend his reach further into a swamp where nothing but crocodiles were waiting. "Self-awareness is important for anyone, especially for women. It was a jungle out there even before this epidemic came up, and now it's getting worse."

Next he expected the question of how long had he been such a sap about women to come up in one form or another, but instead Lee asked, "Do you think Holly's prettier than I am?" She was leaning against the stove with a neutral look on her face, adding, after a suitable pause, "Just because she's white?"

"Whyever would I think that?" His tone was light, but was *whyever* even a valid English word? After what had gone before, this had the sound of something the village idiot would say.

"Just from the way you looked at her. I'm only guessing here, OK? To be frank, I'm just tryin' to define our relationship a little more. As *y'all* know, we nevah have." Mimicking Holly's tone, the last sentence hung in the air for a moment. As Lee pronounced it, *have* possessed two syllables, each clearly articulated.

"And this conversation is going to do that?" Behind his back, Brett's left hand was gripping the overhang of the counter for support, possibly the only source of it remaining.

"Well, it might define what it isn't, and that's a start, because if you're goin' on with Holly like that, then you're not goin' on with *me*." The flash in her eyes was one he hadn't seen before, although he would certainly recognize it if it returned. It could've ignited charcoal from a distance.

Brett already knew there was only one way to look at Holly, one that Holly herself defined. Now here comes the minefield that follows the dismal swamp, he thought, setting down his pen. It was the moment when he would have to sum it all up, thin as it was. A statement that would acknowledge that, while he hadn't been neutered at puberty, he was still able to rise above the crasser forms of feminine enticement, such as those on display earlier in the evening, and in such dangerous abundance. He tried to summon an objective tone.

"Since you ask, I'm happy to deal with this. I would have to say that Holly is a little different, and she's not made in your style at all. She's also not as smart as you are, by the way, but she is flashier. Flashy can be OK at times, like at the later stages of a party, but the problem is that it can lack solidity… ah, in a crisis like this." The last phrase had occurred to him an instant too late to properly bind it to the previous one. He realized that the word *crisis* itself might have several meanings in this context.

From the look on Lee's face, he realized they had

149

entered a slack-free zone, and this improvised response had earned him none whatever. He sensed that an invisible clock was ticking somewhere in the house.

"But I do sense you think Holly is better looking."

"She looks great, OK? And so do you, but last time I checked, being pretty was not a survival skill. It only helps you have more children, which won't get *anyone* through this. In fact, having kids with us right now would cut our odds badly. Ah…not that we're planning to." How had he ended up with that sentence?

Lee seemed uncertain how to react to this. Her brow was wrinkled as she rifled through their mutual experience, hour by hour.

"I just want to know where we are here, Brett, that's all, because we're in a tough spot. Are we together or aren't we?"

A flutter of panic went through him. Exactly what did *together* mean? He well knew he had failed to define it correctly twice in the past. He went for caution. "When I stopped to pick you up outside of Dundee, I wanted to bail you out. I was happy to do it. Remember? The rest of this kind of came together hour by hour." This suddenly felt like way too many hours for a couple who'd never met before to be spending every moment together.

In taking a minute to reprocess this, Lee stayed cool. "Have you made any more choices about us since then? Like where we're going from here?" she asked carefully but firmly, leaning forward and releasing an encouraging smile that appeared to cost her some effort, even if it wasn't her most convincing performance.

"Like did I escalate the choosing process from that point?"

"I guess. Seems like then I thought you only chose to give me a ride because I was desperate. We didn't exchange vows, although I noticed you thought my legs were pretty damn good. It wasn't everything, but you have to start somewhere. I don't know how it works for you, but my brain is at the top of that formation." Her finger pointed toward her forehead.

Lee had failed to mention a humanitarian instinct on his part, which he believed was an important part of the picture. Still, Brett had spent too much time on the open road to fail to recognize a crossroads when one appeared. He had become skilled at avoiding wrong turns because much of his adult life had been structured around not being forced to do things he didn't want to do. Now, he was having trouble connecting the appearance of Holly with the decision point that immediately followed.

When he didn't respond, Lee jumped back into it.

"Maybe you need some time to think about it on your own. You might have to sleep in the kid's room after all, just to keep your mind clear, although I didn't object last night to the idea of your company in the bed next to mine. I enjoyed hearing you breathing. It meant we were both still alive."

Even though he felt he now needed to make a move of reconciliation toward her, since the door was open, instead he found himself trotting out the *chippie* issue again, as if it had been brainlessly waiting for this kind of moment. Why was she coming on like she was so perfect? Hadn't he reacted like any man would to a sexy neighbor? He folded his arms rigidly over his chest, suddenly feeling extremely tired.

"That's not the only thing on my mind," he said. He didn't care for the tone of his own voice once he heard it.

"What does that mean?"

"It seems like you've already made some interesting choices yourself. What about that chip planted in your neck? That's always been a big dividing point for a lot of people. Maybe it still is for me."

Her eyes flashed at him. "What about it? That was *my* choice at the time. Maybe you were just checking me out a little bit too close when you noticed it. Did you see any other imperfections? Were my boobs all right?"

"I would never have one of those things buried in my body, OK?" *Things* made it sound like a deeply foreign object

151

that was possibly alien in origin.

"Because that's all you could *ever* be, Brett, is NC (no chips). I can see it now all over you, so don't pull that Mr. Charlie white crap on me." Her jaw was thrust out like a snake, although her tongue did not leave her mouth. Lee's hands were upright before her, either in an attack mode or a defensive position. Brett couldn't tell which it was. He wished he knew her better. Probably that would never happen now. He wished more that he hadn't ever brought this up. It looked like they wouldn't see the end of this together, despite how far they had already come.

"I always thought those microchip implants were so controversial, once the NSA spying scandal came out, I mean, especially to blacks, who never have that much trust for the system, even in good times. And you can never stomach having a voter ID, either, am I right? So how could you do that to yourself?" He knew this was still going rapidly downhill, but he wasn't sure why. As a person normally in pursuit of calm and equilibrium in his life, he wasn't very tuned in on anyone else's hot buttons. Brett didn't have many of his own, although he might not have expressed it that way. Clearly this was one he hadn't noticed before.

Lee stood for a moment without speaking, her cheeks puffing in and out as if fanning a blaze inside her that was still rising toward its highest temperature.

"Don't go making those assumptions about *me*, OK? Don't be putting me in some group that always acts this way or that way." Her hand made a violent motion of separation.

"But you've got that chip in your neck. Doesn't that mean anything to you at all? Why fling it back at me? Is this the way you treated Ted, throwing the race thing back at him all the time?"

She looked at him as if she were at a crossroads, gathering herself together, still shaking her head.

Brett suddenly felt she was going to be more rational than he was.

"Alright. Here's what it is, so you can just take this

home and suck it up. Think of who's going to hire me once I have my master's degree. My advisor told me that any big company that has federal contracts, or any state or local government that takes federal money is going to require ID implants to get hired starting a year and a half from now. I did what I had to do, OK? Why should some silly regulation block me, when I've worked so damn hard to get this master's degree? Didn't you ever do what you *had* to do? Or were you always above it?" Her voice took on a lofty tone and her fingers fluttered as if taking flight.

A heavy silence settled in around them like blocks of stone, crowding them toward each other. Would they even have had this conversation if they hadn't drunk that rum of Clayton's? Brett was glad at least that the *chippie* issue had finally come out, even as it opened the door to his own past, which under her scrutiny was starting to look more self-indulgent than he had ever thought.

With this, an unexpected insight came to him. What Lee needed was the same thing he needed. Holly and the ID chip were merely the catalysts, and this was more about making some positive statement of where they had arrived at that moment. Lee already looked so much better than Holly that he was happy to do it. He stood up and pulled her firmly into his arms, instantly knowing this was the right thing to do. She didn't resist, but her body was still tense. He left enough space between their faces so he could look into her eyes. "Lee, I choose you at this moment in time going forward. We'll find our way through this and beyond, and then we'll make whatever we can of this, because that's where we belong."

"Thank you. Now I feel better." Even though he had felt her arms tighten around him as he spoke, her voice was no more than polite as they drew apart.

"A lot better?"

"No, but a little. Don't worry about me, I'm OK. I don't always aim as high as I should. You'll find that out."

"I don't know what else I can say. That other stuff isn't important. I'd like to save you, just as I'd like to save

myself. Right now you're saving me by getting me into Outpost. I'd like to meet you on a normal day in a public park and
shake your hand. We'll have a drink or lunch. I'd like to talk
to you as if this had never happened. I'd like to connect as if
we knew we'd both be alive tomorrow and neither of us had
ever thought of this. But I can't do any of that, because I'm
just as desperate as you are." He shook his head as he felt his
eyes start to well up, so he turned away.

Lee looked at him quietly, calmly, as if this was the
new reality, and she had already figured it out on her own.
"I'm very practical," she said. "You'll find that out, too."

"Most women have to be."

"But I need to be anchored, and you seem like you're
paralyzed, but you don't want to be. Let it go."

"Emotionally?"

"Yes, because I deserve better than what I'm getting
here. You're just tripping over a chip."

"I know that. I've never questioned it. I'm trying to
find a way through it."

Silently, as if his mind and voice had gone as far as
they could, his hand crept across the table and seized hers. It
felt more meaningful than the hug.

This was the moment of their tiny improvised
declaration, their commitment, two dollar's worth on no
notice, sparked by the arrival of Holly. They'd been together
almost constantly since they met, and it had already lasted
about fifty-five hours. Once she was out of sight, Holly was
easy to forget. It was no surprise to Brett that he was ready to
commit to Lee for the duration of the crisis, even if hovering
at the back of his mind were the two past near misses with
marriage, Lee's off-putting statement in the bathtub, the microchip, and the questions that these events brought up every
time he thought of getting close to a woman again. He tried
not to think that race was part of it, but it was, mainly since
she was so aware of it.

Another part of this was that Brett was increasingly
aware that most of the power he had once possessed over his

own life had also virtually evaporated. That was the great achievement of the ISIS terrorists, if this was really their doing. Not only was the power of the government mocked and rendered nearly nonexistent, but also that of every individual who had so far survived. Everyone's head was down, and if they weren't running like Brett was, then they were cowering under the table like 1950s school kids in fear of a nuclear blast.

Brett had grown up in a household where his parents hated each other and only pretended they didn't for special occasions, like Brett's birthday parties and their own anniversaries. Occasionally Christmas, but no one could depend on it. Their smiles were brittle enough to form hairline cracks in their teeth. With an example like that, he had never fully trusted his own judgment. Now that earlier kind of judgment didn't matter. He wasn't trying to second-guess his connection with Lee, but with all the pressure they were under, it was hard to see anything clearly. On the other hand, why be rethinking their relationship if *nothing* was going to last? No one could estimate life expectancies anymore.

"I'm glad we worked that out," Lee said with a small, yet satisfied toss of her hair. "Now we're a couple, even if we can't exactly say what that means, but I'm still not putting the twin beds back together."

He ignored this. "We *are* together. When did you know for certain you needed that?" Brett couldn't have said why, but suddenly this was important, looking back on their beginning.

Lee gave him a knowing look, as if playing an important card at the perfect moment. "OK. It was that instant when Holly's head appeared at the top of the fence, with the sunlight collecting in her hair like a golden halo. And when her hand came up, she seemed to be waving goodbye to me before I even knew that I was going, or why." Clearly this made perfect sense to her, but Brett found it hard to connect this to their current condition.

"Good enough, but she's married. Let's factor that in, too."

"Even so, I do think she gets around a little bit, and all bets are off now. As you may have noticed, men like her, and I do hear things. Although you tiptoed past it fairly well, I know you liked her, too. There was also, just for the record, a small episode with Ted when I brought him up here. I never brought him back."

Brett could think of no response to this, although it shed some light on the conversation.

When they finished all five pages of the forms, they had a light supper and walked to City Hall to drop them off. Every supper was light now. Brett's idea had prevailed about not disclosing the gun or the gasoline. Lee had decided that what little it would add to the city's resources wouldn't justify their potential helplessness if they were forced to give them up, should it come to that. He had no doubt that it *would* come to that, even if only to make it easier for Emmett to consolidate his grip on Outpost. In particular, losing the gun would fundamentally change their position.

The clear, flawless evening lacked any hint of the ongoing collapse of everything beyond the city limits of Outpost. One exception was the presence of two city pickups the police had painted black and outfitted with side roll bars and benches. Canvas was stretched over the bars on top to provide shade. They both circled the square twice, each with a cop in the back, carrying an assault rifle. Lee waved in a friendly fashion, all encouragement and smiles. After all, Outpost is a small town. It wasn't going to grow in size if those guys had their way, but it wasn't going to shrink drastically, either. Doing their jobs, which didn't include public relations, neither cop waved back at her.

Aside from a few people slipping their questionnaires into the drop boxes, the plaza next to City Hall was nearly empty. Most did so with a flourish, as if they were promoting a cause or affirming their commitment. Lee and Brett sat on a cast iron bench with a view of the lake across Shoreline Boulevard as dusk settled. While it was almost possible to think the world was normal for a few moments, that didn't matter, since the ugly reality of it was the adhesive that held them together. Otherwise, with a polite handshake they would've gone their separate ways days ago, wishing each other well. Still, Brett somehow sensed a mellowing of her attitude toward him, even if the magnitude of their allegiance was less than cosmic.

"Tell me one big secret thing about yourself," she said, leaning back on the bench and retying one of her shoelaces. "I want to know you better."

He hesitated. "OK. But not anything good, right? Like I've been shortlisted to be the next pope?"

"No. Something you wouldn't usually reveal to anyone you weren't close to. Something that could send me away shivering and covering my chest with both arms in disgust."

"Wow, this *is* trust night. But, OK, here goes. I get stuck easily. Chicken especially can stop its travels somewhere in my throat to rest for a while, and I'm not able to move it on right away through normal means. I'm always afraid I'm going to choke. My dad had it too."

She looked at Brett with alarm. "What do you do when that happens?"

"I go outside to jump up and down on the sidewalk because it's an unyielding surface, or I pound my sternum with both fists like King Kong. Eventually it loosens up. The main thing is not to panic. That's an attractive image, right? This is what you're in for with me at dinner parties, if we ever go to one. How about you?"

She pressed her hands over her face. "Now I can't tell you. Suddenly I'm too embarrassed. I shouldn't have started this."

"Sure you can. I told you mine. That cost me something. We're investing in each other today. Go ahead."

A long pause followed. She pressed her lips together as she centered herself, looking straight ahead. "Sometimes I wake up crying in the night. It's a girl thing. I never know why. My pillow is wet and I flip it over to the dry side. Nor am I ever able to remember any dreams that are connected with those feelings. I don't even feel sad."

"OK. But is that all?" Brett made a useless gesture. It didn't seem like this was on the same scale as his problem, which always felt subtly life threatening.

"I wish it was. Then I need to have sex right away, like in the next five minutes."

Startled, Brett stared at her for a moment. "But, what if you're alone?"

Lee shrugged modestly and turned her face away as her voice fell to a whisper. "I can get by on my own."

"But that's terrible!" He turned away to keep her from seeing him laugh, but his chest was shaking.

"Now I'm embarrassed." She covered her face again. Brett leaned forward in her direction, pulling at her wrist. "Listen, Lee, it was you that suggested this game. You must have wanted to tell me that, because I think you are a *royal* tease. As a psychologist, you ought to realize that about yourself."

"Didn't I tell you my specialty was all about testing, not self-analysis?"

"You do know how to test me, I'll give you that."

"See, I'm a natural. And you've always passed, so far. Even now."

So far, Brett thought; that was the governing phrase. *So far.*

6

On Friday morning after breakfast they signed in to what they were now thinking of as the dark angel information center on the only remaining television channel. The split screen displayed a map with irregular perimeters enclosing the four surviving major cities of the South. The presentation was headed by the words, *Unified Recovery Districts* (URD). The background speaker was not the CO, but a man with a blond crew cut wearing an Army uniform. The banner at the bottom identified him as Colonel Dwayne C. Atkins. He was in the middle of explaining that for the present time, access to the four major intact cities would be restricted to military personnel that had been trained in disease prevention techniques. This would replace the purely local security apparatus that had so far kept the epidemic out. The outlined areas were now autonomous federal districts, similar to Washington, DC, and the state governments no longer had any authority there. Brett wondered how they could do that. Had state sovereignty now fallen victim to the epidemic? The Constitution was only a piece of paper. It had been forgotten before during wartime.

Col. Atkins continued in a drone. Anyone within the URDs was free to leave, but people who left these districts would not be allowed to return for an indefinite period. While every effort would be made to develop self-sufficiency programs nationwide, trading would also be instituted among the four cities, using disinfected Army transport exclusively. Exports from these recovery zones to the rest of the country would be confined to items deemed nonessential to the population inside, or in excess supply and renewable. National communications, such as the network they were now watching, would be routed through one of the URDs, and every effort would be made to sustain a national grid, although numerous gaps were to be expected at this point. Everything was subject to local conditions, which could change by the hour.

"We're on our own now, aren't we?" Lee said in a small sad voice. She sounded like a child lost in the forest as she tried to peer through all the huge dark tree trunks.

"I feel like we always were, since the moment we chose not to return to Highway 36 and continue up to Bridger. It's hard to say this, but I think they have to suspend some of our institutions, or something like that, to preserve what isn't already ruined. Everyone else gets thrown under the bus. They've got to save whatever is savable."

She turned to look at him. "This is your doing, you know. You're standing here in somebody else's house in Outpost, and if you hadn't screwed up the delivery of those four packages the CO wouldn't have anything left to save. You're the only hero that's emerged from this so far."

"So blame the messenger," Brett said. "But don't look for a stamp with my face on it any time soon. Not that national mail service exists anymore. It's the perfect way to spread the disease."

"But then no one is ever going to know what you did."

"Not unless you tell them, but I don't want my fifteen minutes of fame. Who's listening, anyway? You won't see it come up on this channel."

Brett wondered for a moment whether Newton the fishing tackle guy down at the Flats was still alive. If he had examined his copy of the manifest for the packages he gave Brett when this began, then he might have figured it out. The four recipients were all part of the plot. Poor old Newton, he thought. It was more likely that he never had the chance. He was a guy Brett identified with because he had made his way in business alone. He had lived his dream of being an amateur fisherman on the Gulf, supplying fishing gear for other people when he didn't get out on the water anymore that much himself, although he kept his boat in shape. He also always understood the tackle his customers needed to buy for current conditions. Suddenly he could see Newton's body lying in a spray of his own blood behind the counter.

Shaking his head to rid himself of the image, Brett tried to flip through the channels to see if any other news was being released, but no other stations were on the air. "We're down to one channel again. I wonder what's happening?" He pulled out his cell, which hadn't rung in a while. It displayed no signal. "Check your phone," he said.

Lee found hers in the bedroom and brought it out.

"I've got no signal on mine either. I just used it Wednesday night when we got here. But there's still this." She brought out her laptop and booted it in the kitchen, plugging it into an Internet jack in the wall near the table. "No service," she said, after the screen came up. She snapped the lid shut again, too hard.

"I think this must be the beginning of a breakdown

in the satellite grid. Not only are millions dead now, but even healthy people are staying away from work, and some of the communications and power plants aren't running from lack of staff."

He picked up the cordless phone in the kitchen and found it also dead, although the red button light in the base showed it was charging.

"So we've got power because of the hydro plant at the base of the dam," Lee said. "But fewer and fewer people outside this area are going to have it. What's going to make a difference out there is if people have solar panels, or access to wind power, or one of those generators you tow behind a truck."

"And those run on gasoline, so that's not going to work very long."

"I feel like the world is physically shrinking," she said, "at the same time as the population drops."

"So here's the problem. The CO has to maintain access to the public to spread his message, not only his propaganda message, but solid factual information as well. So the government must be shuffling the TV signal over the grid in areas where it's still operating, to keep distributing it as widely as possible. I'm sure now that everything we see goes through Dallas or New Orleans."

"So the feds are dependent on the grid more than anyone. Won't their next move be to take it over and resurrect it where it's failed? Doesn't that mean they'll come after our little power plant right here?"

Brett thought about this for a moment. "I assume Outpost is still selling its excess power, like they always have, but I doubt the government will come after it, because I don't think this hydro plant has the capacity to provide service for a whole lot more customers than it already has in this part of the state. You saw it when we came in. A better strategy would be to get those big plants going again that were built to supply the main urban centers. If they're thinking clearly, they'll probably leave us alone."

"Right, if they are. But what about Clayton?"

It took Brett too long to connect Clayton to this problem.

"Ham radio," she said, after a moment. "The unofficial information source."

"That's right! He's got a steady supply of electricity. If it's only a matter of sending out a signal on a given frequency, he can put it out as far as the strength of his transmitter will allow. You could run it on solar power, you could run it on wind, both sending and receiving."

"He said he had reached Dallas."

"And the forms we filled out from the city didn't ask about ham radio equipment, did they? They're not likely to know that he has it, unless DeShawn says something down at the motor pool. They've got the same communication problems we have. They can run their police radios with no problem, with the transmitter and electricity that Outpost has, but any national broadcasts have to come through the four intact cities."

"So why can't Clayton share it with them?" she said. Brett suppressed a chuckle, but she was serious in asking this.

"Would they let him keep it if he did? I think they'd elbow him aside in a heartbeat. Remember what he said about power? Power is about not having to share anything."

"But what if it's for the common good, Brett? Can't anybody think like that anymore? Does everything have to be so hard ass now? That's what's dragging me down."

"To each according to his needs, right?"

"Why not?"

"I guess I'm really asking this: what if it isn't used for the common good? You'd like to assume one thing, but I'm afraid of another. Clayton would say that he's seeing an awful lot of power being concentrated in the hands of the city government here, which really means in the hands of Emmett. He can justify it by the emergency. I think the answer to the question of what he might do down the road will be revealed by how he handles the power he has now."

"OK. So we can only watch what he does." Her

expression said she had bought this solution.

"That's all we can do."

"Maybe Holly will come back with some sense of that after she talks to him today."

"But will she be able to figure it out on her own?"

"As you suggested yesterday, she may not be as smart as I am in some ways, but she certainly knows everything about men."

"That," he said, "is only raw instinct, blended with extensive experience. Men might act differently when she's not around." I certainly do, he thought.

7

In no special hurry, since she already felt in control of the situation, Holly strolled downtown at ten that morning in her normal abbreviated shorts and halter, a combination that would have embarrassed Jessica Simpson in *The Dukes of Hazzard*, a film Holly had seen four times, mainly to analyze the body language. She knew Emmett usually arrived at this hour because he had told her that two days before while they were lying in his king-size bed at what he liked to call "The Residence." She also knew that in his mind, the name was capitalized, as it was on his personal stationary. She would not have been surprised to see it tattooed somewhere on his body, but if it was, she hadn't located it yet. Emmett had applauded the search. It had been their fourth encounter in bed in as many weeks and they'd captured the rhythm of it perfectly. Not everything in his life was such a thoroughly delightful distraction, he had told her. Holly already knew it. Emmett held few surprises for her, although she liked to think she did for him.

With each step toward City Hall, Doug's image faded further from her mind like a child's dream on waking, and with even less substance. Holly was thinking more of how much she appreciated the high thread count of Emmett's sheets, something that mattered to her since they pampered her delicate skin while she accommodated his rather athletic and invasive manner. Although he was an accountant, counting threads had never mattered to Doug, nor had he ever understood her interest in spending that much money on bed linens. As the numbers ticked away in his columnar dreams, she felt he could've peacefully slept on canvas. Soon he probably would be if everything went right.

Entering the polished terrazzo and stucco precincts of the 1930s City Hall, Holly marched past the stiff bow-tied photographic portraits of previous mayors, mostly in black and white, identically framed in dark-stained mahogany against walls painted in the shade she thought of as old bile. She especially liked the image of the first mayor, Roscoe Belden, with the leering glint that beamed from his monocle. Even before color photography she could detect the flush in his cheeks, and she never failed to stop for a moment in his gaze, imagining Roscoe's very proper hand grabbing her ass. If only life in general was as easy as men were, but other, unexpected elements had recently entered the mix. Holly knew that a big test was coming, and it was not far away. The problem, as always, was to be on the winning side when it came. She had a recent history of landing on her feet, although marrying Doug had been an awkward stumble early on. Was it only her youth that made him look like such a step up? Fortunately, the rough landing hadn't damaged either her spirits or the perfect skin of her knees.

Approaching Emmett's office door, Holly was waved past by the armed sentry. At the door of his inner office, Emmett's secretary, Rosie, who would never see seventy again even on a clear day, gave Holly a glum look.

"The mayor is working at home this morning, my dear—urgent business. He was expecting an email from his mother and he never gave her his office address. I can't imagine why, but you know how he is better than most, I suspect."

Her eyebrows went up on the last word. Rosie was too old to reign herself in anymore, and she knew where the bodies were buried, an enviable combination, for her, anyway.

I know more than you can ever imagine, Holly thought, even though you think you know everything about him. Holly wondered why he couldn't have checked his home email from his City Hall desk. Was he up to something at The Residence? She turned with a mincing step and walked down the long corridor out of the building like a model on a runway. It was not a bad gait, either, for a short girl, and she was certain every security man's eyes were caressing her, as they damn well ought to be.

She relaxed into a normal step as she crossed the parking lot, still mulling over Emmett's absence from City Hall. Four short blocks brought her to his front door.

Standing in the northwest corner of Outpost, The Residence was a smooth 1931 stucco cube with no overhangs or window trim. It was painted pearl gray with tall black steel casement windows divided into small panes. The third story windows were smaller, as befit the lower ceilings of the staff quarters. Outpost's only Art Deco building aside from City Hall, the town's first millionaire, a gambler who had made a fortune in 1929 by being heavily short the stock market going into Black Friday, had erected it. An armed guard at the entrance let Holly in. Without asking her what it was, the guard in the corridor inside took her name in to the mayor, padding softly down the black and white marble tiles set on the diagonal.

As Holly waited she pressed her bare midriff against the molded edge of the alabaster hall table, leaning toward the beveled mirror to check her makeup. She stuck out the tip of her tongue, but before she had a chance to touch up her lipstick, the guard returned.

"Come this way, miss, if you would. His Honor will see you now."

In the living room Emmett sat at an eight-foot rosewood desk facing the two pair of French doors on the façade, which went to within fifteen inches of the ten-foot ceiling. He was wearing a pair of sharkskin slacks and a white shirt with the sleeves rolled up over his elbows. As Holly approached, he slowly turned toward her on his swivel chair. His nested fingers covered the tiny gap in his shirt between the buttons over his navel. Too bad he's not five years younger, she thought, but you have to go where the power is.

"I don't usually have dessert right after breakfast, but in your case I'll make an exception. Hold my calls, Kevin. I'm in a security meeting." Emmett raised his voice on the last nine words. Kevin was attentive but unseen in an adjacent room.

Holly didn't move, stopping ten feet away from his chair, her normal negotiating distance. Her hands rested on her hips. "No whipped cream this time, Emmett," she said coolly. "I mean it. And never again from that spray can with the little tiny nozzle. I always have to shower afterwards, and when I shower, I like to have clean underwear waiting for me when I come out. That wasn't the case last time. You let me down."

Emmett rose and closed the door. "You could've brought a few sets over here, not that you need any. I can clear a drawer in my dresser for you. I won't be skiing for another five months, if ever." The degree of space between his upraised hands suggested how accommodating this offer was.

"Aren't you only too sweet." Her face remained immobile.

"I do know who my fans are." Emmett's eyebrows went up hopefully.

"You have your finger on the pulse of this hick town."

"That's why we're sitting here this morning. I have it on your pulse as well, and I know how to make it *thump*."

"We'll see. Anyway, I came about Doug, my husband." Ordinarily Holly could have filled out a dozen questionnaires without his name coming up.

"Well, he's history, as you suggested yesterday."

"Define history," she demanded, thrusting one hip

out toward him, taunting him.

"A fond memory to some, an inconvenient recollection to others in the event of a tragedy. Mostly it's something to forget about or redefine if you're in politics. But I'd rather make it than define it. Come on over here, Peanut. Tell me some more about your Doug. Is that poor lad flipped out now?" The mayor's smile was serene, framing his perfect teeth, aligned like little porcelain soldiers in his political smile.

"I wonder if he might still come after you," she said, "It's not just getting fired; I think he's on to us." Holly sat down on Emmett's lap and leaned back into his chest. His bear-like paws enclosed her, probing. She was almost finding some amusement in the idea of Doug going after the mayor. Sometimes Emmett was overconfident and she didn't care to be taken for granted. "Y'all might want to watch your back for a while."

"You'd just like to see men fighting over you. That's why I have a security staff. You met some of them coming in. Anyway, I've got other things on my mind too, although you're the most fun at the moment. You're more fun than anything." His breath was close on her neck, and soon his lips were as well.

"At the moment?"

"You know what I mean."

"I do, but I'm wondering about the other moments."

"I only meant that I can't devote as much time to you as I would like." His voice held a subtle note of impatience. "I have my duties too, and we're in an emergency here, in case you didn't notice."

"You have to save the world."

"This corner of it, seriously. No one else is going to until the CO tightens his grip a little more. But I've got a little loose time today; so let me show you my new sheets. They have that same subtle stripe like the underwear you wore on our first date. Took me a while to find it in 800 count Egyptian cotton."

Paced like a marathon, with a focused beginning, a

disciplined center, and aiming toward a flat out scramble at the finish line, their sessions in bed were the only times Holly was absolutely certain of their connection. She worked to stretch them out, barring his entrance until she could hardly bear it. His undivided attention was clear and compelling, and although it evaporated at a certain point, she knew it still lingered in his mind and at the back of his eyes as he looked at her. That was where she always wanted to be. Her competition was the epidemic, rather than any other woman, and her principal strength was that at any given moment she could distract his attention from it, a refuge he always needed. Holly knew all of this without Emmett volunteering it.

   Lunchtime on Fourth Street that day held no foreshadowing of serious trouble as far as Brett and Lee were concerned. He had spent some time trying to imagine Holly's encounter with Emmett—no easy task, since he'd never seen the mayor. As they were sitting down to eat, the doorbell rang. Lee went to answer it. Brett had been having the feeling lately that this was not his home and he ought to stay in the background so she didn't have to explain his presence to every neighbor that came to the door.

   She returned to the kitchen trailed by a man in his thirties whose face looked flushed and bloated from weeping. His reddish brown hair was parted in the middle and his shirt was unbuttoned and hanging outside his pants. The plastic frames of his glasses matched his hair color.

   "This is Doug. Doug, Brett. He thinks Holly's not coming back. She went downtown to talk to Emmett this morning and now he can't reach her. She either turned off her cell or it isn't working." Doug didn't offer to shake hands, his arms and elbows bobbing as if he was swimming through a sea of grief.

   "Is your land line working?" Brett asked, trying to be sympathetic, but thinking his voice must have sounded too businesslike.

"Not anymore. I walked down to City Hall and tried to find her, but no one in the building had seen her. Naturally, they'd all say that. This whole town is so fucked up now it makes me crazy."

Brett looked at him for a long moment, wondering how anyone could miss her. Why would people at City Hall deny seeing her? As they all stood in the kitchen, he was hoping Lee wasn't going to invite Doug to sit down with them. He didn't want to play detective, nor did he want this to go on forever, since it wasn't anything they could fix. When he thought of Holly, the words *wild child* always came to mind.

"Did you stop at Emmett's office?"

Doug nodded. "Yes, but he was in a meeting out of the building. He couldn't be reached."

"Why wouldn't she come back?" Brett looked at his watch. It was just after one o'clock.

"I don't know." Doug's head was swinging back and forth in denial. "Now I think some of her clothes are gone. The closet didn't look the same when I came back home. She didn't come over here, did she? I wish I could talk to her. She's not as tough as she pretends, and I know I could make things right. She's only a little kid, really." His hands were gathered into futile fists and his face was starting to crumple.

Brett began to wonder whether Doug's perspective on his wife was part of their problem.

"Did you have a fight with her?" said Lee.

"No. Yes, but it wasn't that bad. She said some things about me not working full time before and now not at all. She didn't like the trend line, which I thought was snotty. I said she could damn well get a job then herself. It went back and forth like that." His hands made more ineffectual gestures.

"Were you yelling?"

"She was. I never yell."

"What was the last thing she said as she went out the door?" Brett had never read much psychology, but he did understand the significance of having the last shot in an argument. He had learned that from his parents.

"Something about needing a real man in a crisis like this. 'Ha-ha,' I said. 'Try to find one.'"

"And then you slammed the door," Lee said, not guessing much, because if he hadn't, a return volley might have come back at him, and then Holly would've had the last word.

"Yes! All right? I don't know what I'm going to do now. Do you think I should go down to City Hall again?"

"I think you should wait an hour to cool off, then go down and talk to the police. Avoid the mayor. Tell them what you told us. Your wife is missing, no more than that."

Doug looked at Brett like he had no idea what he was talking about. "It'll only get worse if I wait. That's how I'm wired. I'll cool off as I walk down there." He made a series of spiral gestures at his ears, then turned and walked out the front door without closing it. Lee and Brett looked after him for a moment, then at each other.

After lunch ,Emmett's black Ford Expedition drove them isolated behind tinted glass the four blocks to City Hall, where they came up in the elevator from the garage level. It only saved them climbing two flights of stairs, but using it was more about privacy than avoiding exercise. The doors opened opposite the mayor's office. As they stepped out they heard a sudden shout from the end of the corridor and the sound of running feet. Holly whirled to see Doug careening at them as if in a psychotic state. It was as if he had leaped onstage from the wings. An officer stepped between them, then another, both drawing their guns. Without looking back, Emmett and Holly slipped past Rosie into his inner office, where he threw the bolt from the inside, but closing it so quickly still did not spare them the sound of six gunshots.

8

"Have you seen him like this before?" Brett asked about ten minutes after Doug had left. "How long have they lived next to your brother?"

"Two years. It happens now and then. She's been disappointed in Doug for some time, and he's got low self-esteem."

"I wonder how a guy like him ended up with Holly to begin with. Wasn't the competition a little too fierce for someone like that to come out on top?"

Lee looked at him for a moment, trying, he realized, to decide which way to go with this, or even whether he might be making a joke.

"Doug is older than Holly by eight years. Maybe he impressed her with his sophistication. You're ten years older than I am, and I'm impressed with you. It happens. Ask me why."

This offered no parallel that he cared to explore. "Can we call the way Doug acted just now sophistication?"

"It may have looked like it to her at one time, I don't know. It's a small town and I wasn't here then. I guess she didn't come from much. She was raised with four other kids. At least Doug went to college and got his accounting degree. Holly only had a year in sociology, I think, before she quit. Something vague that everybody takes to get some credits when they haven't chosen their major yet. Then the money ran out."

"Has she gone off like this before?" Brett waited a moment before suggesting this.

"Twice that I know of, but she always came back in a day or two."

"Why does Doug stay with her?" If this was a functioning relationship, Brett didn't understand how it worked.

Lee took a moment to look into his eyes. "Wouldn't you give her another chance if *you* were with her?" She waited for his response. Brett didn't feel he was ever likely to be with Holly, but the question still carried some weight. How much self-respect would any man sacrifice to have part of her attention?

"Maybe the first time, but not twice. I couldn't live with that as a pattern, I don't care how she looks. That's no kind of life. You have to live with yourself too, no matter who else you live with."

"From what she's said, I know Holly grew up too sheltered. Then she got married young and inexperienced. Maybe it was mostly to get out of the house. That happens a lot. Girls get married to leave home when their parents, especially their father, is too controlling, and not in a good way."

"Is there any good way to be too controlling? You're saying she didn't know enough when she got married."

"Yes. It's easy to think a woman like that knows she's gorgeous, but that's not always true. She may not see the same face in the mirror that you see when you look at her. She'll always be scanning for the little blemishes, the flaws. Maybe after a while, when she was older, Holly became aware of how much power she had over men. When she discovered that her power extended even to men who were powerful themselves, she might have found that combination irresistible. Like she could borrow some power for herself by getting close to them."

"You're speculating a bit."

Lee shook her head. "Not that much. I've had some long talks with her, and I also know what I'm looking at; maybe a few things she doesn't know about herself."

"This is a terrible time to have your marriage fall apart. Don't we all need every bit of support we can get?"

Lee put her hand on his shoulder. "Don't worry about me. I'm still here."

Brett looked out the front door to see if Doug had gone inside, or perhaps was lying face down sobbing on his lawn, but the only person in view was Clayton. He set down his rake with the tines probing the grass and crossed the street in their direction. They went out to meet him.

"You're the guidance counselors now, I think," he said.

"For what it's worth. I'm late coming into this game."

"What do *you* know?" asked Lee. "You've got that look."

"While Doug was gone earlier an unmarked car from the city drove up and stopped in front of their house. I recognized it because I've serviced it—it was Emmett's back-up vehicle. Normally he uses a Ford Expedition, and this was a black Edge. A woman in police uniform got out and let herself in with a key. She didn't knock first, so she must have seen Doug leave, and she already knew Holly wasn't home."

"So she had Holly's key," Lee said.

"I guess. I hope it wasn't Doug's. She came back out fifteen minutes later with a small white suitcase and locked the house again behind her."

"That's a tough read," Brett said.

"Is it?" Clayton gave him a look that invited him to think about it a little more. "I recall Holly saying that Emmett had a thing for her."

"Well Christ, Clayton, any man in this town would have a thing for her, but that doesn't mean..." Addressing both of them, he caught the look on Lee's face. "Of course, for myself, I'm strictly neutral here. A frothy woman like that would never catch my..."

This brittle thought was shattered by the impact of the aluminum screen door slamming behind them. Brett hadn't learned yet that Lee could be slightly volatile. "Doug did say he called at Emmett's office but wasn't able to see him."

"That Holly is a born troublemaker," said Clayton, with gravel in his voice. "You're startin' to see it now." His head angled a bit toward the door. "My curiosity is piqued by the fact that Emmett must be busier than hell at the moment. How would he find the time to take up with Holly, if that's what's happening here?"

Brett shrugged. He didn't want to consider this.

Emmett was used to multitasking, obviously. "I think I have to go back inside and sort this out with Lee."

"Well, consider one more thing before you do. DeShawn told me the city has closed both the gas stations to the public. They're only for city vehicles now until this crisis is over, although if you have a handicapped sticker, you can get five gallons a month. Have a good day." He touched two fingers of his right hand to his forehead and walked back across the street. How fortunate that Outpost is such a manageable town for pedestrians, Brett thought, making a mental note to stop at the shoe store later and check out their stock of walking shoes. They were probably going fast now, and as with anything else, resupply was going to be a problem.

9

"Sorry about that," Lee said as Brett came in. "Sometimes the fuss men make over Holly sets me off. Is it because she's a blonde? I grew up with a Barbie doll like that and I always felt second rate, even though her hair was brittle and mine wasn't."

Brett gave her a neutral hug. "You could never be second rate. Anyway, I think it's all right. She'll be out of circulation for a while. Doug concerns me more—he had an evil look in his eye when he left."

"I suppose she's all he has. Maybe having her is the biggest thing in his life."

"If he still has her. I'm not sure he ever did. It looks like she's in motion this time. Women who look like that usually end up with men who have plenty of money and no end of privileges. And the way things are developing, that's going to be truer than ever. You don't think Emmett fired Doug to cause this crisis between them?"

"I'd hate to think he was that cynical. We have to trust him through this."

"I know. That's what worries me."

Like Clayton, increasingly Brett found himself trying to predict what was going to happen next. He felt they were in a lull that couldn't last. This was part of his survival instinct. Anticipating events might be a substitute for being able to influence them. What he didn't guess was that it might be inevitable that Doug would turn out to be the second victim of the epidemic to be discovered in Outpost, and the only one whose body was actually found within the city limits. Information was spotty, but a smudge of dark smoke late that same afternoon was announced after the fact to be his funeral pyre. Any services were out of the question, even though he was known to be a nominal Catholic. A poster bearing the most basic information was placed on both entrances to City Hall. Another one appeared on the Post Office building, which now functioned only for local mail, delivered by volunteer carriers because federal paychecks had ceased. None of the federal letter carriers would work without pay, and were threatening to shut down the post office for all service. No one paid any attention, since it seemed pointless. As a public health precaution, no mail from the outside would have been allowed into Outpost anyway, had any appeared.

This was all moving much too fast, but naturally, in the case of Doug's sudden death Emmett couldn't wait for a normal burial; the risk of contagion was too great. The announcement stated that Doug had realized he was infected and died shortly afterward in a remote spot on the north service road that offered no immediate risk to others. Prior to this, he had not been in contact with anyone that entire day.

Brett stared at this announcement with cold eyes. He hadn't noticed this public-spirited side of Doug, but then, he hardly knew the man. The poster ended by saying that, while all residents of Outpost were bereft by the untimely loss of one of their own, they were also relieved that no one else had been exposed. The City of Outpost was not at risk. No explanation was provided as to how Doug might have become infected, since he hadn't left the city in more than a month and therefore could've encountered no one from outside who had contracted the illness. Brett realized he had still heard no discussion in any of the national television reports about how the disease might have been introduced and spread. The name of ISIS had never come up.

Brett didn't spend much time speculating how this would be received, because he knew that under wartime conditions some combatants and even civilians are simply listed as "missing." In epidemics others vanish without their bodies ever being discovered. When a person takes a position against the ruling powers, even for the most valid of reasons, personal or not, he sometimes disappears. In desperate times, certain events defy explanation, and a mature citizenry realizes this and makes allowances. Brett didn't share these thoughts with Lee, although they could talk about almost anything. Some ideas she needed to arrive at herself, and he didn't care to always be playing the role of the cynical, world-weary partner in survival, since it only emphasized the difference in their ages, something she had already brought up in the tub at the Blue Bayou.

"Has Holly returned?" Clayton asked as they later sat behind the house and went back to work on his bottle of rum. It was early evening, another one of their daily neighborhood watch steering committee meetings. The sun was still high but the shadows were lengthening across the yard as they filtered through Holly's trees. Doug had left a little more than five hours before on the way to what had turned out to be his own cremation.

"We haven't seen her," Lee said. "I went over to offer my condolences for Doug's death, but it didn't look like she'd been there. What a sad thing to happen."

"And the way it happened."

"I suppose I shouldn't be sitting with you folks right now," Clayton said, "what with your exposure to Doug today and all." He rose and moved to the next chair, taking his glass with him.

"I think we'll just forget we saw him," Brett said. "We're the only two people outside of City Hall who can contradict their story. If it were true, and he had been infected, we'd both be dead by now too."

"I am sure they really burned his body, though," said Lee. "Otherwise people could see the real cause of his death."

"I would guess he had a bullet hole somewhere vital," said Clayton. "Maybe more than one. This epidemic is going to cover a multitude of sins better than almost anything I can think of."

"Driving up here Lee and I talked about how this disease was like the cutting edge of an axe, and behind it followed a breakdown of civility and law. Now it seems that you only need to have the disease nearby, but not actually present, to get that same secondary effect."

"I don't think we'll ever know what happened," Lee said. "Only that Doug went back downtown and came up against something much bigger than he was."

"From his look this afternoon," Brett said, "most things would've been too much for him. A crisis like this brings out everyone's weakest points. Maybe he threatened Emmett, or he might have had a weapon and tried to harm him. Today it seemed like Doug had a troubled undercurrent running through his personality. Even meeting him for the first time, I wasn't sure what he was capable of."

"Well, he could be tense and unstable," said Lee. "I couldn't always read him, either. Maybe he couldn't handle stress, and that was why he preferred to work half days. Holly told me some stories about him that I'm not going to repeat. Some of the times when she came over he didn't come along. It was like yesterday; she'd say he was brooding about something, some injustice that had been done to him. He often saw himself as a victim."

JOHN SCHERBER

"And that's a good fit for these times," said Brett. "The victims among us will all be vindicated by this. They would've seen it coming in some way or other."

"Well, I would say that you *cannot*," said Clayton, in an ironic tone that made him sound like the judge in a court of law, "especially in a crisis like this, allow threats of random violence to be made against the head of state. The public welfare needs to be upheld above all. Without order at home, how can we defend ourselves?"

"Head of state?" Brett said, raising his eyebrows. "Did I miss another coup?"

"It feels like it, doesn't it? Outpost is like one of those recovery zones they've set up in the survivor cities, except we don't get all that reassurin' Army protection."

"I feel sick," Lee said. "What can we do about Holly? Can't we do something to help her?"

Clayton got up from the table and circled the concrete slab as if he'd been getting stiff listening to this. "We don't know what her situation is, and I suspect that's the last thing we're going to be told. She might be in a holding cell as an accomplice to whatever Doug attempted, or she might be the mayor's new consort. I'm not going to be the one to inquire, although I will ask DeShawn to keep his ear to the ground when he's at work. That's easy enough when he's under a car. Holly might have been seen in one of those city vehicles— she's hard to miss. I wouldn't be surprised if he saw something today. I don't 'spect him back until after ten o'clock, though."

"But wouldn't you think she'd be in mourning? If my husband were killed I'd be prostrate with grief, not so quickly in the arms of the mayor." Lee looked at Brett as she said this.

Clayton sat down again in the chair he'd used earlier, this time as if the risk of infection had passed. "I would hope so, but I don't know her well, and I have noticed that she's veiled sometimes. Not so much in terms of her ongoing flirtations, but what she might do in a desperate situation, I couldn't say. A lot of occasions might come up when your good looks won't help you, and I think that's the trap waiting for Holly. If I were with her, I'd be damn careful. She might have an unforgivin' streak, like what if you didn't pay enough attention to her? What if it were a time of crisis when you didn't know what was happening next? Maybe that's why she isn't wearing black right now."

"You don't know that," Lee said, tentatively.

"No, but I know how I'd bet if I had the chance. Maybe her underwear is black, I could believe that much."

"Aren't you being a bit cynical?" asked Lee.

"Not at all. I'm black myself, and old to boot. I prefer to call it skeptical with good reason." He gave her a broad grin.

Brett was reluctant to look at Doug's death through the same steely prism Clayton favored, but he felt that in his neighbor he saw a man free of illusions, to the degree that was possible. Looking at Holly, Brett had tended to focus, naturally enough, on her appearance. Clayton had prompted him to look at her behavior, and project it onto this situation. But the other side, the unseen side of her disappearance, was Emmett's behavior. They would probably never know what happened at City Hall, how Doug had died, but their earlier talk about what Emmett would do now, when he had greater power, had relevance, and that had already started to play out. Brett had begun as the cynical one in their household, but the Doug and Holly disaster now made him look naïvely hopeful. This gave him no satisfaction whatever.

"In your view, Clayton," he said, "what should we do now? Coming up here we saw a variety of risks, some of which were lethal, judging from the bodies on the ground. We always saw Outpost as a sanctuary. It was the place that had gotten it together just in time—in our minds, anyway. Now, we're seeing another set of risks."

"You're right. In blunt terms, we've become hoarders."

"Oh shit!" Lee said, with a gesture of slamming a phone book down on the table. "I saw this coming from you, too." She pointed a finger in Brett's direction and stalked off onto the grass, which was going to need mowing in a couple of days. Her flip-flops slapped a circular path through it before she returned and sat down again with a more composed look.

Clayton stiffened his back and folded his arms. "If you don't believe me, ask yourself this. Who do you trust? You'd like to trust the government in this situation, right? It's the last resort. *Our* people tried to trust the government—at various levels over generations—and we ended up trusting only ourselves. I think the government will first take from you more than they need to survive, and return to you some of what's left. They'll sell off the difference to get reelected, and call it a more equitable distribution of resources."

"Leveling always appeals to a lot of people," said Brett. "Whoever gets your stuff calls it fairness."

"Indeed it does. It's the one percent versus the ninety-nine, and we'll hear more of that again. Any time you've got something someone else wants you become the one percent. I think that's the real definition of that term. Rhetoric is important now, and it will be increasingly so going forward. Holly—excuse me for saying this, Lee—was something that someone in the government needed, and so she was taken. It's like she was requisitioned. It doesn't mean the whole government needed her, but only that someone of importance did. I 'spect that's going to be a theme we'll hear much more of going forward."

At this point Lee came out with a long sigh. "So now you're looking at Holly as a commodity."

Clayton gave her a frank look. "That's what we're trading in—the physical commodity. Futures don't work anymore because there is no future, not that anyone can make out."

"I'm not sure you answered my question," Brett said. "What do we hoard? Not cash. What's coming next is barter, I think."

Clayton responded with a sly smile. "Well, rum, I believe, would be the first priority, because with it you can relax and laugh at this tragedy, and none of that inspiring brew is made here. After that, of course, would be gasoline, the ticket of escape to a less dangerous place than the one where you are at the moment."

Brett recalled the gallon they'd used to save Dallas, New Orleans, and Corpus Christi, but said nothing.

"We didn't report ours to the city," Lee said, "although we've got fifteen gallons outside of the van tank."

"Then bury it tomorrow. And you've got a gun, an item that may become priority number one before this is over. The whole point is this: both levels of government above us have collapsed, leavin' only the local one. The television will tell you that the feds are still functioning, but I don't believe that; it's only the military now trying to shore things up as they tighten their own grip. The state government here has broken down because it's too much for them to handle. They had already become too dependent on federal handouts, and since those dried up, we never hear from them anymore."

"So it's gasoline and rum," Brett said. "That's simple enough. You could probably even mix them in your tank. It'll be the new ethanol."

"Then food is third. Not barbecued chickens from the supermarket, although I wouldn't mind having one now, but staples. After that, it would be medicines like antibiotics. Good shoes and outerwear, in case we're driven into the hills where we'd have to contend with night. Then, water, lots of pure water, which is heavy to carry. Next, a good woman, who will give you a reason to survive, because you love her and you need some compelling motivation outside yourself to get through this, someone else to protect. A relationship that will take you out of your worried self. Someone who will tell you that you've done a good job today because you both had something to eat and once again, neither of you died. It's a way to go forward when you can trust nothing else, so it's also a way to frame the future. Lastly, toilet paper, because we are a practical people."

"Is that all?" said Lee, "I like it pretty well so far, although I might shuffle the priorities differently." Her eyes caught Brett's and held them for a moment.

"A good attitude would top the list off nicely. By the way, I heard some scuttlebutt earlier on the radio, my ham radio, from a guy in Virginia. He says that judging from the vehicle traffic around Blacksburg in the western part of that state, the government may be holed up in that bunker at the Windsong Estate."

"The Windsong Estate?" Brett said in a flat tone.

"You're not a golfer, I guess."

"No. My father was, but I didn't pay much attention to it beyond caddying for him twice when I was twelve."

"OK. Windsong is a high-end golf resort. The property has a luxury hotel that my informant thinks the feds have taken over too. A military perimeter has been put up around the grounds. It has been, as they say, *secured*."

"Why would a place like that have a bunker? I don't understand. And why would the government occupy it if they did? Couldn't they go to the Pentagon? What's more secure than that?"

"Because the Windsong Estate is exclusive, and it's not an obvious government installation. You'll remember from 9/11 that the Pentagon had a big target on it. Windsong isn't near any major city, which is now an important consideration. The bunker, if I recall correctly, was built in the fifties during the early days of the cold war. It was top secret once and I thought it had fallen into disuse after the Soviet Union collapsed, but then, we're not always kept up to date on everything."

"If that's the case, wouldn't they be creating one of those recovery zones there?" asked Lee.

"Maybe they are, but they haven't announced it to us because it might invite speculation about why they'd be doing that for a place with no great prominence."

"I never thought this through before," Brett said, "but if I had asked myself where they'd go, I would've guessed Camp David. I think that's enough out of the way, isn't it, somewhere in Maryland? And it's got to be secure."

"Maybe that's why they didn't. It's what the terrorists

would anticipate, and if a second wave of this attack develops, they could target Camp David next. They could pass a crop duster over it, sprayin' all those little spores." Clayton's hands formed a gesture wrist to wrist, like the wings of a tiny cherub.

When the mosquitoes drove them inside, they switched on the TV to check the status of the country. Little had changed except the death toll, now approaching twenty-eight million. The earlier station was the only one still broadcasting. The CDC map showed a single orange dot in central Virginia, plus a number on the coast, but it wasn't close to Blacksburg. The next scene depicted the President in his rolled up shirtsleeves walking with his family on a grassy hill as if nothing had changed. He appeared to be moving in slow motion. Was that a subtle editorial comment on his handling of the epidemic? As he reached down with his long arms and tossed a football to a reporter, who tossed it back, only to be caught by a Secret Service agent, his expression suggested an unheard wisecrack. Only good vibes were in evidence throughout. Although he smiled a great deal, he didn't speak, or if he did, his face was turned away and no sound bite was provided.

"To me, that is not reassurin' in any way," Clayton said gravely. "As a golf course, the Windsong Estate wouldn't look like that anyway. Under the conditions we have now, no reporters would be allowed within a thousand yards of him. We're lookin' at some old footage. Remember what I said about Sunday." He paused and held up a single cautionary finger. "If we don't see that man making a provable reference to that date, like holding up a newspaper and pointing to a headline, then he's gone from power. If that's the case, they'll still hold him in the background in the event that they might have to trot him out again for some unanticipated reason. As long as legitimacy is an issue, he's got a ticket to a long life."

"I wonder how many other little enclaves like Outpost survive," said Lee, in a small voice. "People huddled around their single-channel television sets, watching the country die just like we are now."

The next presentation was a brief but uplifting message from the CO himself, who was still not visible. Divine intervention was heavy on his mind. A split screen displayed cities in flames on one side, flanked by the Kennedy grave with the eternal flame on the other. Brett read this as meaning that flames could have a variety of uses, some inspirational, others destructive. One more use in deserted forest clearings also came readily to mind. The background score could have been from Tchaikovsky in one of his more emotional moments.

In Doug, Outpost had already found one of its own citizens to memorialize. Who would be next?

10

The public launching of the Committee for Outpost Perimeter Security (COPS) was called for the following day, Saturday, at one P.M., with some degree of fanfare. This was the sixth day of the epidemic, and people applauded the mayor's quick reaction time. In the flier slipped under the front door of every registered household, at least one adult was required to attend. Brett and Lee assumed that registered referred to families that had turned in the city's questionnaire on time in order to be eligible for survival benefits when it came to that, as no realist doubted it would.

Brett didn't comment on any of this to Lee, knowing that she wanted to believe it was necessary, and believing that made it more palatable. Brett would've felt better about being so skeptical had he been able to offer any alternatives. If he'd been in Emmett's shoes his approach would have been to do what was required, regardless of whose toes he stepped on. This was war, and the epidemic was a way of bringing it to everyone's doorstep, pantry and gas tank.

The setting for the COPS meeting was the high school

gymnasium, the only building in Outpost large enough to accommodate a crowd of that size. It was an eighties-era facility that had been put up at about the time of the peak population of the town. Not that it had been shrinking since; it had only leveled off. The seating in the bleachers on both sides together totaled eight or nine hundred, and on one end, rows of metal folding chairs had been set up to face a podium at the opposite end. Clayton, Lee and Brett found seats in the upper rows of the bleachers.

The speaker's platform was eighteen inches high, and over the lectern a microphone descended from the ceiling on a black cord. Another interesting feature was a line of eight uniformed police seated like a prickly hedge between the audience and the front of the podium. They looked like veterans. After a few minutes, Dr. Marlys R. Johnson, the principal of Outpost High, rose to introduce Emmett as someone who needed no introduction. She withdrew to the sound of applause, hers included.

Mayor Emmett walked up to the microphone. Brett hadn't seen him before. He was a man of about average height, thickly built in a way that forthrightly suggested muscle rather than flab, with short brown hair neatly combed in a crisp military style. Although his head was normal size, his neck could easily have supported one several sizes larger. He wasn't bad looking, although not striking, and he moved with an easy grace that came of natural authority. Even from the bleachers, Emmett appeared to have a considerable growth of hair on the back of his hands and arms. He stood at the podium wearing pressed khaki pants and a short-sleeved pale green shirt without a tie. His manner suggested businesslike informality. Above all, he seemed comfortable in his own skin. Had Brett been close enough to smell it, his aftershave would have been subtle and of the highest quality. His manner and presentation suggested that he was personally quite clean. When the applause ended, Emmett held up one hand, palm outward like a stop sign, and tilted his head toward the microphone, waiting for five seconds before speaking from talking points on a small stack of cards on the podium.

"Desperate times demand desperate measures. (More applause) I'm not the first person to say that in a crisis, but never has it been truer than this afternoon in Outpost. And never was a town's name better suited to its time and its place in history.

"Some of you will remember learning in school that Outpost began life as Gallagher's Northern Outpost, a survey camp that during the days before the First World War planned the dam that now provides our life's blood. In an ironic sense, we unexpectedly find ourselves an outpost once again, this time an outpost of civilization. I need not repeat the reasons why.

"I called this meeting today to ask each of you for your help in ensuring the survival of our community. Without it, we cannot prevail. Make no mistake, a desperate world is poised outside our gates, and it grows more desperate by the hour. What that world lacks is what we have—the cohesiveness and determination of our strong community. My job, simply stated, is to see that we keep it, no matter what challenge develops from the outside." He took a half step back from the podium.

Applause followed. Emmett had picked the right theme.

"I will not comment on what is happening in Washington and the rest of the country now. But my overwhelming sense is that if we are to survive, we will do it best together, and without depending on outside help. We will trust ourselves and no others until we have reason to do otherwise." He thrust out both arms, palms upward, as if to lift everyone from their seats.

This had a familiar sound to the crowd, which stood up and cheered again; it was the warning about the enemy at the gates. It was the line drawn in the sand, the unity theme. Emmett was clearly not about to play the humanitarian card when survival was the most prominent concern on people's minds.

"This isn't bad stuff," Brett whispered to Clayton, who was seated on his left. "A little alarmist, perhaps, but overall, effective." As he scanned the bleachers opposite, he could spot no mass of golden hair. He wondered how many in the audience knew about Doug's bizarre end. If they had missed the posters at City Hall, the smoke of his pyre would have been visible from almost any house in town.

Lee's face displayed a veiled look, as if she wasn't sure how much she could trust what she was hearing. Brett took her hand and she briefly pressed his without looking at him.

The substance of the rest of Emmett's speech concerned specific measures. He had a plan, and he made it clear that he was no mere cheerleader for survival. His voice held more determination than hope. His plans included increased police hiring, relays of spotting crews on the periphery of town to circumvent invasion (termed PRU, the Paul Revere Units), a unified social service agency to deal with psychological stress and family issues, plus a mobile scavenger force to recover supplies from abandoned properties in the areas outside of town. The word *abandoned* implied that the owner had either fled or died from the epidemic. As the crowd left the gym by the side door, the only exit now open, each person was required to stop at a series of desks labeled A – E, F – J, and so on, to pick up his assignment. Brett and the others each stood in line at a different table, and afterward met outside on the shady side of the building. The entire meeting, together with the sign-up process, had lasted only thirty-five minutes. In contrast to the chaotic world outside, it had been thoughtfully choreographed; all the decisions had been made in advance, and it only remained to sign up and carry them out.

"They didn't want me," said Clayton, showing no disappointment after walking away from the desks. "As a city employee, I'm already in a priority job. Being on vacation doesn't matter. They can always call me in if they need me."

"I'm on staff at the stress relief office because of my psychology background," Lee said. "They told me that careful listening is going to be my most valuable skill."

"And I," Brett said, slitting his envelope as if he were a presenter at the Academy Awards, "am a scavenger. I assume that's because I have the van. Naturally I'll sequester any rum I can find. I see now how scavengers might develop some serious trading clout in these circumstances. Conditions are about right for launching a local black market, don't you think?"

"Of course," said Clayton. "I'll stay at home as neighborhood watch, scanning my amateur radio from time to time. I think you've got the riskiest job, walking into places that may or may not be deserted. We don't know what it's like beyond the city limits anymore. It's almost three days since you've seen it. I haven't been outside Outpost in nearly a year." As he glanced briefly at Lee, he suddenly stopped talking as if he'd thought of something, yet none of them said anything about Holly. The concerns of the meeting had thrown her situation into shadow. If asked, Brett would have guessed she was now part of the executive morale division, an elite corps with uniforms provided by Victoria's Secret. What could be more important than that? Didn't everyone have a unique contribution to make to the defense effort? Holly would not have been offended at her assignment, since it related so well to her values.

Emmett had promised that the city would do everything in its power to keep supplied from the recovery zone cities, but how much truck traffic could now risk taking to the roads, threading its way through desperate and infected people, many of them armed? This was an area of the country that had long sworn by the Second Amendment. Emmett's promise sounded like a pipe dream, and more than before, Brett began to see the importance of scavenging as a way of life.

He suddenly had an image of Blake's Nifty Store, full of snacks, liquor and guns. It must by now be stripped and looted.

11

The next morning, Sunday, the first team of enrolled scavengers assembled at the city garage, where Brett met De-Shawn and his coworkers. He was about the same height as his father, but with a rounder face and stouter build. He said he was now clocking close to eighty hours a week. Once there was nothing left to buy, he could always prepay his electric bill with his salary, but he also sensed a time coming when barter was going to be the principal way of doing business in Outpost, or anywhere in the country.

Looking at the other two drivers with vans, Brett tried to imagine himself as part of their team, but failed. One of them was about seventeen years old and delivered pizzas for a living, which couldn't have been much of a living now that food supplies were so low. The other was a low-budget nomad who kept a mattress on the floor in the back of his van. He'd come from Bascombe, further west in the state, and had been visiting a girlfriend in town when the terrorist attack struck. He had chosen not to leave. The garage staff pulled his mattress out and laid it in a distant corner, saying they'd give it back to him on their return. As the luck of the draw, Brett didn't object to this team, but he could only see his role in it as a volunteer responder in a time of national crisis. That was their only connection. He thought of the London Blitz, with half the population of the capital city hunkered down in the subways. People still bragged about being born there.

Brett's was one of three vans requisitioned. He'd be serving in rotation with other van-owning groups after going out with the first sortie. The survey had located more than 120 vans in Outpost. Based on their experience as the first caravan on the road, the overall plan and detail of the approach could be modified. Ten vans in a fleet might be better if they came across a big stash—abandoned, of course. After topping off their gas tanks at city expense, they were given masks, gloves, disinfectant, water, and a fish and chips box lunch from Dante's. A police car with two officers led the caravan, and another brought up the rear. In each of the three vans between rode an armed officer in addition to the driver, so they had a total of seven police officers. The drivers were unarmed; Brett had left his gun with Lee, who declined to touch it. It remained in a drawer in the kitchen behind a clutch of plastic bags and twist ties. He was happy to draw Officer Leon in the passenger seat because he remembered Brett from his entry into Outpost with Lee. Brett thought he might want to talk about her, which could lead to him talking about other recent events. Information was scarce at all levels. Being connected mattered more than ever.

As stated on a handout all the drivers received, the program of the mission was simple: At any operating food store, large or small, they would try to purchase staples. The first priority would be obtaining bulk foods in large, secure containers. To resist the intrusion of vermin, metal was preferred. The lead police cruiser carried $6,000 in cash and an Outpost city credit card, which was to be used first when possible. If the proprietor was unwilling to sell anything, they were instructed to leave without causing a confrontation.

At any unoccupied food store, however, they were to forcibly enter it if necessary and load the vans from a priority list from Emmett's office. They would be taking away no Twinkies or potato chips, for example, and no ice cream bars or soft drinks. In the absence of bulk containers, smaller canned and dry packaged items were favored. Outpost's water plant was functioning normally, so no bottled water was needed. No alcohol or tobacco appeared on the priority list. Items in the vicinity of a dead body were to be strictly avoided for twenty feet in every direction. Each van was furnished a tape measure. Everything was to be inspected for signs of any bloody discharge. The crew was to wear gloves and masks at all times. Upon their return to the garage, their shoes would be retained and disinfected after they left. Each of the drivers and police officers had brought an extra pair to wear home and left them behind with DeShawn in a special locker.

Brett was uneasy about the idea that they'd be entering even locked food stores, which was nothing short of burglary in his mind. The lead car had been furnished with the tools to break in. The argument they'd been given was that it was probable that the owners of these stores were already dead—otherwise they'd be open for business to serve the public interest. With no other valid excuse to be closed, the inventory belonged to the living. Besides, the police were leading their caravan, so who could argue? The fact that these officers were outside their jurisdiction was merely a quibble. Boundaries were already badly blurred and still dissolving.

Lee had wanted to come down to the city garage and see him off, but Brett had sensed the approach of some of this detail and didn't want her to grasp the degree of risk the caravan was taking. If ethical considerations could be honored, their mission mostly made sense to him, and he preferred it to having their own reserves confiscated and redistributed to people who had a better claim on them than they did. Or waiting for the federal food trucks to arrive, a day that he didn't believe most of them would live to see. Assuming the goods they obtained were distributed fairly back in Outpost, being part of the scavengers was not far from what he thought was the best use of his skills.

Brett and Lee had a heartfelt farewell that morning. They hadn't been separated for more than half an hour in five days. Without being gushy, which was not her style anyway, she let him know how important their connection was to her. She made him feel too good to want to check the television death toll before he left, so he was happy not to. There was little emotional nourishment to be had in a diet of undiluted bad news.

"Y'all come back to me, now," she said softly as he backed the van out of the garage and headed to City Hall.

"Ready for this?" Leon said, as Brett drove out through the improvised barrier at the dam end of Outpost. It was a beautiful, cool morning for a scavenger hunt as he executed a serpentine maneuver through four pairs of staggered concrete highway dividers. His was the middle van of the three. They had been told to keep the formation tight so no one could interpose a vehicle between any two of theirs once they were on the road. The caravan was not to break up under any circumstances. Any vehicle that broke down would be abandoned after the food aboard was offloaded to the others.

"Ready as I can be," said Brett. "It feels like we're at war now. Loyalties are breaking down into smaller and smaller units. The final point will be that each of us is on his own."

"So just be glad you're on the right side." Leon gave Brett a reinforcing smile and a firm nod. Life was a simpler calculation for him.

"In my experience, the police are always right because they have the guns," Brett said. He wanted to ask Leon about his take on Emmett, thinking this might open the way to getting information on what had become of Holly, but it was too early in the trip. Brett was too much a greenhorn on the subject of Outpost politics to be at all sure of his ground. It was possible that their future welfare as individuals depended on being quiet and compliant. Insubordination could come later, if Emmett chose to continue his iron grip after they'd survived and he could offer no further justification for maintaining it.

Brett also thought he could press Leon about Emmett once they'd fought a couple of battles. They'd develop more of a connection once he'd saved the cop's life, or Leon had saved Brett's. He tried not to think that the enemy was made up of people no different from them, and how this felt increasingly like medieval times, where the most successful strategy had been to enroll as a vassal behind the walls of the strongest local lord, now named Emmett. Then during an attack they received the protection of his castle and a share in the stored food supply. In exchange, they marched forth in battle formation now and then, like Brett and Leon were at that moment.

"This is like the Middle Ages all over again," Brett said, pulling clear of the last pair of highway dividers.

"I'm only thirty-two."

Brett couldn't see a way to comment on this. Not everyone read as much history as he did.

Five miles down the highway waited an intersection where they could choose to go east or west on a county road named H, or continue south on the route Lee and Brett had used coming in. Discussing this in the garage earlier, they'd decided to go west. A tiny village called Davis Junction marked the crossroads. Lee and Brett had blown through it on the way up, barely slowing, eager to reach Outpost and their dream of safety.

"Have you ever killed anyone?" he asked Leon in the same light tone he might have used asking if he'd ever been to Pittsburg or had a massage.

"No, thank God. I've only fired my gun during target practice. Usually I hit 'em in the heart, though. Eight out of ten, anyway."

"Do you think you could do it?" Brett was too busy keeping his proper spacing in the formation to look at him. He was partly asking this about himself, but now that they were in Outpost maybe it would never come up.

"If someone was trying to kill me or someone else on our side, I know I could. Emmett said this would be a test for all of us, and that some might not survive. Any widows or children of men who gave their lives for the community would be protected. 'Course, I don't have any family myself. My folks don't live here. I came up because they were hiring cops three years ago."

"I'm sure what he said is true. It's good to have him in charge now, isn't it?" This was a sanitized version of Brett's views, but he wanted to draw Leon out. He already suspected that *community* was often a shorthand for Emmett's own interest—more prominent, but now merged with everyone else's.

"I'm a Democrat myself, so I didn't vote for him, but now I think he's the best mayor we've had since I moved here."

"Is he married?"

"No. Well he was, but he got divorced two years ago, when he was still on the town council. Scuttlebutt was that some kind of scandal was connected with it, but I never heard the detail. It didn't keep him from getting elected, though, and his ex-wife left town right afterward. People lie all the time in situations like that, because there's a lot of feeling involved. The worst part of being a cop is when you get called out on a domestic quarrel. When I had my police human relations workshop in Bascombe three years ago, I did a session in sensitivity training."

"His ex-wife probably wishes now that she'd stayed here."

"I wouldn't be surprised. It's going to be pretty rough out there, but who could've seen this comin' on?"

An opportunity appeared to Brett. "Lee and I had a situation like that with our neighbor. Maybe you know her? Her name is Holly."

Leon chuckled. "Sure, I know her. Everybody in Outpost knows Holly. You couldn't miss her. You wouldn't want to miss her, in fact." He folded his arms and leaned back in his seat with a big grin.

"Did you know her husband, Doug?" Here Brett took his eyes off their tight formation for an instant and looked at Leon's face. Although he frowned slightly, he showed no alarm.

"I knew him a little. He did some accounting for the city. Kind of a loner, I thought. I also think he probably smoked a lot of dope."

"But do you know what happened?"

"No. He got the disease, that's all I heard. Then he died, like everyone does. Of course, they burned his body right away. It happens, like with that woman from Bridger who drove up and expired in her car. That's what Emmett would do for you or for me, too, without hesitation. You need to have rules, especially now. You have to think of the common interest. We're all in this together." Without glancing at him Brett could sense Leon was watching his reaction.

"Right. Have you ever been married?"

"No. To tell you the truth, I used to think I might marry Lee, not that I ever got that close to her. Funny now, isn't it, with all of this?"

"I suppose she was with Ted for a long time. You probably never had a real chance to date her."

"That's right. I'd only see her a couple of times a year, and Ted came up once with her. She always came up here for her vacation and usually again at the holidays. Don't tell her what I said, though, OK? I don't think she knows I was ever interested in her. It's all right, but I guess I always thought she had a thing for white guys, you know? Now it's you."

Startled and not knowing how to respond to this, Brett only shook his head. As they drove further south he thought of asking Leon whether he knew anything about the current condition of Marshy Flats, but when they came in on Wednesday, he hadn't suggested that was where they came from, so he kept silent. "What's going on now in the rest of the state?"

"Don't know. We used to have a hookup with the state criminal apprehension people. They gave us help with forensics and with their database, especially fingerprints and DNA, but that Internet link is down now. I don't think we'll get it back for a while. I guess we're on our own."

"So what would happen if someone commits a serious crime here?"

"With our limited resources, I think if you were busted you'd be held in the city jail without bail awaiting more stable conditions. You couldn't even be sent to the county seat in Bascombe for trial at this point. I heard they were already having an outbreak of serious trouble there, with some looting yesterday. Sometimes we can monitor their police communications. I think it depends on the cloud cover."

"It'll be like that until the epidemic is finished."

"Of course. That's why the town council has given

Emmett some extraordinary powers."

"It's like an emergency decree?"

"Exactly. It's to protect the citizens of Outpost. It's for their own good."

Had he been with Lee, Brett would've commented on this, but with Leon he held back. The cop's face expressed a stolid and unquestioning preparedness; he was a foot soldier resisting an assault on his homeland, so his mission was clear and uncomplicated. As they studied the road ahead, his gaze had a wary cast, bouncing from one point to another as the scene changed. Riding shotgun on a mission like this made sense to him, although they weren't encountering much traffic. To Brett the absence of traffic meant gas was getting scarcer, and people were thinking more carefully about unnecessary driving. Soon they'd be seeing horses on the road. Brett had removed his jerry cans before he drove to the city garage that morning and stowed them under a tarp in the curious storage shed at the back of the lot.

"Have you heard anything about taking a survey of horses inside or near Outpost? They might be useful at some point down the road."

Leon only shook his head. As they drove closer to the town, people on foot on the sides of the road occasionally paused to stare at the little convoy of marauders. They didn't seem alarmed, only curious.

After a while the caravan entered a cleared area. Several small farms on both sides of the road struggled with the uneven terrain. They might have been suitable for raising goats or mountain cattle. No one moved near the buildings, but no dead bodies were in view, either. Half a mile farther they entered Davis Junction, population 386. An auto garage built of white-painted cinder block, the first building on the right, was open and operating. It represented an encouraging optimism. People could keep their cars in good running order, even if they could find no gas. They'd still be ready to go when the gas returned and any place was left worth going to. To Brett it looked like a way of expressing confidence that better times were coming.

The street was mixed commercial and residential. Halfway through, a small building twice the size of a double garage announced itself as the Town Hall. It boasted a small bell tower at one corner.

"They've got a little jail in there," Leon said, pointing. "Two cells."

Beside it was parked a retired highway patrol cruiser that had been crudely sprayed in black. These cars are easy to spot; they have a tired and well-used appearance. Their fenders often have a pounded-out look. The driver's door on this one read POLICE, and one of the front tires was flat. It rarely had much use now other than to advertise that someone in town represented the law. It was more like a road sign in weathered sheet metal.

Overall, Davis Junction looked normal, which is to say dull, a little sad, and not self-conscious or even aware of either condition. Comfortable with its fate, it was like hundreds of other tiny towns across the state. Most of its children grew up awaiting their moment to leave without regret for better pastures. The ones who settled in became anchored like weeds in the sandy soil. Eventually they'd wilt, turn brown and die in place. They lived with the certainty of ending up in the small tidy cemetery at the edge of town.

People on the street corners glanced at the caravan with curiosity, but no one ran out to flag it down. The lead police car slowed to scan a tiny grocery store that bore a Dr Pepper logo sign saying it was closed. According to their instructions, they should've broken into it, but the context wasn't right. It was Sunday morning, and some stores, especially in small towns, simply closed their doors while people went to church. Davis Junction did not appear to be in distress, unlike some other towns Lee and Brett had passed through on the way up. Brett found its normal appearance surprising, but certainly temporary, and not reassuring.

"I feel like we're a boatload of pirates sailing into this port and the pickings are too slim to bother with," he said. "So we're sailing on in search of bigger prey."

Leon looked uncomfortable with this characterization and didn't respond. However he may have seen himself, it was not as a buccaneer. At the end of the block, they turned to the west.

"Do you think we should've stopped and entered that store?" Brett asked.

Leon raised both hands as if Brett had proposed a mutiny. "Hey, man, the lieutenant's in the lead car today. You saw that. It was his call and he made it. That's why we didn't stop."

"And you're comfortable with that?"

"Sure, aren't you? It's not up to me, or you either. If I was always second-guessing these things I wouldn't have time to do my job. Believe me, it's better not to think about it. That's one thing I've learned."

"I'm comfortable with it in this case, but I suspect we're going to have a series of situations like that one, and some won't always be so clear."

Leon shrugged and turned to grin at him with raised eyebrows. "That's why we have the lieutenant, isn't it? I mean, I'm not dodgin' your question, but that's the way it has to be. Somebody's in charge and it's not us. I'm the kind of person that likes to go home at the end of the day and hang up his gun. Besides, I don't make the money he does, the lieutenant, I mean."

This suddenly reminded Brett of the CO, the Commanding Officer, General Parker. Through the military, he had furnished a chain of command for the entire country. To anyone with Leon's attitude, this would be more reassuring than alarming. Brett could see how this was its principal value. Starting at harmless levels, it allowed anyone to avoid questioning the logic of whatever came from above. He didn't want to think where this had come up before. It was always called *following orders*.

Brett could also see why Lee would never have welcomed Leon as a boyfriend, had he ever approached her. She would've walked all over him until his back was covered with her footprints, and then blamed him for being an inferior carpet, and not without reason. It wasn't that she was domineering, she really wasn't; it was only that she demanded more initiative than Brett was seeing in him, and Leon could never have held her respect. If you told her about the joy you experienced in taking orders, she would have no trouble giving them, but she had no need to be doing it nonstop. Brett decided to have a conversation with her about Leon after they returned. Maybe she already knew he was interested in her and she'd chosen to ignore it.

A block further, Davis Junction petered out. At the edge, the caravan passed a junkyard with a sixty-year selection of sun-bleached and rusted autos and pickups, then reentered the unending fabric of the pine forest, the greatest turpentine resource in the country. They were headed for Bristol, twenty-one miles away. This was not a terrain or a population that could support a town every three miles. After a stretch of dense conifers, the land leveled out and many more cleared areas appeared. Small, irregular fields of crops were guarded by hobby tractors and rusty implements parked nearby. About five miles out of town they slowed at a tavern in a clearing. On a tall steel pole, the sign at the road's edge read *The High Sign*, under a brewing company logo. A single car was parked at an angle in the lot, as if it had rushed up and stopped in a hurry, and as they approached, they heard the unmistakable sound of a gunshot. Taking the lead police car's cue, they all swung into the drive and stopped, as if trouble was a magnet when you're armed.

After a moment, two men leaped up out of the brush at the edge of the woods and ran back into the trees. They both carried rifles upright. The door of the tavern swung open and a man who must have been the owner stepped out waving at the caravan. His left hand held a rifle pointed at the ground, and his fingers were wrapped around the stock, nowhere near the trigger. Leon and Brett stayed in the van. With his pistol drawn, the lieutenant went over and talked to the man for a moment and then returned to the lead car. As they drove out, the tavern owner shot out the two front tires on the parked car, sent a third round through the radiator, and danced a small jig. Thinking the two gunmen would probably be back, Brett said nothing as they reformed their line. Leon was unperturbed.

"Whose side are we on?" Brett asked.

Leon shrugged. "Truth, justice, and the American way." He was not without a bit of safe irony, but again, how the caravan acted in this situation was not his call. At least they didn't have to decide whether to loot the tavern; alcohol was not on their prioritized list. In this part of the woods, no one probably stocked much rum anyway.

"Things are going well," Brett said as they reached highway speed again. "Don't you think?"

"Sure. Never better."

"What are your expectations for this mission?"

Leon responded with a puzzled look. "Why, we do our jobs and at the end of the shift we go back to Outpost. That hasn't changed, except that we don't usually leave town like this."

That was as close as Leon came to a broader view. But Brett Wallace was not on a shift, nor were the other two van drivers. Theirs was a reality that didn't break down into bite-size chunks so easily. He decided to probe Leon a bit about Holly even though neither of them had saved the other's life. He was tired of waiting for a crisis and the trip wasn't shaping up into anything exciting. He decided to subtly shake Leon loose from the official version of Doug's death "I didn't see you at Emmett's speech yesterday. I thought you might be in that line of police seated in front of him."

"No, I was on duty in town. Those guys working the speech were all the retired officers in their dress uniforms, an honor guard of the reserves. I was furnished a print copy of his remarks, though. They were right on."

"I thought I might see him with that new girl of his, Holly, but I didn't."

Leon's head turned abruptly in Brett's direction, but he kept watching the road as if nothing unusual had come up, even though his statement represented a major shift from what he'd said about her before. After all, driving in formation required more attention than sailing down an empty road. Brett could almost sense the wheels turning in Leon's head, but he still didn't look at him, knowing he was thinking that they'd already talked about Doug.

"No, you wouldn't have seen her there."

"She must be at the mayor's house, then." Brett had no notion where that was.

"I guess."

"When I saw that police woman pick up some clothes from Holly's place, I figured that's where she was going. Was that one of the reserves?"

"No, she was a regular."

Now he's committed, Brett thought. "Sure. Emmett probably wouldn't trust a reserve to do that. I'll bet it's all hush-hush now, eh?"

Leon turned in his direction, a slightly wary look on his face. "You seem to know a whole lot about it."

Brett shrugged. "Well, I am living right next door to her. Holly came and talked to us the evening before she went to see Emmett. Naturally we won't say anything, since she trusted us when she said Emmett had a thing for her, but it is a small town, you know? Everyone knows each other's business. Maybe too much, but there you go. A woman who looks like she does, you're going to pay her some attention, especially when she was all worked up like she was when she left for City Hall."

Brett began to wonder whether he'd already said too much, but he wanted to give Leon the sense that he had other sources, so he might speak more freely.

"She might have been putting you on—that was hardly the only time she's seen Emmett lately. "It's more like weeks."

"I knew I was missing another level to this story! You

have the look of the well-informed." Brett gave him a knowing grin. Leon returned one of his own.

"Like you said, Brett, Outpost is a small town. My Aunt Dar works in personnel and she said it was Holly who got Emmett to fire Doug. Can you believe that? His own wife." Brett fired him a genuinely surprised look. "Now that's one part of this I didn't know. Why on earth would she do that?"

"Because Holly has had her eye on Emmett since he was on the town council. I think she's had her sights set higher than Doug for a long time. That woman made a mistake when she got married so young, OK? It didn't take her that long to realize it, either."

"But even going so far as getting him fired?"

"It gave her an excuse to move on, didn't it? I also heard the bed was already warm at the mayor's residence, if you take my meaning. Don't quote me on that, though. That's only scuttlebutt. In fact, don't quote me on any of this, but since you know so much about it already…"

"Hmmm. Now that makes me want to push this a bit farther," Brett said thoughtfully, holding up his thumb and forefinger an eighth of an inch apart, "but this is one I bet you can't answer. Lee and I have been batting this around between us. She has her own ideas and I have mine. What really happened with Doug when he went down to City Hall the afternoon he died? You gave me the official version, but I already knew he was in a strange mood, because we talked to him right before he left. That man was spinning so hard he was bouncing off the walls."

Leon nodded knowingly. "Well, don't tell anyone I said this, either, except Lee, OK?" Part of Leon's willingness to say this was that Lee would see him as the insider, which was why Brett had mentioned her name.

"Of course. We're all on police business now." That was Brett's credential.

"Like, I wouldn't want Clayton to hear any of this, particularly. Sometimes I think he knows too damn much already. That is one nosey man across the street from you. I know he works for us, and he's not a bad guy to have on the underside of a car, but still, you gotta be careful what you say around him all the same. I'm going to be happy when he retires."

"I hear you. I'm sure he knows way more than he ought to." Brett inserted a significant pause and raised a single finger in the air to punctuate it. "But not way more than you do, am I right? Because there are insiders and *insiders*; some folks are more inside than others."

"As it happened, I was on security detail that afternoon at Emmett's office. A call came up from the groundskeeper to the mayor's secretary, if you can believe that."

"The groundskeeper? How did that make any sense?"

"It didn't at first, but then it turned out that Doug had appeared and made off with some unnamed tool that was potentially dangerous. Their storage is not normally locked during the day and the groundskeeper is only one person. He came back in and noticed that something was missing because a number of the tools were disturbed, but he didn't know exactly what it was at that point. He would've needed to study his inventory list and he didn't think he had time, since he wanted to pass the word upstairs. It was only a heads up with no detail."

"But it was job one for you to respond."

"Totally, with the three others who were on duty. You know how it is. People could come at us from any direction, even inside City Hall. We've been told, and it makes so much sense now, that our job is to keep Outpost pure! That's what we're up against! The invader doesn't even know what he's carrying in his lungs; that's the real problem. He thinks he's a nice guy and he only wants to be safe like we are. And in coming here, if we allowed it, he'd destroy us all. I mean the real problem is that, black or white, he looks just like we do. It's a tough judgment call."

"And so Doug was armed with a lawn tool? Like a hedge clipper?" Brett was thinking he'd been planning to castrate Emmett.

Leon shook his head slowly. "It turned out to be a scythe. He was spotted in the hallway approaching Emmett's office, swinging this crescent blade at his side with an ugly look on his face. Two of the guys at Emmett's door stepped out and shot him, and more than once. What I heard was that the mayor wasn't even there. I wasn't either. I was by the steps at the other end of the hall, and downstairs, so I didn't see it happen. But I heard it, of course."

"I can understand why nobody wanted to take any chances. Maybe Doug was moving too fast for anyone to effectively disarm him. But what I don't get was why it was announced afterward that he'd caught the disease." Brett was also wondering whether this wasn't an act of suicide by Doug. What chance did he have? He must have known the odds because he had worked at City Hall, and he would've seen the way Emmett's security had been ramped up.

Leon became more animated. "I know! I asked myself that too. But what I heard was that Emmett didn't want the story of an assassination attempt put out under these conditions. He figured that a lot of people are going to be discontented anyway with all the hardships that are coming as supplies get short, so why not put it out that the epidemic killed Doug, because that will make people pull *together* rather than give them any ideas. Everybody is already against it. Then Doug is a victim and Emmett's not a bad guy. Doesn't that make so much more sense? Believe me, Emmett's real big on unity. We're all in this together and we need to act like it."

"I can see that. A lot of psychology goes into this too, doesn't it? More than I would've guessed." Brett wondered whether Emmett had a political scientist or a crowd psychologist on staff.

"Exactly! Now you're getting more of a sense of what's really happening downtown. This is another thing Emmett's really good at: keeping his thumb on the pulse of the public. Morale is going to be even more important as this goes on."

"I don't doubt that for a moment. Right up there with food."

On the next curve they came across a truck lying on its side in the ditch across the road. It reawakened Brett into the present because he was still chewing on Doug's sudden demise. The downed vehicle was headed back in the direction they had come, and it bore the logo of a wholesale fruit company in Pine Bend, a town two miles north of Bridger, almost a suburb. Brett followed the lead police car onto their own shoulder as it rolled to a stop.

12

"I'll ask you to wait in the van while we check on this," Leon said as he got out. A streaky reddish film obscured the driver's side of the truck's windshield and side window. The truck's box was rigged for refrigeration, but the cooling unit wasn't running, nor was the engine. In a moment all seven police were gathered around the wreck pulling on gloves and masks. None of them advanced close enough to touch it.

Fresh fruit did not top the Outpost list of needed provisions. Scurvy wasn't an immediate issue, and fruit didn't keep well if it wasn't frozen, canned, or dried. But on the other hand, this truck was the only practical discovery they'd seen that might yield some value for their effort, assuming it wasn't empty. Brett's guess was that an empty truck would've been headed in the other direction. Watching the discussion across the road, he saw the police shaking their heads. Finally the lieutenant waved the van drivers over. They pulled on their masks and gloves as they crossed the deserted highway.

"This is not our top priority," he began, "but we're thinking that if we bring back fruit, then people can eat that instead of something with a longer shelf life, so by extending existing food supplies, it may have about the same effect.

Any thoughts? I'm not married to this idea. We might still find something better around the next curve. On the other hand, if we leave this here it'll probably be gone when we come back. As I said before, I can't split up the caravan."

"This is an insulated box," Brett said, after the other two van drivers offered no response. One was yawning as if he missed his mattress. "It would usually have no internal connection with the cab, so unless the driver handled the fruit himself this morning, it's not likely to be contaminated. To save time, the warehouse crew would've loaded a truck like this at the wholesaler during the night, and the driver would come in and drive off with it first thing in the morning. Then the stores he serves could restock before they open. If the contents are intact, he probably never handled any of it." He was pleased to supply this insight, thinking that no one believes delivery guys know anything other than how to get from A to B on the map.

"So you think we could take a chance. And who are you again?" the lieutenant asked.

"Brett Wallace, in van number two. I use it in my own delivery service. We can always transfer this load to the vans and have it tested when we arrive in Outpost. This bug has got to be easy to spot by now. It's been circulating for six days; they would've known a long time ago what it looks like under the microscope."

"They were going to do that anyway, no matter what we brought back. Some of the guys in the warehouse who loaded this might've been sick."

Privately Brett felt that if they were still functioning well enough at five A.M. to load this truck they were probably OK. A brief discussion followed, and then one of the cops jimmied the lock on the back doors of the fruit truck with a crow bar. A draught of cooler air surrounded them as the doors opened. The truck looked full, with all the boxes lying in rows on their sides undamaged.

One by one they backed the vans across the highway and loaded them with cases of grapefruit, oranges, apples, pineapple, and bananas. They were able to take all of it, and while there may have been some mild bruising, nothing had been smashed. The driver must have slowly coasted off the road as he coughed himself to death. He might even have turned off the ignition himself. Naturally, he would've tried to maintain control to the end.

Back in Outpost an hour later they left the three vans in the city garage for testing. Emmett's crew was on the way to unload. It was not yet noon when Brett turned in his scavenger shoes and walked back to the house in his new ones with a sense of mixed results. Coming in, Lee wanted to rush him with welcome, but he took a quick step back from her, pulling off his shirt and jeans and dropping them in the washing machine. He'd left his gloves and mask at the city garage. The lieutenant announced that they would test them from everyone before they tested the fruit.

While he showered he told Lee what they'd done, not quite yelling over the frosted glass partition. He knew it didn't sound risky or even exciting. Under the new definition, it was only business. "I did some thinking while I was out there," he said after he had dressed and walked out into the bedroom.

"I did too, about how we can make this last."

"By surviving. After what we're going through, that's probably as good as it's going to get."

"Did you ever want more?" she said, brushing her hair back off her forehead.

"Are you thinking about more days of life, more food supply, or what?" He felt like he was winding down after the road trip.

"I meant more of a career, more of a job challenge. I've been trying to look at a life after Outpost. Or am I just a silly optimist?"

"Probably. Do you mean more of a career so I could have more stuff? More prestige? More power? I wouldn't mind having a chicken that would wander around the property and produce an egg every day. That's what more looks like to me now."

Lee looked like she didn't expect this response. "Some of those things, I guess. Maybe that's why I'm getting my master's. It'll give me more of those things than I can get from being a waitress, things I don't have now. Part of it is what I won't have to put up with. I'm not sure what to call them. Some of it is status. I wanted to get more control over my life. I wanted to have a bigger job, with a real company with benefits and retirement and all that."

"And are you still getting your master's, even now?"

"Why not?"

Brett wondered how big a gap there was in how they each saw this problem. Some kind of continuity was important even if neither of them could define a future.

"That's why you don't talk ghetto."

"Right. I don't say 'sup?' and a lot of other things. Thanks for noticing. I worked on that. But what gives you a sense of achievement?"

"At the moment, it's surviving. Life is simpler now, and I've thought about that too. Before, it was a sense of serenity. Living the calm, unworried life. Not having to do anything I didn't choose to do was my way of beating the system. Seems kind of sappy now when even the most basic needs in life are getting scarce." He paused for a moment. "The real irony for me is that now *none* of this is what I wanted to do. The system was ruined by other people, so I have to redefine myself here just a bit."

"But were you always comfortable before this happened? I mean did you have enough to get along on?"

"Enough what?"

"Not ideas, I'm sure you were always OK in that area, but I mean stuff to keep you going, paying the rent."

"I always had enough money," he said. He had never needed that much. Brett hadn't made more than an average income in any year, but living in a small Southern town his rent was only $425 a month and he could see the Gulf from one window of his second floor kitchen while he washed the dishes. Lee's look was asking for elaboration.

"Here's what I think, Lee: your stuff owns you as much as you own it. You've got to carry it around with you. Or if you can't, then you have to store it securely. If it's real estate, you have to insure it or put a wall a round it so someone doesn't ruin it or burn it down or squat in it. Now, I don't mind stuff. I've got a great collection of blues CDs and a heart-stopping sound system to play them on. I've got the old Dobro guitar I always wanted. I own the van that makes me a living. I don't have any debt, but I don't have a house, either, and my furniture is easily replaced. My entire library is on my Kindle, which I can almost stick in my pocket. I could put my music on an iPod easily enough, too, I guess. The point is that it doesn't slow me down. I like all that stuff a lot, but I like my freedom more, so I try to keep it in balance. I don't own anything that restricts my choices." Brett ended this with a weak smile, knowing that not every woman would be impressed by it. At this point he didn't care.

"So you travel a lot?" She gave him an offhand look.

"I am on the road a lot, but I travel for fun hardly at all. Yet I could if I wanted to. The point is, and you heard me mention this before, I don't have to worry about *things*. You've heard people in design say that less is more, right? I believe that more is less—having more stuff means less freedom. I learned this because my family was top heavy with stuff, and that was their burden."

"Then what about a relationship? You said before you'd been engaged. Wouldn't that slow you down and hamper your freedom? Don't you meet a lot of girls as you're going around on your deliveries? They must kind of catch your eye as they bend over to sign the clipboard. You're lookin' down their shirts and all, and you think they don't know it."

He recognized a crossroads when he saw it, even if it lacked any signage. He already knew which direction to take when he came to it.

"Feelings don't weigh much, Lee. The ones I might develop for someone would be as light as the air and solid as rock. I don't see anything in my life now that would hold me back." He waited for her response but she continued to look at him without speaking.

Brett was left wondering where she was going with this. Was she only trying to think of something other than survival? He didn't mind that, but he also didn't know whether some of these thoughts would put her off or not. Although they weren't profound, they weren't all that conventional either, and he thought it was time to let her know how he really felt. He'd always known his values made him a little risky as a boyfriend, but in these times being with him was still safer than stepping out the door alone in most places in the United States.

Lee had started him thinking, and he never avoided reviewing his values from time to time. It was like his roadmap through life, and he didn't always come out in the same place. He had grown up as an only child in a family that had a lot of money, although at first he thought every family was like his. Later, he witnessed as a teenager all the worry and concern his parents spent on keeping the family assets away from thieves and hedged against market downturns, and he decided early on that it wasn't worth it. To him, they didn't appear to enjoy what they had. More than any of their other roles, his parents were full time caretakers of their stuff. That was their main job. They appeared to acquire things to keep them from being acquired by other people. Even though they never got along from early in Brett's teen years on, they couldn't split up and divide their pile, because then each of them would only have half as much as they had together.

When he was sixteen and it was time to talk about where he might go to college, it soon emerged that he wasn't interested in succeeding his father in his business, which made structural steel products, mainly joists for roof and ceiling construction in commercial buildings. He had worked in the plant that summer. This led to a sea change in their relations. The father told Brett he had built the business in order to pass it on to him as his life's work, to create in effect a business dynasty, and it had never occurred to him he might not want it when he was old enough to understand what this meant. Was he not mature enough for his age? Why didn't he get it?

Brett didn't ask why his father had never asked him about it earlier, because he seemed to have picked this time long before. Instead Brett thanked him and said that while that career was a great achievement, continuing it wasn't what he wanted to do with his life. He had more modest ambitions for his own business career, and when asked, admitted he didn't know exactly what that was going to be. He couldn't find a way to phrase it elegantly or with any tact, and he wasn't able to say outright that he'd rather be a writer or a blues guitar player. What he also did not say was that he didn't care to have possessions and business taking over his life in the way he'd watched them take over theirs. Even at sixteen he was certain of this much.

Brett never believed his father had done it all just for him. It was more like a monument to his own business skills and his ego. Brett didn't fault him for that, but he still didn't want it for himself. Not quite eighteen, he moved out of the house the day after he graduated from high school. He worked to pay his own way through the state university. His father sarcastically claimed that with his absence of ambition that would give him a cheap degree he'd never need. In a sense, as it played out, the man was right. Finding his niche, Brett ended up as a micro-entrepreneur in a business that required no academic prerequisites. Having a different ambition from the one his father had for him equated within the family to no ambition at all. They didn't speak about this or anything else for several years. Brett didn't mind the silence.

Four years earlier, when his parents both died within a six-month period, they had left him $200,000 and their good wishes. That was now his cushion. The other nine million dollars went to their favorite charities. Brett had never told anyone that part, but he had silently thanked them for spar-ing him the bother of protecting all that vulnerable money. He would've carried it like a target on his back. Not inheriting their fortune didn't make him an idealist or a person of principle; it only made him free. He hadn't ever regretted the way it came out.

He emerged from this reverie to find Lee still looking at him.

"So when you were dropped by your second fiancée," she began, saying these words with no particular emphasis, "was it because of your attitude towards owning things?"

He struggled to regain his footing in this conversation. "At first it wasn't framed that way, but as we talked about it, that did come up. She didn't want to be limited by my values, by what she called my lack of possessiveness. Clearly, the limitations she thought of were all coming from me. I sensed that she felt her values would have set me free, but it was really the opposite of that. I said I didn't plan to limit her, but I understood how she could see some risk in marrying me. I told her she could still drive a Jaguar if she wanted. In my mind, I always thought we could negotiate something, assuming she was also working to finance her need for consumption, because I wasn't going to sacrifice myself to flesh it out for her. In looking at it like that, I was probably naïve. I think she had already concluded the same thing by the time we had that conversation. I shouldn't have been so surprised when she walked away."

"What kind of job did she have?"

He shrugged, not expecting this question. "She was a waitress. That was how I met her."

Looking away, Lee was silent for a moment. "I guess it doesn't matter much now, does it? Circumstances have made the issue irrelevant. If Outpost doesn't hold, I suspect we'll be on the road a lot more, foraging."

"If the gas holds out. It's hard to forage when you're hitchhiking."

13

"And you brought back three vanloads of goddam fruit?" said Clayton later that day, trying without success not to laugh. They were gathered in the back yard again. "I wonder what old Emmett had to say when he heard that? He must've been spitting nails."

"I was only following orders," Brett said. "Listen, neighbor, it's not how you think out there. These trips are going to be experimental for a while. From the look of it a lot of people outside our gates are still trying to function as if nothing has changed—they're in denial, and that's not going to advance their planning function one bit. It'll look like normal for a few miles, and then you'll hit some rough spots. You can't just go shooting up some little town to take their groceries. They'll all come back at you, and I couldn't justify it anyway. When I was on the road with the convoy, I realized I could only loot a place that appeared to be truly abandoned. It would've helped to find a body out back with flies buzzing over it. It's a much finer call out there than Emmett ever imagined when he laid out the rules."

"It's not his job to sweat the details," Clayton said with a shrug.

"You're saying those people outside of Outpost are just like us," Lee said. "More or less."

"They're like we would be without Emmett; less anchored and focused. They're likely to behave more spontaneously, but they can still act to protect themselves."

"Where we take orders, they can only guess what they ought to do," said Clayton. "And I would imagine too that as we go farther down this road, they still won't develop a plan. They're drinkin' the Kool Aid and hoping for a miracle from the CO. He'd like to convince them that he's really able to deliver one, although we're still light on detail at this point.

I think that's a mistake on his part. It encourages people to 'spect too much from the government. If we've avoided any of those mistakes in Outpost, and that's where the jury is still out, it's that we have a plan in addition to a personality."

"I don't know," Brett said. "I have the feeling we'll start to run into some posses out there on one of these trips."

"Which reminds me," said Lee, brightening. "Did the President put in an appearance today? You said Sunday would be the deadline for that."

"I did not see him if he did, but I can tell you this: if that man made a statement of any kind the network would be repeating it every ten minutes. No, the President is still in seclusion, working his ass off to fix this problem, as I hear, as if he's embarrassed by his lack of action as ISIS grew. The CO will continue to speak for him. Soon, I would think, we'll see the CO in the flesh, but it will most likely be when he has some good news to announce, so we can associate it with his image. When he reports that news, I also predict he will not be doing so in the President's name. The breakthrough will be characterized as coming entirely from his own efforts."

"But what could that good news be?" Brett asked, still thinking he would welcome anything that sounded optimistic.

"I don't know. If they don't have anything soon, they'll probably make something up. Maybe the death rate is no longer rising as fast. Deaths by the million don't have any objective meaning, since it's only when your family and friends die around you that you feel the pain. He could have some of the reports delayed so it looks like the death rate is even slowing."

"Did you pry anything out of Leon about Holly?" Lee asked Brett, after a moment of silence. "At least that's a local issue where we can have some effect."

"I held off for a while until we'd bonded a bit before I brought it up, but yes. Now Holly is in there with Emmett." He went on to describe the situation as Leon had related it. This was followed by another silence.

"So," said Clayton, "they gunned him down right in

the City Hall corridors."

"He was carrying a scythe, if that report is correct. Doug looked wild enough when he left here for that to be true. Personally, I could easily look at it as a suicide, forcing other people to pull the trigger for him. Officially, the mayor didn't want to say Doug was an offended husband, for fear of setting an example among the disgruntled, so they announced he had caught the disease in a way that couldn't be explained. I can see the logic of that. But Holly is another matter, although her tale is closely related."

"It sounds like she provoked Doug's attempt on Emmett," Lee said. "She had to know he could never get through the security downtown, if only to talk to the mayor. I can hardly believe she'd do that."

"Leon heard that Holly had asked Emmett to fire him. These are desperate times," Brett said, with no satisfaction. Privately he believed that people could justify whatever they did and still sleep peacefully at night. "Even when the truth doesn't hurt it can still provide no sustenance whatever. People tried to kill us on the road coming up here for a smaller reason than that. They wanted to kill us for a half tank of gas, for Christ's sake. At least Holly is the Princess Royal now. She's achieved her dream. I'm sure they'll delay the wedding until less stressful times."

"You're right about the gasoline as a motive for murder," said Clayton. "Motivation is now being progressively devalued. In the coming week, tens of millions of Americans will be dying for much less than they did this week. Now it's gasoline, maybe by then it'll be water. Because of the stupefying numbers, death is now trivialized—it's the new normal. As time goes on, life will be the scarcest commodity of all. It'll get more respect if you can hold onto it. That also suits my plan. I've always wanted just a little more respect than I've ever gotten. Don't ask me why. Maybe having a long life will get it for me when nothing else ever did."

"Aren't you upset by this Holly episode?" Lee asked him. She poured a small round for each from Clayton's rum bottle, which was getting low. "Or is it only because I'm a woman that I'm worried? Maybe you think she's in good hands."

"But I don't think she's the victim here, is she?" Brett said, looking up into her eyes. "Unless we don't know everything, which I admit is another likely scenario."

Clayton looked at her for a long moment too before he took a sip of his rum. From the appraising expression of his eyes he might have been considering the differences between her and Holly. Brett realized Clayton had a lot of affection for Lee. Her liking for him was by no means misplaced.

"I think we've reached the point," he said, "where we can no longer trust without question any institution we've trusted in the past, nor even any individual. The names may continue unchanged, but beneath that, a new reality is in motion. That's why new relationships, based on these unexpected changes, are the way to go now. The strongest connections will be those coming out of the epidemic and its effects, not from past history. We sit here tonight waiting for the mosquitoes, and not for the first time, able to talk about a scary situation without flinching. You two are recently together. You have no history before the epidemic. You and I, Brett, have even less, although Lee and I do, so for us, we have an opportunity to deepen what we had. This is what is now emerging as the best way to survive in the present. It is the tipping point of an entire nation, and everything beyond is new and frightening. We must now trust each other with fewer reasons than we had before, because, more than anything, our own need above all is to survive. This is now what we all have in common, and precious little else."

Lee and Brett looked at each other for a long moment, knowing in their hearts this was absolutely true. They also realized that Clayton had mischaracterized their relationship, but that didn't seem worth mentioning. By morning it might be what he thought it was, or never.

"But what about Holly? I keep going back to her situation," Lee asked, but without seeming to discount what he'd said.

"That is a key example of what happens in this process. She has the survivor instinct more clearly defined than most of us, and it has led her, catalyzed by this crisis, straight into the arms of the leader. That's why I don't worry about her now. Long term, her approach may misfire, but she'll still land on her feet. It's one of those new connections I was talking about. I don't believe for a minute that she suddenly decided she needed to dump Doug because he only had half a job, or none. She could have done that long ago. It was more because the world above us, at the state and federal level, no longer functions. Holly fled straight to the core of power at City Hall, the only part of officialdom that now operates here at all."

"Doug even looked powerless," Brett said.

"And that core of power downtown wanted her?" Lee said.

Clayton gave her a broad smile and a chuckle. "Why, sho' they did. They have to relax at the end of the day as much as anyone. Probably more, and our lovely Holly is a party in motion. When you're in charge during a crisis like this, it's hard work makin' up a new and winning reality moment by moment, and I can think of no finer distraction than her sparkling presence. Although she would never visit you in the dungeon if you had the misfortune to stumble, Holly would still be the champagne at your birthday party at the Residence. Right now, more than anything else, I 'spect it will be our baser instincts that survive this quite well, if anything does. Our lust for power and other things, our covetousness of what our neighbor has. Our subtler refinements, however, I refuse to vouch for." He raised his glass. "Nor do I wish to make up any new ones. Refinement is the luxury of a functioning society. Rum is the drink of ribald sailors a long way from the safety of shore and their loved ones at home. Cheers to all of us here in this small and somewhat leaky lifeboat called Outpost."

"That is *crude* stuff, Clayton. You come on like a

genteel hard ass," Lee said.

"Isn't it? This is the time when it all comes out, because those polite barriers of good manners are the first things to fall. Everything is on the table now in a much more undisguised way." He leaned back in his chair with a smile. "I would like to observe the amusements of the CO at this moment. He's been working overtime, like both DeShawn and Emmett."

14

The following morning was Monday, the one-week anniversary of the terrorist attack in most of the country. Brett and Lee began it the same way they had every day since their arrival in Outpost, sitting before the television with a cup of coffee as they caught up with the downward spiral of the battle. It was a grim way to start the day, but they needed to know where they stood. The reference point that morning was thirty-eight million Americans dead.

They hardly ever spoke while they watched these reports. Sitting close together, Brett often put his arm around her shoulders. What he wanted to do most was ignore the problem, even aware of how callous that sounded. As far as he could see, the most important task they had was to avoid adding their own deaths to the total. But the reports were still compelling in their own way, as horrible as they were.

As it dissolved, the scene from the map studded with orange dots became a somber curtain fronted by a podium. Instead of the presidential seal, against a navy blue background, it displayed an oval plaque with an eagle with outstretched wings and a cluster of arrows in each claw. The new image was mounted on a diagonal sash of red, white and blue. A flagpole stood upright on one side. This was minimal indeed, and the symbolism vaguely different. An unseen announcer's voice came on.

"Members of the viewing audience, let me present our Commanding Officer, General Edwin A. Parker III."

"My God, it's about time!" said Lee, pounding her palms on her bare knees. "Here he is at last!"

Brett found he was excited too, but he felt the excitement had been mostly engineered by the long delay in bringing the CO out.

Still, it was almost anticlimactic that they heard no applause and no background music. Within a moment, a tall man wearing the Army Service Uniform walked out to the podium with a vigorous and measured step. On his chest was clustered a square foot of medals and ribbons. He faced the camera and looked the injured American viewing audience in the eye with a calm, confident expression. He wasn't handsome in the way Clayton had predicted, but his jaw was square and his expression forthright, his neck was lean, and he appeared confident and relaxed. His pale brown hair was cut short and he wore rimless glasses that didn't obscure his blue eyes. His age may have been about fifty-five. Neither Lee nor Brett knew army insignia well enough to read the colorful narrative that marched across his chest. His overall presentation suggested he was approachable and competent, while an established crinkle at the corners of his mouth hinted he was not without humor in the appropriate circumstances. Nothing about his appearance was self-indulgent or vain, or aloof and disengaged like the President had often seemed.

"I'd like to begin by reading a message that was handed to me earlier *today* by the President of the United States." The CO's voice held no trace of accent, although Brett thought he detected a slight emphasis on the word today. *Handed to me* suggested a personal relationship. With a fingertip the CO adjusted his glasses and lifted a single sheet of paper from the lectern and began to read.

"He's establishing his credentials," Lee murmured.

"'My fellow Americans. I have requested that General Parker bring you my deepest condolences for your suffering in this, the worst catastrophe ever to strike the United States. As we continue to work behind the scenes with the U. S. Congress to develop a comprehensive program for our recovery, I have also asked the General to outline for you his plan for a communication and power grid consolidation that will guarantee our continued ability to stay in touch with and aid each other, one to one, as this situation develops. Thank you.'"

The CO paused, and with a reassuring smile, slid the presidential announcement to the bottom of the pile. Brett could imagine the original copy coming up for auction one day in a more settled time, like an early working draft of the Declaration of Independence, as if anyone could ever look back on this period with nostalgia. Still, it was an important document, part of the changing of the guard at the start of a new era.

The CO's face expressed a more businesslike note. "Maintaining communications and electrical service throughout this country is at the core of our struggle today. I am therefore announcing that the following measures are being placed in effect without delay:

"The first tier of electricity producers, whether nuclear, solar, wind, coal, or any other fossil fuel system, have been nationalized by the United States Government under the new title, FPA, the Federal Power Administration. The national electrical grid is currently functioning at 37% of capacity. Our goal is to return it to 90% within ninety days. We call this the 90/90 Plan. Rest assured that I intend to keep you abreast of our progress, whether we meet our goal or not. That's why I'm here." He beat out the rhythm of this phrase with his upraised index finger.

"Second, the national television media, whether cable or direct broadcast, have also been nationalized by the United States Government into a single, noncommercial and nonpolitical system, known as the National Media Network, the NMN. Informally we like to call it Information Central. For the present time, this organization will be used to broadcast news and national security announcements throughout all fifty states. As resources permit, other stations will be added under this management, including, eventually, some offering entertainment. Sadly, due to the lack of power resources at many paper production facilities, all newspaper, book, and magazine production has been suspended for now. Indeed, most of those media have already ceased to function on their own because of personnel issues. We've selected key members from their staffs to help us at the NMN. Once it has been restructured, the Internet will also be rebooted under the management of the NMN to provide the broadest possible access to national recovery information.

"Third, the United States Army, Navy, Marines, and Coast Guard have already been merged under a single unified command. This will both improve efficiency and speed communications. It has eliminated the administrative redundancies that they had before as separate services. The new combined entity will be known as Freedom Force One, and under its head will also include a single formerly nonmilitary agency of the government, FEMA, The Federal Emergency Management Agency. Freedom Force One will be directed by myself as Permanent Commanding Officer. Many separate functions previously managed by the old Federal Government have been taken over as well, and will now be handled in a more direct and efficient manner to forward the national interest in this time of great distress. In all of these changes, the provisions of the United States Constitution, insofar as they apply, have been fully respected, and will continue to be."

The CO paused here with a smile that might have accelerated the melting of glaciers even on a cool day. The audience suddenly felt they were going to be OK, as they were meant to. Brett began to perceive the CO's strengths more clearly. His approach was going to include equal parts of benign authority and reassurance. They were all going to be buddies now going forward together, hand in hand. It was like the 1940s, when fighting a war on two fronts required everyone to pull together, to think alike for victory.

The CO's finger pointed forward toward the

audience, reminiscent of an old wartime poster.

"You may feel that all this adds up to a tall order, and I do not disagree. But it is dictated by the times in which we live—that's why we need the cooperation of every American. It is my hope, even my certainty, that these measures will begin the resurrection and continued prosperity of the United States. God bless America!"

The National Anthem came up:

O say, can you see, by the dawn's early light,
What so proudly we hail'd at the twilight's last gleaming...

The song gained in volume as the screen faded to black before the CO left the podium, which dissolved in turn into the Stars and Stripes rippling against a bright, promising sky. It stayed that way until Lee turned it off with a subdued snort three minutes later.

"Now it's time for a pop quiz," she said, quite calmly, as if she were a tenth grade civics teacher. She sat down again with her hands folded on her lap, and looked at her watch.

"Sure." Brett fumbled in his shirt pocket for a pencil without finding one.

"What just happened to the United States of America in the last few minutes?"

Lee had traveled a long way in her attitudes to be able to say this. Brett chewed his lip for a moment, searching for a parallel.

"In the nineties I can remember my father recalling to me his fears on the day when he heard that President Nixon was going to resign within a few hours. Already worried about his money, he thought the government might break up, might collapse, the value of the dollar would crash, but none of that happened. He described how he held his breath as things went on as if nothing much had changed. Nixon boarded his helicopter, waved at the crowd, and Gerald Ford, a former football player, came on as a caretaker. He told me this twenty years later, in 1994. He said he realized on that day that the country was not sustained by its leadership, only by its people. It was not the top level that kept things going; it was the bottom and the middle that were most important and provided the real continuity—the ability and determination to go on no matter what. At the time I felt that had to be one of the truest things he had ever said to me. It was from the heart, an organ he rarely paid much attention to, and the one that ultimately brought him down."

Lee looked back at him with a sober expression. "And you think that's still the case now."

"I hope it is, except that today those same average people are being cut down by the millions with no remedy. Back then, they were undergoing the declining years of the hippie era, but the individual safety of people was not generally threatened. The Vietnam War ended only months after Nixon left. It turned into a time of healing under Gerald Ford, and then a few years later President Carter amnestied the draft deserters. They could freely return from Canada, although not all of them wanted to."

"So it's like that again, the day Richard Nixon resigned."

"In the sense that we've been reduced to our core strength, but worse in other ways. Maybe that has to happen at intervals, just so we know who we really are, not merely who inhabits Washington this year."

Clayton had been remarkably close in his predictions. The CO was not a frightening man, although his announcements could be if anyone analyzed what they might mean for the freedom of communication over time. But few people were projecting them into the future, since it was so hard to make out. General Parker's manner was reassuring, and he seemed both competent and focused on the national interest, two qualities no leader or member of Congress in Washington had displayed within living memory. He exuded no odor of big oil and CIA, as with George H. W. Bush, or of the most corrupt political machine in the country, as with Barack Obama. The CO appeared to be his own man, and it was difficult to see what he would gain from this, aside from personal glory. Was he only the citizen soldier stepping into the breach? But even that seemed unlikely if he was hiding behind the current administration, presenting himself as its spokesman. It was still possible to believe he was really acting for the people's benefit. He also had a sense of humor, one of the critical survival skills Lee had listed. As for consolidating the armed forces to eliminate redundancy, and trimming fat from the government, who could deny the intelligence of that? It made Brett realize that tax collections in these circumstances would be fractional at best. With agricultural and industrial production falling off radically, and the same amount of money in circulation, it looked like a huge surge in inflation was coming.

"I think a lot of people who saw that are now feeling relieved," Brett said, without indicating how he felt personally. "Are you? He said nothing about finding a cure for the disease, although that may be way too early." Lee tilted her head a bit to one side and her eyebrows lifted, as if she knew the answer. He looked into her face, so close, knowing he needed and wanted more from her. It was as if she was now the only person in his life.

"I'm both relieved and scared stiff. Those changes the CO announced make perfect sense. They also turn the government into a military dictatorship, no matter what he said about the Constitution. In a situation where the measures you desperately need right now are also the ones you wouldn't want to put up with in the future, it's hard to be objective. We'll have to trust the CO, at least for now."

"I don't think I can."

"Do you trust Emmett?"

"I did at first. Now not at all, after the Holly and Doug business."

"Do you trust me?"

She turned with a confident look. "You're all I have now beyond my family, and I've trusted you from the beginning. I'm not sure why, but you seem to have no agenda beyond exactly what we're doing."

"Maybe there's no room for anything else."

Yet the CO's broadcast left both of them strangely uneasy as they talked, as if they'd witnessed a life-changing event and couldn't settle down afterward. The old rules had been suddenly suspended and they weren't sure what the new ones were. Lee and Brett both had the impulse to head for a public place to see how others were reacting. It felt like the calm aftermath of a devastating storm and they needed to view the extent of the damage. They left the house with a stiff-legged gait, as if they'd forgotten what normal movement was. There was no sign of Clayton lurking in his yard with a rake. Maybe he was lying on the floor inside, stunned by what he'd seen. They walked several blocks in silence.

During Brett's brief absence as a fruit gatherer with the scavengers, the City of Outpost had inaugurated its new, state-of-the-art local communications system. It had never been large enough to possess its own television station that could be used for that. Part of the installation was a rooftop siren on City Hall that would alert everyone to invaders coming over the hillside, should that be attempted. The alarm would be triggered by signals from the Paul Revere Units. The other part of the new process consisted of a poster, what some would call a broadside, mounted in both of two new glass-fronted steel frames near the front and the back entrances of City Hall. Flanking the current announcement were vertical rows of the prior ones, in reduced size. The clean and finished welding on the frames suggested they might have come from the city garage. The mayor's office must have had a large-scale printer that could take computer output, so they could run off these notices as needed. The citizens could saunter downtown to get the latest news and counsel. It was like the town crier of colonial times. Their landline and cell phones were still not working, and Lee and Brett had stopped trying to find a signal.

Even beyond the need to get out of the house that morning to rid themselves of the heaviness that remained after the CO's revolutionary talk, they liked the poster concept because it would give them an excuse to walk downtown several times a day instead of sitting inside stewing about events they couldn't influence, much less control. As they strolled down to City Hall, Lee introduced Brett to people she knew. He hadn't been in Outpost long, but he sensed a new spirit of community. People were nodding to each other and smiling more than they should, given the downward trend of reality. They even heard laughter. That couldn't hurt, because of what they'd be facing in the near future. The CO had left them in a mood to think about something more upbeat than newspapers and magazines disappearing, and about having only a single television channel. Brett thought he could imagine what the resurrected Internet might look like. He wanted to believe the CO's new plan would help, but how would they get rid of it, and of him, once it had worked and the country was back on its feet, if that could be made to happen? He pushed this question out of his mind, hoping he'd be facing it again later. It was the same group of issues he'd already considered with Emmett's emergency decrees.

Lee looked especially radiant that morning, with her vivid, glossy hair and glowing skin, which caught and reflected highpoints well. Like their relationship, it thrived on contrast. The sunlight set up highlights all over her face and bare shoulders. Had she stuck out her tongue, it would have displayed a star at the tip of it. He realized he'd been getting more and more engaged by the way she looked. He suddenly remembered his conversation with Leon.

"You know, you have an admirer in this town."

"I know it's not you."

"Leon the cop."

"Ah, Leon. Of course, I always knew that about him," she said this softly, as if her voice was coming through a cashmere filter. "Holly said this—and it's true—a girl knows those things."

"And?"

"Although he didn't really come forward and ask for my hand, I could see that Leon was more serious than some others have been, but for me, he was never up to the task, and I think he even sensed that. I need someone strange and new—Clayton has that part of the puzzle correctly pegged for these times. Leon thinks that stability and consistency win hands down. I can still recall an era when they did, but that was last week. Still, a lot of girls would probably want him. It's not like he's going to lose his job in an economic downturn."

"So in his world, those traits would probably still work for most women."

"Leon must think I would go for the boy next store."

"And you wouldn't?"

"I would if he were the last one on the planet. I would usually like to be with *someone*, especially in a crisis like this, but I'd rather go through a much longer list before I committed. I think you would too."

"And yet, you and I met on the road, with scarcely a formal introduction. As I recall, you were hitchhiking with your bare thigh thrust forward as your most prominent and compelling feature."

Lee stopped abruptly and faced him. "I was not doing anything of the kind! I waved at you in the most ladylike manner possible, given the desperate circumstances I was in. I had no way of even knowing who you were, aside from the fact that you were white, and that was chancy enough in itself. You might have been an ogre. You could've had your KKK hood on the seat beside you. It was a hell of a gamble for me."

Brett saw this from her perspective for the first time. "Those are great shorts, though."

She made an indecipherable noise.

They entered the small plaza that defined Outpost's mostly concrete green, where they wanted to see the latest posting of the local news. Here the populace could gather to acclaim the current regime or only to acquiesce in its pronouncements when its charm was fading. The space would've benefited from a battery of old bronze cannon aimed at the lake now to capture the flavor of prior battles. A few small knots of people were conversing with intense expressions. Lee and Brett kept their distance.

"FREE FOOD!" the poster proclaimed in large type. No subtlety there, it was a headline emblematic of hard times. Forthrightness mattered more than finesse at this point. "FRUIT!" continued below in a smaller typeface. Brett's name did not appear as one of those who had brought it in. He'd saved a large part of the world before, and was on record as not expecting any credit. A uniformed cop he didn't know had stopped by the house yesterday afternoon to tell him the lab had picked up none of the current disease organisms on his gloves or mask, or on the fruit itself or its packaging. Since he was still alive, Brett was not surprised. When the cop left he handed Brett his old shoes in a paper bag.

The food distribution was scheduled to begin at ten o'clock in the fruit and vegetable section at Stoddard's Super. That was fifteen minutes away. It would be confined to five each of smaller fruits like the oranges and apples, or one pineapple per family, and would continue until supplies ran out. Another scavenger crew had gone out that morning. Brett had done a little thinking about their foraging venture and decided that the likelihood of finding something to bring back in disturbed areas, like the ones he and Lee had driven through coming up, as with the deserted grocery store, was greatest. This suggested the risk would also be enhanced as the crews went farther out, and as more time passed. Food supplies would be dwindling everywhere. Emmett would be creating that risk if he thought he could generalize on their initial experience, because the world was changing hour by hour.

They walked the five blocks from the village green to the supermarket parking lot and joined the crowd. The two main subjects they picked up eavesdropping were food supplies and the forthright efforts of the CO to rescue the country. The comments tended to be supportive of the general's leadership; no one else seemed as paranoid as Brett was, at least not in public. The upbeat tone partly derived from the previous long spell of incompetence in Washington—people were happy to have someone vigorous in charge now, a person with ideas and the clout to set them in motion. In his prior broadcasts, the images put up surrounding the CO were neither contentious nor partisan, and no opposing viewpoint had been suggested. Had they spelled it out directly, they would have said he was a right-thinking man with the wind at his heels and the right stuff in abundance.

The state had a majority of Democratic voters who were often less than dependable in echoing the national party's views. They displayed a quirky independence that made them naturally run more conservative than their northern brothers. Yet, oddly, Brett had heard none of them yet bring up the fact that the CO was a military man, and one who was now calling the shots in the name of what had been until then a Democratic administration. Party politics had finally been elbowed aside by nonpartisan action.

"There's Clayton," said Lee, pointing to the edge of the crowd.

He was wearing sunglasses and a straw hat with a broad green fabric band, one that suggested neither cotton picker nor field hand, but the raffish character of Clayton himself, or perhaps a New Orleans bookie. He was also wearing a casual and patient look. The group had not formed into a line. Lee and Brett were approaching him when one of the paired doors opened and two uniformed police walked out. One remained at the entry with a clipboard and a pen in his hand, waving people forward. The other motioned them into a line. With only one side of the paired doors open, people had to enter singly. Three feet inside the doors waited a German shepherd with a short leash and an intense look in his darting eyes. His handler was out of sight behind him. Dogs love to have jobs, and this one's task was to be an enemy of disorder in any form.

"Now starts the qualification process," Lee said. "This is why we filled out that questionnaire."

No advance notice of this requirement had been included on the City Hall poster. When Clayton reached the front of the line, the cop found his name on the list, checked it off, and passed him through. Brett and Lee were about six ranks behind.

Once inside, Stoddard's Super looked nearly normal. The principal difference was that the produce department, which was nearest their entry point, had been cordoned off, with a narrow exit gap that led to the rest of the store. No vegetables were in view, and the fruit from the scavenging expedition was arranged on a long row of tables. Lee picked up a pineapple from the display, smelled it, and pulled a single leaf from the top.

"What do you think?" she asked Brett with a smile. "It's ready to eat. Pineapples have long been a symbol of peace and welcome."

At that moment, a teenage boy ahead of them impulsively snatched an apple from the display and bit into it, gleefully spinning out of line in what looked like a dance of triumph. Had he not eaten in a while? Suddenly airborne, the German shepherd leaped past Brett's face, pulling the handler to the floor, where he lost his grip on the leash. The dog hit the boy in the back with both front paws and knocked him face down. The apple bounced off out of sight. Two women in the crowd screamed.

The boy's mother grabbed the dog's tail and it spun around. Brett seized the dog's head as it went for her arm. He leaped onto the dog's back and gripped its jaws with both hands, clamping them shut as it lunged at her again. His legs grappled the dog's torso on both sides under its front legs. Only the rear legs slashed uselessly against Brett's calves. The rest spun away, clearing a circle around them.

The handler was up again in an instant. He seized the leash and pulled the dog back with a guttural command. "Duke was only doing his duty!" the man screamed.

Brett rolled away on his back. His hands rubbed his lower legs. "So was I," he said, quietly. "That was just too much."

Out of the crowd Clayton appeared and pulled him

to his feet. The kid with the apple had disappeared with his family. "Are you all right?"

"Scraped up a little, I think, but I'm OK." Brett glanced at the dog, which regarded him with burning eyes, panting from the end of his leash.

The cop with the clipboard came in, but the crowd was eager to disperse on their own. It had taken less than a minute. He looked at the handler as if to say, "What happened?" but the handler turned away, embarrassed.

Brett found a cart and they took advantage of the opportunity to pick up a few more items. Feeling guilty about Clayton furnishing both the rum and picking him up from the floor, he seized the two remaining bottles of Appleton dark. He observed Lee glancing at him now and then, as if waiting for a response, but he offered none, sensing that it would get into broader issues he wasn't ready to deal with at that moment. He was working to regain his focus.

Some shelves were gapping empty in places. In many others, the front line of product was the only row. Regular oatmeal remained in abundance. Who wanted to boil anything in this weather? Fans of smoked oysters and canned kidney beans were going to have an easier time of this than some others going forward. Brett began to wonder how hard the foraging crews were going to have to work to maintain the food supply. Was it even possible? During his single foray with the convoy it had seemed extremely chancy. He and Lee loaded up as much as they could carry away on foot, just short of the hundred dollars apiece limit. The cashier was still taking credit cards, an act of genuine optimism.

Outside, a table near the other entrance—now the exit—to Stoddard's Super displayed a sign that read, "Last Chance to Sign Up as Outpost Residents." It offered a stack of the five-page forms Lee and Brett had completed earlier, with clipboards to support them while people filled them out. Five or six were working on it. Lee and Brett caught up with Clayton halfway across the parking lot. He made a subtle gesture with his wrist toward a black Ford Expedition with smoked glass that sat parked by the driveway. From its position the occupants could watch both the front and the back doors of Stoddard's. They were close enough to hear that the motor and the air conditioning were running. Gas was no problem for the city government.

"I've been standing here looking for a while," Clayton said, "but I haven't seen a bright flash of blond hair inside. You'd think some glimmer would've gotten through, even with the tinted windows."

They walked back home together. Someone nearby might have said their conversation sounded like muttering.

"You're not becoming an enemy of order, now, I hope," Clayton said.

"You can have too much order, just like anything else."

15

Later, Clayton made lunch for the three of them. He harvested two kinds of lettuce from his garden and sliced one of his apples from the giveaway. Walnuts and blue cheese dressing he already had. It wasn't bad with the Mexican beer he'd bought at Stoddard's. To Brett, it wasn't the most conventional salad he'd ever had, but it worked. Who even expected to be invited to lunch in these times?

"You weren't that far off about the CO," Lee said as they sat down to eat. They were seated in Clayton's covered screen porch attached to the back of his kitchen. The concrete floor was painted dark green in the tone of a Ping-Pong table. When they sat down, the aluminum folding deck chairs squeaked and strained. The well-used, unvarnished pine table looked handmade, and displayed chains of rings from the bottoms of sweating glasses that had weathered the steamy climate without coasters.

"Still," Clayton said, "I thought the CO would have

more of a movie star quality to him, like a bigger chest and shoulders, but he'll have to do, since he's the man now. He spun that announcement about the media and the power grid as if it was all good news. Then he made it seem like the newspapers and magazines had broken down on their own, and maybe that was true. In the general collapse of things, they wouldn't stand out if they had. Yet somehow, I always thought they owned warehouses full of those huge rolls of paper in the event of Teamster strikes."

"It might only be the power to run the presses that's failed," Lee suggested, poking through her lettuce.

"He offered damn little hard information, though," Brett said.

"Well, that's the point. With just a single station you're never going to get more than a little information because they own the only faucet it comes out of." Clayton passed around a plate of stale whole wheat bread from Stoddard's. Fresh baked goods had been among the first casualties of the epidemic.

"Do you think he's dead?" Lee asked.

"The President? Not at all! I talked some more to my amateur radio friends about the Windsong Estate, and they think more than ever that the assembled government that fled Washington—that would be the White House, Congress, and the Supreme Court—is all still present in the bunker. That's about 550 or more people in cold storage. My friends are watching the way military personnel keep coming and going, and looking at the constant run of supply trucks, which is undiminished. One sure giveaway for a population that size is the amount of garbage they generate. Personally, I think that once they were all set up inside, more for their own safety than ours, I'm sure, the CO turned the key from the outside and walked off with a shrug, whistling Dixie. That was it. They would've kept open some kind of airlock for bringing things in and taking them out. The President's cell phone, if he even has one, doesn't work any better than anyone else's now. The government inside is at the mercy of the CO for getting any real information, like the rest of us are, which is to say, they're being told a version of the facts that suits the CO and his plans."

"But why are they safe in there?" Lee asked.

Clayton gave her a grim smile. "They're safe as long as they remain useful as a front to the real government. That's their only value now, but don't underestimate it. That part is not that uncomfortable for them, because they've always been merely a front for the real power behind the government. As it stands, the new government can't see far enough ahead to know when that usefulness might end, so I'd say they'll be OK for the foreseeable future, probably longer then we will. And wasn't that their intention goin' in? Even so, for myself, I'd still rather be out here taking my chances with Emmett, because I'm still able to run in a different direction if it suits me."

"Do you think it's going to come to that?" Lee asked, shaking her head. "I hope not. This town is our last refuge."

"We won't know till it does. The mayor's makin' a big effort, but it all depends on how insightful he is."

"Let me know when that insight starts to break down," Brett said.

"I believe you'll see it on your own. You might be the one tellin' me."

Lee rose and looked through the screen into the yard as if she'd heard something moving. Tall, dense buckthorn hedges blocked any view of the neighbors on both sides. "It seems ironic that their lives are just as chancy as ours are now, being at the mercy of the CO. And they thought they had out-smarted the problem by heading for the bunker." She didn't turn around.

"Or maybe the bug will find its way in there on its own," Clayton said. "No safeguard is perfect. They're go-ing through lots of supplies. Where is all that stuff coming from? If it's not all coming from the URDs, they could have a problem."

Lee sat down again and picked at her salad. If an-other olive was still concealed among the leaves she didn't locate it.

"In that kind of sealed situation none of them could survive once it got started," continued Clayton, "and it would quickly be announced that our esteemed public servants had succumbed to the enemy attack, like our poor friend Doug. Thanks will be offered that they were able to hold out for as long as they did, since every day of life is a gift more precious than the previous one. Then the government will add their number to the millions of other patriotic victims. My guess is that they will all have died in the cause of freedom. Just sayin', OK? But right now they're all still useful in this war effort."

"We all have a role to play," said Brett, without irony.

Clayton paused for a moment to finish his salad. "This bread's way too far over the hill, isn't it? If I could find a productive chicken now, I'd make French toast with what I've got left, since the eggs went first down to Stoddard's. I don't feel like I can waste a single morsel anymore. DeShawn always thought we should keep one or two, chickens, that is, but I never would. I don't care for all that noise in the morning when they wake up before I do.

"Anyway, I have come up with my own idea of what the key phrase was in the CO's speech. You folks probably spotted it too. It was when he spoke of the new Freedom Force One taking over certain functions of the old Federal Government." Clayton paused with a sly look. "A subtle thing, isn't it, but I caught it right away. After all, what discredits a person most in this country? Perhaps you don't know that yet, being young, but *I* do." He paused for a moment awaiting a response from either Brett or Lee that didn't come.

"It is being, or even perceived as being, old. The stock of the *old* U.S. Government, as it once existed, dropped by 90% in that single moment, not that it started from a very high point. And the new CO knew that very well. He built that line on what people were already thinking about Washington. It was like dragging the steel cover over a manhole and dropping it into place. *Thunk.*"

"You're right," Lee said. "He didn't call it the *responsive* Federal Government, or the *forward-looking* Federal

Government."

"He insinuated that it wasn't current anymore," Brett added, "only old and tired, unable to cope. Worthy of respect in the way your grandpa might be as he sits rocking on the front porch, but he was still dismissive of it. And doesn't this new term, Freedom Force One, make reference to the President's personal plane?"

"True dat," said Clayton ironically, with a broad grin. "That's no accident either. Soon he'll be seen wearing the President's jogging clothes. No sense letting them go to waste, just because the *old* chief executive's got nowhere to run to anymore."

"And nowhere to hide, apparently. Do you still like him, the CO?" asked Lee. "He scared me today."

Clayton looked into her face.

"I have no doubt that the CO is very skillful at public relations. Let's say that I don't hate that man, yet. That time may still come, but if he can pull off a recovery, even bare survival with an uncertain future, I'll be the first to credit him with that before I launch my objections."

"I feel powerless, all of a sudden."

Clayton gave Brett a look that said, *you poor baby.* "You probably always had your own power, and it rested on certain assumptions. Is it only this minute that it deserted you? You were fully represented in the past? Your Congressman probably always called to ask your views before he voted on key issues?"

Brett smiled as he shook his head. "I know I never had any power in that respect. But at least I felt I could act intelligently on my own with dependable information. Now I'm at the mercy of people who only tell me what they want me to hear or know, so I'm never sure what to do."

"So now it's like you're married?"

For a moment Bret thought Lee was going to take a swing at Clayton, but she only grinned, even though the grin may have shown too many bright and even teeth.

"How long were you married?" she asked him.

236

"Thirty-three years, and, offered the choice, I believe I would do it again."

"With the same woman?" Brett asked.

"Maybe. She'd surely be among the finalists when I made that choice."

"I mean for all the thirty-three years."

"Yes."

"Then let me ask you a bottom line question. The government has been overthrown. The new military regime will continue to act as if what we have now is legitimate, but we know it isn't. How do you feel about that?"

"Do I regret the loss of our democracy?" Clayton said. He placed one forearm and elbow on the table and leaned forward in Brett's direction.

"Yes."

"Then tell me first when we last had one? Because it looks to me like the political parties are only different in their rhetoric. Their positions on social issues are opposed, but that's only window-dressing. After the election the person who's elected then proceeds to serve the interests of the large corporate contributors and PACs who paid for his election— and aside from the labor unions, they are nearly the same ones paying the election bills for both parties. I've watched this process for a long time, and I realized that this is why nothin' ever changes. Once in office, both parties act the same because they're beholden to the same powerful groups. The parties have become the guardians of the status quo, no matter what their rhetoric tells the rank and file about abortion, gay marriage, and prayer in the public schools. None of those issues damage the pocketbooks of their corporate sponsors."

"And the military pushed them aside because?" asked Lee.

"Because they are so busy serving their corporate masters they couldn't function under this kind of threat. Our system no longer chooses the able and the insightful—people with leadership qualities. It chooses only the compliant on both sides, people who will dutifully return the favor once sworn in.

The paralysis of their ineptitude in a crisis must have been clear immediately in Washington. The military is always the reserve power when civilian government fails. That's true anywhere. Do you think it's only in Latin America or the Middle East? The military is able to act effectively now because they don't need to take campaign contributions, they don't need to consult their masters taking out their big checkbooks in their limousines, and this is what you get. It makes the new *Freedom Force One* the cutting edge radicals in the sense that they're the only ones who can change at all when change is the only thing that helps."

"So the military is as radical as we ever get now," Brett said. "Think of that. The simple ability to act is the new extremism."

"So somebody had to act in this crisis," said Lee, "and the *old* Federal Government had plain forgotten how. They'd gotten out of the habit."

"Long ago. That's how it looks to me, and to the military, too, obviously."

"I'm starting to think this was inevitable," Brett said. Clayton made a noise near to a snort. "Oh, they could've limped on for a while longer if we hadn't had this attack. Don't know whether you saw the new number at noon, but it's now sixty-six million dead. 'Course, that's their best estimate. I don't know how they can be accurate anymore. Bein' within three or four million is most likely as close as they can get."

Nor could any of them think of a possible response to either number.

16

After lunch, Brett and Lee walked back down to the town square to catch the latest news from the City Hall billboard. Between forty and fifty people circulated and chatted in small groups. As a source of information, the plaza was gaining momentum. It looked like the failure of most electronic communications had generated an enhanced sense of community. State and national flags were flying, but no soapbox had yet been erected to encourage public discussion. It might have invited dissent.

The focus of the current excitement was a headline that read, FREE BARBECUE TOMORROW. A list of meats and sausages followed, some raw, but many prepared and ready to eat. Distribution would commence in the morning at 10 A.M. at Stoddard's Super. This time Emmett had signed the announcement at the bottom with a flourish. He was starting to catch on about the political value of giveaways, an idea that had ultimately brought Washington to fiscal ruin decades back, since the federal government had mostly been running up more debt to pay for them. Emmett had his own more cost effective sources, and Brett was part of them.

"I prefer ribs to brisket, don't you?" Lee said, rubbing her hands together. "The scavenger crew must have knocked over a butcher shop with a big deli counter. Abandoned, I'm sure, although the coolers were still running, thank God. I wouldn't mind a little bacon, either. The thick-sliced is best, don't you think?" Although she was trim and carried no extra pounds, Lee did enjoy her food. If strict rationing were to come at some point down the road, she'd be one of the hardest hit.

Even by 9:30 Tuesday, the following day, Stoddard's parking lot was crowded. Many straw cowboy hats were in view, since the morning was simmering already. Brett overheard someone say the meat caravan had been so effective that Emmett was increasing the number of daily vans to four, starting with the crew that had already left that morning. After two scavenger forays, the strategy had been deemed wildly successful. Even though Brett still couldn't see enough volume in what was coming in, he suspected the mayor was taking high fives among his inner circle, which included Holly.

Lee was wearing the same burnt orange tank top and denim shorts she'd been hitchhiking in when they met, with sunglasses and a wide-brimmed white cloth safari hat with a fake rose in the band. The pale pink flower was compressed from traveling in her suitcase.

"I wonder if we're going to get addicted to this," Brett said. "It's like the welfare state, where we stand around waiting for handouts, isn't it? Then at election time we vote for the candidate who promises to give away even more."

"I see your point, but do you have a better idea? Even the bacon and ribs don't move you at all? You've fallen hard for oatmeal now? Come on. This lengthens our survival time. I hope they brought some good barbecue sauce too, with all this marvelous meat."

Lee was right in not wanting to talk about it. How could anyone work productively when no economy existed to work in? At least, not as it existed before. Some businesses remained open, but less than half. People could still see a dentist on short notice or get their car washed without waiting in line. Water and electricity were the only two critical things not in short supply. The hardware store was still open, and most stocks were adequate. Although the guns were long gone, the people of Outpost could buy all the paint they needed, even if few seemed to want much at the moment. They could also get their watch battery replaced in a heartbeat and top it off with a quick haircut next door. It was in some nonessential respects a selective disaster. Still, this alone was not enough to foster an atmosphere of normalcy. Few people talked about the near future.

Brett and Lee came home from Stoddard's with eight pounds of meat, including beef ribs—the pork had gone first—sausage, and bacon. The ribs were ready to eat and the pint bottle of Texas barbecue sauce that came with them was in addition to the eight-pound ration. Enough would remain to use on sausage later. Emmett had learned how to make them feel blessed. But was his expertise developing as well in other areas too, like perimeter defense? Brett wondered for a moment as they cleaned up after lunch whether Holly was making *him* feel blessed. Could Emmett concentrate on her in the way she apparently required? If he wasn't honeymooning with Holly all the time, he may not have been perceived as doing his principal job, in her view. According to Lee, this had been the ruin of Doug. Privately, though, Brett wondered whether Doug hadn't ruined himself. Had Emmett now guided his own charming Trojan horse with a wavy blond mane through the City Hall gates, scattering flower petals on its path?

17

That Tuesday, the ninth day of the epidemic, was also the day the shaky equilibrium in Outpost began to crumble. It might have started because the scavenger parties initiated too much contact with the outside, but no one could have said for certain. The strength and appeal of Outpost had always resided in its isolation. The population in the surrounding area was already too stressed, and the added presence of the scavenger caravans might have pushed people over the edge. Anyone leaving Outpost had to pass south through Davis Junction, which hosted the first crossroad. Emmett's daily caravan of police cars and vans would have constantly reminded those residents of their more privileged existence up beyond the dam; waking up people who may have previously been more absorbed by their own problems. At the minimum, the convoys suggested Outpost had its own supply of gas, and if it had gas, what else did it have that they lacked? There were too many possibilities to count. And then they had the arrogant example of Outpost police cruising their neighborhoods with guns as Emmett's patrols looked for targets to loot. Guns were common, and they could shoot both ways. Brett wondered if Emmett had been too focused on saving Outpost to imagine a potential backlash from its neighbors.

He also began to wonder whether the population around them—and probably everywhere—wasn't starting to contract into feudal demesnes, reeling in their borders hand over hand, throwing up rough-hewn perimeter walls, leaving deserted no man's land spaces between, beyond which more distant neighbors were now perceived as enemies, foreigners, aliens. The people of Outpost had been the first in the area to treat their neighbors that way. They had also been the first in the area to block the entrance to their town, just as the URDs had. They had become the standard bearers for the developing breakdown of civility. It was inevitable that they looked like a gated community in the midst of a ghetto.

While they thought of themselves as organized, forward looking, even principled, and possessing a finely tuned planning function, to others the Outpost residents appeared to define the cutting edge of the new separatism, undoing two hundred years of neighborly tradition in that part of the state. Soon it would probably introduce a new dialect for itself that the surrounding communities would be unable to understand. A secret handshake would follow, a move involving the thumb and little finger in peculiar positions.

Lee and Brett were walking down Shoreline Boulevard after lunch. In defiance of the trend of the world, they were proud to be there, part of which was merely being well fed in uncertain times. The day was already steamy, but they wanted some exercise. Brett missed the workout of his deliveries, the loading and unloading, jumping in and out of his van thirty times a day. Below the parapet the water lay calm and motionless under the glare. Two covered boats trolled along slowly, closer to the other side of the lake. Fish was food, fresh and healthy food. Boats were more valuable now.

From behind them the wail of a siren cut through the humid air. As they passed the Marion Street intersection, where it met Shoreline in a T, a police car with red and blue lights spinning and siren shrieking swerved around the corner, skidding on loose gravel, and turned toward the commercial area. They saw two figures in the back and two in front. One in the back seat appeared to be cradling the other, and the driver was staring out of a shattered windshield that had no glass between him and the onrushing air. Bullets had pierced both the two passenger-side windows. The car sped off toward the tiny emergency hospital, which sat near the edge of Shoreline at the beginning of downtown, two blocks away. Brett put his hand on Lee's shoulder.

"That has to be one of the scavenger caravan escort cars. Looks like they ran into somebody who was ready for them." Shaking her head, Lee didn't want to see it. They picked up their pace, and two blocks past the hospital, found themselves in the City Hall plaza, where, aside from the police, a dozen or so people stood to one side looking at a police car and two vans. The poster frame on the near side of the building was empty of new announcements in the center panel, as if the city was unsure what was coming next.

"*Two* vans?" said Lee. "Weren't they planning to use four today? What went wrong here? Wasn't this going to be easy? Do you think Leon's OK?"

This was too much in the nature of, "Why didn't you tell me before you went out there that this could happen?" Brett could only shrug, imagining himself as one of the drivers in this ambushed wagon train. The lead police car had taken no bullets from what he could see, although one side had a long scrape. Both the remaining vans had a few bullet holes in the sides, and more in the rear doors. Maybe the other two had lost their tires. It had been the trailing police car they'd seen speeding to the hospital.

"Step back, please," one of the cops barked through his blue facemask. They moved away. From the crowd, someone tossed him a roll of yellow crime-scene tape and he proceeded to restrict access to the area. Brett was wondering whether the next input on this event would come from Mayor Emmett, who was now emerging from the City Hall doors, flanked by two armed officers in sunglasses, each with their hands on their guns as if they were Secret Service. Lee and Brett took a further step back. Emmett's unmasked look was grim. Aside from a curt nod, he disregarded the gathering crowd as he approached the vehicles. Everyone was waved back three steps farther as if they were planning to cough.

"Emmett must have asked them to bring the caravan here," Brett said. "Otherwise, wouldn't they have taken it right to the city garage?"

Lee nodded. "He would've wanted to see the vehicles first."

One of the cops lifted the tape with two fingers of a gloved hand and Emmett walked up to the rear doors of the second van. He opened one of them himself before the cop had a chance to reach for the handle. The back was empty. Emmett exhaled strongly and rubbed his upper lip with the side of his index finger as if he was deep in thought—his manner suggested he was aware that the crowd was watching him, but the gesture certainly looked like an error in hygiene. He bent over to inspect the inside of the door at a spot where one of the bullets had passed through. He shook his head as if he was dealing with barbarians.

This is why we keep the town pure, Brett thought, quoting Leon.

Walking up to the lead police car, Emmett passed his hand over the scuff that ran along both doors on the driver's side. Brett thought he heard the mayor say the words *close scrape*, but none of the cops around him smiled, or if they did, it was undetectable under their masks. As he was looking inside the front seat, another police car sped up and stopped. A cop jumped out, ran over to Emmett, and said something in a low tone close to his ear. The mayor immediately stiffened and began shaking his head. He turned stiffly around with a grim look and walked back inside City Hall.

More people collected in the plaza, wondering what they had missed. Small knots of excited conversations started up. Rumors flew through the crowd. Brett looked at Lee; they were both guessing what had happened. The man in the first squad car they saw coming off Marion must have been declared dead at the hospital. Obviously the police had found no safe place to stop on the road after he'd been shot. He'd probably bled to death in the rear of that squad car and they'd now given up trying to revive him. The medics always gave the impression of making exhaustive efforts, and they probably had. Even if the case had been obviously hopeless, they wouldn't want to be sued for giving up too soon. Lee and Brett turned away and slipped through the crowd. A block away she seized his hand with an almost painful grip.

"That could've been *you!*" she said in a hoarse whisper. He knew this would be coming at some point. It had also been his first thought. "What will they do now?" she went on.

"I think the city will have to beef up its defenses. People out there must've been ready for the caravan to do that much damage. If they came after our armed vehicles on the road, they'll come into Outpost too. We started the hostilities, didn't we? Anyway, we don't know whether that was a cop or a van driver who died."

"Does it matter?"

"I guess not. One thing we've got going is that we're more organized than anyone between here and Bridger."

"I wonder what's left of Bridger now."

They walked another block before Lee spoke again. Her gaze was focused on the sidewalk and her arms were tightly folded. "Do you remember Newt?"

"Gingrich? Of course, he lost in the primaries last time around. I don't think he'll try again. I'll be surprised if we even have any more primaries now."

"Not that one. The Newt I'm thinking of was the little girl in the movie *Aliens*, the one who survived when her family didn't. When the rescue expedition pried her out of the ventilation system on that colony planet and asked her about the creatures that had wiped out all the others, she said in her shy little voice, with her eyes really big, as if she had no confidence at all in the people she was talking to, 'They mostly come at night.' How chilling that was."

Brett felt it again, although he hadn't seen the movie.

The attack on the caravan made them both wonder whether an important shift in the balance of power had occurred locally, and whether they'd sleep quite as well in the future. Had Emmett anticipated this? What if his plans had been formulated by the seat of his pants, like they apparently were with the arrival of Holly, or did the elaborate organizational façade he'd erected play a realistic role in determining the fate of all those who lived in Outpost? In any event, the tests had already begun.

On returning from City Hall, Lee and Brett stopped in the kitchen. She bolted the door behind them in the way she had only been doing at night. They didn't speak for a while.

"Don't ever call me Newt," she finally said. "I'm over it now. I don't intend to get spooked like that again."

"It was a great quote, though."

"It was so chilling in her little sing-songy voice. Thank God we're not in that situation. Our enemies are human, and we're better than they are."

"But are we? Better prepared, maybe, but any superiority we have isn't one of ethics, after our scavenger runs. Emmett has us feeling prepared, but what if he isn't as good as he sounds? What if the anger that fueled the attack against the caravan is more powerful than the planning behind our survival program? Those of us who live in town but outside the fortress walls of City Hall itself might pay the price for that miscalculation."

"As a survivor, you're going to have to be a little less evenhanded," Lee said. "We're going to come up against the less fortunate at some point down the road, and they outnumber us."

Brett didn't respond that he thought that encounter might best be made at the end of a gun barrel from now on. The less fortunate were going to be armed and ready for him the next time he went out with the scavengers. This note of indecision led to a quiet and reflective afternoon. Lee did some reading of *In Cold Blood*, while Brett checked the jerry cans of gas in the storage shed. He could only unscrew the caps so many times to know they were still full. Then he took out the cop's .38 revolver they'd picked up on the road and cleaned it with paper towels and some fine grade machine oil he'd found in the garage. It had the essential properties you wanted from a gun: it smelled good, and it felt cold and businesslike. He emptied the free-spinning cylinder and reloaded it to get comfortable with it in his hands. He tested the safety several times, suddenly knowing that they would use this lethal piece at some point. Lee glanced at him occasionally, but she didn't say anything. At about four o'clock Clayton appeared, as they thought he might.

"Let's go out back," Brett said. Often a light breeze rolled off the slope like a blessing this time of day, and one was already waiting for them outside.

"You went down to the garage," Lee said.

"Right. I thought DeShawn would know something, and he did. That boy is the child of intelligent parents, and it shows."

"He's our mole," Brett said.

"Who died?" Lee set down three empty glasses, getting to the point.

"Two of them, one of the officers from the rear car, the one riding shotgun, and the driver of the fourth van, the one immediately ahead of it. DeShawn didn't have their names. They left the van outside of Lawson with the driver's body in it. The shooting was too hot and heavy to be able to recover the body, and the van was too shot up to continue with a new driver."

"So, now we have our first two fatalities in the survival wars," Brett said. "They lost another van too?"

"The tires were shot out. They got the driver out OK, and he's fine. DeShawn didn't know about casualties on the other side."

"I guess they came back with nothing, then," Lee said.

"Nothing but experience. Besides the tragedy of two dead, it was a caution and a comeuppance, but it brought in no new food supplies. I guess Emmett is fuming. He's taking it personally as if it's a blow against his planning skills."

"I'm sure it is," Brett said. "I think that in his mind it's all about him. No one else has any input. He probably thinks he's the new MacArthur, and he's already planning his return to the scene of his defeat." He poured a round from the Appleton rum he'd bought at Stoddard's. "Outpost is still in a good position strategically. At least we've got that. Think of the other towns open on all sides."

"Well, they can't come at us from upstream on the Gunpowder River above where the lake opens out, because it has no landing and you'd have to traverse a run of white water four miles long. So it'll either be a frontal assault at those barriers on the dam end of town, where the caravans come in or leave now, or they'll climb over the slopes here and come down on us." Clayton pointed at the craggy hills above. This close to the dam end of town, eight blocks of houses lay between them and the base of the slope.

"Hard to imagine any force coming down over those shear drops and gravel slides," Brett said. "They'd be likely to get to the bottom much faster than they intended, and then be in no shape to take up positions. If they tried to rappel down, the slopes are too varied. They'd be crawling half the time, and you could pick them off like flies on a picnic table."

"Sometimes people still do it as a challenge, though," said Lee. "I've heard there are a few places where it's possible."

"Emmett's decided to set up gun positions on the two buildings overlooking the barricades. At night floodlights will illuminate every inch of the road coming in. If anyone gets close, they'll be cut down."

"What've we got for weapons?" Lee asked. "Police pistols don't have much range." She was obviously thinking about the people who had fired at the van so ineffectively on the road. They still had one bullet hole near the top on the passenger side.

"DeShawn said that Emmett had picked up two

machine guns and a decent supply of ammo from an anonymous collector in town. I have the feeling they weren't legal, but the mayor didn't have to twist the man's arm to get them, either. The guy's a survivalist. With a finite supply of ammunition, and none of it replaceable, they won't be getting much training, I suspect."

"Old guns," Brett said. "I wonder how reliable they are if they're from World War II? The kind where the bullets are on belts?"

"Korea."

"So they're still over sixty years old. I wonder what else that collector has. Maybe mortars?"

"More machine guns, I would guess, otherwise he wouldn't have given up two of them. I'm sure Emmett walked away with an inventory in his back pocket."

"Here's to freedom," Brett said, raising his glass. Clayton gave him an odd look before he raised his, as if unsure what that word now meant.

"Health and long life," said Lee. "I mean it more than ever."

Without more comment, they sat and scanned the rocky slope for a while. Brett was studying the detail.

"As a courtesy, of course," Clayton added, "the city garage body shop will putty up and repaint those two vans. They'll be good as new."

"Of course," Lee said. "How about the two widows? Will they also be as good as new?"

Clayton suddenly looked uncomfortable in his role as the Oracle of Outpost.

"DeShawn didn't say anything about that, and I didn't ask him. He doesn't get the official stuff any faster than we do, only the scuttlebutt, which often has more detail and less spin."

"I would avoid the entry area of town for a while," Brett said. "Unless I was in a convoy of some kind, and armed to the teeth."

At seven minutes before three o'clock the following morning the first gunfire inside Outpost erupted within Brett's dreams, four shots ricocheting like pinpoints of fire inside his skull. He and Lee both sprung upright at the same instant, clawing at their separate sheets. Brett gradually realized that the shots weren't coming from inside the house, or even in the yard.

"Don't turn on the light," he whispered hoarsely. His right hand probed the drawer of the nightstand between the beds and extracted the police pistol by touch. He knew the safety was on so he wouldn't blow a hole into the wall or either of them by touching the trigger before any other part of it. He rose and crept away from the bed. Holding his breath as he stood at the window, he inched back the curtain to peer out on a black night over the front yard. No moon dimmed the faint pale glow of the stars. The only illumination came from a streetlight half a block down at the corner. Two porch lights flared to life across the street farther toward the dam. Paint a luminous target on yourself, he whispered, shaking his head as he watched silhouettes inside those houses moving uncertainly behind the thin curtains. Let's turn on the lights in the trenches, he thought, because that's where we all are now. But their glow lit nothing prowling the street.

Clayton's house remained blank and remote, cave-like beneath its extended eaves, yet Brett sensed his restless unseen presence beneath the overhang, as his watery eyes probed the vacant pavement. Clayton seemed too focused on events around him to ever have time for a good night's sleep. Brett stood at the curtain for a long time barely blinking, his eyes flickering over the unmoving darkness beyond. He had never stared so hard at nothing in his entire life. The silence was dense. In spite of the barricades, someone must have gotten through, and now the game had changed forever. The front lines had arrived.

A sudden skittery chatter of distant machine gun fire made him jump. The barrel of the .38 in his hand dashed against the glass, but his finger wasn't on the trigger. Outside, no response followed from any single-shot weapons. For a moment, nothing more was audible. But as Brett strained to listen, what might have been in the distance the fading throaty rattle of a motorcycle exhaust rose thin and defeated on the moist night air. Or was that sound only a note of approaching thunder, still too far away to make out clearly?

"Brett! Brett." He felt more than heard Lee's urgent throaty whisper near his ear. Her chest was heaving against his back and her fingers traced a fluttering path from his neck over his shoulders before they connected beneath his throat. He moved the pistol to the windowsill beyond her accidental reach. "Please don't go out there. Please?" she whispered. "I need you here!"

He couldn't respond for a moment, since her tone suggested more was coming. When nothing did, he said, "I won't. Emmett must have this one under control." He automatically mouthed these words that he didn't believe.

When he turned she pressed her face against his neck for a moment. Her cheeks were wet. He set the pistol on the desk and drew her away from the curtain. "Lee, Lee. We'll get through this." He couldn't see her face in the darkness. Then he felt the touch of her lips on the back of his hand.

After a while, alert and restless, she released her grip on him and they went back to bed. Outpost had lost both its isolation and its innocence in that first outburst of gunfire. It had gone from a refuge in the hinterland to an exposed position on the front lines and they both knew it.

They slept no more during the long restless stretch toward morning, breathing silently in a separateness of listening. Edgy in the expectation of the next eruption of gunshots, which never came, they lay with their eyes open, until, near five o'clock, the dawn traced the edges of the opaque curtains in gold.

18

In the morning a murmuring crowd paced both sides of the Outpost entry blockade, avoiding the roadway, where nothing was moving. Brett had made breakfast for Lee and walked her to the high school where she had counseling duty. Describing it as a minor task when the town was about to explode, she was not excited about going. Then, like many others, Brett headed to the scene of last night's battle.

Scattered evidence remained of the violence, centered on a streaked pool of blood thirty feet before the barricades. It was now covered with gray powder clotted in reddish lumps. Four orange hazard cones marked the perimeter of the stain. No one had to be encouraged to avoid it. A battered Harley-Davidson with saddlebags covered in fake zebra skin leaned on its kickstand to one side. The front fender was bent into the flattened tire and the angle of the fork appeared to be wrong. Nearby a police pickup waited with a low trailer in tow. A wide plank sloped up from the pavement to the trailer bed. On the other side of three police cars Clayton stood talking with DeShawn, who was wearing a gray striped mechanic's coverall and a baseball cap bearing the logo of the New Orleans Zephyrs, the minor league team. When Clayton moved away, DeShawn pried the fender off the tire and three other mechanics rolled the motorcycle up the plank and secured it upright in the pickup.

Brett intercepted Clayton as he crossed the street.

"A lovely day in the neighborhood," he said, looking out ironically from under his straw hat.

"At the end of a short night's sleep. Did DeShawn have the scoop?"

"One was killed and one got away. Emmett is going to burn the body, of course, as a precaution. They took it out there half an hour ago."

"I'm surprised they couldn't have hit both of them."

"When they set the guns up, they were too wary of using ammunition they couldn't replace, so they didn't ever practice."

"This was the practice. I suppose that makes sense in a *Catch 22* kind of way. Who was the dead man?"

Clayton shrugged. "No ID. We won't know for a while, maybe never. He was the Unknown Soldier for the other side. The state computers are down now so they can't get the registration records on the Harley, and nothing on the fingerprints, if the guy even had a record."

"Two bikers hardly make an assault team," Brett said. But that statement didn't make him feel more secure—two bikers were more than enough to throw the future into question.

"Right. It looks more like a couple of scouts who thought they might slip in at that hour of the morning. They couldn't take much away with them, but they could check out the scene here. The bikes would thread their way through those staggered road barriers faster and better than cars."

"Firing pistols as they went?"

"Odd, isn't it?" Clayton shook his head. "You've got to keep your hand on the right handle grip because that's your gas. It's spring loaded, so if you let go in a crisis, it turns back to idle, exactly what you don't want when the other side is coming at you."

"So they're firing left handed."

"Exactly. They're taking evasive action, and firing with their wrong hand, in most cases. Shooting, they can't operate the clutch with that hand, because it has the gun, and they can only look ahead because they're threading their way through the barriers. Feels to me like it's the gang that can't shoot straight, or scarcely at all."

"Did we take any hits?"

"No. But I imagine the one that survived will be back with some of his friends before too long. This was only a probe.

Scope out the town, locate our gas stations and our supermarket. They'll never get through the barriers here again. Emmett will double up security after this. DeShawn says he's heard scuttlebutt about putting up a bunker on each side of the road leading to the barriers. They'd be offset, so they wouldn't be shooting directly across the road at each other. But coming up, the invaders would then have to run the gauntlet in a three-way field of fire."

Coming over the slopes to the west now looked better as an invasion route. Yet, that would have the disadvantage of making their vehicles unusable. All the invaders would have to be on foot, but still, Outpost was essentially undefended on that side. Clearly the intruders' first goal would be to commandeer some cars for their escape. If they could maintain secrecy coming in, they could rush the machine gun posts from behind, and then the bunkers, if they'd been built by then.

"Is Lee working today?"

Brett nodded. "Counseling. It's her first time. She was nervous."

"You mainly let people talk about what's bothering them," said Clayton. "She'll be good at that, because she doesn't always run on like I do once I start on some train of thought. Lee knows a lot, although she doesn't always let on that she does. I think you got lucky when you met her."

"Don't I know that? She stepped into my life at a critical juncture."

"She said you were both on a side road above Marshy Flats."

"That's right, but I wasn't running anywhere. I'd left the evacuation behind."

"No? You weren't exactly going back, though."

"I guess you could say that at the moment I met Lee, I thought I was still working, trying to deliver my cargo. That was my business. You probably heard me say that to Holly."

Clayton looked skeptical. "And you were trying to ignore the outbreak? That would've been hard."

"Not at all, I'd only just found out about it, and I was

still hoping to get up to Bridger and drop off my packages. I thought I could get around the traffic slowdown on Highway 36. That's when I really got lucky. I hit the jackpot that day, Clayton."

"Even more than with Lee?"

"I mean in some ways that were more for the benefit of others than for me. Millions of others."

Almost to his own surprise, Brett told Clayton the story that only Lee had heard. Clayton always appreciated the big picture and Brett knew he'd love this key piece of what was still at that time a major puzzle. How had the terrorists delivered all those packages of the bacillus to their widely dispersed destinations? Brett had thought about it ceaselessly since, except for the time he'd spent thinking about Lee and survival. The fishnet floats had been, he felt, the delivery system that was mainly used for the Gulf and other coastal areas. No one would look at them twice. They could unload them by the dozen at Fisherman's Wharf in San Francisco and drive a pickup full of them right into the city. From there, they could wipe out Northern California, Oregon, Arizona and Nevada.

Gloucester, Massachusetts could be the intake for Boston and points north in New England. For the four that entered through Marshy Flats, the source could have been somewhere on the Gulf or the Caribbean, where there were several governments unfriendly to the U.S. In other locations, the packaging would have been designed to fit in with the local scene. In Washington, DC it could have used the portfolios that transported legal briefs or drafts of pending legislation. In Seattle, it would be the one-pound bags that were usually used for ground or whole-bean coffee. This was a plan that had been constructed and carried out in the minutest detail by people that knew the culture and ways of the United States intimately. American converts to ISIS had been popping up all over the landscape with valid passports. They would have had both an inside and an outside crew. If the ones inside died in distributing the spores, no problem, since suicide is a standard feature of terrorist attacks.

Clayton's eyes only got bigger as Brett went through this. "You are the devil incarnate!" he said.

"You flatter me. It's more like the devil repentant, if you can imagine that, and barely in time." He told him of the pyre in the forest near Dundee.

"And Lee was there with you to see that?"

"She was my witness and my support."

He closed by promising to show Clayton the manifest with the packages listed for Little Rock, Corpus Christi, New Orleans, and Dallas. He hadn't been bragging during this conversation, but Clayton's comment on Lee needing to be a listener in her job, had gotten Brett going. He couldn't have vented to anyone else.

"You are," Clayton said solemnly, "both a witness to, and an actor in history. And this will prove to be the biggest event of our time. People will want your perspective when this is finished."

He almost laughed. "Good luck with that." Brett wondered again, knowing what he knew, whether he ought to write something about the attack, his own perspective of not only the delivery system, but the entire story, as told by someone who had lived it on the ground. At that moment a black Ford Expedition with smoked glass on all sides except the windshield pulled up. Brett felt like he'd used up his fifteen minutes of fame and it was now time to step back into the faceless crowd.

After he and Clayton parted company he went home at about 10:30, thinking to read for a while, but he was too restless to get into it. Naturally, he didn't have any of his own books along. He would've been happier delivering something or playing his Dobro, which was still back in Marshy Flats. It suddenly occurred to him that he might at that moment borrow Lee's laptop and begin writing an account of the disaster, starting with that first moment behind the bait shop when he realized the fourth package was gone. He hadn't written a word since just after college, but the idea of taking it up again had never entirely left his mind.

He could also have gone into the kitchen and started an elaborate dinner for Lee when she got back—they hadn't used the barbecue grill yet—but their larder was too spotty. The idea of hummus and sliced pineapple with hot sauce on crackers didn't move him, even with a steamy bowl of oatmeal on the side. Retirement, forced or not, wasn't for him, either. They hadn't looked at the fatality reports that morning so he decided he'd catch up—not so much on the death toll, but on the action in Washington, if that's where the action was now, beyond the cleanup. With all the local excitement he'd been neglecting the national problems. He also didn't mind the idea of spending a few hours alone, which was his normal condition.

When the television picture came up, the first scene to appear was a crowd lining a broad street behind a barrier. Initially Brett thought it was a historical film clip. Lately people in large numbers had been displayed only in piles. He'd last seen an active crowd on television when the world was still young, a week and a half ago. Yet, none of them were in uniform, another shock. The camera pulled back to show a parade approaching, or at least a big marching band. Here were the uniforms. He wasn't certain what was behind the musicians, but it might have been long files of troops.

Beneath several banners, the Marine Band was the first group to advance in their blazing red uniform coats. The first banner read *God Bless America*, and they were playing *The Star Spangled Banner*. The band continued in close formation until it reached the viewing platform, where it stopped, executed a quarter turn in unison, and took five more steps forward to reassemble before halting again.

Facing the musicians from the front row, the CO stood at rigid attention. Thirty feet above him another banner swelled gently against the brilliant sky with the words, *God Bless Our Commanding Officer*. Behind him, in six or eight ascending tiers, stood ranks of uniformed officers that could have been either the regular military or the new government. None wore civilian clothes. From glimpses of the White House behind the viewing stand Brett realized this had to be Pennsylvania Avenue. Today was the second Wednesday of the epidemic, and it was also the Fourth of July, a fact he'd forgotten.

Clearly, the nation needed something to celebrate beyond the anniversary of independence from Great Britain. What he couldn't figure out was where the crowd had come from. They looked like people of all ages, even families. One troop of kids in uniform might have been a fourth grade class. Parents were holding their smaller children up to watch as if this were a historic occasion. Two women at the front row in wheelchairs were waving tiny flags. Was it a piece of theater? Anyone could sit in a wheelchair. Brett began to feel he was being too cynical. All the same, because it was so different from what they'd been seeing every day, it felt uplifting. If only Lee were there to see it. She needed a boost as much as he did.

The Marine Band finished with a flourish. The CO waited for the applause to fade before he held up his hand. His amplified voice erupted like another banner.

"I am *so* proud to be an American on this day of all days!" He waited for the vigorous applause that surged in waves through the audience to fade. "The challenges we face in these times are, more than anything, an opportunity to prove what we are, what we can do, and what we will become after our triumph is complete!" His index finger punctuated each phrase. Another round of wild applause followed. Brett thought the CO was taking a good line. Apprehensive as he was, he realized he felt better about the man than he had about any president in quite a while. None of them had moved him.

"We are the people who *made* this land, and we are no different today, even during this terrorist attack, than we have always been, since, make no mistake, we are made of the same stuff. We are the ones who turned the tide in Europe in World War I. (Applause.) We are the ones who saved democracy in Europe in World War II, to say nothing of restoring hope in Asia at the same time! (More applause.) Was it easy then? Never, not for a single moment!" The CO's voice grew hoarse with emotion. "Ask your fathers and grandfathers who were there, the ones who made it happen. Ask them about Korea and Vietnam. Yes, we have had our ups and downs, but *we are still here!*" After underlining these words, the CO's voice grew measured, inviting a more focused attention. "And did we make bitter sacrifices? Always! Are we distressed now? Yes we are, and to our very core! But only for the loss of our loved ones, not for our future." His voice tapered to a delicate point that everyone strained to hear. "And our hopes are still intact! They are unsinkable!

"Yet even as we grieve, we are sustained by the tradition we celebrate once again today, on the anniversary of the founding of our republic. At the same time, we are grateful for this opportunity to establish a new America on this same date, to recreate it practically from scratch! It is our value system and our way of life that still survives, and will always endure! Our strength is in the continuity of our institutions, the single-minded dedication of our people, your neighbors and mine. Standing shoulder to shoulder in our unity of purpose, we will rebuild on the foundations of the old to create a fortress of the new! Victory in the current crisis is only the first step! What will emerge in the glorious dawn of tomorrow will be the toughest, most experienced and creative nation that has ever existed on this earth in all of history."

As he drew off his glasses, the CO's voice grew cold and dense, drained of any passion other than raw determination. His eyes narrowed. "And make no mistake: we are more resilient now than we have ever been!" He spoke each of these words as if they stood alone. "The cowardly attack we have absorbed is no more than a futile taunt from the envious and the ignorant, from people who face firmly backward to a past that can never be revived. Let us focus on the lesson to be learned here: the future belongs to us alone! And we will prove it!"

In the pause that followed the crowd suddenly went berserk as if on cue.

"Now we pause for a moment of silent prayer. Let us

lift up our hearts to the being who is the Father of us all."

The CO bowed his head. Most others in the viewing stand followed. The flags moved gently in the respectful breeze, but nothing else did. Unseen somewhere in the crowd, a toddler erupted in glee, and the sound of its spontaneous joy was instantly suppressed.

After another moment, the Marine Band took up *America*, and a rich baritone in the stands near the CO belted out the lyrics as if it were the climax of a Broadway show deep into a long and sold-out run. His face did not appear, but the cadence of his voice underlined the wave of patriotic feeling that ran through the crowd. Brett could feel it too, and he nearly put his hand to his heart. As the last chorus ended, the band turned, reformed, and resumed their march up Pennsylvania Avenue. As the last of their ranks passed the podium, an enormous cloud of red, white and blue balloons leaped skyward. Three battalions of Army troops followed the band. After a space of a hundred yards had opened behind them, the crowd surged almost as if on cue from the sidewalks around the barricades and rushed toward the viewing stand, where over the rigid shoulders of his honor guard, the CO reached out to press the eager hands and kiss the lofted babies of his loyal subjects. The flash of camera lights blinded all reason. More than anything else, it was an act of theater that affirmed something was really happening, although in its lack of specifics, few could have said exactly what, other than that it had been a great day to be there.

As stirring as it was, the CO's presentation seemed a bit brief to Brett, but on the other hand, this was an event stage-managed for government-controlled television. No opposing view would be presented afterwards—General Parker could make his position clear with no fear of contradiction by the other side, a side that with each passing day was less and less capable of definition. Who could disagree? It was not obvious who would want to oppose this, given the circumstances. Brett had become accustomed to every chief executive's statements being immediately contradicted. He had also heard that a public nurtured on sound bites and video games absorbs brief messages more easily. If you couldn't make your point in this snippet of time, even less could you bring it across in a two-hour stem-winder of the old style. The CO's handlers obviously knew this. He had surrounded himself with media pros, almost as if he had been prepared for the epidemic.

It did not escape Brett, as he sat there for a while in silence after he'd turned off the television, that for the first time in one of the CO's announcements or appearances, no mention had been made of the current President. Was the CO now running on his own authority? It was a subtle shift, but a shift nonetheless.

The celebration may not have been entirely finished, but it was enough for Brett. Nor did he want any loyal news team to explain what he'd witnessed, even though he had never seen anything like it. The CO had made reference to his relationship with the President in every other speech he'd given. He claimed the President often called him Ed, but now it was as if he didn't need the chief executive any more. It was General Edwin A. Parker III who was now identified with Independence Day patriotism, the annual celebration of the American Revolution, and now, with the triumphant march going forward, even with the future itself. Brett suspected that no one would be calling the CO *Ed* any time soon.

The viewing stand was positioned to enable the cameras to pick up the White House in the background, a kind of patriotic mural wallpaper displayed for its symbolic value. Most likely the venerated and, by now, thoroughly disinfected residence would have only a curator in place, like a house museum where some historic person had once lived at the height of his career and power, but no longer. At nightfall the deepening shadows would reflect the great cadaverous characters of history that had passed over the waxy polished floors of these corridors, and in the small hours of the night, the echoes would replay the moans of the defeated politicians, the cynical laughter of the victors. The groans of women who'd been spirited in through the back door during the Kennedy years, finding themselves in bed with scarcely time to remove their shoes. The frustrated weeping of Richard Nixon, punctuated by his taped obscenities. A long, complex, and occasionally noble tradition was suddenly grounded. To save energy, most of the lights in the executive mansion were now kept off, and the few visible through the windows at night were very low wattage, as if to hold down expenditures for an institution that no longer mattered.

After a while Brett nearly staggered to his feet as he went into the kitchen for a glass of cold water to clear his head. He felt stiff in all his joints, as if he'd recently been too passive in trying to maintain his own life as he witnessed the great crash and upthrust of historic events around him. How does one person take a stand against tyranny on a national scale? And what if the new tyrant is the only person with a real shot at making the country survive? If all his statements and surface mannerisms are benign, how does anyone parse that situation? What exactly was wrong with the CO, aside from the lack of legitimacy in his rise to power? He was a bastard politician, a de facto executive who nonetheless could do the job far better than the gaggle of callow bought-and-sold puppets he had elbowed aside. Was he the new Brutus standing next to the felled body of Caesar, now being dragged out of view of the cameras while a janitor cleared the floor of body fluids? At the age of thirty-eight, Brett began to feel he was either too old to figure this out, or too young.

Standing at the mottled yellow plastic laminate kitchen counter to load more ice into his glass, he noticed a tall plume of smoke rising about a hundred feet into the air above the northern edge of town. It hesitated at that altitude, then rolled over and dispersed to merge with the crosscurrents moving toward the other side of the dammed waters of the lake. This would be from the biker's body, the third to go up in the local crematorium. It defined him as yet another victim of this epidemic.

Brett stepped out the front door to see Clayton standing calmly on the grass watching him. It was Lee's brother's grass this time, where their neighbor waited near the curb with an unmoving rake upright in his hand. Brett couldn't help but smile. "I know I saw a leaf out here somewhere," he said, "but I can't find it right now. Can I get you a tall glass of cold water while you chase it down?"

"Sho' now. I'll come in with you if that's OK, and I'll drink it in the shade. I can always look for that leaf later when this wind dies down a bit." There was no air movement in evidence other than the winds of change, now howling. Clayton leaned the rake next to the doorjamb as he came in. At the sink Brett poured him some water and added two ice cubes. They went out back and sat under the umbrella. It covered the half of the table that Holly's trees missed at that time of day.

"A lot of symbolic props there, wouldn't you say? I'm thinking of the White House as a backdrop." Brett didn't have to ask whether Clayton had seen what he'd seen.

"Right, and I don't know if you were in the service or not, but the Marine Band is the President's house band. You'd never see it rolled out for a mere back office general like that. This CO could've been a staff officer, one who's never seen action, for Christ's sake."

"Watching it, my sense was that we've crossed over today. General Parker no longer needs the President of the United States. And where did they come up with that crowd? Were these people Washingtonians who just now happened to come back home for the show?"

"Well," Clayton said, "I can think of only four places that could furnish a crowd like that without inviting a whole lot of risk. Those cities are all listed on your package manifest, if my guess is correct."

"So they're all URD extras, and the cleanup of Washington was done at least partly with this ceremony in mind. In a sanitized city they could be brought in for a display like this, confined within a narrow disinfected perimeter, and then flown back before evening to be safe at home again in Dallas or Little Rock."

Clayton was nodding before he finished. "It shows

that the new leadership has a strong planning function. That's what we need most now. The old one couldn't have planned anything more complicated than a trip to the bank with a cheery smile and a thick bag of corporate campaign contributions."

"In the CO we're looking at a man who's never accepted a campaign contribution, but do you still like what you see?" Brett asked quietly.

"I do because he's in motion." Clayton exhibited the calm smile of a tolerant man who is nonetheless not easily deceived. "I'll ask them later whether they had my vote or whether anyone had a right to be standing on that podium today. Let's do our survival business first and get it done right. After that, I 'spect the country will be in a very forgivin' mood about all the irregularities that cropped up in the process. If no one else can do it at all, then you don't always have to do it perfectly yourself to be the best and win the game."

"And that's what the CO and his team are depending on, isn't it?"

"Bet on it. I am too."

"I only now realized that something was missing from the screen today," Brett said.

"Right, and I also saw that. The counter box was gone from the bottom left side, that ever distracting roulette wheel of fate as the dead are spun off into eternity."

"Was it too distracting for today's celebration? Too depressing?"

"That, or like the President himself, it was not properly aligned for the CO's new image, which is now being marketed unsupported by the old regime. We'll see if the death counter ever comes back, other than for the dead, of course."

19

At the high school Lee Carter had spent most of the day in a small airless room with high ceilings where the teachers ate lunch, corrected papers, played cards, and groused about Dr. Johnson, the principal. A tiny prison window hung at the top of the wall, out of reach. Under three neon ceiling fixtures, one of which was flickering uncertainly, the walls were painted off-white and bore the marks of numerous bumps and bangs from faculty comings and goings. The coffee maker badly needed cleaning. A corkboard held overlapped announcements of faculty meetings, schedule changes, extra-curricular assignments, union meetings, and garage sales, now mostly out of date because school was not in session. Below it a card prohibited smoking. Behind a freshly printed sign in block capitals that read COUNSELOR, Lee sat at a small bare table in the corner wondering why she had volunteered for this. The only answer she found was that she had to volunteer for something, and the city's choice for her had flattered her developing psychology skills. It was better than waiting tables in Forrest Beach.

Wearing a white silk blouse and black slacks, the best clothes she'd packed, Lee had dressed for credibility, but now felt she was overdressed for an occasion for which almost no one had showed up. She now wished she'd worn jeans and brought a book. By two-thirty she'd seen only two people, and one of them had come to vent her frustration that she'd been given so little free food from the foraging caravans, a condition Lee had struggled to sympathize with, since the per person distributions had been equal. All people had to do was show up with identification and point to their names on the list. She tried to think what mental state was behind this quibble, and when she couldn't come up with anything more than a sense of entitlement, Lee suggested the woman approach the mayor's office directly with her grievance. She tried not to think what had happened to Doug when he had done just that.

Shortly before three o'clock a woman stomped into the office and pulled up the chair before Lee's table. She was of medium height and almost gaunt in a way she couldn't have managed in the short time since the food shortages began. Lee immediately felt the issue was not groceries.

"I've got a serious problem and I want you to listen carefully, OK?"

"That's why I'm here." Lee made her face into a welcoming mask as she pulled a sheet of paper from the center drawer and picked up a pencil.

"You've got to find my sister. I don't care how you do it."

"OK. Your sister is missing. Could she be ill? Was she coughing? When did you see her last?" Lee was thinking of the story given out by the mayor's office of Doug getting the disease and wandering off to die alone to save the town from being exposed to it. It hadn't seemed plausible then, but all the same, if this was a genuine case...

"I don't think so. It looks to me like the mayor's got her."

"And your name is?" Lee had already realized this had to be Holly's sister.

"Denise."

"Why do you think the mayor has her?"

Denise hesitated a moment, her lips compressed. "I know she's been seeing him, and he's ruthless. The man's a pig."

"Have you talked to the police?"

"They're just as political as Emmett. They've been absorbed into his new power structure. The city council hasn't met since this started."

"Look, Denise. I'm here to help people with emotional issues related to the epidemic. This isn't a good fit."

Denise leaned forward and bared her teeth. "You don't think I'm emotional? You don't think this came out of the epidemic? Doug died in this epidemic!" She gripped the edge of the table with both hands as if she was planning to flip it over.

"I realize you're in an emotional state, but the remedy is beyond my sphere. Why not approach City Hall about it directly, not the police, but the mayor's office? You can't believe that Emmett is holding her prisoner. He's got to let you see her if you're right."

"Does he? I shouldn't have come here. You're one of them too." She got up and moved to the door.

A subtle grin crept across Lee's face once she was gone. She had never been accused of being part of the power structure before. Even if it wasn't a perfect fit, it felt good. She could imagine what Holly felt.

20

After his conversation with Clayton, Brett headed for Stoddard's, feeling like he was running late. Normally he went with Lee because the limit was $100 per person, so they could come out with $200 in groceries. But the ceremony in Washington had left him uneasy. The failure of the last scavenging expedition had underlined the problem with maintaining food supplies. It looked inevitable that mass starvation was on the horizon. A poster had been put up at City Hall, where he'd stopped on the way, announcing that a farmer's market was being organized in the parking lot of the high school, but gasoline supplies were still a problem for anyone bringing in fresh produce for sale. One logical option would be to grant the farmers a gasoline ration proportional to the amount of food they brought in, but that would cut into the city's own supplies, and no more was coming in. Another idea was to press horses and wagons into service, but apparently they were in short supply. It must have given Emmett food for thought, an expression he probably didn't use much in public anymore. Brett also wondered who was going to vouch for these farmers being free of the contagion.

The Stoddard's parking lot was busy, and security had been mounted at the driveways going in. People must have started leaving the store with their shopping carts and pushing them home as a way to save gas. A large sign read, *Carts Must Stay on the Property*. Brett had walked because it was easy enough to carry his allotment of groceries a few blocks. Some couples brought three kids and spent $500. No one could argue with that because each of those kids was eating too. All the varieties of sweetened cereals must have been among the first items to go.

Inside, the guard dog was no longer at the entry and Stoddard's resembled a going-out-of-business sale. Maintenance had declined with the inventory. Empty wrappers littered the floors as if people were eating in the aisles. It was now a shopping lunch. Many shelves were entirely bare. People were dumping groceries in their carts without reference to what they were, since they could be bartered later in a street market. A lot of them had furtive looks; desperate and almost sullen as if they were contemplating how much worse this was going to get before it got better, if it ever did. A few kids were crying and more would be later. Being a stranger in Outpost, Brett didn't recognize anyone, and they all looked like they didn't belong in Stoddard's. He felt he didn't either. Brett realized that his sense of being part of a community was gone, an early casualty of the epidemic. He was surrounded by individuals trying to survive against the odds, just as he was.

He was able to get brown rice, lima beans, canned spinach, powdered milk, and three plastic bags of dried exotic mushrooms from France whose names he couldn't pronounce. Two tins of sardines packed in cottonseed oil also found their way into his cart, a kind of slippery packing medium that he'd read some people avoided because it most often came from genetically modified crops. He figured he could go for it this time—so many other things or people could kill them first that he was willing to risk it. Spices to put on any of it were still plentiful. Brett could've bought enough paprika to coat the van from grill to tail pipe and plaster over the bullet hole with what was left over. He added an expensive bottle of Finnish vodka to the cart because he saw almost no other alcohol left other than crème de menthe, and he was still under the $100 spending limit. Rum of any variety was long gone. He could have picked from all the clothespins or mops that he wanted.

Enough window and toilet cleaner remained to keep a dozen households shining for years. As the dust and rain blew through their shattered windows, he thought.

It would've been almost funny if it wasn't so clear that what was coming next were bare shelves behind the bolted doors of Stoddard's. Brett knew this was his final trip. Over the curling wrappers on the floor, the starving rodents would be circling in despair, eyeing each other's necks. Then where would people go to find food? They'd be even more dependent on Emmett. Looking around as he left, Brett didn't spot the black Ford Expedition with smoked glass waiting in the parking lot. The mayor already knew quite well what was coming. Making no judgment, Brett hoped Emmett was ready for it, since that would mean he was planning for other things more grave than that in the future. People would eventually be dying of starvation, and then what—cannibalism?

Looking like she'd spent the day stuck in heavy traffic, although not much was moving on the streets, Lee returned at ten minutes after four and dropped her house keys on the counter. She glanced at the two empty grocery bags folded up next to the sink but didn't say a word. There was an unpleasant twist to her mouth that Brett had never noticed before, even during their arguments. He knew he was looking stressed too, but he tried to let her variety of stress dominate because it was fresher, and he at least had been able to vent with Clayton.

"How was it?" Brett asked in an affirmative tone. Rubbing his hands together, he noted the downturned corners of her mouth and the tense knit to her forehead, almost like a cable stitch. When he got no immediate answer, he pulled her into his arms and held her tightly for a while. After spending his day mostly alone, Lee felt good against him, but she was too distracted to respond. When she started to squirm, he released her.

"I only saw three people today, and I expected a crowd. I don't know why the clinic thought it had to stay open on the Fourth of July. People aren't that desperate yet, or at least they don't want to admit they are. I think it was mainly so Emmett could look like he was doing something."

"But that kind of light attendance must have been good for you, right? Not too many problems? Mostly a slow day?" He quickly sensed that slow didn't necessarily mean good. Being busy at least would have given her less time to reflect and fret. From his own day, he already knew that helpless reflection on events beyond his influence was the new killer of morale.

"Holly's sister came in. She was the last of the three. Aside from being bored, I was really OK until then."

"Ah! And she said? Maybe you can't talk about it, though, being a therapist and all now. It's about professional ethics, right?" He said this to encourage her.

"Screw that. She said to me, 'you've got to find my sister. I don't care how you do it.'"

"Of course, Lee. But that was sensible, right? Maybe what she really needed was a detective."

"She already knew she couldn't go to the police. Practically the first thing she said was that they'd been politicized by Emmett."

"What did you tell her?"

Lee shrugged, pacing back and forth across the kitchen with her arms folded. "What could I say? I was sympathetic, but I told her I wasn't an investigator. I said I was mainly there to listen to people who had problems dealing with the epidemic and all its side effects, and I had no power with the city government." She started waving her arms in a circular motion as she said this, as if she could fly away.

"Then I don't know what else you could've done. Who's going to confront them now? Emmett can shut us down and starve us out. I know it's an old line, but you can't fight city hall. I never used to believe that, but now I do."

"That's what she said as she walked out the door. She tried to slam it but it's on one of those closers that moves slowly enough so the flies can come in after you."

270

"The city controls all the resources now, and besides, Holly went over to Emmett of her own accord."

"That's what we think. We don't know that."

"You know what's going to be the next most valuable commodity, beyond gasoline, even beyond rum for Clayton?"

"What? Drinking water, I suppose, I don't know." She sighed and then shrugged wearily, evidently thinking more about Holly, her escape or her abduction. "I don't even know what we're doing any more, OK? I just want to live through this. Is it support?"

"Information," Brett said, answering his own question with a word that suddenly didn't seem right. "It's getting scarcer and scarcer. Soon we'll all be dullards because we have nothing to base our decisions on."

Lee didn't respond, her eyes distant as she shook her head. When she first came in he'd been eager to tell her about the Independence Day celebration in Washington, but it no longer seemed like the right time. She wasn't ready to let go of the frustrations of the day. It made Brett realize how long it had been since either of them had worked in the real world. The formal economy hardly existed anymore. Barter would be the new economy once people realized their paper money was backed by the full faith and credit of an entity no one could find—the *old* federal government. Effectively, dollars were now backed only by habit and memory. It was a nostalgia currency, about as valid as steampunk. Like Confederate bank notes, soon it would be a collectable relic, but no longer spendable. People would soon start to put the bills into plastic sleeves in little albums.

"I need to talk to Holly face to face. That's the only way I'm going to be able to forget about this." She was speaking to the sliding window over the sink.

Brett now realized that to Lee, Holly had become a metaphor for any woman's survival, for having some vestige of control over her own fate. "OK, I can see that. But does Holly want to talk to you? You're much easier to find than she is. She could've taken a City Hall car over here and dropped by for a chat if she felt any urgent need. I think she might be embarrassed about what happened to Doug. I hope she is. Anyone else would be."

"I don't care about that, Brett. I'll force the issue. I don't like what's going on here."

"I can believe that." If you think this is bad, you should look at Washington now, he thought, not ready to bring that up yet. "Where does Emmett live?"

"I don't know. Clayton would know. He's on top of everything that happens in this town."

"I think we're lucky that he is. So let's ask him, but he already told me he doesn't know Holly that well."

"Then bring that rum bottle along," Lee said. "We'll find out what he does know. I'm tired of getting kicked around and handed announcements and questionnaires."

Six minutes later, after Lee had changed out of her counseling clothes and hung them up, she and Brett resembled a couple of neighbors casually walking across the street to Clayton's house for a cocktail. Back in Marshy Flats social mixing had not been that common among blacks and whites, not that relations were hostile, but their paths and habits were different. Brett didn't know what the norms were in Outpost, but he grasped the current necessities well enough to know that only the present mattered.

They stood waiting on his stoop after Lee rang the doorbell. The brass plate it was mounted in was a bronze image of Mickey Mouse in profile, with the black plastic button standing up as the bulb of his nose. Brett didn't hear any movement within the house. After a moment he rang it a second time and got nothing more. They walked around to the back to see if he was sitting on his screened porch, but Clayton wasn't in view.

Returning to the front yard, they both saw the curtained light in Holly's windows at the same moment. It also gleamed in the bedroom closest to their house, on the shady side. Lee grabbed Brett's arm and started running back across the street. He followed, pausing to slip the rum bottle into their curbside mailbox before he joined her on Holly's front step.

Through the closed hollow-core front door they felt the bone-crushing thump of a rock baseline cranked up to subwoofer dimensions. The outer walls with their turquoise shake siding nearly bulged with the vibration. After they rang four times the door opened a crack. Holly's eye makeup had run onto her cheeks and her single visible eye had a wild look, as if the pair no longer matched. She pulled the door open to introduce them to her own brand of hell.

"So why have I left Emmett?" she yelled before they could say anything. "That's what y'all want to know now, right?"

"I...well, ah," said Lee, half audibly. One hand flapped helplessly in the air as if sudden nerve damage had developed in her wrist as well as her hearing. Her counseling skills had abandoned her.

Holly whirled and reduced the sound system to sub-seismic levels. "Because Emmett's a fucking *asshole*, that's why. All he can think about is that his brilliant foraging expeditions are a failure, and how can he bring in enough food now? He had to break the news to the families of both the cop and that van driver kid who were killed. No food supplies are on the road, and they can't even get ahold of anybody in authority on the outside. You can watch the CO on TV, and from what he says you'd think it's coming together, but it isn't. Maybe it is somewhere, like Washington, but not in Outpost. Nothing is happening here. Especially with the mayor in bed."

As Holly fell into Lee's arms almost sobbing, she appraised Brett's reaction over Lee's shoulder through her smudged makeup. It gave her eyes a bruised look that suited her mood. After she recovered a moment later she motioned them into the kitchen where she poured out two glasses of wine to accompany the one she was already working on. That finished the bottle and she set it on its side in the stainless steel sink. "Now he's got someone taping all of the CO's broadcasts so they can be reviewed for secret content, like he's speaking in some kind of code language. Emmett can't talk about anything except strategy anymore, but he doesn't have one. Overnight he's gotten so boring I could scream!"

"Brett already predicted that the biggest threat here would be starvation, not the epidemic," Lee said in a calm, rational tone as if illustrating what one might sound like. She gently touched her glass to Holly's.

"I did. That doesn't make me profound, but after the first trip I made with the convoy I could see how we might keep the infected hoards out, but we still could never bring in enough food to keep 10,000 of our own people going. We'll end up eating the dogs and cats after a while." He went no further in this prediction as they followed Holly into the bedroom.

Even so, that was going to require a lot of Tabasco, Brett thought, unable to avoid picturing this. It had been in plentiful supply at Stoddard's and he should've gotten a couple more bottles while they still had the quart sizes. Holly looked like she wanted to spit at the idea. He had lost any thought of bringing up the fate of Doug. She was clearly far beyond that, and it wouldn't help now anyway.

Lee looked at her with sympathy. "What are you going to do now, Holly? I guess Emmett is finished, right? At least for you, I mean."

"Finished?" She paused to search for a more graphic word, but nothing else came from her lips for a moment. "He'll be damn lucky if he's not lynched by the townspeople after everything he's promised to do." She made a helpless gesture toward the bed, where her open white suitcase was either half packed or half unpacked. It was round, and for some reason it reminded Brett of Barbie Doll accessories. Small piles of clothes and a makeup bag were scattered around it on the coverlet. Three pairs of frivolous shoes.

Some of Holly's minimal underwear looked like it might be fun in more conventional circumstances, not that they'd ever see them again. Probably an entire week's supply could have been stuffed into a coin purse along with a roll of nickels, but he didn't allow himself to dwell on that image. When Holly didn't answer, Lee went on, all business with a gloss of sympathy. It was as if this was the job she'd been trying to do all day, and the first real chance she'd had to do it.

"Where would you go if you left? This is your house."

"Nowhere. Fucking nowhere, OK? I've blown my life right off the rails, and it's a chasm below."

Brett felt that if he hadn't been there, Holly might have expressed this differently. As far as he knew, this wasn't girl talk. He detected an element of save me in her tone.

Lee looked at him like it was his turn to say something.

"Holly," he said, framing his voice as if he were speaking to an unsatisfied customer, "please listen to me. We all feel like that right now, whether we think we've brought it on ourselves or not." He suddenly wondered if Lee shouldn't be saying this as the designated therapist, but it was too late to stop. "It isn't as much about you as it must feel, it's more about the times we live in. That context has changed everything. All of us have made mistakes recently in navigating these murky waters. Lee and I certainly have more than once." As if he and Lee had been screwing up at every moment. He didn't look at Lee because he couldn't think of a single example to back this up, aside from their occasional squabbles, but he was always good at winging it if people didn't examine what he said too closely.

Lee gave him a glance that was at once grateful and ironic.

"Do you mean that?" Holly asked with an appeal in her blurred eyes.

"I really do. This is all Improvisation 101. It's about faking it from step one and hoping it works."

"And being nimble enough to recalculate quickly when it doesn't," Lee said.

Holly sat on the edge of the bed with her knees turned out and her bare feet turned inwards, resting on an oval braided rag rug, her toes with their hot pink nails curled and touching. She put her elbows on her bare thighs and cradled her chin in her hands. "So you're faking it now too, Brett. I know that, but thank you for saying it. You guys are *so* together. It must be wonderful for you, Lee, to have a boy-friend who's not an asshole all the time. And you've only been with each other how long now?"

"Twenty minutes," he interjected, uncomfortable with the idea that they were in some archetypal relationship, an example to other couples in a crisis. To Brett, it had felt completely experimental from the beginning and it still did. This had been no time to try to define what it was, which he still couldn't have done at any time, and he disliked hearing other people characterizing it when he couldn't.

"It seems like twenty minutes sometimes," Lee said, unsurprised. "We have no history. History doesn't exist any-more. And now no future's on the way, either, so it's a nice balance. I just don't know." She glanced at Brett narrowly as if that was his cue.

"This isn't about history—the future's the issue. So you're thinking Emmett is faking it too?" he asked, feeling like this was the statement Holly had been inching toward for a while. He saw nothing coy or seductive in her expression anymore.

"Well, sometimes I think he is, but at others he can still be quite...powerful, you know? Or he could be, before this got so thick. I don't know how else to say it. Anyway, it doesn't matter, it's over and now I'm *alone* again."

Lee's expression suggested she regarded her with sympathy, but she said nothing more. Brett wondered whether he'd ever seemed powerful to her. She'd called him compe-tent, which had seemed like a breakthrough when she said it, but now that looked more like a starting point, although he could see how competence might be getting more rare and valuable in these deteriorating times.

"Listen, Holly, I suspect that Emmett is most effec-tive in areas where he has some prior experience," Brett of-fered. "The next critical event will be how he handles the coming wave of this assault. I expect it's going to be more about finesse and strategy than mere forcefulness this time."

Although this seemed sensible, even obvious, a sudden chill fell over the conversation as Holly pulled back and regarded him with frank alarm. Her eyes became huge. The startled look suited her, as if a high voltage electrical current was shooting through every part of her body, and not for the first time. She seemed to be subtly vibrating.

"The *coming* wave?" she asked in a voice that had declined into a deathly whisper, although her eyes were undiminished in size. "What are you talking about, like there are more waves of this? We already had the attack, didn't we? It's over. They lost, right? Did I miss something here… or did *he*? That's even what Emmett told me himself. We won! Now it's only the food problem again, which is bad enough." Her eyes narrowed as she spoke the final sentence. Clearly in Holly's view, Emmett, Inc. was now a penny stock, and anyone could snap up a thousand shares for the price of a bag of yesterday's popcorn.

Brett felt reluctant to bring up the subject of crisis strategy again, but how naïve could any of them afford to be? "Holly, we only sustained a probe here last night by two bikers. One of them died coming in, and the other survived to convey the desired information back to their source. My take is that they were spies from a neighboring town or part of a roving gang. Either way, it was a scouting expedition, like ants and bees do every day for a living. When they come back they'll have vans. That's the world we humans inhabit now too. You surely can't think that no more of them are on the way? Or do you?"

When she stared back at him with no response or comprehension, her lower lip quivering, he leaned forward but stopped short of touching her. His voice was nearly a whisper.

"Holly, we still have all the stuff they're looking for right here in Outpost. Can you see why I'm sure they'll be back?"

She put both hands over her face. "So Emmett was wrong again? Oh my god, you mean they really are coming back? I can see it. And I dumped Emmett because he was trying all the time to deal with this, after I called him a wimp and an asshole? All I wanted was a little more of him, and he just seemed to be slipping away hour by hour after the convoy was attacked. How could I have been so mistaken? *I can't live like this every day*! I need some certainty. Brett, help me out here, can't you?" She seized both his wrists.

He didn't respond. Certainty had been lost days ago on the road.

"Maybe you weren't wrong about Emmett when you two got together," said Lee, quickly moving to provide more options for her beyond Brett's statement, perhaps sensing his paralysis. "The choices we all make are important here. The people coming at us don't make Emmett a hero. Only he can do that. Let's watch what he does next. Can't we step back just a little?"

"But now all I want to do is cry!"

"Then have another glass of wine," Brett said, unable to conceal the weariness in his tone, releasing himself from her grip. "Eventually, we can all cry together; only you reached that point before the rest of us. Think of yourself as the emotional pioneer." She looked back at him wildly.

Ultimately they all sat on the floor leaning against the furniture, following Holly's example. With a little luck, any sudden gunfire coming through the windows would pass over their heads. Sensibly, they opened another bottle of wine. Brett had a way of staying rational in times like that—not that there had ever been any—because he felt more violence was coming and he needed to be ready.

"By the way," Lee said, "when I was counseling today your sister came in and wanted me to help her find you."

"She's only looking for food. I expected that."

Brett and Lee only looked at each other.

Holly gradually brought herself around by bringing more wine to pour. She refilled their glasses, serving it deftly with a little turn of her wrist at the last drop from the bottle, almost twisting it off. As a Southern woman, barefoot and wearing shorts too brief for most to go out in—not that they would keep her at home—she had still preserved a pride in her presentation that some would find admirable under these conditions, like wearing a hoop skirt in a tent city of refugees. The wine pouring ritual seemed to calm her like a tea ceremony.

Lee was monitoring Holly as if she was still in her new therapist's role and concerned about avoiding a failure on an early test case. Holly went into the bathroom after a while and returned with her face effectively reconstructed. It must have only now occurred to her that she'd appeared less than presentable for company when she opened the door. Except for her brief outfit, she looked ready to host a dinner party. Her charm had returned as if it came out of the same zippered bag as her eye shadow.

"So you think we can still win if they come back, Brett," she said with raised eyebrows. The line sounded rehearsed.

"I don't know," he said, realizing she would discover how little enthusiasm remained in his voice. "I still have my hopes. I've got a .38 caliber revolver and sixteen rounds. Although I couldn't hold them off forever with that, no one's going to get close to us for awhile."

"Us? A *gun*?" Holly's tone was breathless. Energized, her eyebrows went up.

Brett thought this sounded disingenuous. "But surely Emmett has a gun, Holly."

"Emmett has a lot of guns, but all of them are in the hands of other people. Some are even with the reserves. He thinks he can buy anything with city money."

"I see. So they could still turn against him too."

Lee looked at him sharply, as if she hadn't thought of this—might Emmett be taken down by a palace coup if he stumbled? But Brett wanted to learn more about the inside structure of City Hall. Holly could be his source.

She shrugged. "Like I did. I guess anyone else could too. Why not?" The coolness in her voice was telling.

Brett still wasn't sure what he was looking at in Holly. As soft and yielding as she seemed at times, she also had a hint of the predator in her, in her soft, yielding eyes, in the way her manicured nails gripped things, biting into flesh and drawing blood. She had a subtle way of moving into a man's personal space that could catch him by surprise when he discovered how close she was. She would be shaving him next, grooming him, trimming his eyebrows. He suddenly felt that Holly would have been very effective as a vampire, where all the real and permanent damage was done intimately, at close quarters, only a loving touch away. She also had a way of catching a man's attention and holding it, not yielding it to other people in the conversation.

At that moment, as he was trying to frame the next question, the key one he'd been moving toward, something about what Holly might know about the ammunition supplies in Emmett's possession, the City Hall siren went off in a desperate wail of protest. This was the warning system connected to the Paul Revere Units who scanned the slopes above town, launching the alarm against invasion.

They all jumped to their feet.

"Could this be a drill?" he asked Holly, as if she were the new city spokesperson.

She shook her head, her eyes wide again. "They already tested it on low volume. Someone must have really been spotted coming down the slopes."

"Then I'm going back home for the gun." Brett heard the breathless tone of his voice as he moved to the door.

"But wait, Brett, let's all go over there, then!" said Lee, giving her voice a cheerful, community activist tone. "Why split up now?"

"I would like to be where the gun is, too, if you don't mind," said Holly, quite sensibly, although her voice had taken on an oddly singsong quality.

When they reached the door of Lee's brother's house,

Clayton was already there waiting. He had their rum bottle and local mail in one hand, and held a single finger poised to ring the bell. "I'll take a little of that neighborly gun support now," he said as they came up. "If I neglected to say so earlier, I am a strong supporter of the Second Amendment, even if the rest of the Constitution isn't getting much respect at the moment. Evenin', Lee, Holly."

Inside they drew the curtains and kept the lights off. The sun was already behind the hills but the sky was still more light than dark. Oddly, they heard no shots for a while, as if the Paul Revere spotters had lost sight of the invader. Or was it a false alarm? Had they seen a deer skittering over the slopes and panicked? No one wanted to leave the house to check, and in the absence of phone service they had no way of knowing what was happening. The siren remained silent. Inaccessible police radios were the only local communication system that still worked. Thinking again of all the guns for sale at Blake's Nifty Store, Brett wished they were all armed. What babies they were then. Of course, everyone else was too.

"I don't like the sound of this much," said Clayton, dropping two ice cubes into his glass with a paired clink that was the only other noise they'd heard. "Or the absence of sound, rather. We should hear shooting now, lots of it. These people wouldn't have come over the hills unarmed. I think the city forces have lost track of the invaders."

"Does anyone else in town have ham radio?" Lee asked.

"No. That would be the solution now, wouldn't it? A police radio could work too. Maybe DeShawn can fix us up with one if we get through this. I should have thought of that before."

"You're not going out there," said Lee to no one in particular.

Brett didn't respond. Clayton shook his head. Other than that, they were all listening for what was coming next. It might have been about ten minutes, possibly longer. Time is hard to measure in that kind of situation, and none of them had looked at their watch when the alarm went off. Holly was wrestling the cork out of the throat of the wine bottle she'd brought along when gunfire erupted in the city below in the direction of the dam, and it didn't sound far away. Starting as a few single shots, they were suddenly answered by a barrage of machine gun fire, and then another. Now they knew where the invaders were—the attack was focused on the entry barriers, but this time it came from inside the city. Their hearts were pounding. Clayton gave Brett a sober look and took a longer pull at his rum. "Here we are, then," he said, in the tone he might have used at a wake. "We knew this would be coming."

Holly's mouth opened as if to squeal, but no sound came. Perhaps it was pitched too high to hear.

Brett sat on the sofa with the police revolver resting on the coffee table within easy reach. The barrel pointed to the side away from the others, directly at the front door. The cylinder was fully loaded and the ten extra cartridges were divided between his two front pockets. He wanted to say something reassuring, but only kept listening.

"I just know Emmett's all over this like a cheap suit," said Holly in a hushed voice, tossing her hair and running her fingers through it. His penny stock was now rising. "He has to be." Had the mayor seen it, the confident wave of her hand would have brought a surge of joy to his leathery heart. "I can see him right now standing at the communications controls of police headquarters, directing the action. Trust me on this one," she added before she brought out some other impressive reassurances with appropriate gestures. She raised her wine glass to a level of optimism that no one else could equal, and no one else lifted a glass to match her toast.

A final burst of machine gun fire followed. Even without being able to see it, the exchange sounded hopeless. It was clearly too brief, and then the short choppy bursts of single-shot guns continued, fading as if moving toward City Hall. If the machine guns began firing again, they would probably be cradled in the arms of the other side.

"This sounds very bad," said Clayton. "Excuse me ladies, but we'll be speakin' only the bald-faced truth here in the bunker tonight. I think the other side has now taken out both of our machine gun emplacements."

A plaintive gasp from Holly followed. Brett didn't care to hear this either. From her, it sounded almost sexual, and in this context, it meant surrender.

Lee eased back in the sofa with a look of consolidating her overextended expectations, condensing her hopes into a smaller channel, but she added nothing. Brett looked into Clayton's watery eyes. They held the glittery sheen of observed truth. As they suspected, Emmett, in his planning, had overestimated the barrier value of the scarred and wooded granite hills that had always sheltered Outpost. Coming in, they had looked too rough to manage without climbing equipment, but Brett had approached from a tidal area and wasn't desperate for food when he first studied them, nor had he already been turned back at the gates with casualties like some others.

The last thing he wanted to hear again was the roar of motorcycle engines, but that's exactly what he did hear, and not only a few. Incoming, he thought. He looked into Lee's eyes and shrugged, shaking his head. Clearly if he went out it was going to be as the front line of defense.

"Don't even think about it," Lee said. "Survival isn't about dying on the front lawn."

"We've got no cover outside the house," said Clayton. "If they take you down we'll lose your gun too."

Squatting, Brett settled in at the picture window, pulling the curtain back near the bottom about an inch. The gunfire was audible again but he couldn't see where it came from. The firing sounded almost random, as if a gang of outlaw cowboys were riding down Main Street shooting into the air. He cranked open one of the casement windows a couple of inches so he could get a better sense of their direction. A moment later a rusty Suburban full of people careened up the street. Someone on the passenger side was firing at intervals as they passed.

"Intimidation," said Clayton quietly from over his shoulder. "They'll get everyone to hunker down inside, just like we're all doin' now."

"What is the point of this?" asked Holly, lying on one elbow on the carpet. Any bullet coming through the window would have cleared her with no trouble. She was indignant; perhaps more at Emmett for not putting an instant stop to this, than at the shooters.

"It looks to me," said Clayton, "that they're trying to see what we can come up with for firepower to bring against them. It's about how much of the town they can shoot up without opposition. Call it a touch of terrorism. Then they'll know how many of their own to bring next time. Dusk is coming on now. Soon darkness will give them some cover when they leave, and I don't think they'll stay very long. It'll be broad daylight when they come back again and that's when they'll bring their vans. If they don't get anything out of Stoddard's, and they won't by then, they'll go from house to house, and that's when the slaughter will begin. People will die defending their little hoards."

"OK. So that's how their next visit will go," said Lee. Her voice was dead calm. It could have been a line from a book she didn't care to finish because the ending might be too painful, even though no surprise. In this case, she'd already guessed how it ended.

"Bastards!" said Holly.

"Do you think Emmett will follow them out when they leave tonight?" asked Clayton.

"No, because he's in his bunker now," she said with certainty. "But he'll send a crew out in the morning to reinforce the barricades, thinking that he's done his job. Watch for a new poster to go up between eleven and noon, announcing how well he dealt with this."

"And how it won't happen again?" asked Lee. Silence followed this question.

21

At Lee's invitation Holly spent the night in the small bedroom at the back of the house. After they'd sat around for a while trying to cheer themselves up with only moderate success, she rose to use the powder room and offered a slightly unsteady good night. They'd heard no shooting for more than an hour.

They speculated for a while about what might be coming next. None of them voiced any optimism. Outpost's security had been breached both in front and on its flank. The enemy (the neighboring towns down the road) collectively had more population to draw on than Outpost did, since it was so end-of-the-road, so isolated. Brett's developing view was that no matter what Emmett could assemble now, Outpost was too vulnerable to still be a refuge anymore. They couldn't hold out if the invaders increased the attacks.

Lee and Clayton both objected to Brett's pessimistic view, being more invested in the town than he was, but he responded that, for him, when the invasion forces started to drop diseased bodies on the pavement, then it was over. Outpost would lose whatever remained of its special isolation and become like every other damaged town in the path of an epidemic wind.

"You sound like you want to leave," Lee said quietly. Her expression offered nothing more.

"No, I don't *want* to, but I'm afraid Outpost is quickly going to look too much like other places we've gone through for us to stay here. We've made a good stand, but this has always been about saving ourselves and not going down with the ship. It still is. Maybe that sounds selfish, but no one is going to save us if we can't do it ourselves. We need to ask now whether Outpost is going down next. Emmett's got his forces. They're well armed and trained. They can tip this thing either way. If this town does go down, then we're all on our own anyway. I'd rather take up the fight in a place that doesn't already have a target on it, somewhere more anonymous. As this goes on I think hiding will be more important than shooting back. There's always going to be somebody bigger than we are, Lee, somebody with more firepower."

"And you would give up all this support," she said, "just like that. The food and everything." She spread out her hands as if her palms were full of it.

He looked at her for a moment before he answered. "Lee, Stoddard's is about empty and these guys are driving up our street unchallenged and firing their guns into unlit houses. Where's the support in that?"

Clayton stared at the darkening window as Brett said this and his face clouded over.

"I see some difficult choices to make with leaving," he said, his eyes welling up with tears.

"DeShawn," Lee said.

"He's all I have now."

"You have us," Brett said. "I know we're not family, so it can't be the same. But still…"

Before Clayton could respond, shooting broke out again in the distance. Brett imagined a caravan of invaders pulling up their positions around City Hall and moving back toward the entry barricades. Emmett could have ordered a confrontation as they left, or given instructions to let them go through and then sealed it behind them. One option would've done more damage, possibly made them think twice about returning, and the other would have left Emmett in charge, watching the enemy flee as the last one standing. It wasn't hard to guess what he'd done.

Brett looked up to see Holly standing outside the small bedroom with a bed sheet wrapped around her.

On Thursday morning Holly went home grim and silent before Brett had the coffee ready. After a quiet breakfast he and Lee walked down to the town square to see what was left of Outpost security. Even though they took their usual leisurely pace, both were on edge. Before they left, Lee had described her state of mind as violated.

Security was heavy near City Hall and no one was permitted to approach beyond the edge of the street. They didn't try. Most of the glass on the main floor was shot out on the side where they stood. Closer to the entrance, the glass fronting the new billboard was shattered onto the concrete. Men with uniforms moved about inside, casting wary glances at their neighbors in the crowd.

The twisted bodies of four men lay as they had fallen on the sidewalk edging the green. Along with the anonymity of any nameless corpse, they displayed that peculiar melding against the pavement look of the recently dead. Their cheeks had flattened out in minute and granular accommodation of the textured concrete. Although their vehicles had been towed away, Emmett must have ordered the bodies to remain uncovered in place. Naturally, in different times, they would have been removed as soon as they were declared dead, but here, it seemed, they'd been retained in place through the night to make an important point.

"Examples to us all, aren't they," whispered Lee. "As they ought to be."

Brett's first instinct was to correct her, always a mistake, and he walked that thought back a few paces before he said it, realizing she was right. As an example to other would be invaders, these stiffening victims carried no weight. Who among the gathering forces outside would ever witness their condition to absorb the lesson of their rashness? Emmett had left their remains cooling there for twelve hours, coagulating against the pavement, so that the residents of Outpost would observe firsthand the futility of anyone opposing the mayor, either from within or from outside the town. The message was clear: *Stay the course. Back your leader, as he backs you.*

Brett stood on the blacktop with his hands in his pockets imagining that if someone turned these bodies over they'd have a completely flat side that would remain congealed in that shape, reflecting even the divisions in the sidewalk. Maybe that wasn't true, but that image represented an endpoint for him. It clarified their position by underlining their risk. Only one bullet apiece separated them from these exemplary dead.

"I think we have to leave soon," he said to Lee softly. "We're not going to be able to hold them at bay when they come back, and you know they will. It won't be far off, either. Now they know what we can do. We came up here because we hoped Outpost would be a safe haven. Now it's time to look for another refuge. I don't know what that's going to be, but it's got to offer less of a target, because the absence of a target is the only thing that's going to make any place safe from now on."

She didn't respond or even look at him as he spoke.

"You want to go back on the road, now, after all this?"

"We cannot take on the whole world, Lee. Emmett is not going to be able to prevent these people from going door to door. He's no more than a bigger, meaner version of us, with more guns. Yet, where was he last night? I'll tell you—he was hiding right here in his own bunker. *But we don't have a bunker.* I see now what a mistake those scavenger trips were."

"They seemed like a good idea at the time, especially the meat." Lee finally nodded, but she didn't add anything more in response to this battlefield as they started to walk back home. Her normally full lips were compressed into a line. After a while she started shaking her head. "You're right. I had so hoped we'd be safe here," she said. "I don't have another plan."

"Emmett sold us that idea. Successful politicians always know what we want to hear most. Those who don't know are never reelected."

"But I already felt this was a refuge when I left Marshy Flats. That's why I came this way. I had family here, even though they were leaving for a while. I didn't want to die alone in the Flats. That was the bottom line." Lee was silent again until they reached the corner of their home block, where she stopped. She must have been going over her position point by point as they walked.

"Even so, I don't think I can leave Outpost, Brett."

"What?" He couldn't believe this. "What are you saying? Do you want to be alone again? Outpost will end up just like Marshy Flats!"

"Don't you ever reach a point when you have to stop running?" Her voice was calm, but even as she shook her head, she wasn't looking at him.

"Sure, but it's not when the enemy hoards are charging down on us and we don't have any cover beyond the thickness of a cheap veneered front door. They could shatter it with a rifle butt. How can we stop them from taking what we have and killing us in the process? They can put any number of people into the field and enter each house one by one. Emmett is going to pull back and circle the wagons around City Hall. In that situation he won't care about us. He already doesn't." Brett couldn't help but realize this was much like the federal government taking refuge in the Windsong Estate bunker. Each layer of government would protect itself first. Survival started at the top.

"But it's my brother's house! He trusted me with it."

"Family," he said. "Family is great, Lee, but you can't save his house. He's already OK; he's out of this. That's all he's likely to get until this is finished, and it's far more than most families will come away with. No one in his inner circle has died. How rare is that? How would he feel if he knew you had died in his house, not from the disease, but from being gunned down by looters?"

A light came over her features and she looked at him for the first time since they'd stopped on the corner. "Why don't we go there next then, if we have to leave? His in-laws will take care of us. All we have to do is get to Corpus Christi. We've taken the back roads before and we've gotten through. Now we've even got that gun, which we didn't have until near the end last time."

Brett shook his head slowly. "They're not going to let

us in. Remember the four Unified Recovery Districts? Corpus Christi is one of them, and they're set up to exclude people like us, refugees. We're on our own now."

Lee didn't move another step. "Then I'm not going. You can go, and you can even take the gun. I don't want it; I hate the sight of it. I'm sorry."

"Lee, that's crazy!" Brett felt doors slamming shut all around him. He saw them laughing earlier about having no future, about not worrying because worry would only degrade the time they had left. But how could this be coming to an end so soon? They'd been in Outpost for little more than a week. Brett hadn't known her for even two weeks. And this was it? He felt like the entire remainder of his life had been squeezed into an hourglass and the upper chamber was now nearly empty. How had he missed the flow?

"You're going to end this before you have to, do you know that? Didn't we commit to each other? We can still have more time with our lives! Together we might even survive!" He reached his hand out to her but she didn't move, standing motionless as she stared down the street toward City Hall. Her vacant eyes looked like she had sailed away in her mind. He wondered if this was how she dealt with intractable problems, like an animal freezing in place trying to become invisible to a predator.

They had stopped next to a fireplug with flaking yellow paint. His arms stopped waving and fell helplessly to his sides as he realized how invested he had become in her. She was still silent. Only two cars were moving, both of them police. How could this be finished so soon? He thought of a dozen arguments, but none of them impressed him, so how could they sway her? This was rising from currents that ran deeper within her than merely the moment and their dilemma.

Brett couldn't deny that part of his personality, the loner part, said, of course, this was the way it was inevitably going to be at the end. Yet he had never acknowledged it to himself, never wanted to contemplate that kind of finish.

Whatever the power of two had meant was splitting in half at this precise point. It had a familiar feeling.

Lee finally looked at him again with a set to her unmoving features that defied any further arguments. He found no joy in her face, no triumph, only resignation over her coming loss. He suddenly saw her on the road to Dundee again, only early last week, in her orange tank top and denim shorts, her strappy sandals. He heard her candy voice at the side of the van, charming him into helping her out. He saw them cooling down in the tub at the Blue Bayou Inn. He thought of them torching the three lethal boxes in a steel drum in the clearing, striking a blow against terror. Once, and not so long ago, they had been powerful together. Between them they had found hope.

He thought about their two-dollar commitment. They had never qualified it afterward, or said where or how it might go. It wasn't contingent on time or place. He hadn't meant it as a sacred trust at that moment, but the world had changed so much that it became one of itself. What else was real? Part of that was about what an important piece of their lives they'd already spent together, and how painfully little time they'd had.

In that single moment he saw how it would have to go.

No choice was available to Brett Wallace after all. The realization was like a lump of lead in his heart, but oddly liberating at the same time.

"I'm not going to leave you, Lee. I'll stay here and take care of you. It was going to end fairly soon anyway. When that point comes I'd rather be here with you than have each of us die somewhere off by ourselves."

She didn't respond.

When they got to the door she stopped and looked into his eyes for a moment before they went in. A smile curved her lips and she kissed him lightly on the cheek.

Inside, Holly was back and presentable, sitting at the table with a cup of coffee and a small plate of pineapple chunks.

"I've got my own key, you know. Your brother gave me one before he left."

"We saw four dead downtown," Lee said, "all from the other side. I'm not sure whether we lost any. They were probably cleaned up."

Holly blinked. "What's coming next? I have to know." She now seemed reconciled to a series of battles. Her hand stopped in an upright position with a fork between her fingers. "We're leaving Outpost," Lee said. "You can come with us if you want. I actually think you should. This is already coming apart and it can't be fixed anymore."

Brett stared at her in amazement, but in front of Holly, he could say nothing, even though his mouth stayed open. Lee could tell him later what had happened to make her change her mind. Neither did he say anything to Holly about coming with them because he didn't want to seem overly interested in what she did, and she had her own survivor's instinct. Lee started pulling all the food supplies out of the cupboard. Still stunned, Brett left them to sort it out and walked across the street to ring Clayton's bell.

"I've already been down to City Hall," he said as he waved Brett inside. "Are you leaving?"

"Yes."

"Then I think I'll join you, if that's all right. A caravan is always safer. I have my own car."

"I was hoping you'd come with us. You can see what's coming."

"I surely can, and I'm already packed."

"How about DeShawn?"

Clayton's face took on a more somber look. "DeShawn is going to stay here. He can take refuge inside City Hall because he's part of their crew. They've set up a dormitory in the cafeteria. I don't think the outlaws can capture it. I guess I could stay too, but I want to distance myself from Emmett, even if it's riskier without him. DeShawn will be all right here. The invaders don't want territory, only food and gasoline. Once they've taken everything they'll leave."

"I can see that, but I'm not sure it will be riskier without Emmett."

"When the gang returns they're going to be more interested in the houses anyway. They'll set up an assault on City Hall to pin Emmett's forces down while the rest of their crew plunders the city."

"Come on over when you're ready," Brett said. "We're packing the van now and we've got plenty of extra space."

He walked back across the street trying to track Lee's thought process when she changed her mind. He still didn't understand it. They could always take it up on the road. Right now all he cared about was getting away from the coming attack.

Brett should've known Clayton would be driving something exotic. When he came out of the house twenty minutes later with Lee's suitcase and set it beside the five boxes of groceries in the back of the van, Clayton was standing in their driveway next to a throbbing thirty-year-old Mustang that looked like it had come off the assembly line only twenty minutes before. The base color was lime green, and a blue-violet racing stripe eight inches wide traveled from the grill to the rear bumper. When Holly came out of her house wearing long pants with a sweater tied around her neck, Clayton opened the passenger door for her. Hesitant, she set her suitcase on the apron and stopped with her arms folded. She looked from Brett to Clayton and back, biting her lower lip.

"I've only got two seats in the van," Brett said, wondering how far her reluctance would go.

She gave him a nervous look. "I'd rather be near the person with the gun. That's just the way I am, OK? Humor me."

He knew that Lee would never yield her seat to Holly, nor would he allow it.

Clayton stepped into the conversation. Reaching into his hip pocket he pulled out a small, short-barreled automatic barely larger than his broad palm. He held it up to her with two fingers on the end of the barrel.

"A Beretta .32 caliber. It's not an elephant gun, but it'll do at close range."

"I thought you didn't have a gun," Brett said.

"You never asked. Anyway, it belongs to DeShawn. He insisted I take it when I told him I was leaving town for a while. It's got seven in the clip and one in the chamber. I wish I had more ammunition than that, but he couldn't locate any more in town. It's not a common piece." He reached into his trunk and pulled out two five-gallon jerry cans.

"They're full," he said as he handed them to Brett. "They're a parting gift from DeShawn and Emmett. 'Course Emmett doesn't know it. The man's more generous than he imagines." He didn't look at Holly as he said this.

With no further comment beyond a toss of her hair, Holly handed her suitcase to Clayton and climbed into the passenger seat.

Brett closed the door of the van after checking the straps that held the five jerry cans down. At that moment the gunfire started again. Clayton's Mustang waited for them in the street.

"This is the only thing to do," said Lee. "I know that now."

PART THREE
HEGIRA

1

Despite the addition of Clayton's Beretta automatic to their weapons, Brett felt vulnerable as he backed the van out of the driveway, rolling down the window to hear better. At first the firing was sporadic and all from single-shot weapons. Then, a splatter of machine gun fire erupted and the sound of the single shots began to drift toward downtown in what sounded like a fallback action. He paused before the house, thinking that initially the battle would track up the entry street as the invaders came through the barriers and confronted the main force of Outpost police. They would've needed at least one of the machine guns to drive the defenders back. Clayton and Brett both got out at the same time and stood between the vehicles. The time was just coming up on eleven o'clock.

"I see an opportunity developing here," Brett said. "Like you suggested before, it'll be the point when they've all gotten through the barriers and are pushing toward City Hall, but before they've fanned out into the residential streets. I think they'll have to force the police back inside City Hall first, if they can, and that'll tend to hold them together for awhile."

"You sound like a strategist." Clayton stood with his arms folded, staring off in the direction of City Hall, his head cocked to listen.

"It's dictated by geography and the situation. They're going to need to focus their mass in order to break through the police ranks on the street. Once they've got the police pinned down in City Hall, they can pull some of their number off and start working through town."

They decided to move down Fourth Street to the last intersection where they could still turn down toward the security point and leave. This was four blocks away. The firing was growing heavier as it traveled downtown. They kept near the curb so they could appear to be parked if any of the invaders broke off and came up Fourth.

Ten minutes later, standing at the top of Lafayette and looking down on the barricades, they could see that no one remained to guard the entrance to Outpost. The shooting was sporadic and all coming from the direction of City Hall. They started down the gradual slope. No one was on the street, lending it an eerie deserted feeling with the gunfire in the background. Brett could imagine the shaded faces behind the blinds, the muffled breathing as their neighbors awaited the next assault. Why was no one else leaving? He wondered if people had used up their gas, or were they still banking on some misguided confidence in Emmett? It was still possible that he might come up with something. Brett looked in the side mirror back at the Mustang. Holly's face was stolid, reflecting nothing of her connection with Clayton. He wondered how this was going to play out once they found a place to settle in, if they ever did. Those two could work it out between themselves.

A minute later they threaded their way out through the highway barriers, which were blown over as if the invaders had come through with an earthmover or a large dump truck with a front loader. Brett counted six bodies in easy view, two of them in uniform, but he was mainly watching the road for more activity. As they cleared the last barrier and gathered speed, Lee gave a great sigh. The expression on her face that followed was mixed, and it didn't seem like the time to ask how she'd decided to change her mind. That could wait until they were farther out of town.

They left Outpost on the only road going down to Davis Junction, the same one the scavenger caravan had used earlier, and the one the invaders had just come up on. Brett didn't expect much trouble because any militants from the area would most likely have attached themselves to the marauders in the center of Outpost. Joining the momentum of that booty-driven hoard would be irresistible. Nothing unusual materialized on the road other than an abandoned pickup on the shoulder four miles down. They were driving about seventy. The road held no other traffic and had few curves.

Davis Junction looked deserted, which suited them. As if they were expecting a counterattack, no businesses appeared to be open. This didn't bother Brett; but he didn't want to take a defender's bullet in the head as they drove through. He longed for armor on the front and sides, and bulletproof glass. The small grocery he'd seen on their earlier scavenger visit was standing open. Trash lingered on the threshold but he saw nothing moving within the shadowy interior.

At the highway intersection they turned west. Brett wasn't sure it looked like enemy territory, but they were heading further south and now west from Outpost, so he knew better what to expect. Emmett had been so clear about the sanctity of the perimeter of his town that Brett felt increasingly exposed. Behind them Clayton and Holly traveled with the air of a much faster and more prestigious vehicle that should properly be leading. Brett dearly wanted to be a fly on the window inside that classic Mustang, but he consoled himself with the thought that he could pry some of the conversation out of Clayton another time once he'd found a good bottle of rum and a place of safety. Neither one of those was at all likely.

They had decided earlier to catch the first road going north toward the state line, thinking to eventually find a place to stop in the thinly populated areas inside southeastern Arkansas. The only nearby city of major size was Little Rock, one of the URDs, and they'd have to stop before they got close, since as a URD city, Little Rock was sealed. If it got too rough on the highway they could run for the tiny side roads again.

"This is going well," Lee said, her voice empty of

conviction. She scanned the empty streets as they ended with the town. "I'm feeling naked right now."

"All I can say is that this is safer than Outpost. The brigands are all up there." Brett knew if it didn't work for all of them, he'd be cast in the role of the new Emmett, the well-meaning but shallow leader who didn't possess the insight or creativity to pull it off when it mattered. A man whose skills began and ended with bravado.

"You're sure about this?" she said in almost a whisper.

"I want to get away from this territory. I feel like we're in Afghanistan. Anything can happen, you saw that." The phrase, *it's for our own good*, occurred to him, but he didn't want to sound like one of the people in power.

After the turn to the west, they passed *The High Sign* tavern five miles out of Davis Junction. Only the sign itself remained; the building was burned to its foundation slab, which hardly showed through the charred debris. Had the liquor bottles been removed first? Or had they been heated to boiling and then exploded to fuel the flames? Shaking his head, Brett saw again the happy owner, shooting out the tires on the car parked in front as they drove the convoy away. That car was gone now. Was the owner's incinerated body hidden within the piles of blackened trash?

"I wonder what happened there?" asked Lee, not expecting an answer.

"It's like the Old West," he said, avoiding the detail, which he didn't think she'd find reassuring. "Think of it as the new folklore, the growing legend of the republic reborn and how it came to be what it is today." He wondered if he was editing events too much for her.

Lee gave him an odd look. "You're going to think I'm crazy, but I already wish we hadn't left Outpost."

"I'm sure. It's the devil you know. This one you don't. I don't either."

"I feel like I don't even recognize this state, and I've lived here for ten years."

"So you would've stayed on to shoot it out? With

sixteen rounds and a dead cop's .38, and Clayton's .32 with eight bullets? Maybe Holly could've called Emmett for help from a police cruiser driving by. It would've made the Alamo seem like a cakewalk from what I saw and heard."

She looked at him without responding for a while. "I think you're getting a little stressed, too, Brett. Am I right? I'm sorry I flip-flopped like that, but it was real. I said what I thought, OK? That's all I can do."

"Don't be sorry. This is dangerous terrain. But am I stressed? Probably, even certainly, and why shouldn't I be? I don't know any more than you do. This isn't therapy at the high school, OK? We're down to four people now, one of whom is already a little twitchy, and it's not you or me. I don't have to tell you that. I'm glad she's riding with Clayton because he's steadier than any of us. I wish I had his nerves right now."

"I think she'll settle down once we're farther out of town. That thing with Doug and Emmett threw her off her game."

"Do you really believe that?" Brett tried not to sound overly incredulous, but her statement made him ask himself, and not for the first time, what Holly's game might be.

"I believe the first part and I'm hopeful of the last."

"We're all hopeful. That doesn't mean were all believers."

"You sound ten years older than you did two weeks ago, but you don't look it. You look the same, but none of us are the same, are we?" She looked away from him, out her side window at the pines flying past. "We'll *never* be the same."

They turned north on a county road labeled A21. The woods didn't change much even as they moved higher among the rocky hills. Pines do well in many environments. Maybe humans would too, those who were left when the epidemic was finished. After a mile or two Brett's mind was clearer but he still wasn't ready to dig into his recent history with Lee. The right moment would come down the road.

As the tires hummed along on the blacktop they

were silent for a long time. That far from Davis Junction, the road and the surrounding forests looked undamaged and almost normal. The only difference was that more trash had been thrown on the road and shoulders. Some of it lifted in greeting as they blew past. Few buildings appeared until they approached Bristol. About three miles out, two small farms faced each other across the road as old neighbors. Catching each other's eye in the fields, some of the owners' children had probably intermarried. It was hard to tell how prosperous they once had been because both homesteads were now gutted by fire. Four more farms appeared in this condition before they entered the town of Bristol itself, twenty-one miles out of Davis Junction. It was about five times as big and looked to be in desperate condition. No one was in view on the streets. The few cars at the curbs all displayed broken glass.

In the block-long downtown section the stores were mostly looted. Two had been gutted by fire. Beyond, many of the houses stood open and about one in ten had been burned. Bristol was a war zone, and its cratered condition suggested the combatants and the population had all moved on to safer terrain. Brett wondered where that was.

"This could've been done by the same wrecking crew that's now in Outpost," Lee said.

Halfway through the town they passed a small supermarket with one concrete block sidewall collapsed into the interior. Above, the roof sagged like a tent missing a third of the poles. Littered with food wrappers and flattened drink cups, the adjacent parking lot was empty of cars.

"My god!" said Lee. "Let's move on. This is horrible!"

"Now you're missing Outpost more."

"Yes, but I'm also wondering if it looks like this too. We're homeless now, aren't we? Two of us out of how many millions?"

Brett picked up speed and they were soon at the edge of town. A21 continued northwest, but it was a parade route of destruction. Every building along both sides appeared looted, and many were burned. Scattered bodies defiled the ground, ragged and picked over as if crows had been tearing at them for days. Lee covered her face. "Go faster," she said. "Tell me when it's only forest again."

After they had navigated about ten miles of this misery, thinning as the spaces between settled properties grew in length, Clayton flicked his headlights behind them. They pulled over to the shoulder and got out. They'd seen no other cars coming toward them in five or six miles.

"We've hit a rough spot here," Clayton said. "A21 is looking like the route Sherman took during the Civil War." Holly stood next to her side of the car looking depressed.

"I think we should get off this road as soon as we can," Lee said. "This is not what we're looking for." Holly nodded with a grim set to her lips.

Brett opened his map. It indicated a turnoff a few miles ahead to a route that had no towns marked on it, although it may have gone on for thirty miles or more with few intersections before it dead-ended. "This heads back in the direction of the river valley above Outpost. I don't know; it's a tiny road. It might be no more than trees up there, and have nothing on it for us at all." His fingers danced uncertainly on the page. A look at both Lee and Holly's faces told him nothing.

"But maybe it has no targets on it, either," Clayton said. "We've got enough supplies to hold us awhile. We can take a chance and go further on. At the moment, shelter is more important, and we clearly have to get away from this." He made a vague gesture that included the devastated route they'd just driven through.

"Let's do it," Holly said. "We haven't passed anything left alive for miles on this road and it's creeping me out. Why doesn't anyone bury those stiffs? It looks like Jonestown around here. Pass the Kool Aid." She rubbed her palms vigorously on her thighs.

Brett didn't suggest that the usual buriers of stiffs were now probably all stiff themselves. No one advocated continuing on A21. Clayton and Holly took the lead as they drove off.

To Brett's relief, they went faster than he had when he was leading. He knew he'd been too tentative, too cautious. He'd been waiting for another ambush.

"Are we going to get beyond this soon?" Lee asked. "I had really hoped we'd be able to hole up in Outpost until it all cleared up. Now I think it's going to be like this everywhere."

"Let's hold off judgment until we see some of this side road."

She gave him a weak smile that seemed salvaged from some time in the past; it was not very fresh.

Ahead, the turnoff appeared and the Mustang swung onto it with no hesitation. The surface was gravel, but smooth and well maintained. Brett was relieved. It made him feel ready for the conversation he'd been holding at bay.

"I would like to know why we're here today, on this road, at this hour," he said, quite softly, and with no urgency, after they'd gone about a mile without seeing any corpses or ruined farmhouses. He paused for a moment and glanced at her. Lee's face was blank. His attitude grew more definite. "Because I would have stayed back there with you. If Outpost was where you wanted to make your last stand, and that meant we went down together, I was ready for that, I really was. I had made that decision." He didn't go on to say what he thought of the wisdom of it. Wisdom hadn't counted for much recently, certainly not enough to get them through this, but connections were everything.

Lee looked at him in surprise. "But that was *why*, because it meant you loved me. You just didn't know it yet." She folded her arms with a satisfied look, but it was inward, not directed at him.

It came over Brett in a rush that this was true. For a moment he could hardly speak. "*Of course* I love you. How could I not love you?" Brett tried to look both at Lee and the road at the same time. It didn't work. Too long in either direction and he was sure to miss something critical.

"I'm glad you said that to me, Brett. Any woman needs to know that."

"You're right, I just hadn't said it to myself yet." Brett's voice tapered off. He was already starting to feel like a sap and the blood pressure was throbbing inside his head.

"I knew it at the moment when you said you'd stay with me and we'd face it together, not until then. I had almost said it to you that night we were attacked the first time, but I felt like I was already too far out on a limb and I didn't trust myself."

"Jesus! We could still screw this up, we could still blow this, even if we didn't catch the disease and no one killed us. We could ruin this relationship ourselves! Or I could."

"I know. That's always the way it is, don't you think?" She placed her hand on his knee, working it as if the joint had frozen up from driving.

Ahead, Clayton slowed and drifted onto the shoulder. Brett pulled over too and stepped out. Their conversation was unfinished.

"Holly has to pee," Clayton said with a neutral shrug and leaned against his rear fender.

Lee got out and stretched her muscles, pushing against the side of the van to loosen her calves. Her look asked why Holly had chosen that moment to interrupt their conversation. Holly had already gone off into the brush, squatting invisibly in the pines. The whole picture lent the situation an element of almost touching normalcy, like a Memorial Day picnic excursion to a remote location. Unconsciously Brett was recording these things in his mind as if to relate them to a future generation yet unborn. What if he survived to write that book? Details like this mattered. He suppressed a laugh. When would that ever be? He heard an irritated squeak followed by a slap hitting bare skin from within the woods. A moment later Holly walked out buttoning her pants and shaking her head.

"How will we know this place of refuge when we find it?" Lee asked Clayton.

He thought for a moment. "First, as we drive up, we'll see no dead bodies in the yard with clouds of flies above them.

The house and outbuildings will bear no bullet holes or scorch marks. No neighbors will be able to watch us as we take over the property and settle in."

"So it'll mostly be about what it's not," she said.

"It will also be defensible by two handguns," Brett added, "and ideally, it will have some of its original food supply remaining."

"Original?" said Holly, not liking this.

"The stash it had before its owners went off to politely die somewhere else. We don't want a shootout." Brett knew this sounded cynical, but how many idealists had survived so far, other than the ones who'd launched the terror attack, now at home in bed after a full meal?

They drove off feeling more confident. Before they left Outpost, they'd agreed to avoid Bascombe, the county seat, which had been another option upon leaving Bristol. According to Leon, that town had experienced its own outbreak of violence. Nothing would've improved in the time that passed.

"You look happy," Lee said after a long silence. Her face held a provocative look.

"You have no idea. I can't believe it." He shook his head, but found no more words to add. There would be a better time for finishing this conversation, where watching the road wasn't part of it. He took her hand in his.

For some time they encountered nothing more, no buildings or clearings, only the thick pine woods. The gravel road was always in shadow between the narrow, weedy shoulders. It gave Brett mixed feelings. Maybe the only way to avoid the violence now was to have nothing worth taking. The absence of corpses and burned out farmhouses was good news, but could they still find a refuge if no more settlements appeared? If they didn't, four of them sleeping in the van would be uncomfortable for a variety of reasons. Shuffling the possible sequence of warm sleeping bodies in his mind, he could only predict an unsettled night all around.

The first lane came into view about eight miles along

the gravel road. It was covered with undisturbed and prospering weeds three feet high. Anticipating a ruin, they didn't stop. They needed a well-maintained refuge with electricity. Food was not an absolute necessity, but it would be a big plus. Supplies were getting low and they didn't expect to see another functioning food store until the epidemic was brought under control. That could be never. They might end up using their .38 police special and sixteen rounds of ammunition to hunt raccoons and jackrabbits.

After nearly twenty miles they'd seen only four more lanes. On inspection, none of them had led to anything that looked promising. Only one was inhabited, which was encouraging, although they didn't approach the house.

Six miles farther on they encountered a narrow opening that broke the tree line. They slowed to give it a detailed look. A car length inside, a chain crossed the lane, and beyond, parked on the right near the trees with enough space for another car to pass, was a small white two-door Chevrolet. No buildings were visible from where they stopped. Clayton pulled into the lane and Brett paused on the shoulder. They all got out.

"What do you think?" he said to Clayton.

"There's a blanket of debris on that little car." He put on his straw hat and pointed.

Pine trees produce and shed volumes of small-scale debris, which is why it's so quiet walking beneath them. Over its roof and hood the hatchback Chevrolet was spread with a thin but even scattering of brown needles and broken twigs mixed with the wispy castoff coverings from the buds and pinecones. It was also garnished with more than a few bird droppings that may have acted as a binder to this developing blanket.

"It looks like that car hasn't been moved for a couple of weeks or more," Lee said, "but that lane gets regular use. Let's give it a try. If we knock on the door of the house and someone answers we can say we need directions to Bascombe. Put Holly and me in front and they probably won't even shoot us."

"I like that idea," Brett said. "We can't be too careful." Locking the vehicles, they edged past the chain and walked down the lane. Clayton and Brett both had their guns in the back of their belts. Ahead, the property opened into a broad yard with a well-kept lawn that needed cutting, which they took to be a good sign. On both sides, ancient mossy oaks graced the borders, the land behind rising in broken stony outcroppings. It was all screened from the road by a stand of pines and inclined gradually toward a precipice overlooking a valley. From their maps they knew that below ran the Gunpowder River, which, miles farther downstream and to the east, fed the artificial lake next to Outpost, and whose controlled outflow powered the hydroelectric plant beneath the dam.

On the left stood a well-kept spacious two-story country house built of timber and fieldstone. A broad porch fronted the yard, and across the lawn, it overlooked the upper rim of the valley below. On one end a porch swing awaited the return of a more relaxed time. Overhead, a series of four black iron lanterns with a hand-forged character lit the porch at night. They were done in an Arts and Crafts era design, but they weren't old, except in spirit. The place felt like peace.

"Now I'm just praying so hard that these folks are on vacation in Lithuania," Lee said. "All the return flights have long since been cancelled, and they've left the entry key under the doormat with a nice note. This is where I want to be." Holly stood with her hands on her hips surveying the scene. No sound came from inside the house and listening hard brought no sense of movement or awareness of their arrival.

The aura of serenity spoke of long-nurtured isolation and calm repose. This property was either a retirement refuge or some busy family's far-off getaway. Brett and Lee revisited the same sense of coming home that they'd had entering Outpost the week before, but it seemed with more reason now. That small city suddenly felt like a lesson in social failure, a ruptured utopian colony like Amana or Oneida. Don't get ahead of yourself, Brett thought. He was suddenly aware of the tension in his neck and shoulders. Without urging, Holly and Lee mounted the steps of the porch, both swinging their hips in the same motion. Holly instinctively put her best leg forward. She rang the bell and placed her right hand on her hip as she waited with her response, a move she'd been rehearsing to perfection since the age of ten.

Nothing followed, which was exactly what they all hoped for. They rang again. As he stood next to Brett on the flagstones fronting the wooden steps, the outlines of a wry smile formed on Clayton's lined and freckled face.

Two tapering square half-height columns flanked the steps, each topped by a clay pot of ferns, now dry and wilted. After the third unanswered ring Lee turned around and lifted the edges to check under each of them, but found no key. Holly raised the doormat. Nothing again, other than a startled family of black spiders that fled in all directions, provoking a muted squeak from her as she hopped back. Clayton and Brett climbed the steps, thinking the occupants had had enough time to come forward and defend their property. Clayton's pale fingers probed the dry potted ferns and found nothing. No other obvious place to hide the keys offered itself.

Clayton put his back to the door, and with his right elbow sharply smacked the lower corner of one of the three panes of glass. When half of it shattered and blew inward, he put his arm through, avoiding the razor edges, and turned the deadbolt latch inside.

"You look like you've done this before," Brett said as he opened the door.

"I admit nothing. We're in the damn house, OK?"

After sticking their heads in all the rooms to make sure it was empty, Brett and Clayton left the house for Lee and Holly to explore as they went back to the road to retrieve the vehicles, the road sign that betrayed their invasion. Clayton lifted his trunk lid to expose a mobile repair shop and a variety of tools perfect for break-ins like this one, as well as a variety of other useful tasks. He selected a stout crowbar from the bottom of the box. Inserting the claw along the edge of the post where the chain was anchored, he made a quick lifting motion. The links on that end dropped to the ground.

"They were never ready for us," he said. They both drove in, happy to attract no more attention from the road, although no one had passed while they worked to get in. They parked behind the trees, invisible from the road, at the opposite end of the property near a tool and garden shed that was linked to a garage stall.

"Do you know what preserved this place?" Brett asked.

"Sure. It was that little Chevy made it look like someone was still living here."

"And the other part must have been that no one very formidable went past. I like that part best."

Brett entered the house while Clayton went back and reattached the chain with a piece of wire from a coil he had in the trunk. Lee and Holly were both in the dining area. In a moment Clayton rejoined them.

On the circular pedestal table a note was centered on the blue and white paisley print oilcloth, computer printed in block letters:

SUNDAY.

ANN!
HI, YOUR DAD AND I HAVE GONE INTO BRIDGER FOR A COUPLE OF DAYS. HE'S GOT A DENTIST APPT TOMORROW TO HAVE A ROOT CANAL (UGH!). WE'LL REST FOR A DAY AND DO SOME SHOPPING BEFORE WE COME BACK. TAKE ADVANTAGE OF LAST NIGHT'S CHICKEN IN THE FRIDGE AND HELP YOURSELVES TO ANYTHING ELSE. THERE'S ALSO SOME BEER FOR GABE. WE'LL SEE YOU ON WEDNESDAY. LOVE,

Mom was scrawled in cheerful loops beneath the message in a violet felt tip marker. Lee opened the refrigerator. On a plate covered by plastic wrap she found the leftovers of a fried chicken dinner. A bowl next to it contained parsley potatoes. The lettuce in a plastic zipper bag was pulpy and brown on the edges. There was no need to smell any of it to know it was all far past the point when it could be eaten.

"That's nearly two weeks old," Clayton said in a weary voice. "They must have been overtaken by the detention in Bridger as they rested on Tuesday from the dental work."

"Ann and Gabe never made it out here either," said Lee. "That's clear from the chicken." Three untouched bottles of dark beer in the refrigerator door still awaited the absent son-in-law.

"It was the week of missed engagements. I was due in Bridger myself that Tuesday." Brett placed two fingers on the note. It was eerie to witness this final family communication that had never reached anyone. The scene read like the whole tragedy in miniature. As personal and intimate as it was, it was also nearly every family's story, in one way or another.

Holly walked over to the pantry cupboard and threw open the doors. It held enough food to keep them for a couple of weeks, at least, which made sense at this distance from any supermarket. She took an empty box from the bottom shelf and began to pull all the spoiled items from the fridge, sniffing them carefully when in doubt. In a nearby corner a low wine rack held sixteen bottles of red.

"Looks like we've stepped into someone's abandoned life," Lee said. "This is almost too painful." Mixed emotions struggled on her face. This house was the perfect place to come to earth.

Kitchen flowed into dining area into a living room with broad valley views. Heavy beams supported the story above. Wide rustic planks faced the walls with battens covering the joints. They were dotted with small tight knots and full of character, painted a warm pale green.

Brett pulled open the country pine armoire. The music assortment inside ran mainly from early opera to late opera with a garnish of Christmas music and hits of the sixties at the bottom. He could have used some blues; a little bottle-neck guitar would've been good for settling in. He suddenly missed his vintage Dobro. Brett was now relaxed enough to see himself sitting on the porch rocker picking out a few lazy tunes. Big Bill Broonzy came to mind. "Lawd, my baby's leavin' this mawnin'…"

Along the fireplace wall, finely finished bookshelves flanked the fieldstone mantel to about eight feet high. The house owners had not been e-book readers—they had relished the physical papery feel of real books in their hands. On one side was fiction, the other nonfiction in equal quantity. Most of it was history, with forays into politics and social analysis. The bottom shelf held a section on travel. Brett saw guides for Prague, Trieste, and Machu Picchu. From midway down he pulled out a volume titled *American Government at a Crossroads* and paged through it. Crossroads? Little did they know, he thought. The copyright date was 1977, and he knew the key themes would be Nixon and Watergate. With no warning a hand came to rest on his back with a proprietary feel to the fingers as they traced his spine.

"Too sad, isn't it?" Lee said close to his ear. He felt her warm breath on his neck. "This is all that's left of their lives. They drove off to their deaths on the way to a dentist appointment, of all things. As if there could be any meaning in the final days of any of us. It always goes like that, an appointment we missed or didn't return from. The day we die is often a day of broken promises. Don't try to find any significance in your passing beyond that. It's more like an interruption than a conclusion."

Brett digested this for a moment, trying not to picture his or hers. In the element of unfulfilled commitments, it re-sembled life, perhaps his own. He looked into her eyes for a moment.

"I was there when my parents passed," Lee said. "It was like that for both of them. 'Are you sure I turned off the stove?' my mother said to me. Her hand gripped my wrist.

That was the last thing she said to anyone."

He put his arms around her, pressing her to his heart, amazed at how important she had become to him, even though he still didn't feel he really knew who she was. His hands traveled upward from her waist, reaching her shoulder blades, pausing to caress her neck below her hairline until his index finger stopped at the subtly harder object beneath her skin at the base of her neck. Holly was still working over the refrigerator with a damp sponge and a kitchen cleaner spray. Her glance met Brett's for a moment over Lee's shoulder. Clayton had gone upstairs.

"I guess we're their sole heirs now," Lee said. "It's tragic, but I still don't mind inheriting this house."

Half an hour later they were moved in and settled. Upstairs, the house offered three bedrooms and two baths. From both the two large bedrooms in front, French doors opened to a balcony atop the porch overlooking the valley. Although they couldn't see the river, they could hear it scouring its rocky path through the ravine. Other than that subtle watery sound, silence held sway throughout the clearing around them. It was easy to believe they'd slipped into a safe zone overlooked by all the combatants.

"I think we can relax now," Lee said some time later, sitting down in a chaise on the porch, a glass of ice water in her hand. "We hit the jackpot. I like this sense of anonymity. We're finally too far away for anyone to notice us. You won't even need to carry that gun around anymore."

"I'm not sure I can let it go." Brett wasn't as confident of their safety as she was, or had he heard something else in her voice?

"To tell you the truth, I can't stand the sight of it. Ever since you took it off that dead cop it's been on my mind."

"It could be the one thing that saves us."

"If only."

"You saw the same things I saw coming up here."

"I know. You don't need to tell me. I saw more than I wanted to."

"What is it then? That cop was dead. He's not going to miss his gun. He never even drew it. The flap was open, but it was still holstered." He turned to look at her, but she only stared off over the valley. "Tell me what's on your mind, Lee. I feel like it's not this."

She took a while to answer.

"I had a cousin who was killed in Corpus during a gang shootout. He was only fifteen years old. He wasn't part of the action, he only happened to walk out of a drugstore into the line of fire. Some kids were shooting up the street. When they took him in, the one who shot him said he didn't *try to do it*. That was his excuse. Ever since then…"

She took a deep sigh that was nearly a shudder. "I'm sorry," he said, reaching for her hand. "I understand your re-action, but I'm going to have to do whatever I have to do to protect us. If the shooting starts out here, I think you should find a safe place and get out of sight. No one will blame you. We don't have enough guns to go around anyway. I don't know what else to say. It's a different world, now. You know that too."

"Yes I do. The toughest and the smartest are going to make it. I wrote that list of survival qualities myself. But writing a list is not the same as being on it."

"The luckiest are going to make it too. I'm lucky and so are you."

"Clayton's lucky."

"And Holly's a hard ass survivor." His voice was more hushed as he said this. Holly had left the kitchen and gone upstairs.

"You're too hard on her. She's alone now. You can't know what it's like to be a woman alone in rough times. There's no feeling like it. I just had it come home to me earlier today back in Outpost, before you said you'd stay with me."

"I know. We'll see how this plays out now that we have her with us all the time. I have my doubts."

"But we couldn't leave her back there in Outpost; she'd just lost Emmett."

"And she'd also lost Doug, with his body in ashes and bones out in the maintenance building parking lot." Holly had never mentioned his name again. Brett could see how Lee didn't want to leave Holly unprotected, but he still thought she might be more formidable than Lee suspected. He made a mental note to ask Clayton for his take on her, after driving up this far in the intimate quarters of the Mustang. No radio stations were left anymore to divert them from having a real conversation, and few things remained to talk about beyond shelter and their next meal. Clayton was never in the mood for mere chatter.

"How's this going to end, Brett? I feel like it's closer now and breathing down our necks."

Knowing this was true, he gave her as good a smile as he could summon. "If it can be done, we'll do it. If not, we'll die trying, and I see no shame in that. We'll give it everything we can summon. For myself, I only want to go on with you. I'd like to still be around to see where we end up a long way down the road, if we can pull that off. After all we've been through, I have more curiosity than fear now. If someone comes at us, we'll take him down. That's all. That's why I'm keeping this gun in my belt."

"I knew you'd say that." She continued to look out over the valley.

2

Later in the afternoon Brett went to pace off the property. He was searching for markers, looking for fences in the brush, and scanning the woods and outcroppings at the edges of the property for natural barriers to watch besides the lane they'd come in on. He was already too conscious that night would be soon approaching, although it was barely evening yet. He walked off as far to the left as he could before the landscape became choked with spiky underbrush fronting a rocky ridge. Then he traced the edge of the hillside, where the sun occasionally flashed off the tumbling water below. At the point where the forest began again, he paused and was overtaken by the thought that because resources were running out everywhere, this would probably be their last stand. Here, in this peaceful place, they would decide their own fate or have it decided for them, but he sensed that, however things went, this was the end of the road. Each of us, he thought, faces this point at some time in his life. Oddly, at that moment, Brett was as close to being at peace as he had ever been. It may have been the stark simplicity of the few survival options that remained. Too many choices can be confusing and stressful.

It was no surprise, then, that he heard no one creeping up on him as he stood there, until abruptly he sensed a presence close behind him. The small hairs on the back of his neck stood up. It could've been anyone. His hand found the pistol grip. But before he could move beyond that, a female form curved against his back and two hands met on his chest. A soft breath moistened the skin at his collar, and what felt like a tongue flickered on his neck. Brett didn't have to look at those hands to know it was not Lee.

"You think you can have anyone, don't you?" he said quietly. Although he hadn't exactly expected it, he realized he wasn't surprised at this encounter.

"Yes I can." Holly's voice was a whisper. "I can have *you*, for example. I could have you on this patch of grass right now. Do you want to be over or under? I'm flexible."

"You're also very confident."

"I know who I am. So should you, by now. If you don't, y'all will surely find out in the next ten minutes."

"But why me?" He couldn't help but picture this action on the lawn.

"I need to be where the power is. If I've learned anything at all since this epidemic started, I've learned that much about myself. I only wish I had known it earlier, I could've saved myself a mistake or two in my life."

"Then save yourself another one this time. I'm not your man. Clayton's got a better grasp of our problems than any of us. He has more power than I do."

Her voice grew softer, more enticing. "But y'all have that cop gun, Brett. It's bigger, and you've got twice as many bullets. Anyway, Clayton isn't my style, and you are, especially now in this crisis. I think you're *reliable*, and suddenly that's very sexy. You can't imagine how much you're turning me on just by trying not to listen to this, even though you know what's going to happen." Her voice sank to a whisper again on the last few words. He found himself straining to hear them.

I'm right up there with competent, again, he thought. With the high marks all around he was getting from the women, he was soaring. Next one of them would conclude he was OK, or even fairly good. "It's a bad time to change horses in midstream, Holly. You ought to consider that."

"Hell, I don't even *have* my own damn horse any- more! That's what this is all about!" He wondered whether she meant to say it that way, or it had only popped out.

"But *I* do, and I was talking about myself. I'm really interested in Lee right now." He thought he could still try to be kind to her about this. Since their community was down to four people, it wouldn't do to have a rift in short shorts streak- ing through the middle. He honestly wished that she'd start up with Clayton. It would take the heat off him. Besides, Clay- ton was one of the most insightful people Brett knew, which, on second thought, may have been enough to make him avoid Holly.

"This wrongheaded thing you have with Lee will pass soon enough. She's too serious for you. You need someone who's *fun*. I'll bet you're talkin' about books with her all the time."

"Not exactly. We talk about the future, too. We're in this together."

"That's still all just talk." Holly batted the idea aside like a tiresome insect. "Anyway, I don't see why you'd want to be with some little black gal. Her brother's even darker than she is. Is that really what you want in a *woman*? Think about it! I'm the real thing, Brett! I'm blond all over." Like a tongue, her tone caressed him.

Brett wished he'd been looking into her face as she said this. It was such a cheap shot that he couldn't believe she was serious, and he was unable to come up with a sufficiently devastating response.

To him, Holly was the kind of girl you might eagerly go home with after a party where you'd had too many drinks, or set up in a condo near the office if you had more money than sense. You might buy her a two-year-old lower-end Porsche, but you'd never marry her, nor would you live with her or introduce her to your family. She was too much fun; she was all dessert. She was, as Clayton had put it, a party in motion. But beneath the balloons and the crepe paper, the pink and white frosting, other much less festive aspects of her personality lurked ready to uncoil with a startling hiss. Most of all, Holly was no one Brett would ever blow up his life for, even before it had taken a strange and unexpected turn for the better on the road to Dundee and Blake's Nifty. He could easily imagine Lee walking in on this conversation. It was time to break loose and end it. But with her exquisite timing, Holly was there before he was.

"What if I took all my clothes off right here, right now?" she said with a seductive but determined note in her voice that meant she would damn well do it with or without his permission or anyone else's.

"Mind you don't catch a chill, then, girl, if you're out here like that. The sun'll be going down in an hour. At these altitudes it can cool off pretty fast as the shadows get longer." As her fingers struggled to keep themselves entwined, Brett firmly unclasped her hands from his chest, turned, and walked toward the house without glancing at her again. As he moved away he thought she said something about her sexual needs, but he wasn't sure, and he didn't dwell on it. However, once inside, he couldn't keep himself from sneaking a look back out the window to see whether she'd really done it.

If Holly was looking for more ways to make trouble between Brett and Lee, he knew that no shortage of opportunities would be developing. Lee had always acted at once protective and skittish about her, and he knew they hadn't seen the end of her maneuvers. Holly's field of potential targets had narrowed uncomfortably. Next time, he could see her picking a moment of crisis to take her shot. Crises are easily amplified, and the refugees were far from being home free, no matter how secure this sanctuary in the forest felt at the moment. Even ten minutes earlier it had looked much safer.

Inside the house Clayton and Lee were settling in. Earlier they had all flipped coins for the bedrooms. Lee and Brett drew one of the masters and Clayton got the other. Holly was miffed to be in a small bedroom at the back of the house with a view of the pine woods twenty feet away instead of the deep views over the valley. She referred to it as the baby's room. Clayton didn't offer to switch, but he did say he'd share his room with her. After all, it had two beds. She had tossed her hair back and walked away without comment. It made Brett wish again he'd heard some of their conversation in the Mustang coming up. He couldn't imagine what kind of accommodation they had come to. He wondered whether Holly might be capable of only one kind.

Brett switched on the television. With all the chaos in Outpost, it seemed like a while since they'd seen the news. A sign asking the viewer to please stand by filled the screen. No background music was playing. The new NMN system seemed full of pauses, primitive fits and starts compared with the old standard networks. He waited, seated on the sofa. Holly came in without glancing at him and went directly upstairs. She was fully dressed. The screen image cut to the podium as the announcer's voice came on.

"This message was first broadcast this afternoon at one o'clock eastern time."

The CO entered from the left and paused at the podium, a broad grin on his face.

"This is a moment I have been anticipating for some

time. My medical advisors told me it was coming, but I almost couldn't bring myself to believe them. First, I must give you some very grim news indeed. The death toll from the epidemic has now passed two hundred million souls. That's right. A number that is nearly incomprehensible to most of us. I don't need to elaborate on all the other effects of this disaster, since we are experiencing them first hand in the loss of our loved ones, our businesses, and in the breakdown of law and order throughout the land.

"The good news is that the end to this calamity is now in sight. The rate of new infections, by all measures, is dropping sharply. The estimates I've received from the CDC suggest that we may lose as few as fifty million more people before it stops entirely. A sobering number still, but one we can survive nonetheless. The epidemic is playing itself out. I won't go into the reasons for it—I'll leave that to the experts, but I've been told this is a natural phenomenon, and one that many in the health sciences have predicted.

"My message for you today is to hold on, to maintain yourself in place as well as you can because the end is definitely in sight. Do not give up hope, because if you have survived to hear this message, your odds of getting through this disaster alive are better than they ever were, possibly as high as fifty-fifty.

"I will be updating you more often as this plays out. Let us pause a moment to give thanks to our Heavenly Father..."

Brett didn't wait for the moment of silent prayer to end before turning off the set.

"Heads or tails," Clayton said, his voice a low growl, pursing his lips. "Not too bad. We started with 300 plus million people, say 310, so we've got about 110 million left. The CO is right; our chances are better than even if only 50 million more die."

"Jesus," said Lee, and walked out of the room shaking her head. Holly followed her. Brett hadn't heard her come back down to hear the broadcast.

"It's still going to be a fight for what's left," Brett said. "A lot of people don't have the resources to survive much longer. We're going to have to mount security tonight. If the disease numbers are dropping we'll probably come to a point where being murdered for our food is likelier than dying from the epidemic. It'll be like the second wave of this. "

Clayton shook his head. "I hate to see it come to that, but then I haven't enjoyed hardly any of this. We'll need to post a sentry for twenty-four hours."

"Did you notice the outside lights?"

"Sure. They're in the eaves on three sides with a few spots aimed into the yard. The porch has its own lighting, as you saw."

"It's as if the owners of the house saw this coming, or something like it."

"Something like it," he repeated. "What would that be? This place is more isolated than anything we've seen. Maybe these people were paranoid."

"I think you and I can each handle four hours a night, right? Lee's got a problem with guns, and as for Holly, I'm not sure about her aim. I've been feeling her sights trained on me lately and I'm still standing."

Clayton looked at Brett for a moment. "Maybe you're thinking she might shoot Lee by accident. I've seen the way she looks at you, too."

Lee reappeared a moment later, saying she'd been going through the belongings left behind by the owners.

"Anything interesting?"

"Yes, I found a gun in the closet! I didn't touch it."

"Really! What kind?" Brett leaped to his feet.

"I don't know, a big one. It's long and it's in a padded case."

Brett bounded up the stairs. In the back left corner of the closet, standing up behind cold-weather clothes, he found a padded travel case containing a Remington 30.06 bolt action with a scope. It was not a gun that would lay down a rapid field of fire, but a well-placed shot would bring down virtually anything that moved in that part of the world. In a case on the shelf above he saw a cleaning kit and two unopened boxes of Setpoint hollow point cartridges at twenty to the box. "Halleluiah," Brett said softly. "This is going to be our ticket out of here alive."

The rifle was clean and in fresh condition, with nothing in the four-round clip or the chamber. It would more than offset the shortcomings of Clayton's Beretta .32, which Brett thought of as a lightweight gun. Anyone would wonder whether it would reliably take down an intruder of substantial size, even at close range, and how long did you want to delay your best shot? It was most likely wisest to go for a headshot, and that was rarely the biggest target in view in a panic situation. It could, however, still be a credible deterrent if you aimed it at an intruder and shouted that you had drawn a bead on his forehead.

3

Brett took the first shift that night, ten-thirty until two-thirty. It wasn't that he was eager, he just didn't expect any trouble and wanted to get some experience handling the new artillery and watching the yard at night. From the road the property appeared as it had when they'd come in, except that they'd scrubbed the little white Chevy clean of debris to suggest it was in regular use. They'd even pulled out the garden hose and scoured the bird droppings off the front and back glass. Their own vehicles were hidden near the garage on the far side of the house, behind a screen of trees.

He knew from the note on the kitchen table that the house hadn't been disturbed as it stood empty for two weeks. But things changed rapidly in those times and it would only take one carload of determined marauders to wipe them out if they weren't ready. Luck had taken them a long way so far, but it was like a tank of gas: you couldn't run on it forever, and it could easily go dry in the most inappropriate situation.

Brett didn't turn on the television or play any opera CDs because he wanted to be able to listen for movement outside. This was not the time for *Der Rosenkavalier* or *Fidelio*, or even Lead Belly, and the grass made for a silent surface underfoot. All the windows were open and no lights were on inside the house. Every five minutes or so he got up from the windows at the front corner and checked the perimeter. It was as he returned from a scan out the windows at the back, the ones nearest the pine forest that screened them from the road, that he found himself face to face with his latest security risk. She was not armed with a gun, but dangerous nonetheless.

"We're in a security mode, now," he said. "I should shoot you."

"Go ahead. I surrender. That's an awfully big gun you've got now, bigger even than that cop gun you had before. My lord, I wonder what I ever saw in Emmett. I can't imagine, but then, that was a much earlier time. I think of this as the endgame, now, don't you? Who you end up with will count for a lot."

Brett had wondered the same thing about Emmett on several occasions, but for different reasons.

"I have my own room now, as y'all well know," she added, "in the back. I'm not sure you saw it, but it's quite private and there's a lock on the door. At first I thought that being there was a disadvantage, but now I've had time to re-examine the possibilities. I'm sure you've had a chance, as you sit here in the darkness, to do the same, imagining me upstairs. Have you thought at all about how little I wear to bed? Some folks might think it indecent. Others might look at it as an opportunity too good to miss."

Brett pressed his lips together and swallowed hard. People don't always want to answer with the truth, even when they're not in politics.

"I'm on duty now," he said in a coarse whisper. He couldn't see her clearly in the reflected glow from outside, except for the light that collected in her hair. She was facing him as he looked out on the porch. "You wouldn't want to bring on a disaster by distracting me, would you?"

"Surely not." Her hand touched his cheek, which distracted him. "I'd rather distract you at a different time. I came down to apologize for the way I acted before. It was immature and possibly insensitive. I wonder if I didn't even seem a little pushy."

"OK, I accept." Spitting this out, he didn't take his eyes off the yard. Outside, the chorus of crickets was still chirping in the heat, while the moths seared their wings against the hot porch lamps.

"I know I came at you the wrong way. I should've seen that, and I would've, except that I've never known anyone like you before. But I want you to know I can be serious, *very* serious."

He wished he could see her body language, but it was too dark. That was always the main feature of her presentation. "I did believe you were serious about Emmett, brief as that was." He couldn't help but add this.

"Being serious doesn't mean you're always right, Brett, only that you're trying to be."

This was a quick return, and adding his name made it more personal. "No. I've been wrong too."

"See! I also wanted you to know that I didn't mean to say anything negative about Lee. She's a great person, and she's supported me in some tough times with...my former husband. I can see why you might like her."

The formerly alive and now nameless Doug, he thought. Interesting that she didn't use the word *late*. He also didn't miss how much she understated what she thought his own connection to Lee was. He turned and walked to the side windows on the fireplace wall, then to the back of the house, and on again to the kitchen where he stared into the blank wall of pines. He wasn't carrying the rifle. He had set it aside when Holly came into the room.

"I don't have to tell you these are tough times," she

continued. "But isn't it nice to know you still have choices? I mean, it's not too late for you and me. Sometimes it's even easier in a crisis like this to see things more clearly. Everything that doesn't matter gets stripped away."

Returning to the book cases, Brett was about to pick up the gun again from its position angled into the corner nearest the front door, when he found Holly's body pressed against his like the yin half of yang, a barrier both to sanity and judgment. This was serious indeed, just as she had said. Sentries have died for less, he thought.

Of course, he couldn't fail to notice that she was made differently from Lee. That was the first thing. She was four inches shorter to begin with. Her breasts met his chest in a lower place. In that tentative light, what he hadn't been able to see in the way she was dressed was now fully clear as his hands traveled her back, and lower. A first effort spider web woven by a novice could have been no thinner than what she was wearing, no less revealing of the texture of her skin. As Brett gathered her against himself, as his hands traveled over her neck and face, his fingertip touched her exquisite teeth. When she tilted her head back to receive his tortured kiss, he said instead, "So you still think you can have anyone, don't you?" He didn't know where he found the ability to say that, but tough times require tough choices. It was too bad that he couldn't tell Lee later how stalwart he had been.

Their lips failed to meet once again as she moved closer but suddenly pulled back. She ran back upstairs. Holly, Brett thought, what a great piece of work you are, what a truly dangerous woman. He hoped he would never meet anyone like her again. Of course, the lucky side to this was that Lee had not awakened and walked in on them. He whirled to face the windows, suddenly aware of how distracted he'd become. The remaining two and a half hours of his shift passed without incident as he considered how they were going to survive this while they waited for the CO to save the country. Brett had studied their food supply and estimated they could last three weeks at most, with rationing.

"All quiet," he said to Clayton, when he came downstairs at 2:30. Brett handed him the rifle and he gave Brett the .38. He checked the safety and then stuck it in his belt.

"Nothing?"

"Right. Nothing is good. I didn't have any trouble staying awake. I feel like this is our last stand. We've got no Emmett between us and the world."

"I'm not sure we ever did, but that was a comforting illusion for a while. The man talked a good game, at least."

"I feel like we're wrestling at the bottom of a pit." Brett was thinking of Holly, with her constant jockeying for position.

Clayton was silent for a moment as he scanned the yard. "We all have different needs. This situation tends to bring them out more than some others might. You've already observed that I have a compelling interest in making sense of things, not that it's always possible. But I am still driven to try."

"You must have felt the absence of sense early on. I've often felt it myself."

"That's right, although for a brief time many years ago it appeared to me like the sky was opening." Clayton scanned the side windows as he spoke. "It was a time when it suddenly became possible to attend the white man's college, and I was lucky enough to get in with a scholarship. I even came out with a degree in business."

Brett said nothing, wondering about Clayton's long-time job, long enough to retire in a few weeks with a pension, as a mechanic for the city of Outpost.

"What I did *not* reckon on was that upon getting out with my brand new diploma, I would still be black. No doors opened for me, although I knocked on many. Not much had changed, even with the widespread appearance of change. So I traded on my love of cars, which had driven my life since the age of ten, and I became a mechanic. Given a little time and the right set of tools I could make even an old car get up and purr."

Brett suddenly felt Clayton peering at him, although he couldn't see his eyes.

"It's not been a bad life, even if it's not the life I expected or hoped for. I could never have been an entrepreneur like you, even on that small a scale. I found I had quickly developed zero interest in hearing the word *no* all the time. The city garage was as good a place as any to come to earth. DeShawn was pleased to follow my lead, after starting out by passing me wrenches at home in the garage."

"I could only have been an entrepreneur," Brett said, shaking his head. "I never could take orders."

"Right. And now you have Lee. She won't intrude on your need for independence."

"She might be my best connection ever. If we make it through, I'll be one of the few people to come out of this better than when it started."

"What does she want? You must have asked yourself that more than once."

"Once you move past the race issue, where I'm a novice, her needs are simple. She wants to live and to improve her condition. To stop waiting tables and get a real job with some status."

"And Holly?"

"Well, you know something about Holly." Brett turned away. "She needs to be near the center of power, and she's willing to share her assets. She'll give a little if you will."

"And she possesses the means to make that power connection happen, most of the time."

"I do believe that's the case," Brett said, hearing a certain weary tone in his voice.

"And is it the case here with you?"

Now he truly wished he could see Clayton's face, but the reason not to turn on the lights was even more compelling. As he tried to make sense out of Holly, Brett knew he had landed in the middle of Clayton's calculations.

"She's mistaken in thinking that I have any power," he said. "I've never aspired to power in the past and I don't now, other than what is required to survive this."

"Yet, this is a small group. You may have more power than you know. I'm a light sleeper, and I kept my door open to listen for trouble. I heard her come back upstairs tonight at about midnight. I assumed she'd been makin' her pitch to you. Maybe you caught it, or maybe it went over your head."

Brett paused for a moment before he answered, looking out over the yard where nothing moved within the range of the lights. "It wasn't aimed at my head. It was more of a low ball. You could say she tried. She thought she could convince me she was serious."

"She is serious, about some things."

"So am I. Holly is tempting, but we're not on the same track, and as you said, I have Lee. She and I are still sorting things out. I'm not needy and I'm not looking for an adventure, not of Holly's kind, anyway. I've got my hands full with staying alive. Besides, I was on duty."

Clayton walked the perimeter barefoot, pausing to look out each of the windows. Like a tongue of black lightning, a bat flitted without warning at the edge of the porch lights and retreated.

When Brett came back upstairs, Lee was sleeping like it was an earlier time. She lay on her side with one arm under her pillow, her hair half covering her cheek. What trust, he thought. She woke up and turned her face to him as he climbed into the bed they were now sharing, although they hadn't yet moved beyond comfort and consolation.

"What time is it?" she yawned into her question.

"A little after three."

"Any trouble?"

"Nothing moving outside other than a bat."

"You and Clayton had a talk, or did he not get up on time?"

"We talked about the state of the union, and its future."

"And?"

"It's only the four of us now. We've got food for three weeks, more or less. If the CO is right about the epidemic tailing off, we've got a chance."

"And then what?"

"I think you and I should go back to Marshy Flats, if we can, and if that also makes sense to you. Our stuff is there, our friends, whoever's left alive. Once the epidemic is over, it'll be all about rebuilding. That's more within reach. I don't think, for all the rhetoric, that anybody in government has been able to even slow this thing down. It's been running its course unchallenged."

She settled in against his chest. "I'm glad."

"Glad?"

"Glad we found this place. Glad I found that gun, even."

"Glad to go back home if we can?"

"I guess, even that, although it feels good here."

"I'm just glad I found you."

4

As they relaxed more day by day, yet not completely, a week passed without incident or intrusion. Their refuge looked like the right choice, although the food was dwindling by the hour. Many evenings they played poker, using dry pinto beans for chips, having agreed that they would be the last staple they'd eat. Holly was quickly far ahead in the tally. They kidded her that she'd have to share when the other food ran out. Brett often felt her speculative gaze upon him, and in those moments he never looked back at her. She made no more approaches, and Lee seemed unaware of the wayward current between them. He wondered if this were true; it was also possible she was only trying to hold things together in their gang of four.

After an early discussion about how much they

could eat at any given meal, each of them stuck to the group decision without protest. The CO gave three more broadcasts during this period, each of them more optimistic. All the major electrical plants had been cleaned and disinfected, so the power grid, he stated in the second one, was now back up to 68%, and running far ahead of their estimates toward the announced goal of 90/90.

In the last one they heard, on Saturday, he announced that the government truck fleet, made up of many thousands of unused Post Office units, leased vehicles, and military transport, would be in motion by the following Monday, with sanitized crews bringing food and other supplies to population centers across the country. Monday was the three-week anniversary of the terrorist attack. For the present, these convoys would be heavily armed and ready to sweep away with no discussion any challenge they met on the road.

This was the most fundamental problem for these four exiles too, one that had them nailed down. When would basic public safety improve? The CO had suggested it was best to stay in place if your situation felt safe, but whose did? How could anyone make that call, since the reality on the road could change in a heartbeat? At one moment the risk was invisible, and in the next, someone was in your face.

They talked about this endlessly. One idea was to leave on Monday—that was in forty-eight hours, with Lee and Brett heading back down to Marshy Flats, and Clayton and Holly returning to Outpost. They had no idea of the condition of either of these towns and no way to find out. They tried their cell phones several times each day, but none were yet operating. One optimistic note was that if the government was taking to the roads in a forceful way, then they ought to become more secure. Federal escort troops would eliminate the nests of armed looters.

They decided to take the chance. Brett would have the rifle and the .38, and Clayton and Holly would take the Beretta. Clayton felt the speed of the Mustang could keep him out of trouble on the relatively short trip back to Outpost, and they could afford to be more lightly armed. By her expression as he said this, Holly didn't agree, but she kept silent.

Later they spent some time siphoning gas out of the little Chevy, dividing it between the van and the Mustang, surprised that it still had any. In a way, that suggested they were safer than they thought, because that car was an obvious target. As they drained the tank Brett watched the road with one eye, but no one passed.

Lee came out and stood with them. "I'm already getting nervous about Monday."

"I think we all are," Brett said. Clayton nodded slowly.

"It'll be the first step back to normalcy," he said. "We need that. I do, anyway. I want to see my son, to know he's all right. I want to walk through the door of my own house and sleep in my own bed without worrying about the street getting shot up."

Beyond this, none of them speculated on the condition of Outpost. They spent the rest of that day unusually silent, counting down the remaining hours.

Shortly after two o'clock the following morning, Sunday, as Brett was watching the overgrown lawn through the front window, grateful for his next to last nightshift on sentry duty, the thick trunk of the nearest oak in the right side of the yard lit up for an instant and then faded to darkness. The other trees nearby did not light up. This could only mean that a car had pointed its nose into the lane and cut its lights. He had heard no engine sound. It might only be someone turning around, but why cut his lights? They weren't moving when they went out. Who had any gas now to be out cruising without a specific purpose? What purpose made any sense at that hour? He jumped over to the base of the stairs and yelled Clayton's name. Here we go, he thought, hoping Lee would have the good sense to remain in bed through what must be coming.

He slid the safety off the Remington and scanned the windows at the front and side of the house. His heart rate felt like it had doubled. Above the subtle chirp of the crickets, the humid silence almost hissed in his ears.

Brett knelt at the corner of the great room. From there he could fire out the front windows through the porch, or if he stood, through the fireplace wall, where a small casement window, about eighteen inches square, opening through the bookshelves, admitted ventilation on each side of the chimney. Could their return fire penetrate the walls in front of him? The outer main floor facing of fieldstone was only a veneer. A lucky bullet could pass through the mortar. There was no way to know what the invader might be carrying. He pictured splinters of the plank surface exploding outward from the wall and piercing his shirt or his face. The outdoor lights on all sides of the house were switched on and no one could approach from any side unseen, but he couldn't look everywhere at once.

Clayton had rushed down without his shirt and now waited at the front on the kitchen side with the police .38 in his hand. He'd given Holly the Beretta .32. Dressed in a light robe, she also came down and went to the back, scanning the yard nearest the woods from the narrow vertical window of the powder room. The casement window was open–she would shoot through the screen.

Brett knew that Lee was upstairs worrying, unable to shoot anyone. It was not a time to try to sell her anything. She knew her comfort zone, not that this was about comfort. Brett wondered if the unknown owners had somehow foreseen this kind of action when the house was built. Maybe it had once been a refuge for moonshiners and the walls were lined with quarter-inch sheets of steel. In his mind he heard the twang as the bullets bounced harmlessly off and dropped inert and flattened into the hollow space within the walls. They'd end up as big around as counterfeit lead quarters. Strange images and foolish ideas for the end of days, he thought. But what were the proper thoughts to have at death? He already knew this was the final tipping point. He reminded himself that according to the CO, parts of the country were recovering and they were next if only they could make it now, through the hardest part. Fifty-fifty, he had said—a simple flip of a coin would decide it after all they'd been through.

Winning the toss, the other side must have run their best sprinter first—and that made sense—because Brett had heard nothing approaching until a kid in shorts took him by complete surprise as he raced past him toward the front. He did not fire at the house with the long-barreled pistol in his hand, nor did he even raise it. He appeared to be running for the front door, but he was moving so fast he couldn't make the tight turn on the dewy grass as he came around to the front. Startled, Brett's first shot was like a mule kicking him in the shoulder, and the round drove off harmless across the darkened valley. People can't aim correctly when their attitude is total surprise. It lends a useless twitchy quality to the motion of a finger on the trigger. Brett was learning this second by second, almost synapse by synapse. He hadn't fired a gun in years. He didn't know if the kid had even heard it, but nothing slowed that boy, he only bent lower and kept on coming.

Brett had a line of cartridges ready on the windowsill. The clip was full. He had already thrown the bolt and chambered a new round faster than he could think. Tracking the kid for an instant in the scope as he approached the porch, Brett's second shot took off the upper part of his face in a bloody spray that was luminous in the porch lights. An awkward silence followed as he spread-eagled his final movement onto the lawn a dozen feet from the steps. His now empty left hand made a subtle waving motion twice and then stopped with a shudder as the pistol traveled on, end over end through the long grass. Brett was gripped by a wave of nausea as he pulled back the bolt to chamber another round. He couldn't believe he'd just killed someone, but that was now the real meaning of survival. And there's our fourth weapon, he thought, out there on the lawn if we can get to it, not that Lee would ever use it.

A shot rang out from inside the back of the house, Holly's station in the powder room, and then an empty click followed, and another, capped by a string of vivid obsceni-

331

ties. Clayton sprinted past with the .38 in his hand. Two shots were returned from outside. Brett didn't move. He couldn't be drawn away from the corner where his view included both the front and the approach at the side nearest the lane. Holly was yelling something in frustration when another shot came from the back. Clayton fired twice and got no further response.

After a moment of calm a man in bib overalls approached one careful step at a time from the side of the house waving a white tee shirt over his head and pointing toward the body he knew must be lying in the front yard. As far as Brett could see, the man wasn't armed, but he still kept the rifle fixed on the intruder's chest. "Clayton," he said softly. "Can you cover this guy when he gets to the front? I think he wants to pull the body away." Collecting the dead suggested it was over. Brett didn't buy that.

"OK by me," Clayton said. "I don't want to touch it." He took Brett's place at the porch window while he moved to the small bookcase window in the back corner, nearest the lane. "I cleared that Beretta, by the way. There's one in the chamber for her now."

Brett pulled the window inward and stood to one side resting his left hand on the sill, listening hard, feeling like something more was coming. The air hung tense and sticky around him as he waited, scarcely breathing.

Cocking his head to the opening, Brett heard nothing more than the crickets in the woods. Each second ticked by almost as a distinct, standalone unit of time. He heard nothing more from Clayton and didn't dare look over at him now, and apart from the crickets, the silence felt like it was building in layers. Holly was quiet in the back, watching as he was. Nothing came from Lee upstairs, but he could sense her listening, her cheek pressed against the plank floor above. He reminded himself to breathe.

Abruptly the crickets fell silent too, as if a final switch had been thrown. Brett realized what was happening. Someone, or more than one, was inching toward them through the cover of the trees. He stared at the forward edges of the pines, lit by the house lights. Within, the bristly darkness was opaque. The guy out front swinging the tee shirt had to be a diversion. Brett didn't look in that direction.

Sudden movement caught his eye at the margin of the trees. Two men rushed out hunched over nearly double. The first one had a double-barreled shotgun in his left hand, almost scraping the ground. The Remington was already leveled, resting on the top shelf of the bookcase. Brett took a bead on the runner's shoulder and pulled the trigger. As if hit by a truck, the man was lifted from his path. He spun over onto his side and instantly onto his back, where he didn't move again. The one behind him tried to stop, and in a wild stumble, he seized the dropped shotgun from the grass and reversed course back into the pines before Brett could chamber another round and aim. Behind Brett, Clayton fired two shots into the front yard with no warning.

"The sucker went for that pistol on the ground as soon as you fired," he said into the ringing silence.

Ten seconds later they heard the sound of tires spinning in the loose gravel of the lane, a tearing screech as the treads bit into the harder compacted surface on the road, then the extended wail of the engine revving too high as the car raced away in a low gear, followed by silence. Gradually the crickets started up again, taking back control of the shattered night.

"Looks like three dead out there," Brett said. The rounds still echoed singly in his head. His voice sounded almost normal, but his hands were shaking so badly that he had to set down the rifle for fear of firing it again accidentally.

"You OK?" said Clayton softly.

"I'm OK, maybe a little twitchy. You?"

"I'm better now. Was that only the first round of a bigger battle?"

"I hope not. What would you do in their shoes?"

"I believe I would try a different house next time," Clayton said, his voice growing more relaxed. "They lost three out of four, and no one could keep that up for long. The last guy standing will be looking at other choices now, I 'spect. Nice elephant gun, by the way. You can be on my side any time." His hand gripped Brett's shoulder.

Lee called from upstairs. "Is it over?" Brett took her hand as she came down one step at a time. At the same moment Holly came into the room, the Beretta dangling at her side.

"Well?" Lee said. "Did they run away? I heard a car."

"Three of them didn't," Brett said. "One did."

She put her hands to her mouth. "You killed three of them?"

"I killed one of them," Clayton said.

"Why?"

"If you want to survive in these simpler times," said Clayton, "you must be either a scavenger or a killer. We chose scavenger. You know what they chose."

"Fuckers," said Holly, practically spitting out the words as she pulled the belt of her robe tighter. "They deserved it. Trying to kill us for our food. Imagine." She set the Beretta on the kitchen counter with evident relief. Clayton walked over and switched the safety on. The .38 was still jammed into his belt.

Brett stood silently at the window, looking into the front yard where the two bodies lay unmoving. The conversation behind him faded; it was as if he were alone. What a thin veneer civility is, he thought, barely covering the dark and dense layer below it. That is where we find ourselves now. He suddenly felt like he was standing at the edge of eternity. Was this what elderly people felt? With the knowledge that their lives would soon be snuffed out in a heartbeat, all their hard-earned knowledge, all their experience, all their humanity lost. In the process of saving his own life and that of the others, he wondered what he had lost in the last ten minutes. It was not innocence; he hadn't felt innocent in a long time. He couldn't say what it was, other than that it was also something that could not be replaced.

After an indeterminate amount of time, the touch of

Lee's hand on his shoulder pulled him back to reality. By the clock it was nearly half past two, and it already felt like the longest of nights. No one could imagine going back to bed. They kept the outdoor lights on and the inside lights off as they all sat in the great room, waiting for another sortie. The presence of the three bodies outside in the front and the side yards suggested a scene from wartime. They couldn't ignore them, nor could they deal with them until daylight. Holly disappeared upstairs for several minutes and returned dressed. She carried a wet cloth in one hand and a plastic bottle in the other.

"What's that?" Clayton asked.

"Rubbing alcohol. I'm going to save that damned pistol out there. Y'all can give that silly Beretta back to DeShawn if we ever get back to Outpost. Maybe he'll have better luck with it than I did."

"Be careful with that thing out there," Brett said. "It's not only the germs."

Holly responded with a level look that suggested she might be a little more competent than he imagined, and in different ways. "I know where the safety is," she said. "My daddy had guns."

Brett stood and watched her as she walked out the screen door. The porch light glinting off the finish made the gun clearly visible about twenty feet from the first body, and she didn't glance at the dead man as she picked it up with the rag and brought it onto the porch. There she emptied the cylinder and worked it over point by point with the alcohol under the lights, keeping the cloth soaked and forcing it into each seam and hollow. Then she cleaned the cartridges. Holly was not a sentimental person, Brett thought once again, but he already knew that for other reasons. She now had the power in her own hands.

After she cleaned it Clayton went out and asked to see it, along with the rag. It was a chrome finish revolver, dinged and worn in places but still a formidable piece.

Popping the cylinder out, he sighted down the

barrel into the porch light. "A big gun," he said, "and still fairly clean. Smith and Wesson .44, a classic." He looked at the cartridges and reloaded the cylinder. "Factory loads, too. Good job." Holly went back in to the powder room to scour her hands. Brett started a pot of coffee and Clayton went back to take up a position at the windows. The night had several hours remaining.

At six o'clock Brett went into the kitchen and made a second pot of coffee. Three more pounds of it awaited them in the freezer. This was an ongoing break because they'd run out of it in Outpost. Although they'd been using them since their arrival, he cracked one open to find out if the eggs were still good—there was no way to know how old they were. They also had some bacon left that he thawed.

As he worked, Brett expected to be in a grim mood after the night's assault—he had never expected to kill anyone, to say nothing of two men he didn't know—but if he wasn't happy, he was certainly relieved, although he couldn't clear his mind of the image of the kid he'd shot in the head. Even so, they'd had their first big battle and survived. Because it was so simple it was easiest to see his own role as that of a soldier in the trenches; the nameless enemy came at you and you fired your gun. You lived or you died.

"I found a lawn tractor in the shed," Brett said after breakfast. He'd been unable to talk about death while they ate.

"I know," Clayton was clearing the table. "The first thing I looked at was these people's tools. It's got gas in it too, and I saw two full jerry cans hanging on the wall. We won't have to use any of ours."

"I thought we could loop a rope around the bodies and tow them one by one into the woods. Maybe dig a grave, or if not, at least get them far enough away from us so we can think about something else." Abruptly Lee and Holly got up and went upstairs together as if they'd suddenly remembered another appointment.

"You don't even want to know who they were," Lee

said, looking back down the stairs.

"We already know," Brett said. "They were the enemy. Anybody that tries to sneak up and kill me in the middle of the night receives no honor in death regardless of how good his reasons. Those guys are only casualties. Sorry." The women were out of earshot for most of this, but Brett felt better saying it.

"You're starting to sound like the CO," said Clayton.

"Now I'm pleased and insulted at the same time."

"You notice I didn't say you reminded me at all of the President."

"No. Nor do you."

At the end of the property on the far side of the house, recessed into an alcove within the trees, the garden shed was attached to a single garage. The building's architectural features mimicked those of the house. Brett waited by the bodies in the shaggy grass until Clayton appeared. Three coils of coarse rope were looped over the handlebars of the garden tractor, and two shovels rode in the rack behind him.

It was easy to avoid looking at what was left of the face of the first invader, but hard not to step in the scattered remains of it. The body was lying face down. With a stout stick Brett lifted one foot off the grass, and Clayton looped a rope around the ankle and tied it to the rear of the tractor. Brett walked alongside as they found a path into the woods. The motor made too much noise for conversation, and they were both lost in their own thoughts.

Brett shook his head as he and Clayton located another trail in the pines, one that angled off toward the valley, trying not to hear the bumps and bounces of the very dead body behind the tractor. He pulled up at the edge of a cleft in the hillside. About twelve feet wide at the top, it tapered to a close twenty feet below.

"What do you think?" Brett said. "This could work."

"We can put them in there, cover them with some of these rocks, and throw down a load of dirt after that."

They brought the other bodies up to the edge of the cut.

337

Clayton stood looking at them for a moment, his hands folded atop the shovel handle. "The dead are wiser than we are," he said. "They have answered the question that's lingered at the back of their minds for their entire lives—how does it end?"

"And that's wisdom? A single instant of insight followed by an eternity of forgetting?"

"I'd like to think of it as closure. Don't we all want that?"

That was the funeral. Clayton and Brett both shoveled a dozen loads of dirt over the bodies. They found no more to say, and they were finished by about ten o'clock on Sunday morning. It wasn't perfect, but no one would stumble on the remains by accident.

That afternoon was an uneasy period they spent killing time. The silence around them was troubling. They would've departed sooner but the federal trucks were not yet moving. They'd packed up most of the remaining food and loaded the vehicles. They watched more television hoping to pick up last minute reports before they took to the road again. Every few minutes one of them got up and looked outside, although a daylight assault seemed unlikely.

At three in the afternoon the same white-coated commentator they'd seen earlier analyzing the nature of the epidemic came on. His use of the term *fulminant* had stayed in Brett's memory as such a grave but yet frivolous way to describe the cause of death for two hundred fifty million people. They'd been distracted earlier, and he wasn't sure whether they'd heard everything the CO had been announcing lately. Maybe they'd gotten weary of being reassured that things were improving even as they were being attacked. He stood at the podium and scanned his notes.

"Most of you have already heard that the rate of new infections has fallen to nearly undetectable levels, possibly as few as eighty thousand a day or less. Although the government cannot claim credit for this in any major way, we did antici-

pate it. We are confident that it's happening for three reasons."
He turned toward a prepared display board and aimed a
laser pointer.

"First, there exists in any large human population a
group of people who possess a higher than normal degree of
natural immunity, even to a new disease of this startling level
of virulence. We don't fully understand the reason for this, but
we've observed it in the past in a number of different situations. It may stem from something no more complicated than
basic genetic variation. In other words, in this situation, some
genes are better to have than others.

"Second, as the population drops through mortality,
the sheer number of interactions, and therefore individual
exposures, drops with it. People who have not yet been exposed to the epidemic are now less likely to be, since they will
encounter fewer people who have it. This effect is enhanced
if they live in isolated regions or are simply holed up in their
homes to avoid contact with others."

"Or are fucking flat out in hiding in a place like this,"
added Holly, "and shooting anyone who tries to mess with
them."

"Third, the phenomenon exists in nature where the
predator organism does not fully render the prey population
extinct. In other words, you don't kill off your victims completely. For the predator, being inefficient in this way is actually adaptive behavior, since it leaves a portion of the victim
population alive to regenerate for a future recurrence of the
epidemic. In our case, however, it leaves enough of us standing to develop and distribute a vaccine in the near future. This
process has been underway almost since the first day of the
outbreak.

"We have seen these patterns before, which makes
us more confident that they're repeating now. Witness the disastrous epidemic of smallpox, measles and other common
European diseases among the native populations of the
Americas in the sixteenth and seventeenth centuries. Without
any previous exposure they had no immunity, and the popula-

tion dropped by 90% in most cases, but no further. We have a similar situation here, somewhat altered by the miraculous diversion of the initial infection from the four survivor cities of the South, now called the Unified Recovery Districts. The total salvation of those cities has boosted our overall national survival rate to about 15%."He paused with an ironic look.

"Some have attributed the salvation of the URDs to divine will; others to blind chance. One of my subordinates even brought up a comparison with Noah and the ark. Fortunately, my job calls for no special judgment in this regard. Personally, and as a scientist, however, my estimate is that it came about through a simple failure on the part of the delivery system to successfully infect those four cities. Call it human error if you will. All of us screw up at times, and we don't like to talk about it. It usually appears to be from simple ineptitude or forgetfulness. To me, this random incompetence of humanity is one of our saving graces, and never so charming and appropriate than in this, the greatest catastrophe in the history of mankind. If the salvation of those four cities did come about because of the actions of one such anonymous individual, whose name we will never know, I would like to thank him, no matter what his intentions or his naïve missteps. I'm quite sure that he's not even aware of his role in this. I think of him as 'the Unknown Blunderer,' and as such he deserves a monument greater than that of the Unknown Soldier, even though he was working for the other side."

Brett sat on the sofa for a while with his lips pressed together in an extremely thin line, unsure whether to be flattered or not. In the past he had been charming, and occasionally, inept, but rarely at the same time. Apparently he shared some typical human traits with others, random incompetence being prominent on that list. In the progress of the disaster, his low-achieving kind of humanity had been of some inadvertent but important use to the population at large. Brett wasn't sure whether to be proud of this because of its outcome or insulted at the slack way it was characterized. Calling him a blunderer, at least, offered the possibility that he still might have been well intentioned at the critical moment.

PART FOUR
HOMECOMING

1

Forty miles above Marshy Flats the skies unleashed a torrent of rain that streamed over the highway like a fluid skin. Arcs of spray rose behind the van's wheels. The pale, luminous clouds cast an eerie light over the familiar landscape. It was late Monday afternoon and they had been driving all day.

"It's a rebirth," said Lee, her face almost pressed against the side window. "The world is clean again. Next we'll have a rainbow. I don't think I can bear it; I'm going to cry." Her face crumpled and she covered her eyes with her hands.

Brett studied the distorted image of the road as the windshield wipers struggled to keep the glass transparent while the rain continued all the way to town, as if guiding them home. He had driven back into Marshy Flats along Beach Avenue more times than any other route in his life. This time it was like returning after being kidnapped, and he was surprised to find himself still alive. As they dropped to the city speed limit forty minutes later, the clouds sailed past them as the wind drove the rain out over the Gulf.

Marshy Flats had never been anything much, mainly soft and friendly, laced with a mineral scent of the sea, and more than a little slow, especially on a hot afternoon. For Brett, it had always been a comfortable place to settle into and pursue his worry-free lifestyle—it was undemanding. Now, as the rain streamed away, it looked and felt badly injured, almost curled up upon itself, but no worse than any other place they'd driven through. Yet because it was home, seeing it in this condition was especially tragic. Without realizing it, he must have hoped it had somehow escaped the destruction. Of course, no cities had except the URDs.

The Gulf Shore Market on the northern edge of town had been burned along with two cars in the parking lot near the entry. No fire fighters would've remained to attempt to save it. A few twisted girders and joists lay where they'd fallen over the pile of blackened rubble on the concrete slab. Seeing the distorted joists exposed reminded Brett of his father's business. They passed half a dozen other burned buildings, but saw no bodies on the streets or sidewalks. Other shop fronts had lost window glass and several had entry doors hanging open. As a public health issue the bloodstains from those who died in public must have been scoured away already, because none were visible. Lee and Brett had been gone for just three weeks.

"I'm still glad to be back," Lee said in a voice more optimistic than convincing. "It's our new start, even like this, OK? I'm just going to think about the future from now on, because you and I certainly have one."

The eerie atmosphere of Marshy Flats suggested a movie set, with only a few actor extras in view to give it the flavor of a real town. Aimlessly walking about along the streaming gutters, they glanced up at the van with startled looks as Brett drove past. How had he come by his gas? Lee fell silent, her eyes wide as if she'd never seen this place before.

Unaware of the tense set to his jaw, Brett drove the van slowly, as if on an inspection tour. The air carried the acrid odor of wet charred wood, more than other towns they'd gone through that also had fire damage, but part of that was from the day's downpour.

At the base of Beach Avenue the shallow rolling dunes were deserted. Fifty feet on, the Gulf rested smooth and gray

right up to the undulant line where it lapped the shore. Farther out, the rain still lashed and puckered the heaving water.
The clearing sky looked much like it had on the morning this
all began so long ago. They pulled up to the line of railroad
ties. Half buried in the sand, these timbers edged the parking
strip at the beach. Brett sat motionless in the van, his hands
locked on the wheel, feeling like a different person. He knew
this place so well, how could it now appear so foreign and
remote? The beach was free of debris. It was the only thing
that looked exactly as it had before, yet he sensed that the
surface of the world had broken loose and shifted. His gaze
swept from one end of the sand to the other. He was suddenly
startled to realize that Newton's tackle shop was still open for
business. Brett jumped out and ran inside without closing the
van door. There he found old Newton himself behind the gray
weather-beaten counter, looking back at him in shock through
his thick lenses.

"By God, you made it too!" His voice trembled as he
grabbed Brett's hands in both of his.

"How did you do it?"

"Hell, Harold and I stayed on my boat through the
whole damn thing." Harold was his half blind fourteen-year-
old black and white bull terrier. "I got to do quite a bit of fishing, much more than I usually get a chance to. It wasn't all that
comfortable, but we made it. You adapt. I learned to like sushi,
and Harold even learned how to pee over the side, at his age."

Newton told him the electricity had been on again
for three days after being off for fourteen. They chatted for
a while about conditions in town and promised to have lunch
once Brett got settled in again. He walked back to the van feeling like they'd been through the war together, although serving
on different fronts. It was only as he drove away, pointing and
chattering to Lee about how it had all started right there behind Newton's tackle store, that Brett realized no place would
have survived in the Flats to have lunch at anymore, with the
population reduced to a fraction of what it had been. The
expression was only an emblem of a lost normalcy that would

be a long time in returning. Even if Brett had remembered it when he was inside, he wouldn't have felt ready to mention the four fishnet floats to Newton.

Going home was not easy, but they weren't expecting it to be. Brett's apartment door had been jimmied open and the rooms roughly gone through, but the only things missing were the sound system, his laptop, the treasured old Dobro guitar, and the contents of his pantry cupboard and refrigerator. Apparently with the power out for two weeks, his small flat screen television hadn't been worth bothering with, but taking the sound system had been a firm bet on the future. He felt now that the television wasn't worth much either, especially since they had only the single channel from the NMN.

Miraculously, all his blues CDs remained. Even in the Flats, and in desperate times, they were not everyone's first choice in music. His landlady had once described these artists collectively as "a bunch of old black dudes howling down by the water between slugs of Sauterne." Brett hadn't responded, but privately he thought that some of those old dudes wouldn't have objected to that description.

Lee found her apartment door still locked and her belongings intact. Her refrigerator was, as she later reported, revolting. On the way over she had refused to let Brett drive down the street where Ted had died in his garage. She didn't say that it was because she didn't want to think his body might have still been there, but Brett guessed that was the reason.

One of the other things Newton had mentioned was that the population was down to about 150, and people were being encouraged to settle into the better undamaged homes and take over their upkeep in order to stabilize the town. A national program was in the works to recognize these squatter's rights on properties they occupied where no owners or their heirs had returned within a given period. With communications so fragmented, no one could figure out any effective way to track down missing people, so occupancy was only tentative for the first sixty days. A refugee's registry was being talked about, but many areas of the country still had no basic telephone or electrical service, and no gasoline for travel.

As Emmett had done in Outpost, the city government had requisitioned the only gas station to serve official vehicles during the recovery. It had since been reopened to the public for minor auto repairs and oil changes, even though it no longer had any gas on hand. Brett and Lee were surprised to find food distribution was genuinely expected to begin soon. Traveling mostly on back roads, they hadn't seen any government trucks coming down, but there were many other towns with a higher priority than the Flats.

After a survey of vacant properties, when they showed their local ID they were allowed to settle into a white four-square colonial with four two-story columns across the shallow portico. It had an attached garage at the back and broad water views from the principal rooms. The house had belonged to Stan Bremer, the town pharmacist. Brett had known him, of course, because he'd handled deliveries for his business, but he had never been in his house before. He wondered whether the Bremers had fled in the same exodus he and Lee had been caught in, but then stayed the route only to die in Bridger.

Stan's familiar Cadillac Escalade was no longer in the garage, but his wife's Jeep Liberty was, and it somehow still had a full tank of gas. This became Lee's car. She immediately remarked how spacious it was after her Beetle. Brett parked his van next to it, amused to notice the bullet hole near the top every time he went around to Lee's side. He had no plans to repair it. At fifty-eight miles an hour it made a curious whistling noise that now sounded almost optimistic or even cheerful, although they didn't use either vehicle much because so little gas remained. They were seeing a lot of bikes on the streets.

Now they were able to chuckle at the thought of people shooting at them, although on the trip back to Marshy Flats they'd had no trouble. Brett assumed it was because the closer-in areas had been thoroughly sifted for provisions and the marauders had moved on for better pickings in the more rural northern parts of the state. This they knew from bitter experience.

Coming back, they had avoided Highway 36 until near the end, turning onto it just as the rains began. Because they didn't want to go through Bridger, assuming it was mostly gutted by fire, ironically they'd come back by way of Dundee instead. Brett didn't stop to retrieve his packages at the Blue Bayou Inn, thinking that most of the recipients would be dead. The motel was closed and looked even more desolate than before.

Sadly, Lee's blue Volkswagen was gone from the side of the road when they passed. They both had some sentimental feelings about it, since it had served as their introduction to each other. Brett had promised her he would willingly come back for it once more gas was available.

Stan Bremer's house was a step up for both of them. Although Brett's well-seasoned Dobro was gone forever, it even came with a better sound system than the one he had lost to looters. Stan had also been a more stylish dresser than he was, and many of his clothes fit Brett, although he wasn't tempted to wear the white pharmacy coats. Lee packed the belongings of Stan's wife, Sherry, into boxes without trying anything on except some of her jewelry, and they carried them into the garage. Sadly, no one was left to give them to—used clothing of all kinds was in great oversupply and would continue to be for years to come. Most of the few people they saw on the streets were well dressed now, even if they had nowhere to go. They made the reviving town appear more upscale than it ever had, although people often appeared more shocked than prosperous.

Stepping into the detail of the Bremers' lives was like seeing the epidemic in microcosm, and they couldn't help but be reminded of the house in the woods they'd just left above Outpost. They were surrounded by the pharmacist's vacated lifestyle at every turn. They knew what gum the family had chewed, what brand of tooth-whitening toothpaste they preferred, what coffee they drank and what magazines they read in the bathroom. One closet held a minor pharmacy of prescription meds.

By far the most difficult part of the house was the daughter's bedroom. Brett didn't remember the girl, but found a collection of pictures of her and her friends on the white painted dresser. She looked about eight years old, and in the most recent shots she'd been learning to smile without revealing her lost front teeth. Neither of them could bear to clean out her belongings and wrap up her life, so they closed the room and tried to forget about it. From her school notebooks they learned her name was Eve, but unlike her namesake, she had not begun life at the start of a new world, only toward the end of a badly battered one.

Finding enough to eat was not easy in the beginning, although they did better than most. Food supplies were still scarce through the first few weeks after their return, although Stan had a roomy chest freezer in the basement. Brett opened it without thinking on the day they moved in, and the stench of what must have once been three hundred pounds of steaks, seafood, and frozen vegetables was unearthly. The putrid mass was now refrozen in distorted blocks, many fused together, but a noxious cloud still hovered in wait beneath the lid. He thought of it as a coffin, and wanted to have it hauled away as it was, but during that period no one was available for tasks of that kind. It lacked any priority, since among the acres of ruins, diligent searchers could still sometimes find good watches and gold jewelry. Trash and building rubble were two of the few commodities not in short supply.

In the pantry, cereal and packaged mixes of various kinds were plentiful. The refrigerator was not as bad as they expected, and they still had two sacks of food supplies from their previous refuge. They grew accustomed to eating corn flakes with water for breakfast. Soon after that, a variety of staples began coming in again from México and Canada. Both countries had sealed their borders soon after the outbreak. A week after they arrived, a makeshift supermarket was set up in Tim Grober's old auto repair garage. It felt dark and shabby, but the garage was one of the few buildings big enough to accommodate it that was still standing. Most importantly, they could buy small quantities of food again, although the limits on the total amounts were reminiscent of Stoddard's Super. Even though their stay had been brief, memories of Outpost were still vivid and would always remain so. Brett and Lee talked about it often, as if rationalizing an episode that had gone past too rapidly to make any sense at the time.

"Is suddenly having all this stuff going to change you?" Lee asked one evening as they sat in the screened gazebo behind the house with a bottle of Stan Bremer's excellent white wine. He had kept a small cellar in the basement, and his three hundred bottles had survived well in an area with stable temperatures. "I don't want you to start worrying about anything now that you're a more solid citizen."

"Oddly, I think it's OK, about the house, anyway. I truly did pick up the scavenger instinct in Outpost, so I'm not bothered that we're stepping into the Bremers' shoes. Besides, all this stuff is free. Without any cost, it's lost its cachet. Because almost anyone can have this, it's got no value anymore as a status symbol. It says nothing about our position in the business world or our education. I'm an unemployed delivery guy with a degree I've never needed, and you're an out of work waitress with half a master's. So what? We're both survivors now, and that's the only meaningful title left to have."

Lee gave a small shrug. "Like Clayton, I always thought I wanted just a little more status."

"Look around you—you've got it now."

"I don't have much money," she said, "and even if Paul's Place was to reopen in Forrest Beach and they wanted me back, I don't know where we'd find the gas to commit to making a thirty-six mile round trip five days a week."

"I know, but we've got no house payment or rent, and I still have my cushion, the money I got from my parents, and it's in two New Orleans banks—in the heart of the URD. We can coast for a while." He drew her closer and kissed her neck. "I think we need a break. This is not going to be about money. Let's think about us, and try to figure out our values and how they've changed."

"Have yours? She looked at him in surprise, as if she thought his had been so locked in before that the epidemic would leave them unaltered.

"I think they have. I know you always thought I was a radical and unconnected to the culture, but I think now that since almost everything we depended on has been destroyed, I've gotten more conventional. I know that's ironic, but I want to settle down with you." He gave her an ironic smile. "On Tuesday we'll have known each other for five weeks. That's a milestone of sorts. I'd like to get to know our surviving neighbors, too, even though the houses on both sides of us are still empty. I'd like to have some real friends. Eventually give a barbecue party now and then. Does that sound so boring? Even if it does, why not? After all, I'm on record as being competent, even reliable."

"Then join Rotary." She smiled at him ironically over the edge of her glass.

"I don't know about that, but I would like to feel settled once more and not under threat all the time."

"You're singing my song, Brett. You're sounding like hope." She took his hand and kissed it. They had been lovers since the first night in their new house. It felt like the first time they could explore their relationship as their main priority, and now they were nearly two weeks into their honeymoon, and still dating.

That night as they were lying in bed under the ceiling fan, with the warm breath of the Gulf bathing their bodies, Brett nuzzled her breasts. The only sound was the subtle lapping of the tide. The Bremers' 800 count Egyptian cotton top sheet was pushed down to the bottom of the mattress.

"Something is on your mind," she said.

"I wasn't quite honest before when I said none of this would worry me."

"Really? You could've fooled me. You've been sounding contented and relaxed ever since people stopped shooting at us."

"I'm more worried now than I've ever been in my life, but not about our stuff, or this big house, or getting enough food, or my business ever coming back."

"Then what? Tell me. Not your health?"

"I'm worried about you."

"I'm not goin' anywhere, babe. I'm at home with you now." In the darkness Lee kissed his cheek.

"I'm worried about us, that we won't have a future, or that we won't be happy, or that something will happen and we'll lose this…all the usual unlikely things that people worry about if they're disposed to worry. I'm worried something will change again."

"But that's not you. You don't think like that."

"I feel that I am now. It's almost a revelation, like I never really had anything to worry about before."

"I thought you chose that. Does it upset you?" She raised herself on one elbow and looked into his face.

"In a way, it doesn't. It makes me think that the reason I never worried before was that I wasn't committed to anyone the way I am to you now. It was the way I kept some distance between myself and everything in my life. I can see now that's why I never got married, why those two engagements blew up. I hadn't really made a commitment to either of those women. Not like this, anyway."

"So you're happy to be worried."

"You could say that, as odd as it sounds. I'm glad to want something enough to worry about keeping it."

A realization gradually came over him. Brett had all his life worked at avoiding those things he didn't want to do, and in the process he had never done a single thing he deeply wanted to. Now, in this ruined world, he was about to start.

2

And that ruined world was truly in motion around them again. Indeed, Brett and Lee gradually began to sense a light-hearted camaraderie among the people they talked to on the streets of Marshy Flats. It felt like palpable relief. People were finally talking about how certain they had been they wouldn't survive, and the unique moment when they realized they might have a chance. Although the Bremers were not among them, nearly a hundred more residents had found their way back to Marshy Flats in the two weeks since Lee and Brett had returned. The population approached 250, and the people returning could be identified by their stunned expressions, their exclamations of shock and dismay as they turned corners and encountered yet another gutted building. Yet, it was with a constant sense of discovery and delight that Brett and Lee came across friends and acquaintances that had survived when they didn't dare hope they would. The Disaster, as it was now being called on government television, had created a clear dividing line between the past and the present, even as it had reduced the divisions and barriers among the survivors.

The tickers of death had stopped spinning, and the last numbers Brett heard estimated the remaining U.S. population at around forty-nine million people—about the same as England without Scotland or Northern Ireland—so the CO's forecast had been a little optimistic. Only one in six Americans had survived the epidemic. Going forward the nation would have to be more cautious when picking a fight with someone overseas. Oddly, the CO had not spoken much lately about revenge, or even justice. Although the Islamic State was still talked about as the prime suspect, rebuilding was still his new theme, a message people clung to for obvious reasons.

Retribution would have to come later and from a much stronger position.

Nearly every city and town had its own public crematorium. Lee and Brett saw this from a primitive government-made documentary from the NMN on how various parts of the country were coping with recovery. Clearing the dead was a fundamental health issue. The production had an improvised look as if filmmaking talent was now scarce. The Marshy Flats facility was out beyond the baseball diamond on land no one owned anymore. A memorial was being planned on the site for the 511 people whose bodies had been cremated there. Someone had erected a small square of plywood nailed to the top of a two-by-four with this total and a short nonsectarian prayer. Oddly, with a survival rate of nearly 25%, Marshy Flats had done better than the country at large.

A tiny shop-front mental health clinic was about to open for people who felt guilty about surviving, or were obsessively mourning their loss. Lee and Brett didn't plan to use it, although she had volunteered to help with screening and counseling.

Would they have felt guilty if they'd chosen to stay with the crowd going into Bridger on that first day, helplessly watched people die by the thousands, and then survived after seeing that? The conversation about guilt was one they hadn't had yet. Instead, they'd been proactive and engineered their own survival, chancy as it was. Nor had Lee ever mentioned the two men Brett killed in their last refuge. He hadn't found a need to raise the issue, either, since it had bothered him less than he expected, and he was still working out the reasons for that. He'd held onto the Remington, now hidden in its padded brown case up in the rafters of the Bremer garage, out of sight. He had concealed the .38 in the nightstand on Stan Bremer's side of the bed, since he was not fully certain things were totally calm yet. Once things were, he planned to offer the rifle for sale, but not until then.

Oddly enough, even though a few worries lingered, Brett was happy now, happier than he'd been before the

Disaster, and he had thought he was happy then. He was in love with Lee in a way he hadn't known was possible before. Once they dated a little more, he planned to ask her to marry him. If she was up for it, maybe they could have a couple of kids. They'd probably have the perfect bronze skin and wavy black hair she had, but they'd grow up to be sturdy entrepreneurs like him. The coming decades would be a perfect era for new businesses since it was an unfamiliar world that offered many gaps to fill, and it would be the only kind of world their kids had ever known. That prospect wasn't worrisome; he and Lee could fill them in selectively about the past. Surely some important lessons could be absorbed from it, just as some other discoveries about how people had behaved in desperate times were better forgotten. Nothing useful could be learned from them now. Brett often thought that, after all, when you've been through what they had and survived, what forces coming from outside themselves could ever worry them again? In its own way the world was a brand new creation.

Brett had heard that the only church in town was organizing to reopen with a monthly service, but not as the First Baptist it had always been. The old pastor had not survived, and like many other churches, it was going to be operated by military chaplains. They were now planning to call it the United Freedom Church. It would have the new Freedom Force One flag hanging above that of the state government, which was also going to be resurrected within the next few months, possibly with a few structural changes. Brett was thinking that he and Lee could be married there. Naturally, it would be quite a small ceremony. Hopefully the mail service would have resumed by then so they could send out invitations. Email didn't seem classy or formal enough for a wedding invitation, and he was confident that she'd say yes when he proposed.

Freedom was a word on everyone's lips in those balmy recovery days. The country was gathering momentum, especially since the CO had renamed it the United States of Freedom. Most people were eating again. If a debate followed about whether Americans should now be called Freedonians, like a lot of other secondary issues, it didn't make the NMN news. Brett heard General Parker's speech on television several times, since nothing else was available to watch, although a revived weather channel was about to be added, a much-needed resource on the Gulf as hurricane season developed. The delay was always about finding adequate staff for any venture. It was a new beginning, the CO announced proudly, and it was only appropriate that the country should experience a symbolic rebirth through a change of name, almost like a baptism, even as it continued to staunchly embrace the principles of democracy that had always made it the greatest nation on earth.

The President, he added, had personally approved the name change, and only regretted that he was still too engaged in grappling with the problems of reconstruction to attend the announcement in person. The viewer was encouraged to imagine him with his sleeves rolled up, the back of one hand sweeping the sweat from his brow, lending a hand with the other. Indeed, continued the CO, the President had very much hoped to deliver the news himself, but under these demanding conditions, he wasn't able to do every single thing he wanted, and he knew that most patriotic and right-thinking Americans would understand. He considered himself to be blessedly fortunate to be able to delegate many of these more routine tasks to the CO, who had been his right-hand man during the Disaster, and would continue to be.

General Parker said all this without blushing. Lee remarked that he was awfully good at this part of his job and getting better every day.

Still, Brett was surprised to hear him mention the President's name again, as if the man really were actually back there behind the scenes, pitching in for the benefit of all his fellow citizens. Maybe he was. He had always been skillful at seizing his main chance, which now would've looked mostly like playing along with the new powers that be.

As Clayton had predicted, the November election

was postponed until an unnamed date, but not, of course, cancelled, because elections formed the cornerstone of the democracy of this reborn nation. Both major political parties dutifully delayed their conventions in response. This announcement was made via the little ribbon that ran along the bottom of the screen, just after the delivery schedule for the food trucks on the coming day. No one actually announced it aloud. Clearly, too much remained to be done in restoring the country's health to pointlessly divert a lot of energy to re-electing people who were already serving in office, and doing such a great job to boot. Congress, after all, had overcome its ceaseless wrangling, and no hint of squabble, or indeed, of anything else, was heard from it anymore.

Continuity was more important now than it had ever been in history. When life was so fundamentally disrupted, hadn't people come to depend on nothing whatever changing at the federal government level? The only detail that differed was that most departments in Washington now functioned and politics appeared to be sidelined. Many people attributed this to the President's unparalleled skill in delegating tasks. It felt like he had developed real leadership qualities at last, and just in time. Of course, a huge crisis can often bring that out in people with real potential.

Privately, Brett remarked to Lee that he did not expect to hear the President's name ever mentioned again. He had received credit for the backstage rebooting of America's operating system, and he was ready to assume his place with honor in the annals of history, which were even now being rewritten to receive him in a fashion commensurate with this unique achievement. Aside from the 260 million dead, the system itself had experienced no losses. This was a testimonial to its durability and resilience. He would be the one given credit for providing the continuity that brought America through the Disaster into a shining new future. In due time, it was hinted that people should watch for his face on the new half dollar, replacing both Eisenhower and Kennedy, and now worth about four cents of the purchasing power of the *old* federal currency. This would happen once the mint could be staffed again.

By this time the email system was also up and running, although the informational parts of the Internet were not, and Clayton had written to Lee and Brett that his ham radio sources in western Virginia had informed him that the traffic of official vehicles around the Windsong Estate had dropped to nearly nothing. "You can draw your own conclusions from that," he wrote, as he knew they would. Lee suggested the old federal government had been moved somewhere else. Who, after all, wanted to continue living in a dreary bunker after it was no longer necessary? Brett wasn't sure, although he concluded from this that emails were not being censored yet; a good sign, although he knew it was not likely to last.

Clayton went on to write that although many commercial buildings and homes in Outpost had been burned, and more than 300 people had lost their lives in the struggle with the invaders, Lee's brother's house was intact, as was Clayton's. It was mostly the better houses that had been destroyed, aside from the mayor's. Best of all, the disease had never taken hold in Outpost, and the single case recorded among residents, that of Holly's husband, Doug, had led to no others. The town council, meeting for the first time since the outbreak, had authorized a bronze memorial plaque in his memory to be mounted on the base of the obelisk that honored those who had died in constructing the dam. Emmett was taking credit for the overall victory and was applauded for doing so.

Since Lee's online university was located in Dallas, one of the URDs, she expected work on her degree to resume shortly, and she spent much of her time hitting the books. To Brett, she seemed even more serious than before, although that was a little speculative since he hadn't known her then.

As the summer days began to shorten, they heard frequently from Clayton, and were always glad to have his calm and reasoned take on things. They speculated that the flow of rum into Outpost had resumed. He had used up all of his vacation and was finishing his last days working at the city garage before he retired. DeShawn was doing well, he added, still working at his side, only with no overtime now. Upon his father's retirement he would be promoted to assistant manager, an important position.

They did not hear as often from Holly, except that she was reunited with Emmett, for which she offered neither explanation nor excuse. She was now working part time as a volunteer in a city-sponsored nutrition clinic for children who had become malnourished during the Disaster. There were quite a few. She had lost more than a pound and a half herself during the acute food shortage that was still going on in Outpost at her return, and she professed not to miss it at all, wearing its absence as a badge of honor. It was, in a way, her contribution to the community's survival, her pound and a half of flesh as she described it. In her spare time she was redecorating the Residence for Emmett, giving it a more uptown feeling even while preserving the Art Deco flavor. She was proud to add that she had kept the long-barrel .44 Smith & Wesson as an emblem of her role in the struggle to survive. In her few messages, she always made a point of giving Brett her love separately at the end, knowing that Lee would see it.

Even though Brett was not in the least fooled by his trappings of legitimacy, he gradually gave up complaining about the CO. Everyone had to admire the man's ability to sweep aside the rancorous political rant of the past and get things moving again. If Americans didn't seem to have as much personal freedom now as they had before the Disaster, they did have a functional government that didn't feel too oppressive unless a person believed he was entitled to have a real voice in its decisions. But on sober reflection, which Brett had been doing a lot of since their return to Marshy Flats, he couldn't remember a time when anyone *did* have a strong voice in the *old* government, either, unless they were one of the big campaign contributors. Although the irregular course of this transformation still made him slightly queasy, over all it wasn't hard to see the outcome as a net gain for the country.

Simply stated, they had survived, they were eating better, and they were moving on.

Since their return to Marshy Flats, and especially since the food trucks had begun their circuit of salvation, Brett had more time to gain perspective on the events since June 25, the day he picked up the shipment from Newton's. He tried to take the longest possible view.

Brett had come out of his upbringing with a sense of having to look at the world through his own eyes. Even in his twenties, when he examined the way the government operated, he saw a system that often didn't work. It had been co-opted by the people who paid the campaign bills. Yet, he had still continued to believe in the *idea*, even when he knew that the process of democracy itself had been derailed. He couldn't tell for how long. Without articulating it, he still hoped that someone would eventually step forward to restart the system of voting for accountable candidates and return it to operational status. That person would find the magical solvent to loosen the rusty, unused levers of democracy, and it would function once more. It *could* work; Brett knew that it could. Hadn't it already worked for two centuries? Hadn't it been effective under a variety of extreme challenges? This, of course, had been the most devastating shock of all, but coming into it, he'd still had confidence in its elasticity.

Now, only the question of the CO remained. Until this point, the lingering, but still critical, idea of democracy survived in the abstract, even if the practice was long gone. That idea was hope.

But Brett was still plagued as well by a sense of a large tradition lost, of an era that had slipped away unseen in the night while everyone in full, or at least partial confidence, slept. It was a loss much different than the demise of two hundred sixty million people, and far more abstract, but in its own unrecoverable way, it was still too sad to endure. As they always had, populations could regenerate, but inspiring traditions, once lost, are gone forever.

Brett realized that the old America had gone the way

of the ancient Egyptians, the Hittites, and the pre-Columbian Maya. Like them, the Americans had worshipped false gods with no result, and eventually their story, once the data had evaporated from the disk drives and the cloud, could be obscurely deciphered only from fractured tablets, crumbling scrolls, and discarded books rescued from rubbish heaps. Historians would write papers on what had made them stumble at some critical fork in the road, on how the Americans had disappeared from their role as the masters of the past, the scholars of history, and in so doing, relinquished their grip on the future without seeming to care, or, in most cases, even to notice. Thinking of this, Brett was reminded of the refrain from *Dixie*, "Look away, look away, look away..."

Remembering the Maya, in dismay future anthropologists would study ruined American ball courts for a clue as to how it all went wrong. Was the losing team really killed at the end of the World Series, or was that no more than lore and legend? After all, the outlines of Fenway Park and Yankee Stadium were still easily discernible from satellite images taken from space, although, even when standing on the pitcher's mound, they were not all that clear anymore from the ground. This is the value of perspective, and time ruthlessly provides it whether or not it is wanted.

The Commanding Officer: it always came back to General Parker. Had it been a revolution? If the word means a change of government by other than constitutional means, then it certainly had. Yet, it never required the clash of opposing armies, or vast hoards of rebellious citizens sweeping through the streets with torches, no burned and bloody barricades except to protect hoarded food supplies. Throughout, people had been more concerned with hunger than politics. No guillotines had been erected, since the terrorist attack was reducing the population faster than any other means could. The old government had fallen quietly with a turn of the key at a distant golf resort, almost without protest, and from none of these more traditional assaults.

Ironically, at the end the Washington establishment

had succumbed neither to treachery nor radical ideology, but collapsed when confronted by simple *competence*, an unsuspected enemy, yet one more powerful than any other on the scene, a true stealth invader, one long overlooked and never imagined to have any meaningful role to play again in the current era.

How long the Commanding Officer of the United States of Freedom planned to continue in power, few could hazard a guess. Neither was Clayton able to come up with an estimate. When Brett asked for her thoughts on their present status, Lee replied that the Bremer gardens were in need of some serious attention, and neglect had never been part of her character, either in her treatment of her life plan, or of her man. She was at last done thinking about politics and survival, and was now prepared to get her hands dirty, more with flowers than vegetables, since it was late in the season, but not too late for a determined person to still make something blossom in the earth where few things had of late.

Yet Brett was certain of this: the CO would stay tirelessly at his post for as long as he felt he was needed. After all, it was for the good of the nation, and having nothing more to worry about from Washington was not a bad way to live in the new post-Disaster world.

On a day late in high summer of that tragic year, with the Gulf lying limp and yielding as if in exhaustion, Brett sat outside in the gazebo, facing Stan Bremer's laptop on a green-painted picnic table. Afternoons were still steamy now as the season advanced, yet tempers were cooler, and expectations had risen. The looting and shooting had stopped a while back, and the incinerated piles of the recent dead had been bulldozed like Indian mounds into a rolling park-like landscape behind home plate, where Marshy Flats, never a force in the fields of sport or politics, had lost many other contests as well. Grief was everywhere, but so was the relief of survival, and it was increasingly seeking a voice.

Lee emerged from the Bremer house, now the Wallace/Carter house, carrying a cold mug of beer, and she set it down next to his elbow. Using the same chilled fingers, she caressed his forehead with a loving but possessive touch and then leaned over to give him a kiss before she went back inside to her books.

He watched her walk away as if she were the embodiment of change in his life, one he found personally even more profound and intimate than the epidemic, and he smiled as he shook his head. Many years would be required to adjust to what had happened, but in this calmer time, he saw a place to begin. Recalling himself pausing at the back door of Newton's Bait & Tackle on a morning late in June in Marshy Flats, gazing out over the Gulf as he stood next to his van, Brett knew what he wanted to say, and this was the time to begin the story as no one else could ever tell it. There were millions of other versions of this narrative, most of them now lost, but he could only start with the one he had lived:

A colorless haze hung over the Gulf of Mexico, he wrote, *visible mainly as a thickening of the air in the distance. Gulls traced loops against the flat windless sky, and on the simmering sand, shorebirds stalked about on stiff legs among the solitary tufts of beach grass. The single dock was empty of boats that morning...*

www.ingramcontent.com/pod-product-compliance
Lightning Source LLC
Chambersburg PA
CBHW030811260626
47169CB00001B/286